A SECRET PRINCESS

~A~ SECRET PRINCESS

MARGARET STOHL & MELISSA DE LA CRUZ

putnam

G. P. PUTNAM'S SONS

G. P. Putnam's Sons

An imprint of Penguin Random House LLC, New York

First published in the United States of America by G. P. Putnam's Sons,
an imprint of Penguin Random House LLC, 2022

Visit us online at penguinrandomhouse.com

Library of Congress Cataloging-in-Publication Data is available.

Book manufactured in Canada

ISBN 9781984812049 (hardcover)
1   3   5   7   9   10   8   6   4   2
ISBN 9780593531594 (international edition)
1   3   5   7   9   10   8   6   4   2

FRI

Design by Eileen Savage and Suki Boynton
Text set in Winchester New ITC

For Emma, May, and KK
—M. S.

For Mike and Mattie
—M. de la C.

Prologue

British Raj, 1858

*M*ary Lennox met a genie once.

It came to her when she was eight years old, in the depths of those five dismal days between when her mother, Mrs. Lennox, was alive and when Mary knew for certain that she was dead.

Mary knew her mother in that distant, reverent, and mysterious way that others knew creatures of myth. In fact, when Mary woke that first morning to find her mother gone, she was quick to assume she had just left, as she often did. A socialite to the last, her mother found the seclusion of motherhood in Calcutta indescribably dull. Every night, Mrs. Lennox would leave their bungalow of hushed voices and long shadows to scent out entertainment elsewhere. Sometimes Mrs. Lennox would return home the morning after a night of dinners and parties.

Sometimes the morning after that. One could never be entirely certain, least of all Mary. Mr. Lennox was rarely home himself; too many new fortunes to exploit.

On the second day of her mother's vanishing, Mary asked her ayah where her mother had gone.

Her ayah was a woman of callused fingertips and herb-scented skin, charged to mind Mary since the day of her birth. She was younger than Mrs. Lennox, but with four children of her own, and Mary often wished she could have been her fifth. Because she knew, in some unformed way, that she—like her family—truly belonged neither to this country she loved so dearly, nor to this woman she loved even more.

But her ayah would tell Mary many things. She would tell her stories of how the sun came to hang in the sky, how the sea became so wide, how the stars became so bright. Even so, she never lied. Not until now.

She looked Mary in her eyes and did not blink when she said, "She will return soon."

On the fourth day, Mary stood before her mother's portrait and studied it intently. She'd begun to lose bits of Mrs. Lennox. Her eyes: a dark and luxurious blue, while Mary's were the dusty brown of desert sand. Her skin: an angelic alabaster, while Mary's was a jaundiced yellow. Her voice: light and pleasant to the ear, while Mary's was grating and loud. Now, these were not opinions Mary's young mind had formed about herself. They were widely known and discussed regularly by Mrs. Lennox and her husband, when he was not too busy chasing his fortune as a merchant to join them. Even then, Mary's mother seemed indifferent to her only child; Mary remembered clearly watching her mother cover her ears during dinner upon hearing her daughter's laugh for the first time. From that point forward, Mary endeavored not to laugh in her mother's presence.

On the fifth day, the genie came to her.

Mary saw its blurred and fleeting image through the tears she shed into her pillow that night. It was a figure that could have been mistaken for a person if it hadn't been for the living embers that served for eyes, the whipping flame that served for a tongue, and the crackling black magma that served for skin.

It sat at the edge of her vision, perched rather primly on a damask chaise and smoking a long, queer pipe.

"I'm dreaming," she said immediately, before her mind could draw its usually fantastical and far-from-reasonable conclusions.

"Oh yes," the genie said. Its breath smelled of burnt bread, and its voice snapped like a campfire. "Or, at least, that is what I'm sure they will say when you tell them you have seen me."

The hungry curiosity that had earned Mary the name *pishi* from her ayah now came creeping forward.

"Am I not dreaming?" she asked. Even though she was cold

with fear, an excitement like the genie's eyes burned in her chest.

"There are many tears in this city," the creature said in answer. "But yours must be the loudest. I was passing through, minding my own business, and I was struck by a pitiful mewling coming from that very window. I thought perhaps it was a creature in pain. Tell me, what has a little British girl to cry about on such a cool night?"

"My mother's gone," Mary said.

"She is," the genie confirmed.

Little more was needed for Mary.

When spindly tears leaked from her eyes, she knew they weren't from sadness, but from a righteous and heartbroken anger.

What will become of me?

"Great things, little pishi," the genie said. "That is my gift, to dry those angry tears. You will see the world's wonders through a keyhole, flee across the countryside, earn the love of a prince and the friendship of a princess, tell stories that echo through the ages, and more. All of the great adventures and ambitions of your heart will be fulfilled. But, as with all things, there is a price."

"What price?" Mary asked. "My father is rich. Whatever it is, I can pay it."

"*Oh no,*" said the genie. "The cold coins of an empire will not pay this debt."

Anxiety rushed like lightning down Mary's back. She knew what story she'd fallen into, and she knew how it ended. How many of the characters in her ayah's stories had paid similar debts?

Still, she did not hesitate. "I shall pay it."

The genie's grin chased away the lurking darkness with a hearth fire's glow.

"Be brave, Mary Lennox," it said. "That is the payment I demand of you if all of these wishes are to come true. Be brave. Go forward into your destiny, and never look back."

Seven Years Later
Manchester, England

THE HEELS OF Mary's boots clipped against the stone floors with military procession, casting an echo that extended forth like a bugle call. People halted and moved from her path, struck with bewildered expressions. She did not spare them a passing glance. Her arms swung at her sides, hands balled into fists and eyes set before her, never looking back.

And if she felt like Joan of Arc, marching into battle, it was not completely unwarranted.

Because her head was mostly shaved.

Morning had broken upon the cloistered halls of the Select Seminary for Young Ladies and Gentlemen and filtered through thick-paneled windows to cast pools of light on the gray stone before Mary's feet. For a moment, polite society's premier boarding school for the children of the nouveau and the mercantile was once again a medieval citadel, and Mary wasn't the fifteen-year-old bane of Headmistress Minchin's existence, but a Knight

Templar robed in divine virtue. The Lennox family crest had "I'll defend" on it. At her hip, she could feel the heavy weight of a long-sword touched by angelic fire. It was as strong as Excalibur itself, and on her chest was a burning heart.

The grand doors to the seminary's dining hall opened before her and rose-colored light shone in from both sides, transforming it into a majestic throne room. Mary's snooty classmates were now bickering courtiers. Her teachers and governesses were black-draped clergy. And at the far end of this throne room, flanked by the most gallant of knights, was a princess called Sara.

Mary felt eyes upon her as she walked swiftly and proudly down the narrow columns between dining tables. Laughter ceased and morphed into shocked whisperers. Young ladies pointed, young gentlemen laughed, and the teachers looked as if they might swallow their tongues.

Sara Crewe was the only one who saw her and smiled. Which made sense, since Sara's dark curls were the only others in the hall that had been shorn off.

Next to her, Cedric Errol—unshorn—looked like he might cry.

Mary wore her proudest grin as she sat between Sara and Cedric at their secluded end of the dining hall. Outcasts by nature, the three were occasionally ridiculed—more often ignored—by their stylish peers, and thus pleasantly left to their own devices. But not today. Today, the three might as well have been Dumas's musketeers brought to life. Mary actually liked the sound of that.

Before Mary could even pour her morning cup of tea, Cedric was admonishing her.

"You are absolutely raving mad," he said.

"Is that how you must greet me every morning, dear Cedric?" Mary asked before biting into buttered toast. "Why not a pleasant 'good morning' or 'how fares the weather in the girls' dormitory'?"

Cedric was born to be an old man, forever squinting over the rim of his spectacles and shaking his metaphorical cane at rambunctious youths. He even laughed as adults laughed: short, low, and slightly bitter. But still, he laughed, and Mary considered that to be a morning's good deed.

"Mad you may be," Sara said, grasping Mary's hand. "But what you have done also makes you my dearest, truest friend."

Sara's brown hands glowed with health and beauty, in stark contrast to Mary's own thin fingers, her skin transparent as the dried palm-leaf manuscripts found in the temples of Thailand and Indochina. It made her squeeze her friend's hand all the tighter.

"What manner of true friend would I be to let you suffer in this way?" Mary asked. "Minchin is a beast for what she has done, and I mean to hold her to account. Cedric, you are a Judas for not joining me."

"I doubt it would have the same impact, Mary," he said.

"It's the thought that counts, as you well know. How will injustice and cruelty be overthrown if not through brotherhood and unity? How will evildoers be stopped if not by the love of dearest friends? Who was King Arthur, truly, without his brave and loyal knights of virtue?"

"Are we to be the knights of virtue to your King Arthur, then?" Cedric teased. "I must say, I thought he would be taller."

Mary was not deterred.

"The world's ignored and inspired are our King Arthur, Cedric," said Mary. "All we do, we do in defense of them."

"Hear, hear!"

Sara raised a glass of buttermilk above her head, her once-proud mane of black hair now patchily sheared close to the scalp. Cedric raised his glass halfheartedly, and Mary lifted her own above wilting yellow hair that was now cropped in fits and starts about her ears. She only slightly regretted using the scissors without a mirror.

The glasses clinked together.

The next sound to fill a room shocked into silence was the metallic song of Minchin's silver chatelaine, forever at her waist and weighed down by two dozen iron keys. It was a slow and fearful rhythm that followed the headmistress, like the chains on Marley's ghost. All eyes became fixed on plates and cups, all hands folded demurely into laps. All except Mary, who kept her head defiantly raised and her hands tented before her on the table.

"Mary, don't," Cedric said. He may have had no knowledge of what she meant to do, but he knew she always meant to do something.

She winked at him over the lip of her teacup.

Headmistress Minchin climbed the steps to the table at the far end of the room where all heads of departments sat, raised upon a dais like a vicar in a pulpit. A pair of plain silver pince-nez sat at the end of her pinched nose, forcing her to look both above and below at the same time. It created an unsettling sensation for the student or teacher caught in the crosshairs of her gaze. Minchin stood as if the straightness of her stance held back the red tide of the end times, and perhaps for her, the prospect of disrespectful and uneducated children inspired the same sentiment.

"Good morning, children."

For such a slight woman, she had the voice of a mountain, which bounced about the high-ceilinged room. She loomed over them.

The children echoed, "Good morning, Mistress Minchin."

The headmistress's head swiveled from one end of the dining hall to the other, assessing and observing each student and teacher, as if her skull were a piece of clanking machinery. If one listened closely enough, one could hear the screech of unoiled hinges, metal on metal.

"This morning, we give thanks for the strength of our minds and the resoluteness of our character. Here at the Select Seminary for Young Ladies and Gentlemen, we pride ourselves on producing impeccable members of this, our grand empirical society. Young men of honor, fortitude, intelligence, and gallantry. And young women of poise, beauty, purity, and—"

Mary heard the hitch in the headmistress's voice—what might have been a gasp in a woman with significantly less "poise"—and knew she had been spotted. She then heard that metallic screech again, the harsh cry of a train coming into a station. Mary imagined a great smokestack rising from the top of Minchin's head, billowing forth foul-smelling black coal smoke. The image made her giggle cruelly.

Minchin drew in a thin breath and said in a low, rumbling voice, "Obedience."

"Saints above, Miss Lennox! Does your belligerence have no bounds?"

Minchin's parlor had been converted from the citadel's old chapel, and the dense stone walls, narrow windows, and low ceiling that met in an arch above their heads always seemed like more of an inquisitor's cell than a place of prayer. It was very cold and damp, and the small coal basket in the corner was never lit. Mary liked to think that Minchin enjoyed the damp cold. When she was particularly at odds with the headmistress, she would imagine her as a moldy post in the middle of the North Sea, happily battered by frigid waves.

"Are you listening, child?" Minchin asked, catching Mary's drifting attention. "Or do you simply choose not to hear me?"

"It is quite impossible not to listen to *you*, Mistress Minchin."

Mary stood before her like a soldier preparing for court-martial. She might even prefer it over this endless, senseless admonishment that did nothing but waste Mary's time. Because Mary hated their headmistress just as she had the endless parade of decorated British generals swanning their way through her mother's drawing room, tossing their cloaks at the housemaids and bullying the porters.

"You know that our dress code is strict here at the seminary, Miss Lennox," Minchin said, as if Mary needed reminding. "Young women are to wear their hair long, brushed, and tied back with a blue ribbon."

"I am aware," Mary said. "That is why I was so surprised to see Miss Crewe yesterday after church with all the hair sheared from her head. I thought, why, the seminary has such a strict dress code, I best keep up appearances, lest I'm caught out of fashion."

"That exception does not apply to you, clearly."

For all of Minchin's abject, hypocritical cruelty, Mary had to appreciate her resolve. She did not flinch when faced with the reality of how wrong she was.

"I do not concur," Mary said with the fluidity of a barrister before an assembly. "Miss Waldon, who instructs us on beauty and grace, often comments on the listlessness of my hair. Its hay-like texture, lack of luster, and general undesirability are well known. If anyone deserved to be shaved, it was me, *clearly*."

Mary's fists craved a lectern she could beat them against to finalize her point.

"I shall not explain myself to you, Mary Lennox," said Minchin, dismissive and completely unaware of the dragon she'd awakened.

"No, but you *must*!" Mary was shocked at the strength of her own voice, as was Minchin, obviously. She had not spoken so loud outside of the confidence of her friends in years. It terrified her. It empowered her.

Be brave, Mary Lennox.

"You cut off Sara's hair because it offended you. Just as her heritage offends you, as her money offends you, as the trueness of her heart offends you. She has been nothing but kind and respectful to everyone she has met at this dreadful salt mine you call a school, and you see that kindness as above what she deserves. You call her a little princess out of spite for her parents and the money you take from them. Do not look upon me with such cow eyes, Mistress Minchin, you know it to be true. Sara may have too pure a Christian spirit to defend herself, but I have no such qualms. Both Sara's hair and mine will grow back, and you will doubtlessly cut hers again. And I shall doubtlessly cut mine. And again and again, on we shall go, you and I. You will either leave my friend be, or every Sunday from now until eternity, I shall take my cropped mess of a head, walk into St. Peter's Square, scream in Persian, and shout to the heavens, 'I am Mary Elizabeth Lennox of the Select Seminary for Young Ladies and Gentlemen under Mistress Minerva Minchin's care! Send your daughters there, and they'll turn out just like me!'"

Mary gasped for the breath she hadn't taken since beginning her speech. Before that fateful night after her mother's death, she would not have spoken so much in a month. Now, here, in a dreadful room before a dreadful woman, the words poured forth from her mouth as they poured forth from her pen.

Minchin stared at her with incredulous fury. Mary saw the

challenge in her eyes, and—much against her own powers—grinned like a cat with a mouth rimmed in cream.

She rose so slowly from her high-backed chair that Mary could hear the stirring of her petticoats and the crinkle of fabric stretched taut. The headmistress was an unreasonably tall woman, and Mary could see that now. Shrouded in her shadow, Mary felt like a very brave but very stubborn rabbit, standing before a towering wolf.

When Minchin spoke again, the words struck Mary in the chest.

"The day will come, young Miss Mary, when your father's money will not protect you from the ways of the world. That sour and vicious mind of yours will lead you a bridge too far, and you will learn what so many other spoiled little girls have learned: The fires of your heart do not matter. The strength of your so-called conviction is but sand before the winds of society."

The headmistress moved suddenly and swiftly past Mary. She could feel those winds of society beating at Minchin's heels and was resolved to stand strong before them. She turned when she heard the loud hinges of the old chapel's door open and saw the headmistress standing with her hand on the knob.

"You will go to bed without dinner tonight," she said. "And you will wake without breakfast in the morning. After classes, you will be confined to your bed for the remainder of the day, and if I hear even a *prediction* that my instructions have not been followed to the letter, there will be consequences of biblical scale for you and your little princess. Am I quite understood?"

Mary refused to give Minchin the satisfaction of an argument and simply nodded her head.

"Very good. Off with you, Miss Lennox. I shall send Becky along presently to deal with that tragedy on your head. Oh, and do dislodge yourself from Master Errol. He is an afflicted soul, and I don't want your horrendous influence rubbing off on him."

It is quite too late for that, Mary wanted to say, but kept it to herself. However, that did not mean she would sacrifice the last word.

In the cramped doorway, Mary turned and looked up into Minchin's mousy face, staring past her pince-nez into eyes gray like stale river water.

"We have a destiny, my friends and I," she said. "And no one will hold us back from it. Certainly not you."

Before Minchin could take in a breath to speak, Mary dipped into a curtsy, turned on a soldier's heel, and put the headmistress at her back.

1

*M*emory is a liar. It can hide truths in fantasies, make the misery of one time appear to be the happiness of another. It mutes faces, words, sounds, and sights. It covers everything in a delicate lace that softens the harshest of realities. Take, for example, the morning of January 7, 1865, when Sara Crewe first arrived at the Select Seminary for Young Ladies and Gentlemen.

Memory will tell Sara that, on that morning, the rising sun was filtering through lilac fog, and the seminary's pale stone rose up in the distance like something out of Tennyson. In truth, there was no sunshine through the icy rain. The fog was not a pastoral lilac, but an industrial yellow, and the seminary was no castle, but a fortress. Sara looked out of the window of the smart carriage her father had rented for the journey and found herself shocked by the sight of row homes and factories and turning gyres. This was nothing like the England she'd imagined.

"Is it always this wet?" she asked. "And cold?"

Captain Richard Crewe sat close beside her; even after such a long journey, the smells of dancing lady orchids and sea spray clung to his shirt. It was a trick of the brain, to be surrounded by gray and cold while the senses danced with sunlight and color.

"England has seasons, the same as almost anywhere else," he said. "In the winter, it is cold. In the summer, it is warm. But, yes, it is almost always this wet."

Sara cut her sharp green eyes up at her father, who hid a grin behind his beard—thick, black, and struck with shocks of gray like lightning in a storm cloud. Captain Crewe's ability to maintain frivolity in the midst of anxiety was one of the traits Sara loved most about him.

Sara was not laughing, however. She was sure her father had tried every trick, joke, and story he could think of, but since she stepped onto the dock in London, nothing had stirred the stone from her face. She supposed being angry was easier than being sad.

"I'm stronger than you think, you know," Sara said quite suddenly, no longer hiding behind the conversational pretense of the weather. She stayed facing the grim outside world, but she could feel her father's eyes on her face.

"Oh, Sara." His voice was the heartbroken sound of wind through bare trees. "Dear heart, that's not why—"

"Isn't it?" Sara asked, turning sharply on Captain Crewe. "You think that I am too soft, too . . . spoiled. But I can help run the hacienda—"

"I know you can," Captain Crewe said, harsh and cold. "And one day, we shall need that from you. But not today."

Sara knew from that tone, as final as the closing of a curtain, that the conversation was over.

CAPTAIN CREWE TOLD the carriage driver to let them off at the end of the long drive leading to the school. With the fog gathering around them and pulling at the hems of their clothes, they began to walk. It was an unsettling landscape to Sara. No sun, no color, no birds or animals at play. Not even the sound of children laughing at this so-called school. Somewhere, a church bell chimed the hour, and the deepening sound reminded Sara of the crashing of the tide in a gale. Thinking of the tides and sea storms crushed something in Sara's heart anew. What was a place without an ocean? What chance was there for happiness without the sea?

The old gray estate that housed the seminary rose before them like the base of a great mountain. Lights blinked on and off behind tiny windows that looked down at them with a cold and assessing nature. It was a grand, judgmental building. A craggy old man sitting alone on his hill and looking with suspicious eyes upon the world as it rapidly changed about him.

"'Time's glory is to calm contending kings,'" Captain Crewe said, staring up at the seminary. "'To unmask falsehood and bring truth to light, / To stamp the seal of time in aged things, / To wake the morn and sentinel the night, / To wrong the wronger till he render right—'"

"'To ruinate proud buildings with thy hours,'" Sara interrupted. "'And smear with dust their glittering golden towers.'"

"You've been studying," Captain Crewe said.

Sara refused to accept the joy that her father's pride often gave her.

"Well, I had to do something on the way here."

"Aye. By the time I return to fetch you, you'll know more Shakespeare than I."

"Who is to say I don't already?"

Sara and her father traded glares until the corners of the captain's lips quivered. His sober countenance only held up for another moment before he threw back his head and laughed. It was a loud, prideful, and utterly joyous laugh, and above all else, it was the thing Sara loved most about her papa. Richard Crewe was the German-Irish son of servants, a war veteran who made his fortune in the Far East, and a person who chose independence over food, education over shelter. He was a man who had no right to laugh after all he'd endured. And yet, he laughed like a man born with all of the eases of the world at his disposal. Quite forgetting the decorum her Filipino-Spanish mother had drilled into Sara to ensure she could never be denied due to bad manners, Sara hurled herself against her father and wrapped her arms securely around his chest.

Sara pressed her temple against the beat of her father's heart until she felt his hand grasp the back of her neck.

"Come now, little Sara. Truly, you must be the most solemn child . . . Please, my love, if you keep this up, I'll be forced to take you directly back to Manila, and your mother will have both our heads."

Captain Crewe attempted a laugh, but it was hollow. It made Sara cling to her father all the tighter.

"Sara. Sara, that's enough of that, you hear?"

With a gentle yet jarring force, Captain Crewe grasped Sara's shoulders and pulled her back to where she could stare directly up into his face.

"What has happened to my brave little girl, hm?" he asked. "The one who chased a hawk from the baby goats at the age of three, who scolded her cousins for sitting idle at six. Why, when you were no taller than my kneecap, you crossed through the jungle with no more than your wits. The one thing Sara Marie Crewe has never been afraid of is an adventure, and I won't have her starting now. Straighten your back, dry your eyes. Show them where you come from. Who are you?"

Sara did as she was told—straightened her back and dabbed her eyes—and said, "I am Sara Crewe, daughter of Richard Crewe of Munster, Ireland, and Munich, Bavaria, and Matea Reyes of Manila and Pampanga, the Philippines."

Captain Crewe smiled, and Sara thought there might have been tears in his eyes.

"Yes, you are," he said.

The sound of quick steps on the gravel turned both their heads. Materializing out of the sickly yellow fog was a black pillar of a woman. The minimal light was caught by and reflected off the heavy set of keys that hung at her hip. She was dressed all in black, as if in mourning, and her dark hair was pulled back in the monarch's tight bun. She began to speak immediately, even before she was fully upon them.

"I thought I heard footsteps on the lawn," she said in a surprisingly deep voice. "This ridiculous Manchester fog. I hope you did not become lost on the way to our quaint school, Captain Crewe. I promise, in the height of spring, this estate is as beautiful as—"

The woman ceased speaking almost immediately upon seeing them fully. Her mouth hung agape; breath caught between two words. Sara could practically feel the heat of the shock and confusion playing behind her eyes. It was an expression Sara had become used to since setting foot on English soil. This woman was expecting a flaxen-haired, rosy-cheeked girl of proper British stock. She glared at Sara and her father as if they'd eaten these imaginary people and now dared to stand in their place.

Finally, the woman managed to speak.

"Captain?" she asked warily, as if afraid of the answer. "Captain Crewe, I presume?"

Sara's father removed his bowler hat and bowed his head gallantly.

"Pleased to make your acquaintance, Headmistress Minchin. And this is your newest pupil, Miss Sara."

Sara dipped into a curtsy, fluid and elegant, as her mother had taught her.

"Charmed, Mistress Minchin," she said.

The mistress in question attempted what Sara thought was a smile. Instead, it more mimicked a chittering mouse drawing its lips back over wide teeth.

"Yes," Minchin said. "Charmed. Absolutely charmed."

From her mouth, the word *charmed* was biting as a curse.

SARA AND HER father followed Minchin through the tall main doors of the seminary. Sara expected a flood of warmth to chase off the cold of the outside, but she was shocked to find that the interior of the citadel was the same temperature as the exterior. She burrowed even deeper into the mink scarf tucked around her neck.

"The child does not much care for the cold?" Minchin asked this of Captain Crewe, even though she was looking directly at Sara.

To Captain Crewe's credit, he did not address that statement as the slight Minchin was probably hoping it would be.

"The Philippines is a land of sunshine," he said. "Sara has never known cold."

Minchin's smile was of genuine malice this time.

"What blessings," she said. "Some children are born, live, and die only knowing cold. Well, I'm sure Sara will have ample time to adjust to the seasons here at the seminary. Our winter is quite robust."

Minchin strode on, and Sara's eyes began to adjust to the changing light. The ceiling of the entryway was vaulted as high as a cathedral they'd visited in London. The sounds of laughter, talking, and many footsteps seemed to gather from throughout the building and collect there, for even though there were no pupils in immediate sight, Sara could hear them. It brought the image of ghost children chasing each other about the rafters to Sara's mind.

The floors, ceilings, and walls were all of the same monastic gray stone; the only light shone from flickering sconces. Very little had been changed from one century to another. In one way, Sara loved that aspect of her new home. When her parents told her she was to be shipped off to an English boarding school, her first thought was of castles and battlements and abbeys. As Sara walked the halls with her father and the brittle Minchin, Sara removed her hands from her muff long enough to brush her fingers against the walls as some fleeing princess, delicate lady, or resolute nun might have long ago.

"I shared in my correspondence that Sara is quite intelligent," Captain Crewe said. "I expect for her to have a thorough education."

"Oh yes," piped Minchin. "We do pride ourselves in providing the necessary foundation for any young lady of means and grace. Our girls must master several languages, at least one of the fine arts, the intricacies of home life—"

"When I said education," Captain Crewe said, "I did mean a *true* education. Sara's mother and I have already taken steps to secure her with the trappings of good breeding. I rely on this school to make her familiar with more collegiate matters. Languages, yes—she is already quite conversational in French—but also the sciences, geography, history, literature. Things she will truly need in life."

The note of sarcasm in Captain Crewe's voice was sharp to Sara's ears.

The headmistress endeavored to straighten her back even further and lifted her chin defiantly. As a trader in these trappings of good breeding, Sara was sure she took the speech with some offense.

"I cannot speak for the Philippines, I'm sure," she said. "But here in the queen's own country, we understand that if a young woman is to aspire toward anything, it must be house and home, where she is needed. Beyond this, yes, I am sure there are collegiate matters, as you say, that she may undertake. But she will find that all that truly matters lies within the confines of the four walls of her own dwelling. But, yes. I suppose since Sara is such a special child"—Minchin looked down at Sara from what she believed was a physical and moral height—"we may make allowances."

As THE TOUR concluded in the heavy, wet air that hung all about the seminary, Sara stood silently and watched her father speak of dollars and cents with the peckish-looking woman. They discussed a timetable for payments, addresses where invoices were to be sent, and a lawyer in town that he'd employed as a go-between for matters that required immediate attention. She turned back to look up at the looming manor. It seemed to reach out to her with long, sharp fingers, snagging on her gown and binding her to it. She had a sudden and desperate urge to cry out, to flee, to run all the way back to the Philippines if that's what it took. But her feet kept their place even as her spirit rattled against her ribs like a prisoner rattled against their chains.

"My solicitor at Barrow and Skipworth will be along presently with the full amount," said Captain Crewe as he creased his billfold and returned it to his chest pocket. "But if there is ever any need, do not hesitate to contact me. In any case, we shall be back in the summer, to see Sara's progress."

"Oh, I'm afraid that's quite impossible." The headmistress said this in an unnervingly casual tone, all while counting crisp banknotes with the efficiency of a merchant.

"What?"

It was the first time Sara had spoken since arriving at the seminary, and it was a disruptive sound even to her own ears.

Minchin managed to give Sara her full attention when she said, "Parents are permitted on campus just for a Parents Day ceremony in the autumn, and the school operates year-round. Students only leave under very special circumstances. We believe that this arrangement allows for as few distractions as possible, thus expediting a pupil's education through routine and focus. It is an unorthodox approach, but we have found it to be quite effective."

"I assume you include holidays in this . . . approach?" Captain Crewe asked.

"Yes, of course," Minchin said. "Many parents send gifts and greetings for the season, but rarely do I allow a student to leave for something as fleeting as a local holiday. We still employ all the usual festivities, I assure you. Easter service, philanthropy during Christmas, and all the rest."

Sara understood this perfectly, but she could see her father grasping for an explanation that seemed less absolute, less final.

"Allow me to be sure I am understanding things clearly," Captain Crewe said. "Apart from these Parents Day ceremonies, when are her mother and I meant to see Sara?"

"During Convocation," Minchin said. "At the age of seventeen. Only then is a seminary student deemed fully prepared to rejoin society."

Sara turned devastated eyes up to her father. She withdrew her hand from her muff and clung to his coattails like she did when she was a child.

"Papa, please," she whispered, ignoring all of the lessons on decorum that he and her mother had painstakingly imbued in her over the years.

Captain Crewe inclined his head to the mistress, excusing them, and gently drew Sara aside. She felt a choking swell in her chest, but she held down that urge to cry. Her voice—usually even and strangely calm—shook with the effort.

"Papa," she said with urgency. "Das ist keine Schule, es ist ein Gefängis."

Captain Crewe raised a dark, bushy eyebrow at his daughter and once again looked on the edge of a smirk.

"German now? Has it really come to that?"

German was a language solely for Sara and her father. They spoke it while only in the gravest of confidence, a fact that often angered Mrs. Crewe, who could only pick up bits and pieces. But Sara felt the danger pressing in around her, and her most powerful instinct was to escape, by any means necessary.

"Do you not find this place inexplicably odd?" Sara asked. "A school with no holidays, no education, and no students from what I can see."

"Yes, it is rather unorthodox," Captain Crewe said, glancing back at Minchin, who'd begun to tap her foot impatiently. "But it is the only boarding school of note in this damned country that will accept you. Or rather, accept your papa's money."

Sara refused to accept that as an excuse.

"Then why not Spain? France? Switzerland? America?"

"Do you assume that your mother and I have not explored all options?" Captain Crewe answered, affronted. "You are a brilliant girl, as durable and beautiful as a narra tree. Wherever you are planted, you will thrive. But this is not just concerning an education, my princess. The day when you should marry is fast approaching, and all the cosmopolitan education in the world won't rival a British title."

Sara followed her father's logic in only a cursory way. He was a sensible man—his words and reasoning often made sense—but he might as well have been speaking in Farsi for all Sara understood.

"Papa," she said slowly, as if speaking to a child. "If their schools refuse your money, how do you imagine their families will accept your daughter?"

That seemed to freeze the captain's blood. He stood still and rigidly tall. The child in Sara saw the stony look in her father's eyes as disappointment. However, the more astute side of her—the side that said little but saw much—recognized only hurt.

"You do drive to the heart of things," he said. "Times are changing again in the Philippines, Sara. All that your mother and I have done could be taken away in an instant. Here, in this cold, dreary place, you will find protection. Little can touch an English duchess in this world of ours. You will grow lovely enough to catch the eye of any stuffed lord or earl. And you are wealthy enough to secure the best of them. I shall ensure that."

Minchin coughed in what she probably hoped was a demure way, but the crudeness of the gesture shattered the private moment.

"Captain, I must insist," she said. "Young Sara needs time to become familiar with her new home."

At that, Sara felt her heart beat once, hard, in her chest. Again, every atom in Sara's body screamed at her to protest. To fall onto the ground and rave like a tempestuous child. To resist this new home as a body resists a virus. But she withheld. She smoothed her gown and lifted her chin. She stilled her trembling lip and poured cold iron down her back. When she and her father returned to Minchin, Sara thought it would be very difficult for anyone to sense the terror in her heart.

"I expect all our requests in regards to her care and upbringing to be addressed," Captain Crewe said. "If there is ever a concern, my representative speaks for me."

Minchin dipped her head in answer. The captain then turned his full attention to Sara.

"I shall send you books. Great, big, fat ones like you like:

English, French, German. Perhaps even one or two by those cynical Russians that you favor."

"Truth is not always cynical, Papa," Sara said in solemn answer. This inspired a laugh in the captain, a gasp from the headmistress.

"Oh, do not be shocked, Mistress Minchin," Captain Crewe said, still laughing. "Sara's mind is sharp and known to cut deep on occasion."

The mistress appeared sincerely terrified by the prospect.

"Well, then, I suppose I am off," the captain said. "I'll be back in—what is it, October?"

"November," Minchin said with a quickness. "November, Captain. Details will be shared promptly."

November. It was only just now the start of January. Sara calculated the days in her head, lining them up in a row as a captive might on a cell wall.

"November, then. There, that is not quite so long, is it, princess? The time will fly by. With all your studying and entertainments, why, you won't even have time to dwell on Manila and your old papa. Come now, let us not dawdle. Give me a hug for luck on my journey home."

Sara did not hesitate and threw herself quite inelegantly against her father. She heard the breath forced from his lungs, followed by a chuckle. In childhood, Captain Crewe had always encouraged Sara to hug him with all her might, to knock him over if she could. Of course, as a small child, she never managed to unseat Captain Crewe. But she wasn't a child anymore. With shaking fingers, the captain gently drew Sara away. He cradled her cheek in his large, callused hand, a hand that Sara had clung to every day for the entirety of her life. She refused to cry, not in front of the dreary headmistress, who continued to look at them as if they might transform at any moment into the congenial white family she'd expected. And Sara refused to cry in front of her father. To him, she was a mooring in a turbulent sea, and she refused to display any behavior that contradicted that sentiment.

Sara stood with Minchin as they watched Captain Crewe make his way down the drive. His shoulders hunched against the wet, and the black tails of his overcoat flapped about him like the wings of a raven. Memory would tell Sara that the sun victoriously broke through the blockade of clouds, and bathed in a ray of gilded light, Captain Crewe turned and blessed her with a smile. Yet, as has already been established, memory is an unscrupulous liar. Captain Richard Crewe did not turn to look at her one last time. He drew farther and farther from her, fading into the writhing screen of fog. Sara opened her mouth to call his name, but only a gasp left her throat before her father became lost to the gloom.

Sara exhaled the breath she didn't realize she had been holding and watched it crystallize in the air before her.

Sara turned her head to see Minchin's eyes—now malicious and judgmental, where only a minute ago, they were the very sparkling image of compliance—glaring down at her.

"Do you not speak, girl?" she asked, not bothering with forced charm, which Sara appreciated. If this was to be her home for the next two years, then it was best that she knew where she stood.

"I am quite fluent in several languages, Mistress Minchin."

The woman's lip turned up in a sneer.

"The Queen's English will serve," she said.

Without waiting for Sara to follow, Minchin turned and vanished through the open doors of the seminary, which gaped before her like the mouth of a ravenous, cruel, and cunning monster.

This we do not for ourselves, she reminded herself. *But for those who came and those yet to come.*

2

$\mathcal{S}$he has a French maid and everything."

"A maid! Heavens, the seminary has become quite posh, hasn't it?"

"She has practically her own wing of the manor. Not only a bedroom, but a study and a sitting room and a dressing room and a—"

"That seems not at all fair. Why, my father is the Viscount Herbert, and I don't have a French maid. Or any maid for that matter."

"Well, Lavinia, perhaps if *your* father had seventy-five thousand pounds sterling a year, you could afford a French maid. In the meantime, you will have to settle for Becky's dirty hands on your frocks like the rest of us."

"I saw them bring in her trunks and dresses yesterday afternoon. Such clothes! Finer than what my mama wears, and she's a duchess."

"I thought your great-grandmother was the duchess, Margaret."

"Same difference. What's a few generations removed, my papa says."

"Your papa the camel merchant, you mean?"

"Llamas! I told you, it's llamas!"

"And she's . . . Tropical. *From the Wild Tropics.*"

A great gasp rose and fell as if guided by a conductor.

"What?"

"No one mentioned that."

"Is that permitted? Rather, is it proper?"

"With seventy-five thousand pounds a year, I suppose anything can be made proper and permissible."

"I intend to write my parents immediately. They would never agree to me—their only child—rubbing shoulders with some uppity goatherd's daughter from India. How are we expected to make good matches when—"

"The Philippines."

Eyes in shades of milky blue, green, and pale brown turned toward Mary, who was grateful for an end to the girls' harsh clucking. She sat slumped in her desk chair with *Moby-Dick* unfolded in her lap. The girls were assembled early for their daily French class, gathered in herds positioned haphazardly throughout the room while awaiting the Monsieur, their teacher.

"I do beg your pardon?" asked Lavinia in the nasal tone that she thought was aristocratic when it was truly just snobbish.

Without lifting her eyes from her reading, Mary repeated,

"The Philippines. Her name is Sara Crewe, and she is from the Philippines. Not India."

Lavinia's already dark eyes narrowed until they gleamed dangerously like the depths of some long-abandoned well.

"Oh. And I reckon you would know, being the queen of Bengal yourself? Tell me, what is it exactly that your father does? Does he even exist? In the three years you've been here, I daresay I have seen neither head nor tail of the man."

"Perhaps he is actually out earning his fortune, instead of sitting idle and spending his money on ballerinas and actresses."

Lavinia was on her feet in an instant. Her face was red with affront, and Mary had to hold back a laugh.

"Has anyone ever told you that you look just like a tomato when you're angry?" Mary asked. "The resemblance is uncanny. You should travel with a carnival. I am sure you would have a dazzling career on the stage."

"You ridiculous gypsy!" she shrieked. This time, Mary's laugh could not be contained.

"Gypsy? I do wish. My life is far too dull as it is. Rather a lot like yours."

Lavinia advanced on Mary in a blistering rush, a winged fury. She knew the snob wouldn't strike her, but the image of the slight girl exchanging fisticuffs like a Liverpool pugilist filled Mary with bubbling amusement. She laughed brazenly in Lavinia's face.

"Ladies!"

A sudden gust of arctic wind came through the room, causing

much shuffling in the process. Every student found her seat and drew her eyes downward in the graceful supplication trademarked in every seminary girl. All except Mary, who kept her eyes defiantly raised and staring directly at Minchin. Mary never had a nemesis before coming to Manchester. There was something romantic and dangerous about the concept of an enemy, so she eagerly leaned into it with Minchin. When she first arrived at the seminary, she put forth a sincere attempt to be pliant and respectful, a small dot that could be easily overlooked and left alone. Yet, Minchin's nerves were so sensitive that the slightest irritation caused overblown reactions. It amused Mary to no end to cause such frustration in the headmistress.

"Ladies," Headmistress Minchin said again, with a pointed look at Mary, "I wish to introduce you to your new companion."

For one so young, there was something oddly striking about Miss Crewe. She seemed beyond her age, beyond any age, if that made sense. Mary tripped about in her head for the correct word and landed on *regal*. Mary looked about the room at her peers, who glanced up through lidded eyes, and saw their curiosity, their fascination, their envy. Mary imagined that most—if not all—of the girls had never seen someone with skin like Sara's before: a rich, healthy brown that seemed to glow as if dusted in gold. Or at least they'd never seen someone with that skin in those clothes.

The hens had not been wrong. Sara's ensemble was that of a duchess, or rather, an American heiress. A dress of navy velvet, petticoats that crinkled and brushed when she moved. The buttons were polished silver, the sleeves trimmed in lace. She wore no jewelry apart from pearl earrings that hung like raindrops from her earlobes. On any of these other girls, such an outfit would seem ridiculous, like a child dressing up in her mother's party clothes. Yet Sara, slim and small and elegant, stood as graceful as a dancer in a music box. On her, it all seemed proper and necessary. She was dressed for her station, which was somewhere very high above them all.

"All," Minchin continued. "This is Miss Sara Crewe of Manila, Philippines. A great distance away, indeed. I shall expect each of you to afford Miss Crewe all the respect and dignity for which the fine young ladies of the Select Seminary for Young Ladies and Gentlemen are known. Now please greet your new peer."

As one, the class rose, curtsied, and intoned in a meld of singsong voices, "A pleasure to meet you, Miss Crewe."

Sara curtsied as well, sweeping the hem of her dress behind her, making the petticoats rustle like the wings of small birds. She lowered herself before them, as if bowing to the queen herself. It made Mary blush in an uncharacteristic type of shame when she thought of her own rigid curtsy, which had once been compared to a flamingo with a broken wing.

"The pleasure is mine," she said, an accent dancing below the evenness of her tone like a goldfish beneath a still pond. Her eyes rose to pass over them, and they were a color that Mary thought she'd never see again; the shifting blue-green of a tropical ocean.

Minchin nodded, pleased by the superficial display, and turned back to Sara.

"I understand that your father takes your education very

seriously and considers you to be some kind of savant. I intend to see this proven for myself. Miss Herbert!" Lavinia stood as quickly as a summoned soldier. "What are you learning currently, in this class?"

"Subjunctive phrases, Mistress Minchin."

"Thank you, Miss Herbert. Do you know your French subjunctive phrases, Miss Crewe?"

Sara's brows rose slightly, and Mary read the hesitancy in the expression, and the confusion.

"Yes," Sara said slowly, uncertainly. Minchin clearly heard something to judge in that.

"Well, we shall see. Monsieur Dufarge has been instructed to give you special consideration once he arrives. Now please take a seat."

Sara curtsied again and made her way down the long row between desks to take an empty space at the back. The eyes of the girls followed her, including Mary's. She wore perfume, something floral and delicate. Mary was sure some of her classmates were scandalized, having been raised to think that only Parisians and women of loose morals wore perfume. But Mary was fascinated. Life at the seminary was a gray and muted affair. Miss Sara Crewe was a flash of color across a blank canvas. Mary glanced over her shoulder to look at the new student, and for a second, her eyes met Sara's.

Monsieur Dufarge rushed into the room, clearly quite late, and stopped short when he saw Minchin looming in the doorway. He was an agreeable man, ruffled and thoroughly French.

"Ah, madame!" he said, screeching to a halt before her. "Will you be joining us this morning?"

"I have brought you a new pupil, monsieur," she said, gesturing toward Sara. "Miss Sara Crewe. Her father claims that she has extensive knowledge of the language. I would like to see that demonstrated before going forward in her curriculum."

Without leaving room for argument, Minchin rooted herself in a high-backed chair normally occupied by the Monsieur. Resigned, the French teacher set down his satchel and coat and approached Miss Crewe. Mary turned in her seat to watch the young girl's reaction. A slight, pleasant smile, eager and accommodating, ready to answer whatever was asked of her. The readiness to oppose, to fight—which was so constant in Mary—was nowhere in Sara's expression. When Monsieur Dufarge made it to her, she rose smoothly and curtsied once more.

"Monsieur," she said in greeting.

"Mademoiselle Crewe," he answered. "It is my great fortune to make your acquaintance." Sara smiled and Mary could see that the Monsieur was instantly charmed.

The two launched into a conversation that Mary could not follow. Their exchange in French was fast, casual, and second nature. They talked about the weather in Manchester, Sara's traveling experience, the food in the Philippines, and that was all Mary was able to pick up. There were murmurs throughout the room, and even Minchin looked momentarily impressed, in an indignant kind of way. When the conversation ended after some time, Monsieur Dufarge shocked them all by grinning and deigning to kiss Sara's hand. He beamed like a stranger in a strange land who has suddenly met one of his own. He turned back to face the headmistress and looked positively delighted.

"Madame," he said. "Mademoiselle Crewe has not simply learned French; she *is* French. Her accent is exquisite, her grammar, flawless. She might as well be a *dictionnaire* considering her flexibility and aptness of word choice. There is not much more I can teach her, madame. In fact, Mademoiselle Crewe could teach a class of her own. My younger pupils might quite enjoy it."

Minchin's mouth opened and closed like a great, gasping bass. Mary's laugh was short, loud, and obtrusive. Soon, Lavinia was giggling, and when Lavinia giggled, the whole host giggled too.

"Silence, young ladies," Minchin said in a tight but even tone. Then loudly, "Silence at once!"

The hush that settled over the classroom was immediate, but the drawbridge was already down, and the disobedience creeping in. Mary saw the realization of this pass over Minchin's face. Realization, and something else, as well. It was not the frustration that the headmistress found with Mary—something one felt when teaching a stubborn pupil—but something colder. It was envy. It was fear. It was hate.

SUPPER WAS A buzzing affair that afternoon. The entire dining hall was absolutely aflutter with conversation about the dazzling and odd Sara Crewe, who sat alone in the center of the great room. Mary also sat alone, which was not an unusual occurrence, watching the anxious mutterings of her classmates. This was the one time when the girls of the seminary and the boys of what students came to call the college gathered together, and their shared rumors and speculations about the new girl were morphing before Mary into some living, breathing thing. Sara was different from other new students, and not just because of her color and not just because of her money. Her foreign origins, her aloof demeanor, the way she seemed to humbly float above everything played to the school's wildest imaginings. Her arrival was a stark breaking of the status quo. Eventually, something would have to give.

When Mary saw Lavinia stand, an air of superiority draped about her, she knew that the moment had come.

Conversations ceased and all eyes turned to the drama unfolding before them. The room watched Lavinia approach Sara's table, licking their lips like dogs before a bone. Sara smiled politely at the girl, as she had with every student who'd glanced her way or passed her on their rounds from class to class.

Lavinia answered that smile with a tilted head and a pursed, calculating expression. "Was your mother a whore? My parents said all the girls in the colonies are whores."

Lavinia's question shattered like glass against a stone floor. Mary watched Sara's face, looking for fractures. At first, she thought there were none. But what her ayah once called her cat's eye looked closer. There! In the corner of Sara's eye. A twitch, so fast it was almost undetectable. But it was there.

Sara wiped the corner of her mouth, folded her napkin, then set it with some resoluteness before her on the table.

"The Philippines is a colony of Spain, yes, but my mother is a lady," she said. "Her family, the Reyeses, are one of the biggest landowners in the country. I don't believe we've met—"

"I only ask, you see, because when my cousin Cecile visited San Francisco in America a few years back, she said that all the prostitutes wore shawls like that."

Sara's hand briefly rose to touch the pañuelo she was wearing.

"It's a shawl," Sara said. "In the Philippines we wear them for modesty. It reminds me of where I came from."

"And where is that, precisely? Some sugar plantation? Banana farm?"

Sara's smile was tight-lipped and didn't reach her eyes.

"Would you please sit down, Miss . . . ?"

"*Lady* Lavinia," she said. Mary knew that for the lie it was. Lavinia's father might have been titled, but she was certainly no lady. "And, no, I don't think I shall; is it cotton, then? Or tobacco?"

"Banking," Sara said. "My family is in banking. And real estate. And shipping. And we own several newspapers. Is that what you are trying to ask me, Lady Lavinia?"

Mary's eyes briefly flew to the long table at the head of the dining hall, where the school's teachers sat, Minchin senior among them. All saw this disaster building, and all kept their seats. The headmistress didn't even glance up from her potatoes and roast. Perhaps she found some obscene satisfaction in knowing that a favorite student was doing what she could not. Mary's fingers closed tight around her fork.

"What about your smell?" Lavinia asked, completely leaping over Sara's question.

Miss Crewe's polite veneer began to slip. Mary could see it in the sharp twitch at the corner of her mouth, caused by a prolonged attempt at an insincere smile.

"My *smell?*"

"Yes, I've heard the Filipino people are malodorous. Are you?" Lavinia leaned over as if to check, but before she could, Mary was up, out of her chair, and sliding into the seat next to Sara's.

"May I sit?" she asked. Sara looked at her, and beneath her surprise at Mary's sudden presence, there was gratitude, and welcome.

"Yes, please," Sara said, holding out her hand. "I'm Sara Crewe."

"Mary Lennox." Mary gave Sara's hand a firm shake. "Pleased to make your acquaintance." Mary finally acknowledged Lavinia, who stood with the remnants of her grand scheme lying deflated around her. "Oh, still here? Best run along, your dinner will grow cold."

Lavinia looked like she might speak—or scream even, which Mary would have much preferred—but mercifully, she accepted the checkmate and returned fuming to her herd. And like with the closing of an opera curtain, the other students took that for the end of the show. They went back to discussions of clothes or books or pairings or difficult courses. Sara Crewe was still a strange and fascinating point of conversation, but not the *only* point of conversation. At least, not for now.

"I am awfully sorry about Lavinia," Mary said to Sara. "She makes a point of challenging every new girl, especially those who are wealthier than she. But like any other warlord, she respects battle lines. She will leave you alone until she feels she has a better position from which to attack, now that you have an ally."

Sara smiled, and Mary felt the sincerity of that smile in her chest.

"I am grateful for an ally," Sara said. "So far, everyone has seemed content to gawk at me like an exotic bird in a menagerie."

Mary shrugged and said, "That is to be expected for the long term, I'm afraid. I have been here for three years, and they still think I have some jungle disease. And perhaps I do. A contagion of the brain. An infection of perspective. A rare case of *I've seen the world beyond Grand Britannia . . . itis.*" As Mary stretched to reach the bread basket in the center of the table, she caught Sara staring at her with pitiful disbelief in her periphery.

"Three years?" Sara asked. "You haven't been home for three years?"

A brief flame of jealousy ignited in Mary. The word *home* meant for many students what it meant for Sara, apparently: parents, tradition, familiarity, love. For Mary, however, home was none of those things. It was an address on the quarterly letters she received from her father. A place she would most likely never see again and knew so little about that she could barely imagine it anymore. She took a bite of a yeast roll and swallowed it jealously.

"Home is in India, presumptively," she said. "It would be a great act and expense for my father to ship me, or himself, back and forth every year. He is so busy, after all . . . The same can be said for many of the little ones." Mary pointed to a table of giggling young girls, all between the ages of five and seven. "Most of their parents live abroad. Home for them might as well be a steamer ship."

"Why, that's awful!" Sara said, gasping. "Those girls mightn't see their parents for another ten years or more!"

Mary shrugged again, but this time, she felt a significant weight on her shoulders. "Some parents prefer it that way."

The look in Sara's eyes was not belittling pity—something Mary had seen in the eyes of many of her teachers when another month would pass with no word from Mr. Lennox, or another Parents Day where his lawyer came to check on her instead of the man himself. It was, rather, an empathetic sadness. Mary had been on the receiving end of a multitude of human emotions and perspectives, but had rarely seen empathy. Not even when her mother died.

"You're quite peculiar," Mary said, unperturbed. Sara grinned.

"So are you," she said. "I saw you reading *Moby-Dick* in Monsieur's class. And India, how exciting! Do you miss it? What was it like growing up there?"

For all of Mary's fifteen years, she had never been able to claim a "friend." She had her ayah, who was certainly her companion, her teacher, her champion, but never her friend. An only child surrounded by children she wasn't allowed to play with, Mary had grown up believing that friendship was something rare and to be avoided. Now, sitting next to Sara Crewe, she saw the appeal of friendship and resolved to pursue it to its fullest conclusion.

3

"Where's the French maid?"

"Pardon?"

"I was told to expect a French maid," Mary teased.

Sara watched Mary walk slowly throughout her room, touching everything. It was Sara's first Sunday at the seminary, and the evenings after church and supper were left free for the students to fill as they wished. Mary was insistent on seeing this palace that the new girl was apparently living in. In reality, she had a single room with tall windows, a bed, a vanity, a wardrobe, a writing desk, and a tea table. No salons or libraries or dressing rooms. The only great difference from the other students was that Sara had her room to herself, instead of sharing with another girl, and that alone was a great expense. They really were incredible, the rumors concerning her that stirred about the seminary like a typhoon.

Over the past few days, Sara had formed a series of opinions about Miss Mary Lennox. There was a weakness to her body, a sickness that could be seen in her sallow skin and eyes set deep in her head. Sara was morbidly reminded of the image of a man she'd once seen in an infirmary, dying of starvation. Skin stretched taut over a round skull, limbs long and bony, a small presence, worn down enough to be transparent. Something of that starvation lived in Mary's eyes. She was well-fed and provided for, yet she hungered.

"I certainly don't have a French maid," Sara said as she unwrapped and combed her hair for the afternoon. "I've never been tended to, not by servants. Papa says such positions stink of bondage."

Sara's face was to her vanity mirror, but in the reflection, she could see Mary stop in her analysis of Sara's small traveling library and turn toward her.

"Truly? But who minded you whilst your parents were occupied?"

"When I was a child," Sara said, "my family looked after me, mainly my aunties. As I grew older, I had chores. Along with my mother, I laundered my own clothes and cooked my own meals. Oh, don't look so insulted, I'm sure you're familiar with the concept of doing for one's self."

Laughing, Mary stuck her tongue out at Sara and said, "Of course I'm 'familiar with the concept,' *Miss Crewe*. It just seems all rather fantastical. Like a gryphon or unicorn. I mean, a self-reliant lady of means and breeding, whoever heard of such a thing?"

Sara wasn't quite sure how much satire was in that question, and how much true disbelief.

"My parents have what you might call dueling philosophies," Sara said. She looked herself over in the silver-backed mirror, at her thickly curled hair, the sun-bleached streaks beginning to fade. "Papa taught me to be independent and educated. Mama taught me to be elegant and cultured. Or whatever she thought that meant. Both thought their philosophy was the only philosophy, so I became a student of both."

Mary ran at a trot and launched herself onto Sara's large four-poster bed. "How exhausting!" she said, swooning dramatically. "It must be a terrible imposition, being so perfect."

Sara knew that Mary was teasing her—over the last five days, Sara had come to understand that teasing was Mary's first overture toward affection—but the gibe struck deep.

"Not perfect," Sara said. "Refined. Fire-tested."

They were silent for a moment. Sara could see Mary splayed out on the wide bed, her booted feet swinging back and forth girlishly. The only sound was the beat of Mary's heels hitting the wood of the bed frame. Sara had just finished plaiting her hair in the way her mother preferred to keep it straight and pliable when Mary spoke again.

"If you could do anything, be anything, what would you be?"

Sara crossed the room and flopped down next to Mary. Together, they looked up at the tapestry that hung between the posts of the bed. It depicted a Grecian meadow and milk-skinned nymphs with rounded edges dancing sensually to the flute of a satyr. The nymphs were always white women with burnished, golden hair. So were the mermaids, and the princesses, and the queens. No one was brown-skinned or dark-haired. None of the women looked anything like Sara.

"An actress," Sara said at last in answer to Mary's question. "If I could be anything, I would be an actress. If I could be anywhere, I would be on a stage, reciting Shakespeare and Aeschylus and all the great tragedies. I saw my first play—*real* play—in Manila when I was a girl, and I knew then that it was the only thing I was ever meant to do. Does that sound terribly dull?"

Mary shook her head emphatically.

"No, not at all! If anyone was ever to be an actress, it would be you. You have a natural presence."

Sara was touched by Mary's compliment. Ever since their first meeting, she had a sneaking suspicion that she didn't give them out often or receive them herself.

"You are kind to think so," Sara said. "What about you? Where would you be if you could be somewhere else?"

Mary seemed to sink back into the bed at that. She tilted her head like a curious cat and squinted her eyes, deep in thought. Obviously, she'd mused over this question often. Something about that broke Sara's heart.

At last, Mary said, "On a ship with a course set for a place that's wild and untouched. Bound for an adventure, disappearing over the horizon. Like the heroine in an epic drama."

Sara closed her eyes and allowed herself to see what Mary was seeing. Crystalline waters. Warm sea spray. A sunrise so brilliant that it hurt your eyes to look upon it. Nothing behind you and everything before you. And there was Mary, standing confidently at the helm, laughing like a pirate.

"May I come with you?" Sara asked. Mary looked at her with frightening seriousness. Everyone said Sara was solemn, but Mary seemed to hold the matters of her heart and luminous imagination with the greatest care.

"Would you?" she asked in a quiet voice.

"Of course," Sara said with all truth and sincerity. "It would be the greatest honor."

Mary's smile was filled with purpose. Sara did not doubt that one day, and one day soon, Mary would be standing on that ship, chasing that horizon. And Sara was not using flattery when she said that it would be the greatest honor to stand beside her.

4

$\mathcal{M}$ary's time volunteering in the seminary's infirmary reaffirmed much of which she already didn't like about hospitals.

For an institution that housed over two hundred students year-round, the seminary's infirmary was a sad affair. It was a dark, narrow room crowded with hard cots. Mary herself had been housed there in her first weeks at the seminary, when Minchin was determined to find out just why her skin was so jaundiced and her hair so limp. She suspected a tropical illness of some kind, but the common consensus was that Mary needed to eat more fruit and spend time outside, far too gradual a correction for Minchin's impatient taste. Eventually, she resigned herself to Mary's appearance and resolved to correct Mary's character instead, a task that was proving to be much more troublesome. A town doctor from Manchester visited the infirmary once a week, but otherwise, the sick and injured were cared for by other students. Most were assigned to the infirmary as a kind of punishment. Sara was the first one who ever volunteered. And if Sara was volunteering, Mary was volunteering as well, to be with her friend.

"It's only an hour a day," Sara said in response to Mary's doubtful scowl when she was told.

"An hour that could be spent on something much more productive," Mary countered. Sara would smile and shake her head, but never argue. Mary could stand up to an argument; however, Sara's quiet, polite assuredness was impervious to debate. All Mary could do was accept her fate.

In truth, the infirmary was more boring than unpleasant. Mary was at least expecting some excitement: broken bones, gashes to the leg, a case of consumption or two. Instead, her shifts mostly consisted of wiping runny noses and fetching tea. Sara insisted on their taking the evening shift. Morning shifts carried the chance of exclusion from class, possibly even an extended breakfast. Evening shifts took place in those liberated hours between dinner and lights-out, and only the mad or truly despondent would give that up to mind children brought low by the flu. As Mary sat by the cot of a sleeping boy one night in the midst of a spring frost, she wondered which of the two described her.

He didn't have the flu, from what she could tell. For that one small deviation from the norm, she was grateful. His brow didn't perspire from fever, his lungs didn't rattle with every breath. His inhales were shallow, whispery things, and his eyes whipped frantically behind his closed lids, but otherwise, there didn't seem to be much wrong with him. Miss Amelia—Minchin's younger sister, a shy woman prone to great sighs of longing—was the teacher assigned to give some matter of authority to the infirmary, and she told Mary only that the boy was very ill and not to be disturbed. She refused to say what ailed him, but Mary's hard-earned interest was sufficiently piqued.

As she watched over his fitful sleep, Mary became steadily more determined to diagnose his mystery affliction. He was older than most of the students who ended up in the infirmary, closer to Mary and Sara's own age. His skin was pale, but not from any malady of the skin—something which Mary had experienced personally—but more from simple lack of exposure to sunshine. He had long fingers that twitched in sleep, and Mary could see dark smudges on his fingernails. She initially thought that he suffered from some form of flesh disfigurement that left men with blackened stumps where once there had been hands, arms, legs, and other more sensitive appendages. Mind you, she had never seen such a thing in real life before. But she had read plenty of books about pirates, sea travel, and the perils of adventure. She had a strong, but perhaps misplaced, confidence that she could identify the flesh-eating disease on sight if given the opportunity. However, Mary had seen this boy three times before, and while his fingernails were often stained black, the skin of his hands had yet to flake away as the stories often described.

"Perhaps he's just a messy writer, like you," Sara had said good-naturedly when Mary posed the inquiry. It was true, when Mary was chasing an idea on paper, she didn't once stop to consider the neatness of her penmanship. Miss Waldon had worked herself into proper fits over Mary's insistence to write not erect and poised, like a proper lady, but hunched down over her paper, gripping her pen with clumsy fingers and smearing ink all over her sleeve and palm. Mary saw the logic in Sara's explanation of similar marks on the sleeping boy but remained doubtful.

Then there were his legs. They were like the legs of a rabbit, kicking and twitching beneath the quilts of his cot. At times, Mary thought he might jolt himself awake, but he never did. She was reminded of a dog she'd seen once sleeping in the cool shade of her old bungalow's portico. The dog was so lost in sleep that Mary could practically see the wide fields stretching out before him, could feel the pulse of his legs as he ran. Watching this boy's legs become active in similarly random spurts, she began to wonder what manner of dream he was lost in. Was he running toward something, or away? Did the world stretch before him, or close in around him? Were his legs strong as they carried him over great distances, or was it for him as it often was for her in dreams: no matter how fast or how far he ran, his legs would weigh him down and his steps would become mired in sand?

It was while following the trail of this thought that Mary noticed that the boy's eyes were open and staring curiously at her.

"Hello," he said. He didn't sound shocked or put out by her odd analysis of his sleeping form. Mary, on the other hand, started with embarrassment.

When she was able to collect herself, she said, "Hello. You've been asleep for some time. Do you know where you are?"

The boy chuckled, but it was a dark laugh more appropriate for someone who'd lived much longer and had seen much more. He lifted himself into a sitting position, groaning with the effort and carrying, Mary noticed, all of his weight on his thin arms.

"I believe I am still at the Select Seminary for Young Ladies and Gentlemen in Manchester. Unless God is truly merciful and this whole sorry affair was no more than a bad dream."

Mary chuckled as well, just as darkly.

"No such luck, I'm afraid," she said. "Besides, if there is a God, I imagine He'd have more pressing uses for His mercy."

The boy cocked his head and looked at her as one would look at a beguiling insect.

"You don't think there is a God?" he asked as he reached for the gold-rimmed spectacles that sat on the table by his cot. He put them on, and his face transformed from that of a child with a small frame and dark eyes to some odd cross between a young boy and an old man. Mary could see the wrinkles in the corners of his eyes and the perpetual frown lurking in the corners of his mouth. They were characteristics she sometimes saw in her own reflection.

"I don't think there *isn't* a God," she said. "There just isn't enough to prove that there is."

The frown that the boy carried briefly turned up in a novel grin.

"That is an interesting opinion," he said. "How did you come by it?"

"Well, I didn't find it on the side of the road, as your tone seems to infer," she said. "Just simple powers of deduction. I grew up surrounded by all manner of gods and demigods and rituals. Everyone prayed, and everyone suffered. Or died. Or thrived. Nothing made any difference. If there is and has always been a God, then prayers would be answered, not ignored."

The boy looked impressed. "I don't believe I have ever heard a young lady say something so peculiar."

Mary snickered and felt her eyes flash, like a cat with new prey in sight.

"Perhaps you should associate yourself with a more diverse group of young ladies."

Then Mary had the awareness to realize that this boy was in the infirmary, and she was charged with his care and comfort, not starting theological debates. He'd just woken from an obviously trying sleep, and she had done nothing but challenge his beliefs and cut down his arguments since the moment he opened his eyes.

"Forgive me," she said. "I've been inconsiderate. May I fetch you anything? Water? Tea?"

The boy waved off her remorse and her question.

"I shall sleep again soon," he said.

Mary assumed she should take that as a cue to leave the boy be and let him rest, but she was hesitant to abandon the conversation. She was rarely able to communicate so casually with the boys from the college—the girls were intentionally separated from them for all but two hours of the day—and she found that there was something in the smoothness of their exchange, however brief, that she enjoyed.

"I haven't seen you before, in the dining hall or about the school," she said. "Have you been at the seminary long?"

The boy shook his head. "Only for a fortnight or so. I had an accident on my first day, so unfortunately, I've seen very little of the place."

Mary's impulses screamed for her to latch on to that word *accident* and pursue it, but she withheld. She knew from personal experience that explaining the subtle and strange ailments of one's body could be a vulnerable task, especially with strangers. If she delved too far, she could easily scare him away. Instead, she focused on the obvious.

"What is your name?" she asked.

The boy grinned, a true grin this time, not a snicker or a satirical scowl, and said, "Cedric Errol. Of Yorkshire. And you're Mary Lennox, correct?"

Mary had enough training in the mannerisms of polite society to feel scandalized.

"I am," she said, almost blushing. "Either my reputation proceeds me or we have met before, but I don't recall us being introduced."

The boy, Cedric, flushed in mortification after his drawing-room faux pas.

"I beg your pardon. No, we have not been introduced, but I have heard your name and seen you about during my few waking hours. You are the only student I truly *see*, you and the other young lady. The charming one who smiles a lot."

"Sara," Mary said. "Sara Crewe. And that is an apt description."

"Yes. Miss Crewe," Cedric said. "She seems very nice."

"She is."

"As are you, of course. For taking of your free time to watch over me."

"It is nothing," Mary said. "I do little but watch you sleep, anyway."

They passed then into the natural silence that comes with a lull in any conversation between the newly acquainted. Mary had a host of questions loaded on the edge of her tongue like bullets in a chamber, waiting to be fired. The most crucial, what was your accident? But that would be the very peak of rudeness, leaping upon someone with such a personal question. She knew that much, at least. So she settled on the most adjacent question.

"What's wrong with your fingers?"

Cedric looked at her with something akin to terror, then cut his eyes down to hastily examine his fingers.

"What?" he asked. "What do you mean?"

Mary thought it was obvious.

"The black smudges. It's some kind of flesh-eating disease, isn't it? Is that what caused your accident?" She grilled him like a prosecutor salivating over a forthcoming confession.

Cedric looked upon her again with another selection from his revolving door of expressions, this time the fear one possesses when facing the potentially dangerous.

"They're charcoal smudges," he said slowly. "Surely you . . ."

Mary understood his words, but she always had difficulty accepting a conclusion that she did not come to on her own. Cedric must have seen this in her eyes, for he reached over the edge of his cot and pulled a large leather portfolio from beneath the mattress. It was stuffed full with loose paper, to the point where the thong keeping it closed was straining with the effort. He laid the portfolio open upon his lap, and a world of sketches and drawings spilled out. They were some of the most fantastical images Mary had ever seen. Machines and devices drawn with such heightened detail that she felt she could reach into the paper and grasp them in her hands. Then there were softer, more intimate landscapes depicting rolling hills stretching uninterrupted into the far distance. Still lifes, but not of the endless bowls of fruit that Mary and her peers were forced to draw, but true fragments of an existence. A half-eaten dinner. A stain on a cotton shirt. The upturned carcass of a bee. A bouquet of herbs bound with string. They were all unique and strange and utterly wonderful.

"These are masterful," she said without a hint of flattery. "Truly. And there must be a thousand of them."

"Not quite a thousand," Cedric said. "Closer to five hundred, I would say. And more at home. Charcoal stains the fingers, you see." He held up his fingers for Mary's inspection. She took one in hand, turning it over to catch the minimal light. She didn't stop to realize that she had never touched a boy's hand before.

"Oh, you're awake!"

Cedric snatched his hand away from Mary as quickly as if he'd been stung. Mary's first instinct was to giggle at his propriety, but she held back. She turned to see Sara standing behind her, beaming. Sara was a girl with an outfit for everything, and the infirmary was no exception. She looked like a proper Florence Nightingale in a high-collared cotton gown with an apron tied around her waist and a bonnet on her head. She carried a tray crowded with teacups and a round-bellied kettle before her.

"They're charcoal smudges, Sara," Mary said, completely disregarding whatever conversation Sara was attempting to start up with Cedric.

Sara shook her head and said, "I thought as much. Honestly, Mary, you read too many novels." To Cedric, she said, "We have had quite a vigorous debate—regarding you, I'm afraid. The great mystery patient of the infirmary. Like the man in the iron mask."

Sara sat on the edge of his cot, close to Mary. Seeing the way Cedric smiled politely while still retreating farther against the headboard, Mary wondered if this was a frightening experience for him, being pinned in by two young girls who had passed many a breakfast creating outlandish stories about him.

"Nothing so dramatic," Cedric said. "Just the sickly son of a British landowner. One of a hundred, I would think."

"You're much more than that, certainly," Sara said. She was always quick to raise someone up, even beyond their own opinions of themselves. "I'm Sara Crewe, by the way."

He nodded in welcome. "Cedric Errol. Is that tea you're holding hot? A chill has come through here."

Mary felt it as well. A sudden iciness that dropped like a cannonball in a pond. Her first winter in Manchester, the cold just about drove her mad. It crept into her bones, and in the depths of one particularly horrid February, she thought that she might never be warm again. Now, although she still much preferred the warm of the summer sun than the cold light of the winter one, she saw the magic that dwelled in the geometry of ice and gray trees.

While Sara poured Cedric a cup of the tea she was carrying, Mary crossed to the nearest window, through which the cold passed unencumbered. The moon was full and strong enough to shine through the heavy snow clouds that dropped their delicate bounty upon the earth. The world outside glowed silver and the untrodden ground sparkled like a diamond-studded wedding gown.

"It's snowing," Mary said to no one in particular, but she fully expected Sara to drop everything and rush to the window. She was not disappointed.

"Oh my," Sara said, sighing. Her eyes were wide and shone with a kind of gratitude. Sara was just as opposed to the cold as Mary, but ever since January, she'd plant herself at the window if there was even a hint of frost. Mary was no longer quite as enchanted, but she could empathize.

"It must be the last snow of the season," Cedric said. "Rather unseasonable, actually." Mary turned and was surprised to see that he'd stayed in his cot while she and Sara gathered at the window.

Well, Mary thought. *Perhaps snow has become as mundane to him as wind and rain.* Then the oddest concept entered Mary's head.

She turned to Sara. "Have you ever been skating? You know, on the ice?"

"When would I go skating in the Philippines?" Sara asked, her raised dark brows creasing the skin of her forehead.

"Neither have I," Mary said, ignoring her friend's sarcasm. "I wonder if the lake has frozen over."

"In the three years you've been here, you have never gone skating on the lake right outside your door?"

"Oh no. Too crowded with all of the other chickens out there, clucking and laughing. Besides, who would want to skate in the sun when you could skate in the moonlight?"

Sara was quick to check Mary when her ideas led her down improper paths, but always with a smile.

"Mary, it will be lights-out in less than an hour."

"Exactly! And you know the teachers do not check beds. They go to sleep soon after the students."

"Will the front door be open?"

"Probably not. But perhaps the kitchen door—"

"Yes! For the grocer, who comes before dawn. They keep the spare skates in the boathouse. I can't imagine Minchin keeping it locked."

"We would have to be quick. An hour, at most."

"That should be more than enough time."

"What is happening here?"

Mary and Sara broke from their scheming, remembering briefly that there was another person in the room. They both looked back to see Cedric's eyes darting between them. Even his wary expression could not mar the delicate symmetry of his face. He reminded Sara of a Diego Velázquez portrait she'd seen once at an exhibition. Suprisingly handsome but in a cold, almost melancholy way.

"You cannot possibly be discussing what I think you're discussing. Correct?"

Mary glanced at Sara, who gave a grinning, shrugged consent. "Well, that depends," she said. "Do you want to come with us?"

"Come with you where? Out *there*?"

The fear in Cedric's eyes was something Mary instantly recognized. The anxiety and apprehension that came with stepping out of the relative safety of one's own home. She saw that anxiety take hold of him and was resolved to break him of it, as an evangelist preacher might resolve to banish a demon from a human soul.

"It's decided, then. You're skating with us. We may need you, after all. As a native of this frozen isle, you will doubtlessly have more experience than we foreigners."

Cedric looked down at his smudged fingers and grasped at his quilt. A shadow seemed to cover him suddenly, a sadness palpable enough to make Mary gasp.

"Please do not be so quick to assume," he said quietly.

"You're joking!" Mary said, loud and oblivious to the new tension in the room. Sara touched her elbow, detecting that tension easily. Mary didn't even slow down. "You say you're from Yorkshire, so I imagine you've had a lifetime to skate. What's wrong, have you fallen one too many times?"

It was easy for Mary to slip into cruelty; it was perhaps the only lesson her mother had unwittingly taught her. Though Mary hated nothing more than a bully, if she wasn't careful, she could fall back into speaking as one, even though she told herself it was only a bit of rough humor. Her ayah had been instrumental in checking that cruelty, but just as with speaking in French or playing the piano, if taught early enough, such lessons were very difficult to unlearn.

Mary saw the results of that lapse now in Cedric's face, which resembled that of an old man more than ever.

"My sisters had ample opportunity to skate in Yorkshire," he said in a voice both small and heavy. "But I never could. It is why I'm here in the infirmary, actually. You see, since I was very small, I have been afflicted with these . . . tremors. When they come, they render my legs almost useless. A few months after an attack, I should be able to walk once again. Slowly, with a limp and a cane. But they come closer together now, so I mostly use that chair."

Mary darted her eyes to where Cedric pointed and saw that what she'd assumed to be a mundane sitting chair, with a curved wicker back and worn leather armrests, actually had large brass wheels where back legs might normally be. Seeing it in its truth, Mary felt a darkness creeping from the chair. The trench in its red leather seat where a body would spend hours sitting, the notches in the wood, the dull shine of the brass frightened Mary somehow. And shamed her.

"We are so sorry." Sara threaded her arm with Mary's and patted her hand as a kindly governess might. Mary was once again grateful for Sara's selflessness; her willingness to share in Mary's embarrassment.

Cedric shook his head with a tight smile. It was a reaction that Mary assumed Cedric had used many times before when facing the ignorance of others.

"There's no need, really," he said. "One does become used to things."

That was such an elderly response. The type of thing Mary would expect a man five times his age to say. It struck her with a kind of disgust, that a young man—practically a child in Mary's falsely mature eyes—would resign himself so easily. Indeed, it lit her from the inside out with a prideful anger. This, none of this, would do.

"So, you're coming with us, then?" Mary asked. Cedric looked at her with eyes creasing in a confused hurt, and she felt Sara pull at her elbow.

"Are you mocking me?" Cedric asked. His voice was hard, striving to hold back the beginnings of a soft, angry sob.

In that moment, Mary despised herself. She almost stumbled over her words when she said, "No! No, not at all. I mean, at this point, you *must* come with us."

"But I cannot skate," he said. "I've never learned. Even if I had the strength of my legs, it would not be possible."

"We can learn together," Mary said. "We could use those single-person sleighs that they keep for the little ones. I'm quite resolved now, you see. And very little can turn me once I have made up my mind."

"She's right, you know. Stubborn as a mule," Sara said, stepping forward. Her wide hoop skirt moved ponderously, like the bulk of an elephant. "Besides, now that you know of our scheme and are a fellow conspirator, you must join us. Or we shall simply have to kidnap you."

Mary saw Cedric's eyes bouncing between the two of them,

searching for the lie or the joke or the tease. Mary was also a child who'd lived always in the company of adults, and she understood his confusion when judging the seriousness of his own peers. Finally, a light flared behind his eyes, and the water that had been brimming there was blinked away. Cedric smiled. It might have been the most brilliant and effervescent smile Mary had ever seen.

MARY WAS ACTUALLY surprised by how smoothly it all went. She admitted that it was one of her more haphazard and fly-by-night plans and would only succeed as a result of the failings of others. Thankfully, those failings occurred like clockwork.

It started with the end of their shift in the infirmary. Miss Amelia came right at the turn of the hour to escort them back to their rooms. Mary assured Cedric that they'd be back before midnight. He still found it all to be ludicrous and said as much about every thirty seconds, but his excitement hung about him like a cologne.

Mary and Sara were led to their separate rooms; Mary shared hers with another student, while Sara was given the world's freedom in her own parlor. Mary went through all the motions of the nighttime. She danced around her roommate—a pug-nosed local girl who'd managed to live her entire life within ten miles of the house in which she was born—and made herself ready for bed. When one of the teachers came through to conduct lights-out at 10:00 p.m., Mary was sitting up in bed with a book on her lap and her roommate already asleep. Mary stuck to her role, going all the way to the point of pulling her quilt up to her chin and closing her eyes in mimed sleep. In the silence, she listened to the wind bluster against the old windowpanes and the steadiness of her roommate's breathing. She gave this about a good thirty minutes, then she was up.

Moving like molasses in order to not wake her roommate, she dressed fully in her warmest, most comfortable clothes. The bedroom doors were never locked except for the rooms of the very young children, who were prone to waking and wandering from the nursery at all hours. Mary slowly opened her bedroom door, holding her breath as if that would magically keep the ancient hinges from screeching. She created just enough of an opening to squeeze herself through, then as she closed the door behind her, she whispered, "Good night, pug face."

The harsh and unaesthetic origins of the seminary were most obvious at night. The cold of the outside crept through the porous gray stone and created a chill so heavy that it felt as if the entire building had existed under some icy dome. The ceiling of the hallways was high and the few wall sconces had long since been put out, so the space above Mary's head writhed with a living darkness. She endeavored to be as quiet as possible, but even the steps of the smallest field mouse echoed like those of a giant within such halls. Mary told herself that she wasn't scared. She walked these halls every day. The shroud of night did nothing to change that fact. She found herself humming an unfocused tune to keep the ghosts at bay.

When Sara's silhouette appeared at the landing of the stairs they used to ascend and descend from the dormitory floor to the main floor, Mary exhaled with relief.

"Why are you early?" Mary asked once in earshot of Sara. They were approaching the boys' dormitory wing and had to proceed with particular caution. The old gardener, Mr. Hanley, patrolled these halls with a militant efficiency, or so the few girls who'd attempted to sneak into the boys' dormitory and lived to tell the tale had said.

"I couldn't wait," Sara said. "I feared I would fall asleep if I stayed any longer. This place is awful fearsome at night, isn't it?"

"I kind of like it," Mary lied. "I feel like an assassin sneaking through the bowels of a palace to dispatch a tyrant king."

"Oh yes," Sara said, unfurling shoulders that were previously hunched against the night. "I rather like that. Or prisoners escaping confinement in some lightless cell."

Mary laughed and said, "That's not too far from the truth." Then, close enough to see the shine in Sara's eyes, Mary took a moment to really take in her friend.

"What on earth are you wearing?" she asked, forgetting for a moment to keep her voice low.

Sara glanced down at herself, affronted, then back up at Mary. "I'm dressed for skating."

"You're dressed for tobogganing."

"What is tobogganing?"

The image that Sara presented brought to mind a Swedish elk hunter. She wore a thick, dark blue woolen coat with fur at the cuffs and collar, all over trousers—*actual trousers*—and deerskin boots. A bowl-shaped cap with fur-lined wings that turned her face into some kind of winged gargoyle completed the ensemble. An outfit for every occasion, as Mary had always believed.

Sneaking through the school together felt much better than sneaking alone. The shadows weren't as long and the sounds weren't as malicious. There was a power to it, in fact. In the silence, it seemed to Mary that she and Sara were the only ones in the fortress, the only ones in the world. She felt like a spirit or sprite, suddenly playful and curious. She laughed, and Sara laughed too. Finally, something exciting!

The door to the infirmary was unlocked, just like the rest of the building, and moonlight shone through the windows in long, straight beams. All the other ill students were deep asleep, only stirring to cough or sneeze softly. Cedric was sitting up straight in bed, on top of instead of under his quilt, more animated than Mary had ever seen him. He'd also changed clothes. Instead of the wrinkled nightshirt that everyone in the infirmary wore, he was decked in a full outdoor ensemble. Mary had no idea how he had managed and wanted to ask for an explanation, but something pricked her like a pin in the back of her mind, warning her that a question like that could be taken as rude and even obliviously mean.

Instead, she said, "I'm sorry we're late."

"You didn't get caught, did you?" Cedric asked.

"Surprisingly not," Sara said. "We were the opposite of caught. Nothing is locked in this place. Why, if Mistress Minchin woke one morning to a completely empty school, it would be no one's fault but her own."

"Good thing for us," Mary said. She then stood in what Sara always believed was a pose reminiscent of Robin Hood, stance wide and hands on her hips, looking between Cedric and the wheeled chair. "How should we do this?"

Again, not very polite. She knew that as soon as the words were out of her mouth. Yet he didn't seem to notice. In fact, he answered just as casually.

"Just push it closer to the cot, if you please," he said. Sara did as asked, and once close, Cedric lifted himself by his arms and slid with surprising elegance into the chair. He gave the wheels a tentative push and they glided quietly along the stone floor. He looked up at them with a comfortable, confident grin.

"Lead the way, ladies."

"I AM SINCERELY hoping this wasn't a bad idea."

Cedric sat in the tall, one-person sleigh—blankets stacked around him—and watched Mary and Sara fumble with the skates.

"A bad idea?" Mary said. She pushed her foot down until her toes bumped the front of the steel-toed skate. "I mean, perhaps it was not my *best* idea . . ."

Sara laughed and her breath gathered in a cloud about her head.

The night was sharp with cold. Indeed, the air seemed to sing with the sound of cracking ice. The high moon coated everything in silver, and the light danced on the lonely, frozen lake. Theirs were the only tracks in the uninterrupted snow, apart from perhaps the hurried tracks of a squirrel or wayward fox. Nestled within the shadow of gray trees and skies, the seminary looked more like a medieval castle than ever before.

Mary secured a final shoelace, then moved to stand from the bench set a few steps off the lakeshore. The ground shifted below her and her arms pinwheeled. She felt like a big, flightless bird. But an exhilarated big, flightless bird. Sara stood with a bit more elegance, but not nearly the same amount of confidence. Her hands reached out, grasping, and Mary clung on. Sara smiled in her direction, but there was wariness in her smile. Perhaps she was starting to think, like Cedric, that this was a bad idea.

The plan was to use his sleigh as a weight, something to stabilize them on the ice. It made sense in the infirmary, but now, with nothing below them but frozen lake ice, which could give way at any moment, the flaws in the logic were starting to appear. There was no chance at balance; the skates were worn and uneven, catching on bumps in the ice. It was impossible to feel grounded, and every step seemed a great unknown. Mary held on to the handle of Cedric's sleigh with white knuckles and cried out every time she felt her feet waver beneath her. Of course, Sara caught on to it all immediately. Her mother had dedicated significant expense and time to her dancing lessons, so she was well-equipped for physical challenges. After only a few minutes pushing the sleigh along with Mary, she was making small steps on her own, then longer strides until she was effortlessly gliding across the gleaming surface of the lake. Her enthralled laugh skipped over the frozen water like a stone, making her friends laugh, as well.

In that moment, the night seemed to pause and float undisturbed in time. The sound of their laughter was a music as old and natural as the forest itself. Seeing Cedric flushed with excitement from the cold and Sara spinning and dancing as if on the very air itself, Mary found herself stunned by her own childish, foolish happiness.

5

Dearest Papa and Mama,

As I write this letter, there is a warm August breeze wafting through the rafters, bringing in the fragrance of far-off wildflowers. The summer sky is bright here. We can see clear over the hills until far past sundown. Mary says that the summer horizon is magical. She claims that if one makes a wish at the very moment when the sun vanishes behind the earth, that wish will come true. But Mary is full of such fancies. To her, everything is a mystery or a drama or a myth or a ceremony. That, in part, is why I cling to her so fiercely. To her, the direst of circumstances are predestined acts of fate that are bound to work out in the end.

We sit now in the old chapel at the far edge of the property. A true ruin, Papa! Something as old as the Romans and the Normans and all of the English conquerors. Its crumbling walls, tarnished mosaics, and ivied ceiling are beautiful in their age. Mary has taken to calling it La Petite Maison to throw off those who wonder at our absence every free afternoon. I would spend all day, every day, out here if I could. The classrooms and dining halls seem quite dull compared to this place, which is slowly submitting to the wilds from which it came.

Oh, and I have formed a wonderful acquaintance with the young boy I mentioned in my last letter! (And not like you're thinking, Papa. Not like that at all!) Cedric Errol may be one of sweetest and most tender-hearted young men I have ever met. He is not much for spontaneity, but once convinced of a good time, he can be great fun. He has the saddest affliction, Mama. He gets these terrible convulsions where he shakes so hard that it's as if I could hear the bones rattling in his skin. He uses a wheeled chair mostly, but he will not be deterred from pursuing adventure. The last thing that Cedric will ever accept from friend or foe is pity.

However, the boy is a mystery. He claims to call somewhere in Yorkshire home. Mary and I managed to find the place on a map. It seems to be a very remote, rocky place far to the north, almost in Sir Walter's Scotland. He might as well be from

Faery for all of the information he provides us as to his origins. He is always sharply dressed in the latest fashions of the highest quality. He is well-read and speaks almost as many languages as I. He creates the most wonderful drawings, full of brilliant landscapes and fascinating machinery that I cannot decipher. It makes me sad that he receives no letters, and sends even fewer. Still, that makes him even more wondrous, I think. He's like a changeling left on a widow's doorstep.

I miss Manila terribly. I miss our home. I miss the sound of Mama's cello in the morning and the smell of Papa's cigar smoke in the evening. I miss our library with its hundreds of books. I miss our garden full of herbs growing knee-high. I miss the sound of frogs. I miss everything bright, colorful, and sun-kissed. But I feel so very grateful, Papa, as I am sure you knew I would. Mary and Cedric have turned what I was sure would be the loneliest months of my life into some of the best. This experience of having true friends— people my age whom one can be most at home with— is strange and wonderful. But still. The sooner I can see you again, the better this all will be. This far from home . . . I'm thrilled at the adventure of it all. But I am worried by how comfortable it has become. I feel like Persephone sitting at Hades's table. One bite of the pomegranate, and I shall never see you again.

Mistress Minchin is a terror, but nothing I cannot abide. As you say, Mama, fine manners and good breeding will outmatch any bias. And although she sneers at me as if I were a foul smell caught in her nose, I am on my best behavior in her presence. By the end of it all, I trust we shall be great friends. Well . . . maybe not friends, per se.

I was sorry to hear of the horrid business that you described in your last letter. A part of me had hoped that we had seen the last of the protests and upheaval last year. As you say, Papa, such things are never concluded, not until equality is ensured for all. Even so, I pray that you remain safe. You are not a young rabble-rouser anymore, Papa. For my sake and Mama's, please take care and leave the fighting to those with room in their lives for such risks.

I must run soon. The sky is turning purple and they will come searching for us. I promise, Mama, I am not getting up to too much trouble. I outperform in all my classes; Monsieur has even followed through on his desire for me to teach French to the little ones. I believe I am quite good at it. Indeed, if this grand plan of yours to catch a lonely earl falls through, I might make a successful governess. That is how Jane Eyre found her lord, anyhow. I do not see how the same could not be possible for me.

Mary sends her impassioned thanks for the volumes of penny dreadfuls you sent in your last care package. I personally can't abide the morose things, but she eats them up like sunflower seeds. It breaks my heart to think that the only parents who deign to send her anything other than quarterly letters that read like business correspondence are not even her own. Mary says she hates him, her father, but after seeing the excitement that fills her when his sparse letters arrive, I cannot believe it. It's as if she waits for him to change from this cold, distant man into a kingly father within the course of a few sentences. You will see, when you come. Such dreams dance within her, as well as a confidence that those dreams shall, and should, come to light. There is always a risk, as you know, for dreamers like that. The disappointment may yet break her.

Please give my love to Lola and the cousins. I miss them all dearly and am counting the days until I see them again.

Your loving daughter,

Sara Crewe

P.S. Forgive the inconvenience of translation, but I suspect Mistress Minchin has been opening my letters, so I have taken to writing in French, for

which, I assume, the headmistress has no eye or ear.
Perhaps I shall write in Latin next time, and really
give her the vapors.

"I DON'T BELIEVE I ever want to be married," Mary said loudly, proudly, as she flipped through the pages of a large book recounting the lives of Henry VIII's six ill-fated wives.

"You say that now," Sara said. "But when that perfect young man appears, you'll be singing a different tune."

"There will be no such young man. There will never be a young man that I deem worthy. For goodness' sake, look at how this so-called king treated the women he supposedly loved."

"Maybe the lesson there is to avoid marrying the king of England," said Sara.

"I am just grateful that I shall be entering society with you," Mary said. "The potential suitors will be so taken with your charms that they will pass me over altogether."

"Or they will see that your quick wit and clever tongue is the greatest prize in any potential wife."

"Don't move, if you please. The eyes are a point of contention for me."

Sara snapped her mouth closed and resumed her pose in quarter profile, staring into the middle distance. Cedric sat close by in his chair, sketching furiously on a thick sheet of paper. For months, he'd been begging Sara to sit for a portrait. Now that her hair was growing back after Minchin's display, he all but insisted.

"Why have you never asked to sketch *my* portrait?" Mary asked, perched on the tall bishop's chair that she'd claimed as her own personal seat of power in the abandoned chapel, now their makeshift headquarters.

"Do you think you could ever sit still long enough for a portrait, Mary?" Cedric spoke without shifting his gaze from Sara's face or pausing the frantic movements of his hands. Sara was always amazed by his automation. He saw and drew without a break, fluid and minutely organized.

"I disagree!" Mary said, as strongly as any parliamentarian. "Why, just last week, I stood still as a statue when Miss Amelia almost caught us taking biscuits from the kitchen."

"Well," he said. A smile ran away from the corner of his mouth. "Mischief does inspire the most uncharacteristic of actions in us. Especially you."

Mary made her tongue long as she jutted it out at Cedric, a very unladylike image.

Sara watched him in her periphery and for a moment saw a handsome young man under his exhaustion and suspicion and doubt. The leanness of his face made his eyes appear large and expressive. His smile, when offered in all its sincerity, was something brilliant to behold. Even in the relatively brief time Sara had known him, his shoulders had widened and his neck seemed longer, thicker. The little boy fell away like the chipping paint on the walls of this chapel. A charming mural lurked underneath.

Cedric blew softly against the paper, and charcoal powder collected on his lap.

"What of your tragedy set in the diamond mines in India?" he asked. Then, quietly, "I rather liked that one."

"Oh yes, of course. *Bejeweled Paramour* will be my grand debut—"

"Is that what we're calling it?"

"—still, all writers worth their paper and pens work on multiple projects at once. Who would I be, to hold myself to one story, one world?"

"Quite right!"

"Sara, please, don't encourage her."

Sara's gaze connected with Cedric's and he winked, making her squirm in her seat from the mirth of it all. For Sara, watching the two of them exchange blows was like watching two bare-knuckle boxers. A friendship of sharp jabs, skirting punches, and the bloody smile common to fighters who feel at home in the ring.

Sara heard Mary close her book, then stand. She crossed the floor of the chapel to the pew where Sara sat for her Errol portrait. Mary looked over Cedric's shoulder, down at the sketch, then back at Sara, then down to the sketch again.

"How did you do that?" she asked.

He didn't look at her when he asked, "Do what?"

"It is the strangest thing. I know the charcoal is black, and the paper is white, but you somehow manage to make her eyes dance with color."

Cedric snorted in his usual, dismissive way, but Sara could see a shade of humble appreciation rush up his neck.

"Such poetry, Mary. It is not all that difficult, actually. I just draw what I see. Sara is a fascinating subject."

"Honestly," Sara said, feigning a breathy, overwhelmed tone. "Mr. Errol."

A strong wind rose and rushed through the rafters of the chapel, stirring Mary's hair about her head. Even a month after the unfortunate event, when Sara looked at her friend and saw her short, almost boyishly cut hair, she was filled with a deep sense of gratitude. Mary never did share the conversation she'd had with Minchin after she appeared in the dining hall with Sara and Cedric. She only said that things were taken care of and Sara need not worry about Minchin's cruelty again. Sara knew that such a thing was impossible; the old headmistress had yet to see the extent of the harm she could inflict on Sara, and there was an assurance that she could, and would, push that boundary until one of them crumbled under the pressure.

"It's getting cold," Mary said with a shiver.

"Well, it *is* October," Cedric said. "It will be winter soon."

Mary groaned, and the sound echoed up and up into the ceiling, bringing to mind briefly the small choirs that must have raised their voices in praise in this chapel once.

"How can the summer be over already?" she asked. "It was August just yesterday."

If only, Sara thought. Indeed, the seasons crept along with belligerent slowness in her opinion. The months until Parents Day had turned to weeks, and soon would be days. Days as long as years. Sometimes, Sara would wake in the night crying because she missed her parents so terribly. She'd start roughly awake after suffering through a bad dream and for a moment not know where she was. Once, she even called out for her mother, paralyzed with terror. Then she would look about the room, which was somehow both cheaply and luxuriously decorated, and she would remember. Her own bed was thousands of miles away, and it would be two years yet before she spent a night in it again.

The early-evening air was split by the sounds of someone making their way, rather ungracefully, through the overgrown brush outside the chapel. Preceded by some very unladylike, whispered curses, Lavinia Herbert appeared through the rotted old church doors. Her usually pristine gown was muddied and cut, and even her hair held evidence of the difficulty she'd had arriving at the location. The expression on her face told Sara that she would rather be scrambling over a pass in the Battle of the Pyrenees than standing there right at that moment. Her eyes, squinted with suspicion, looked over the space with barely veiled disgust.

"I cannot believe," she said, "that this musty old place is where you all insist on passing your time. I almost broke my neck getting here!"

"How ever did you find us, Lavinia?" Mary asked. "I thought this place was a secret." She looked to Sara and Cedric. "Isn't it a secret?"

Lavinia tossed her long, spun-gold hair over a shoulder. "Oh, hardly. Everyone knows about your so-called Petite Maison."

"I am afraid she's right, Mary," Sara said. "It is rather common knowledge."

"Even in the boys' dormitory?" Mary asked Cedric.

"*Especially* in the boys' dormitory," he said. Then a quiet blush dusted his cheeks and his eyes dipped. "I am hesitant to say just what the opinion of this place is in the boys' dormitory."

Mary looked truly surprised, which Sara found rather sweet.

"I do not want to spend any more time out here than necessary," Lavinia said with a wide gesture of disregard. "Minnow wants you, little princess."

Minnow was a cruel little name she used for Minerva Minchin. It was a skill of hers, finding diminutive ways to be spiteful.

A familiar chill rushed through Sara. Lavinia took a sick pleasure in being the bearer of bad news. Sara knew that from personal experience. Still, she stood up from her seat and smoothed the wrinkles in her skirt.

"Have you had enough time to finish?" she asked Cedric. He blew once more over the paper and brushed the side of his hand across the surface. Sara reached for the paper, but he snatched it playfully away.

"I'll show you when you return," he said. "Leave you with some anticipation."

Sara followed Lavinia silently. She focused her eyes on the ostentatious blue bow the girl wore high in her hair. It bounced and bounced, calling for immediate and rapt attention. On their way, fellow students paused to wave at Sara or wish her a good day, many of them being her own young French-language students.

For every kind smile or enthusiastic wave Sara received, Lavinia would give a terrible frown. Lavinia was popular as well, but in the way dictators were popular. No one waved at her as she strutted through the halls. They'd duck their heads and cross out of her path. Unlike Mary, who had the vengeful spirit of a Spartan warrior, Sara carried no ill will toward Lavinia, for all her snakelike spite. More pity, truly. It must be a terrible burden to have confidence so low that you had to attack others in order to survive. Like a lost, sick dog backed into a corner.

"It's bad news, you know."

Sara blinked, and realized that they had stopped within the cavernous expanse of the seminary's rotunda. Sound seemed to take shape in that moment, spiraling around them and climbing up into the rafters. It gave Sara the sensation of standing in the midst of a whirlwind. That is when she saw clearly that Lavinia was looking at her with a frightening kind of glee. The very personification of the eye of a storm.

"What do you mean?" Sara asked.

"The reason old Minnow wants to see you. It's not good. I fear it may even be . . . unfortunate."

Sara could do nothing but stare. What possible response could she make?

"I saw your father's lawyer leaving her parlor, and he looked positively downtrodden. Terrible to think what would make such a dour man appear even more forlorn. I admit that I am awfully curious." Lavinia's hand suddenly jutted out from her side to clutch Sara's arm in a mockery of companionship. She squeezed enough to leave a mark. "You *must* tell me all of your news as soon as she's done with you. I promise it will stay in the deepest confidence."

Sara suddenly couldn't abide it anymore. She was tired of dancing around Lavinia. If there was something to be settled, let it be settled now.

"When did I become your enemy?" she asked. Her voice was straight, even, nonconfrontational. Sara didn't want a fight with her. But she did want an explanation. Lavinia, in a surprising show of bravery, turned to face Sara fully. Passing groups of students whispered when they saw the two standing facing each other, as if prepared to duel.

Leaning forward, teeth drawn back in something of a snarl, Lavinia said, "The day you were born."

Sara should have been deeply offended by such a vile statement of hate. But expectation dulled the sting of offense. It was something Sara's parents dedicated significant time to talking about with her. When one expects the words out of someone's mouth to be ignorant or cruel, or even evil, the acceptance of such words becomes easier. The pain was less. Not significantly less, but less.

"It does not have to be that way," Sara said. "I carry none of the disdain for you that you seem intent on carrying for me. We could easily be friends."

Lavinia crossed her arms tightly under her chest. "Unlike

every other soul that lives and breathes under this roof, Sara Crewe, I do not want to be your friend. I am still having difficulty understanding how someone such as you could be accepted to this or any school in a civilized country. You come from *nothing*! No family, no prospects, no legacy! I mean, who *are* you? What are you? Just some *island girl.*"

Sara was working very hard to maintain a stoic expression, but it was a considerable strain. She felt the muscles in her jaw clench, the veins above her eye jump, and the tremor in a lip that desperately wanted to curl. Instead of laying every curse she'd ever heard on the streets and in the hills of the Philippines on Lavinia's head, Sara forced herself to smile.

"I hope that you find happiness someday," she said, with a lifted chin and a straight, unshakeable spine. Instead of fighting the constraints of her corset, she leaned into them, allowing her body to become erect and taut with confidence. "And if not happiness, then something that will lift this darkness from your heart. I would pray for you, if I thought it would help."

Lavinia didn't even have the vulnerability to look ashamed. Perhaps she wasn't.

"No need to guide me like a lamb on a leash," Sara said. She dipped into a quick and superficial curtsy, then walked briskly past the girl. "I know the way to Mistress Minchin's parlor."

"Oh, Minnow's not in the parlor." For what she hoped was the last time for some time, Sara turned to acknowledge Lavinia. "She's in your room."

SARA HEARD THEM before she saw them. The door to her room was open, and from within came the sound of rustling clothes and porcelain against wood. She hurried her steps.

When she turned into her room, she almost couldn't comprehend what she was seeing. Minchin was examining Sara's leather-bound encyclopedia, given as a special gift from her father, with a transactional eye. Behind her, Becky was gingerly taking Sara's clothes from the armoire and packing them into large, hay-lined boxes. When she saw Sara standing in the doorway observing the ransacking of her things, Becky looked guilty, not an uncommon expression for her.

Becky was a curiosity on the seminary's campus. So quiet that some students assumed she could *not* speak, Becky worked in somber service to the school and mainly to Minchin. She was stunted in her growth from lack of nutrition, and her pale face was afflicted by what Sara came to know as phossy jaw. Sara was uncertain what that meant, other than that Miss Minchin forced Becky to cover the lower half of her face with a veil. Sara was more disturbed by the cause of Becky's disfigurement than the results of it. Apparently, Becky had spent the first ten years of her life making matchsticks in the one-room flat she shared with her parents and five siblings in Manchester. Most of her family died of cholera. The rest died of typhoid. Becky was the only one left of a family gone to dust to the point where no one in the school even knew her last name.

After some time, Sara fought through the shock and found her voice.

"Am I going home?"

Minchin didn't even seem caught unawares when she glanced up from the encyclopedia to look at Sara. She ran her long, pointed fingers over the gilded edges confidently, possessively. Then she tossed the book into a box with the care one would use to toss a sack of flour.

"Home?" Minchin said. "No. No, I am afraid not. Come in, please, Miss Crewe. Do close the door behind you."

Sara swallowed to moisten her dry throat and did as she was told. Now, stepping fully into the room, Sara could see that this pillaging had been going on for some time. The heavy shipping boxes were not just filled with her clothes, but with her books, her scarves, and things of tender preciousness, such as the large seashell her older cousin had fished out of the sea for her before he died of yellow fever. If these things were packed in the many trunks and luggage containers her father had purchased specifically for the journey from Manila to Manchester, Sara would have had no doubt that she was going home. But her luggage was nowhere to be seen. Just like when her father left her in the shadow of the seminary, Sara felt again the tilting sensation that comes with a complete lack of control. The personal effects of her life churned about her, out of reach and in the covetous hands of those who would do her harm.

Sara looked down and saw that her hands were shaking. She

clasped them before her, then waited patiently to accept this newest turn in her fate.

"Your father's lawyer visited me this afternoon, Miss Crewe," Minchin began. She moved slowly through the room, drifting like some great ship about the island of boxes and loose items. "Apparently, there has been a terrible accident in your homeland."

Sara froze, bracing for the worst.

"There is no painless way to say this," Minchin said, although she looked utterly content and absent of any pain. "But your own dear parents are reported to have died in the recent volcano explosion. Your father's lawyer says all their lands and holdings have been destroyed."

Sara continued to inhale. She breathed in and in and in, but she could not breathe out. The air built in her chest until she heard the rapid beating of her own heart in her ears. The strangest reminiscence came to her. She recalled the first time she swam in the sea. The swell was rough, and by all accounts, she shouldn't have been out amongst it. But everyone around her knew how to swim. She would stand on the shore with her feet deep in the sand and watch them leap about like dolphins. So, without alerting anyone of her plan, she walked into the water and tried to swim. A wave rose above her, groaning like a giant, and then another and another, beating her down again and again. She was a strong swimmer in a still creek or pond, but the sea was something alive. It met her childish determination with a primordial fury that she could never hope to match. She didn't have the time or breath to scream. The last thing she remembered before fainting from exhaustion and lack of air was staring up from beneath the waves. Her chest burned and the silence closed in around her. She swam for the surface, but it only stretched farther and farther away.

Now in a room halfway around the world, she exhaled. But the constriction in her chest did not go away.

"I . . ." She closed her mouth. Then opened it. Then closed it again. Her tongue was heavy, and she felt that if she tried to speak, it would fall out onto the floor and land like a stone.

"I need to go home," she finally said. Her voice was small, weak, and sounded very far away, even to her own ears.

Minchin leaned forward and said, "Pardon? Do speak up, girl."

"I need to go home!"

This, Sara screamed. And she was not one to scream. It was a terrible noise that brought to mind the wail of hungry, desperate children. Becky actually yelped and dropped the petticoat she was holding. Even Minchin—glowing with victory—looked momentarily frightened. The only sounds in the room were the bellows of Sara's breathing. Her head felt light. Her feet were unsteady. She desperately needed to sit down. She reached out with grasping fingers for something to steady her and touched only air. Before Sara could see the earth rushing up to meet her, Becky was there, holding her hand.

"Shush," Becky said in a soft voice. "Shush, now. It'll be all right." Sara nodded, clinging to those words like wreckage in the sea. Clinging to them for dear life.

Minchin suddenly regained control of herself. She puffed up her chest in the usual pose of self-importance and delusional grandeur.

"Going back to the Philippines is out of the question," she said. "The place is a disaster and there is nothing to go home to."

Sara shook her head and kept shaking it.

"No," she said. "No, I need to bury my parents. If they are truly . . ." Sara closed her eyes and struggled to say the word without breaking into a hundred million pieces. "*Dead*. If they are truly dead, then I must do my duty. As a daughter."

"Well, that is noble of you," Minchin said. It sounded more like a criticism than a compliment. "But I think the Spanish government will take care of that."

She said that with such casualness that Sara thought she might fling herself at the headmistress and pummel her with her fists. But of course, she didn't. She squeezed Becky's hand.

"In any case, it is not your duty anymore," the headmistress said. "As an orphan, your responsibility is to no one. And no one has responsibility for you."

"But I have relatives. My grandmother, my cousins—"

"From what Mr. Barrow has gleaned, no one in your family survived. Any lands, holdings, or properties are all buried underneath the ash. You have nothing, Sara Crewe. And no one."

Sara heard those words, but through some wonderfully stubborn will, she allowed them to bounce off her. Again, she felt the situation getting away from her, the control slipping through her fingers. She had to assert herself, get ahead of it. She gave Becky's hand a last, grateful squeeze, then released it. She collected herself and tried to ignore the rattling in her chest and fogginess in her head.

"Even still," she said, working quite diligently to sound respectful, "I clearly cannot stay here. I thank you for the time you have dedicated to my education, Mistress Minchin. If you would be kind enough to connect me with Mr. Barrow, I shall do what must be done to make my way home. I am a citizen of the Philippines. My country should decide what is to be done with me, if indeed something must be done."

"You're a guest of the British Empire," Minchin said with a bite at the end of every word. "And as I said, traveling to the Philippines is out of the question. There is also the matter of your debt to this school."

Now Sara began passing through sadness and into anger. She was there when her father paid her tuition, in its entirety and with cash. She saw the quarterly invoices for her lessons and clothes and the care of her person. There was no debt. If anything, the seminary owed *her*.

"My father paid my tuition in full," she said.

"But what of the room? The board?" Minchin asked while gesturing about her. "Your meals, which must be specially prepared, your extra lessons with the boys' teachers? Your additional piano lessons and cello lessons and singing lessons and dancing lessons—"

"Things I did not ask for!" Sara said. The pressure came

through her voice now. "You insisted that this was what my 'status' at the school required. My father was perfectly willing to have me treated like any other student here, exposed to what any other student would be exposed to. You cannot possibly hold your insistence on displaying me like a china doll against me."

"It was your father who wished to display his wealth with improper ostentatiousness, not I," Minchin said, thrusting a finger against her chest. "He wanted you treated like a princess, and so you were. I understand that you must be under considerable emotional disturbance at this moment, so I should not hold your ingratitude against you."

"And for that, I am endlessly appreciative," Sara said with a roll of her eyes, not even attempting to hide her insolence. "But the point stands, I must return to the Philippines."

"But you cannot. In truth, I have every right to turn you over to a debtor's prison. Hundreds of pounds owed to me that I shall never see. However . . . I do pride myself in maintaining a Christian spirit. Considering the debt and the sad fact that you have nowhere else to go, I shall allow you to remain at the seminary."

This, Sara was not expecting. She expected Minchin to leap at the chance to escort her through the thick front doors and watch the back of her walk away.

"With conditions."

Now, this, Sara fully anticipated.

"What conditions?" she asked.

"The debt must be collected somehow," Minchin said. She held her hands out, palms up, and shrugged as if this were a great inconvenience to her. As if Sara weren't the one standing in what was once her room, having just been told that her parents had been killed. "That, I cannot dismiss. These fine things of yours will help, certainly. But they will not clear the ledger. The rest, I propose you pay back in wages. As I am sure you've witnessed as a student, there is much need on this great estate. Cooking, cleaning, managing the grounds, caring for the students. You are a very bright girl, Sara. I am sure you can easily rise to the occasion."

Sara stood straight while accepting this news. This *proposition*. There was something smoldering underneath it, a cruelty that she'd actually assumed Minchin was too dull to be capable of. It was devious, malicious, and humiliating. And possibly Sara's only option.

"When will I know that my debt has been paid?" she asked.

A smile like that of the Cheshire cat cut slowly across Minchin's face.

"When you need to know," she said. "You may even continue teaching French to the young girls." She clapped, as if coming upon a brilliant realization. "You may take over Miss Amelia's class! Lord knows, she has never been the best with languages."

Sara swallowed and nodded her head just to keep it from lolling off her neck.

"Where am I to sleep, then?" she asked. "If not here? What am I to wear, if not my clothes? What of my education?"

"Do not make such a dour face," Minchin said. "It is not as if I would have you sleep in the kitchen by the fire. You will live in the attic, with Becky." Sara looked down at Becky, who averted her gaze. "As for your clothes, you may keep what you are wearing now. Anything else will be provided for you, by the school. When you need it." Sara was wearing a simple pinstriped cotton frock. Perhaps the simplest thing she owned. An interesting turn for Minchin, that this terrible revelation didn't come on a Sunday, when Sara would have been wearing all her best for church. "Your education, you may continue, if you wish. You can do your studying alone at night, after your chores are completed. That will come out of your wage, though, of course."

Of course.

Sara just then realized that she had yet to cry.

"Will I have time to consider all of this?" she asked. Minchin had the proud audacity to laugh.

"I hardly see what your other options might be," she said. "But you may have the evening to decide. Just know that if you make the wrong decision, you might as well leave this place and never return, because apart from what I have offered, there is nothing else that can be done for you."

WHEN SARA RETURNED to the chapel, the crescent moon was rising. She was so quiet upon entering that Mary actually jumped when she saw her standing in the shadow of the doorway.

"Hell's bells, Sara!" Mary exclaimed. "You just about scared me half to death. Where have you been? Cedric is being a terrible tease and would not let me set eyes on your portrait until you returned."

Sara stepped into the light and saw the faces of her friends fall.

"What happened?" Cedric asked.

"You look terrible," Mary added, stating what was surely obvious. "Did you get lost coming back here?"

In truth, Sara had gotten lost. When she left the place that was once her room, pursued by Minchin's solution to the new problem of her destitution, she walked out of the seminary and kept walking. She walked and walked. She walked to the edge of the property, walked until the lawn faded into the garden, faded into the woods, faded into the wild forest. She walked over ankle-deep puddles and through cutting hedges. She stumbled once and fell headfirst down a hill, only stopping when she collided with the base of a fallen tree. She walked until the sight of the seminary was far behind her. She walked until she saw nothing before her, and nothing behind. She walked until her feet ached and her legs burned from the effort. She walked and had every intention of walking forever. Then the chapel's old steeple appeared over the tops of the trees and called to her, and her steps turned toward it. The closer she drew, the more her mind cleared. The more she felt. The more she remembered.

She walked through the chapel doorway, saw the only two people she had left in the world staring back at her with beseeching eyes, and suddenly the weight of it all was too much. She collapsed.

6

*I*t took some encouragement, but after a time, her friends were able to pull the truth from Sara. And it was dire.

"This is unacceptable," Mary said, fuming and pacing a trench into the centuries-old flagstone. "We cannot allow this. This cannot be permitted to stand!"

She was furious. Even more than when Minchin cut Sara's hair. Now her dearest friend was being trussed up like a prize stag to be paraded around in the depths of her loneliness and desperation. When Sara most needed the protection and benevolence of the school, which was under every obligation to raise and defend her, she was being thrown to the proverbial wolves. Mary was so angry that she couldn't be still. Her stride had to go in circles lest she take off straight for the seminary and give Minchin and the whole sorry lot of them everything they doled out, and then some.

She had said as much since hearing the full story and in a thousand different ways, but Sara remained silent. She hadn't moved since walking into the chapel and collapsing to the floor. Even when Cedric and Mary picked leaves from her hair and cleaned the mud from the heels of her shoes, she'd barely blinked. That bright spark of what Mary had always seen as some kind of ephemeral purity in Sara's eyes had gone dull. Her mouth was a firm, straight line; there was neither a frown nor a smile nor an openmouthed wail of despair. She looked so much older with this mask of numbness. It sent a shiver through Mary when she looked at her. It was like looking at a living corpse.

"Well. We must do something," Mary said again. The only response came from her echoes up in the rafters. The voices of somber angels, both applauding her righteousness and mocking her naïveté.

"What can be done?" Sara asked slowly, with long, gasping breaths between each word. The very act of speaking seemed to take considerable effort and cause terrible pain. Cedric sat by her and for most of this sad witching hour had done nothing but hold Sara's hand. Sara clung to it with an inhuman strength that no other iota of her being seemed to radiate. Every inch of willpower was concentrated in that one hand's grasp on another.

"We can go to your father's lawyer!" Mary surged forward, feeling the inspiration of what she was sure would be the answer to this whole mess of a problem. "If he acted in your father's interest, he must be obligated to act in yours. Honor must demand it if not decent legality."

Sara rolled her bloodshot eyes at Mary. "Honor or legality means very little when there is no money to bolster it. My father is believed dead. My mother is believed dead. My entire family. No, dear Mary. I think the only case that man may defend is that of the school, and the apparently staggering debt I owe them."

"My father, then," Mary said. She rushed to Sara's side and was soon holding her other hand as tightly as Cedric. "He has money, more money than he knows what to do with. Whatever debt is owed, he can pay it. I can make him pay it."

Sara made a sound that could possibly be called a laugh, if not for the way it clattered about in her throat.

"You are more than I deserve to even offer that," Sara said. "But even if the debt was to be paid, it is impossible for me to return to the Philippines now. I don't have enough money to get to London, never mind aboard a steamer and halfway across the world. This place"—her eyes drifted up and around her, her gaze becoming crowded with fear—"this is my home now. I should be grateful. Mistress Minchin had every right to toss me out."

"What kind of Christian would she be if she did that?" Mary asked. "I hold no candle for the faith, but with all her talk of goodness and virtue . . . If she had any soul at all, she would erase this so-called debt and allow you to live out your time here as a student, as it should be! You are her *best* student! I can count on both hands how many parents have entombed their children here because of you and your accomplishments. How does she intend to explain your going from star pupil to scullery maid overnight? No one would believe her. The parents will never allow it!"

"Oh, Mary!"

Sara was up now, exerting more energy in a second than Mary

had seen from her in an hour. She walked farther into the old church, up and onto the raised dais where an altar and a pulpit once stood. The silhouette of her back was stiff and hunched in the low light.

"For all of your bravery, there's so little that you really understand," Sara said. A cold wind ran through her voice. "This is exactly what every parent that has a child in this place would want: the uppity island girl put in her place. 'How dare she outshine the descendants of lords and earls and despots? How dare she buy her way into this school, this country?' It will fit their expectations, my parents' deaths. And my debt. 'Of course, all that money was just for show. How could we ever assume that they were decent, respectable people?' Lord, I do not even know how to begin to find what remains of my family! If they're not among the hundreds dead already. My friends. My neighbors. Everyone I have ever known."

A sob broke through Sara's flimsy barrier, and even from a distance, Mary could see how it racked her body. She curled into herself like a wounded animal, and everything about her said *alone, alone, alone.* It was a death by a thousand cuts for Mary's heart. Instead of crying as she herself wished to do, she turned this boiling-over frustration on Cedric.

"And why have *you* been so quiet?" she spat, as if one word from him would have settled the whole matter.

"Sara has a point," he said. Before she could rise up over him like a black wave, he added, "Even if we could assemble enough money to erase her debt, where would Sara go from there? She is not of age to come out in society. And without a dowry—"

"You sound as if you've given up on her already!"

"Not at all. But we must think in realities. For God's sake, Sara's parents are dead! No childish fancy is going to make that go away."

Mary bristled at the insinuation that she was either childish or fanciful.

"I *know* that," she said. "I do. But I also believe that no amount of hand patting or tear wiping is going to make the situation easier to bear. Why think in realities when you could think in hope?" Then Mary fixed him with a critical and appraising glare. "What of your parents, Cedric? Could they be of assistance? I can do my best to cajole the money out of my father, but if you have a home only a train ride away—"

"I have no home, Mary," he cut her off coldly, absolutely. "None that I could easily return to at any rate, just like you."

"You mean to tell me that you will do nothing to keep this terrible thing from happening?" she asked, fearing the answer even though she knew what it would be.

True to form, he straightened his spectacles and tented his old-man hands. "It is already done."

For a fleeting, blink-and-it's-missed moment, Mary hated Cedric Errol. But the moment passed. Indeed, in days to come, she would forget it had ever happened.

But that didn't mean she was backing down.

She announced to the room, "I have a plan!"

Sara actually groaned from her lonely altar. "Please, Mary, no more plans."

"You haven't even heard it."

"I'm sure it will be brilliant. And ludicrous. And utterly impossible to achieve."

"That just shows what you know."

Mary rose and crossed to Sara, taking her hands and clasping them tight.

"I am writing what is sure to be greatest play of the decade," she said without a shred of doubt. "The heroine will be beloved for generations, and that role *has always* and *will always* be yours. Parents Day is only weeks away; we can rehearse and practice and prepare, then stun them all. Producers are parents here, art patrons who will pay us for the honor of staging our plays."

Sara did not break, but Mary could see reason and hope waltzing in her eyes. She didn't believe it could be, not yet. But she would.

"Do you truly think that after all this, Mistress Minchin will approve of a command performance of your play in front of the most important figures at school?"

"Well, who said she has to approve it? Or even know about it? In the early days of theater, players would just assemble in public spaces and perform. She cannot deny us our right to express ourselves."

"You seem to forget that Mistress Minchin is a feudal lord who would rather cut off our thumbs than allow us the right to express ourselves," Cedric said, raising his voice to be heard. Some nerve he had, speaking up after all this time.

"You hush!" Mary snapped. Then to Sara, "Just one incredible performance, and we'll be off. We won't need parents, or schools, or anyone else's money because we'll earn our own. No dowries. No stuffy old men and frigid old women telling us who we are and what we must do. We shall be the Player Princes, the finest theater troupe across three continents, and everything will happen exactly as we wish."

Sara spoke with her eyes downcast, focused on the muddy hem of her cotton frock, now the only article of clothing she had in the world.

"You have such confidence in the fates?" she asked.

"I don't give a fig about the fates," Mary said with a dismissive brush of her hand. "I have confidence in myself. And in you. And in Cedric."

He perked up at that.

"Me?"

"Yes, you," Mary said. "We shall need you to create the larger-than-life scenery for this and every subsequent performance."

Cedric's mouth hung open, and Mary rushed to cut him off before he hurled one of his reasonable assertions over the plan like a bucket of cold water.

"You said yourself that you don't have a home worth returning to," she said. "Well, neither do I. And, Sara, although we shall never, ever be able to replace what has been lost, *we* can be your new home. Your new family." She cocked her head and gave Cedric a pointed look. "Right?"

He met Mary's gaze, unflinching. Mary threw a challenge, created a height for him to ascend to.

Followed by the odd, paradoxical sound of his industrial

chair's wheels against age-old stone, Cedric approached them. He gave them a smile, then held out his hand to Sara. From the height of the raised dais, she reached down and took it.

"Of course, she's right," he said. "We, the... Player Princes"—he swirled the phrase around in his mouth—"will be each other's family from now on. Relying on each other above all else. And this play of Mary's will be the thing to propel us up and out of this place forever. Of that, I am certain."

Cedric looked toward Mary, and the pride she saw in his face was enough to stop her breath. This figure of such sensibility and strength saw her, even if only for an instant—a girl of dreams and adventures and plans gone awry—as someone worth believing in. All right. Perhaps she didn't hate him so much after all.

She felt Sara squeeze her hand, and was shocked to see, when she focused on her again, that she was crying. Mary instantly panicked.

"Oh, Sara," she said in a low voice. "Please don't cry. I didn't mean for you to cry. You are right, of course, it's a ridiculous plan and it will never work—"

"I am not crying because of that," she said. Then, through the tears like a sun peeking through storm clouds over the ocean, Sara smiled. "I am crying out of gratitude. I am crying because of how blessed I am to have friends like you."

Mary inhaled, mainly to hold back her own tears. She then straightened her back and focused her ready mind on nothing but the task before her.

"Well, dry those eyes," she said. "And steel yourself, Miss Crewe. We have work to do."

7

*O*ver the first few days of Sara's new situation, she began to see the students of the seminary in all their vain, dry, uncompromising ignorance. It started on that initial morning, following a horrid night that never seemed to end.

After departing from Mary and Cedric, Sara climbed what felt to be miles of stairs to the very height of the school. The attic was broad, covering the width of the building, but the low ceilings made it feel like a closed coffin. She had to walk at a hunch just to pass through the miniature door into the nook that she would be sharing with Becky. Sara knew what prisons were, so she would not insult the imprisoned by making a comparison. But the shock did bring to mind rooms and houses designed to break the spirit and reduce self-worth down to the point where people would be prepared to accept anything. There was a cot—more of a straw mattress, barely even a frame—pushed into the corner. Crowded into the small space was a stove that seemed unused, or incapable of use, along with a scattering of old furniture not fit for the downstairs. A chair with a broken leg. A table that drooped in the middle. A low upholstered chair with its stuffing leaking out. And a lone, stubby candle protruding from the mouth of a milk bottle. It would need to be replaced soon. Possibly tonight.

The room was filled with a gray hue that came through the attic's only window: a thin, dingy skylight that showed nothing but muted sky. No sun. No stars. Even the light of the moon did not reach this place. The desire to leave washed over Sara. Passing in quick, dizzying succession, images that she associated with home swam before her. A bright, high-ceilinged house with sun-filled rooms that smelled of earth and sea. Her nana, soft arms always outstretched toward her. Even the ornery tabby that slept in the pool of light that landed on their west-facing porch every afternoon. Her heart reached out for each memory, only for them to dance out of her grasp. Gone. It was all gone.

She closed her eyes and prayed that the last twenty-four hours could be erased, wound back like a spool of thread. She knew it was impossible. The past stayed in the past. The dead stayed dead. Decisions stayed made. But, oh, how she prayed. More than she had ever prayed before, after a life raised in the shadow of a church, a priest, and the Catholic assuredness that if you prayed hard enough, God would hear you. She fell to her knees, clasped her hands before her. Her face was cracked and dried from all the tears she'd shed that night, and the salt of new tears made her cheeks sting.

"Please," she intoned to the vibrating air. "Please, please, please, please . . ."

She did not pray to be spared the hard work stretching before her. She did not fear drudgery; she did not shy away from labor. But a lifetime without her parents, that was too much to bear.

She did this for some time, until sleep came for her. She had hoped to dream, curled up on the hard, wide-planked floor. But she didn't dream. Even nightmares left her in peace. And for that, she supposed, she should be grateful.

She woke to the sound of skirts rustling and the firm grip of a hand on her arm. She opened her eyes to see Becky learning close over her, fully dressed for the day in her veil and a black maid's uniform.

"Miss," she whispered with that same deference that she'd shown when Sara was the star pupil and not an indentured servant. "Miss, you must rise. It will be morning soon."

"Morning?" Sara asked in a voice made scratchy from sleep and crying. The color in the room hadn't even changed between sleeping and waking.

"Yes, miss. Dawn. I was told by the mistress to wake you for morning chores."

Ah, Sara thought, even through the fog of her confusion and grief. *So it begins.*

BEFORE THE SUN was above the eastern horizon, Sara had helped Becky stock and start the fires in the dining hall, clean the chalkboards in every classroom, scrub the foyer with soap and lye, prep breakfast for Cook, and set out morning tea for the older girls who would be graduating that year. Sara had yet to eat a morsel or wet her throat with water, and already she was worn thin.

"I cannot believe it," she said to Becky while hanging freshly washed linens in the light of the early-morning sun. "How is it that Mistress Minchin has allowed you to handle so much on your own?" The chill of winter was upon them, and Sara could not help but shiver in the thin dress that was meant for afternoon teatime, not chores.

Becky, despite it all, laughed, even as her thin, pale hands moved with expert quickness and efficiency. Sara was glad to hear that it was a beautiful laugh, one unhampered by the frustration and tragedy that no doubt followed in Becky's steps like a sheep followed a shepherd.

"It ain't so hard," she said. "Once you get accustomed. I am thankful for the warm meals, the roof over my head, the clothes on my back. If Mistress Minchin hadn't given me this opportunity, I'd most like be on the street."

Sara felt a sharp stab at her heart. Sara's misfortune was less than a day old, but Becky knew nothing but misfortune and still found a way to show gratitude. They stretched out a white sheet between them to fold tight at the edges.

"I am sorry," Sara said. "I did not mean to make light of the work you do, the life you live here. It must be a terrible insult, to hear this princess demean everything you have worked for. This former princess."

Becky's arms landed at her sides so suddenly that Sara's ends of the sheet were almost dragged from her hands.

"Now, miss, don't say that," she said. "Whatsoever happens, you will always be a princess. To me, and to a host of others here. Don't let 'em wear you down."

Sara nodded, hearing Becky's kind words but regretting that the girl felt the need to say them at all. Together they lifted a basket of folded sheets and carried it from the row of laundry lines behind the school to the kitchen. It would all have to be sorted before being brought upstairs so the students' linens could be changed while they were in class. And it wasn't even breakfast yet.

THE DINING HALL was awash with activity, which ceased as soon as Sara entered. Every eye was upon her, keen and sharp with hungry anticipation. Even those students whom she'd tutored or inspired or comforted salivated at the smell of her grief. Sara felt a rush of déjà vu. Here she was again, a bloody steak presented to a pack of hyenas that knew nothing but their own appetite. Out the corner of her eye, she saw something flitting in the air like a hummingbird. She turned her gaze and saw that the hummingbird was Mary's hand, waving over the heads of the others, beckoning. Cedric sat with her, radiating his usual calm assurance. There was one thing that had not turned on its head within the course of the sun's rise and fall. Their special table. Their corner of the world where nothing changed, where she could sit down and tell Mary about the awful dream she'd had the night before. Mary would conceptualize ways to work it into one of her plays. Cedric would shake his head and smile and express how glad he was that

Sara was feeling better. It lifted Sara's spirit just thinking of it. She smiled and took a step toward her friends, but a hard hand on her arm broke the mirage. Sara turned to look at Becky, who managed to radiate sympathy, even through her cotton veil.

"No, miss," she said. "We *serve* breakfast. After, we eat."

Sara nodded and the ringing in her ears shook her very brain in its skull. Of course. It was foolish to think she could sit down to breakfast like it was any other morning. She turned back to her friends. Mary's hand had stopped waving, and Cedric was reaching out to settle her, or perhaps comfort her. Sara tried to express through her eyes, wide and apologetic, that everything was different now.

Sara was ashamed of herself for how little she'd paid attention to the bodies floating about her before this morning. Becky and the one or two other girls that Minchin had exacted a penance on rushed between tables, refilling teakettles and adding fresh bread. Before, she would smile and mouth a thank-you, but never did she really observe them. Heads always down in deference, hands always fast and sure, cringing when admonished or insulted, but never looking their assailants in the eye. Sara tried to manage that same level of professionalism but found it difficult. Especially with Lavinia raising her empty glass above her head every few minutes, shouting "Princess, I need more milk! Princess, I need more juice! Princess, my tea is cold!"

It felt like someone was playing with a loose thread on Sara's nerves. The more she answered one of those shrill summonses—no better than what she would use to call a cur—the more she wanted to take Lavinia's tea and dump it in her lap. And no one raised a hand to defend her. Those same students who only yesterday had complimented her on her French or praised her dancing. All they did was stare. Or avert their gaze. Some even laughed.

And Minchin lorded over it all with her nose lifted and a look about her face that said, "Yes. This is the way. The way it always should have been." As if Sara were a clock that, until recently, had ticked out of time.

Breakfast was the hard end of a baguette and watered-down tea from leftover leaves left stewing next to the kitchen stove. They had only minutes before the chores would begin again, then minding the young children, and errands for Cook, errands for the teachers, errands for the students . . .

"Miss?"

Sara turned her head so Becky wouldn't see the tears.

"I'm fine, Becky," she said. "Please, don't mind me."

AND SO, THE days passed, one leading neatly and unremarkably into the next like a line of tin soldiers.

Wake, work, sleep.

Wake, work, sleep.

Eat when you can. Rest if you must.

Her only respite was the nights when the three could gather in the chapel ruins, cloaked in the late evening while the rest of the world slept, hard at work on their salvation. Mary would burst upon the scene like a prima donna, her arms heavy with loose sheets of paper speckled with ink splatter. Even her fingers and cheeks were stained blue. Sara often assumed that was Mary's favorite aspect of writing, the physical evidence of it. Baptism by ink and quill. She would peel off several leaves of paper and pass them around, out of order and utterly indecipherable. Mary's handwriting was that rushed and inconsiderate scrawl of the only child, legible to virtually no one but herself. Often, Sara would ask Mary to identify a word or a sentence, and Mary would stare at it for several seconds, and Sara could practically feel her thinking, "Now, what *did* I mean there?"

Yet, in time, Sara found a beautiful clarity in Mary's handwriting. It was something entirely new and almost rather clever. A strange and novel bridge between formal British schooling, the practical results of growing up surrounded by a language of symbols, and an innate impatience. Cedric jokingly referred to the pages and pages of writing as hieroglyphs, which made Mary beam with pride.

Night after night, even when Sara was so exhausted that she only needed to prop up against a wall to fall asleep, they rehearsed and attempted to breathe life into Mary's vision. It was a chaotic vision, bursting with youthful zeal and ambition. Even Cedric, a greater doubter than Thomas, would be swept away by the gushing romance, overwrought drama, and derring-do. The parents would be stunned, that was for sure. Stunned, and a bit concerned for the mind that would assemble such a thing. Even though Sara's reason told her that this play would not save her, not save any of them, those nights performing for a hidden audience thrilled her so that the truth of her circumstances seemed a distant storm, rumbling on the horizon and still too far away to cause her harm.

Then there were days when that storm was no longer distant, but bearing down upon her with gale force. Take the days when they sent her on errands in the city. These were not errands in the congenial sense of the word. First, a list from Cook as long as her arm, stops at the greengrocer, the butcher, the baker, the apothecary. Then a list from Minchin, mostly items requested by the teachers, or personal whims that Sara was sure she'd invent in the moment just to add more to Sara's load. All of this Sara would be required to carry from town to school, and in one trip. She'd begin early, after morning chores, and some days not return until dusk. She'd end those days with deep, swollen grooves in her shoulders, blisters on her feet, and spasms of pain racking her back. Each time she returned bent under the weight, Minchin would stand before her in the foyer, cocking her head and quirking an eyebrow so finely plucked it was barely there.

Without speaking a word, she would ask, *Have you had enough?*

Sara would inhale, shift the weight until she nearly groaned from the pain, and say just as silently, *Not quite yet.*

THERE WAS ONE Wednesday, three weeks into her captivity, when Sara's list of errands was particularly trying. She managed to grab a moment's rest huddled on a bench carved into the side of a building, and her tears melded with the rain until the two were inseparable.

"My word, child, is all well with you?"

Sara jumped, for it had been some time since an adult in this pitiless land had spoken to her with concern. She sniffed, wiped at her eyes, and saw a man standing before her. He was tall and lean of form, dressed in a rich black suit and carrying a wide umbrella aloft. His skin was the red of old brick dust, and his beard, thick and black, reminded Sara of her father. On his head, instead of the bowler that many local gentlemen wore, there was a bright orange turban. The sudden presence of color in the bland landscape siphoned of all variety made spots appear before Sara's eyes, like she'd been staring for too long at an open flame.

"I say, are you quite all right?" he asked again.

She saw a kinship in his accent. He was clearly not a fellow Filipino, but he had also put considerable effort into erasing any vocal indication that he was something other than British. Accents of non-native English speakers were usually the first things the bigoted used against them, to claim they were ignorant, to validate the bigots' feelings of superiority. Sara's mother had gone as far as isolating her daughter from anyone who spoke with the slightest diversion from the Queen's English until she was eight years old and well established in her languages to ensure such a thing would never be used against her. Sara imagined this man's parents had employed similar strategies.

Sara suddenly remembered that she'd been asked a question. "Yes, sir," she said. "I am quite well."

This gentleman looked anything but convinced.

"You do not look quite well," he said. "You look as if you have walked a mile over brimstone with a demon dancing on your back."

Sara grinned sadly at the aptness of that appraisal. "Nothing so heroic, no. But I suppose I have walked many miles today. And for several days prior."

"Yes, I can see that," he said. "Please take no offense with what I am about to say, but when I saw you sitting here—alone and wet and shivering from cold—I had the strongest impulse to ask after you. Something said to me 'she does not belong here.' Was that instinct incorrect?"

Sara said nothing, for what could she say? Instead, she hung her head and focused on the wrinkles in her dress that would never, ever iron out.

The man made a huffing noise of decisiveness, letting a plume of hot air out of his nostrils like a horse teasing for a gallop.

"Right. Come with me, then. I am treating you to luncheon. Is this your basket?"

Before Sara could stop him, the gentleman lifted her basket, exclaiming at the weight, tossing it over his shoulder, and making off down the street. Sara was frozen in place, staring at his swiftly moving form. He turned back to look at her and said, "Come with me, please."

For a moment, Sara had the good sense to be frightened. Here was this odd, fast-moving man, making off with her belongings and beckoning her to follow. This man could easily mean her harm, as so many men did. Yet, much against her better judgment, Sara felt herself rise. Felt her feet move from a slow walk to a trot between raindrops. She felt herself taken into the shelter of his umbrella, and she felt her soul exhale, assured that she was once again in the presence of an adult who, for the first time in a long time, might make everything all right.

ONE DOES NOT really know how hungry one is until presented with warm, filling, delicious food. Sara began eating as soon as the bowl of stew, steaming from the heat, was set before her. She ate so quickly that she scalded the top of her mouth, but she didn't hesitate. Almost instantly, the strength returned to her limbs, the vibrancy to her skin. Weeks of scraps and leftovers had left her weak, and with one proper meal, she knew what it meant again to be strong.

The gentleman did not speak as she ate. He sat with delicate poise, like a man in a portrait; back straight, leg crossed over the knee, umbrella closed, and his hand upon its tiger-head pommel. What an odd pair they must seem to the patrons of this genial restaurant. The lordly Indian and the lowly urchin. Again, sense and an animal's instinct told her to be frightened of him, wary of his intentions. But then another plate would arrive, and she'd forget.

After a time, when Sara's hunger finally started to be quenched, the man spoke.

"I despise this place," he said. His head swiveled like the top of a lighthouse, casting its light on the whole of the restaurant. "Look at them. Placid faces, rolling eyes. Anything that is not as it has always been is deemed dangerous and disturbed to them. It is like living in a nation of the willfully ignorant."

Sara listened to this proclamation, saw the contempt on his face, and finally thought to ask, "Who are you?"

The gentleman's dark beard split with a white smile, and a stab went through Sara's heart at the similarities she saw between him and her father.

"I suppose I have been remiss in introducing myself," he said. "I am called Ram Dass in this land. I was sent here by associates in India to observe how things are managed in this country of yours."

With biting clarity, Sara said, "This *is not* my country."

"Yes, of course. I see that now. Where do you hail from, then, young Miss . . . ?"

"Crewe," Sara provided. "Miss Sara Crewe. My parents sent me here from the Philippines for my education, or to find a titled husband. Whichever came first, I suppose."

The gentleman—Mr. Dass—looked Sara over and quirked a thick, dark eyebrow.

"Have the English fallen to such depths of depravity that they have created schools of peasantry?"

Sara's laugh came out like a blunderbuss, a loud and shocking burst. So surprised was she by the sound that she actually covered her mouth, as if stoppering a leak. Laughing in the presence of strangers, especially those dressed as finely as this gentleman, was strictly forbidden and deemed improper. Sara even looked about, half-expecting her mother to appear. But of course, that was impossible.

"I was attending the Select Seminary for Young Ladies and Gentlemen as a student, some weeks ago," Sara said, once composed. "My parents have since met with terrible accidents, and I now serve at the headmistress's pleasure."

Sara could feel Mr. Dass's hazel-flecked eyes bearing sympathetically down upon her, but she could not bring herself to meet them lest she break into tears at the sight of his pity.

"I am so very sorry. The Philippines, you said? Yes, I had read in an English paper about a volcano eruption—"

Sara simply nodded, still unable to speak the words aloud.

Mr. Dass leaned back into his chair and did Sara the courtesy of looking away, out the window and onto a street that still shimmered from the day's heavy rain.

"This headmistress, is she cruel to you, then?"

Sara's instinct was to say immediately, *Yes! She torments me, drives me to exhaustion. She takes a sick satisfaction in my unhappiness and I fear I shall live the rest of my life under her reign.*

But instead, she said, "She has been kinder than she has any right to be. There are debts that are owed in my name. If not for her, I would no doubt be in debtor's prison."

It wasn't entirely a lie. But it wasn't entirely the truth, either.

"Is that wholly the case?" Mr. Dass asked with narrowed, assessing eyes.

"If not, that is up to me," Sara said.

Mr. Dass had the cruel presumption to laugh. Sara's jaw dropped in affront and indignation.

"How is that funny, may I ask?"

"Forgive me," he said. "I am not laughing at you. Not truly. It is just that I have had so many relatives and friends say something similar in dealings with the English. There is a strange belief among us humans that we are responsible for the cruelty of others."

Sara saw the sense in that, but still, her pride was wounded by his candor.

"My friend Mary speaks with that same frankness," she said. "She says that respect should only be reserved for those who earn it through action, not through standing or rank."

"Your friend is wise."

Chuckling, Sara said, "She is. And unstoppable. She believes that one must always defend themselves, even when they're wrong. There is a part of her that refuses to acquiesce, and whilst I admire her for that bravery, I also fear for the day when she confronts something that she cannot oppose through belligerence."

"Belligerence is necessary at times. As I am sure your parents would tell you."

Harsher than she intended, Sara clipped out, "Belligerence also comes with consequences, as I am sure my parents would also tell me, if they could. Screaming and rallying can bring down wrath. When you do not fly into a passion, people know you are stronger than they are, because you are strong enough to hold your rage. It is better not to answer your enemies at all than to answer with anger."

Mr. Dass kept his head turned inward, toward others in the

restaurant, which he observed with that same critical and disappointed eye.

"My father was not a wealthy man," he said. "And yet he was prone to gambling his meager earnings on games of chance. My mother was a woman of holy patience, and she managed to make excuses for his behavior whilst tucking us in with empty stomachs. Eventually, as all must, things came to a head. My baby sister was very ill, and we had no money for medicine. My father's income would not be enough, so, as the young man of my household, it was decided that I must contribute to the family. Mind, I was only seven at the time.

"There was a young English gentleman in need of a manservant. A Master Samuel Carrisford. My father made a quite shrewd arrangement with him. I was to serve Master Samuel from that point until the end of creation, as far as my father was concerned, and my wages were to be sent directly to him. I had seen goats being sold. Chickens, monkeys. But never a person. Not until I myself was taken from my home and family and told that I would never see them again.

"Master Samuel was not a cruel man, not by any means. In fact, he rather doted upon me. I was required to do little more than arrange his clothes, tidy his belongings, prepare his meals, and accompany him into town. In exchange, he gave me the best home I had ever had. A warm bed, plenty of food to eat, new clothes. He even taught me to read and write in English, gave me access to his wonderful collection of heirloom tomes. Ever since I was old enough to think such thoughts, I had hated my father. But in those months and years in Master Samuel's service, I found myself grateful for my father and his role in freeing me from a very hard life.

"We lived quite companionably with each other, Master Samuel and myself. We spoke freely of his business and the politics of the day. We ate at the same table. He trusted me with many of the intimate affairs of his life, and I felt a kind of love for him. The foolish child that I still was, I thought this would go on forever. And then the time came for Master Samuel to marry. Overnight, everything changed. This Mistress Carrisford was a proper Englishwoman, no doubt, and she saw Indians as no more than human pieces of furniture to be ordered about, used, demeaned, and ultimately ignored. I went from what I believed to be Master Samuel's closest friend to little more than a hook on which to hang his hat.

"I felt in those days just as I am sure you do now. Grateful for what I had because I was deeply familiar with the alternatives. Respectful of a man who had given me no reason to view him as an enemy, respectful of an institution that I was taught to view as the pinnacle of human existence. Fearful of a future that was suddenly so uncertain. I watched myself reduced to the dust that these people believed me to be no better than, and I watched silently. And when that day finally came that I could be silent no longer, I made such noise that the sky shook with my sadness, with my rage. That rage called me to where I am today, to take ownership over my own existence."

Ram Dass leaned over the small table between them to look directly into Sara's eyes. His glare captured her, held her, and poured something profound into her.

"Allow others to treat you as if you are nothing, Miss Crewe, then you will be nothing. No amount of respectfulness or politeness or gratitude or decorum will change that."

Sara let these words settle over her. There was no mockery in Mr. Dass's eyes, no patronization. Only the sincerity that comes with experience. Sara did not answer him, only nodded her head.

He inhaled, and the air about them shifted from the gray solemnity that had grown with his story to the pleasant small talk of strangers that they had shared earlier. The glint returned to his eyes, and the levity to his smile.

"Would you like more?" he asked, gesturing to the empty plates before her. "Tea? Or something to take with you?"

Perhaps it was her full belly and subsequently more lucid thoughts, but Sara suddenly realized where she was and how long she had been there. The day would be over soon, and she still had so much left to do. The roads could be impassable by foot in the dark, and she had a rehearsal that night. She searched about the restaurant for a clock, suddenly terrified that the world had somehow managed to turn three times over in the brief hour she'd spent at that table with Mr. Dass.

"Oh no," she rushed to say. "No, no, no, you have done more than enough for me. Please know, if I had anything worth offering you other than my thanks—"

"I would gratefully decline," he said. "Your simple thanks is silver and gold. May I escort you to your next destination?"

"No, thank you," Sara said. She rose from the table, and Mr. Dass rose with her. "I have been foolish, allowing the day to run away from me. Indeed, I forgot, briefly, where I was. Who I was. But now I remember. And for that, I am more grateful than had a thousand meals been laid out at a royal feast."

Ram Dass inclined his head in acknowledgment, then gently took her hand to lay a brief kiss across her knuckles. It had been so long since she'd been shown such deference. The image was almost comical, considering her ragged clothes and unkempt appearance. It brought to Sara's mind a lesson from the gospels about doing unto the least of these.

"Thank you for allowing me to share in your day, Miss Crewe," he said before handing her a calling card made of thick, highly embossed paper of the best quality. "And if you should ever require anything, anything at all, please do not hesitate to look me up at the Duckworth Hotel here in Manchester. If there is more I can do to relieve you of these hardships, I shall."

Sara knew he spoke truthfully. If she came to him within the hour and begged for help, true help, he would offer it without hesitation. Something in her demanded that she take him up on that offer, for there would very likely never be another. Yet, she tamped down that part of herself, and lifted her chin in a show of confidence and contentment.

"You are kind, Mr. Dass," Sara said. "But no. I do not think I shall. As you say, the time for me to take control of my own life may be fast approaching."

Mr. Dass's smile broke with the sun through the clouds outside.

"And when you do," he said, "you will stun the world."

8

*T*his is ridiculous."

"You're ridiculous. Pass me that sewing needle, will you, Sara?"

"Where on earth did you learn to sew?"

"Well, when one spends much of their time sitting, one finds ways to occupy their time. My sisters often left their embroidery about, and they were only too glad to have me finish for them. Do try to keep still, Mary. If you wiggle again, I cannot ensure your safety."

"I'm not wiggling, I am flinching! From pain! The Spanish Inquisition utilized more humane forms of torture, I am sure."

"Now you're being dramatic."

"*You* are being dramatic!"

Mary stood stock-still on the seat of a chapel pew. A mismatched patchwork of linens, old skirts, and a quilt swiped from the laundry hung about her, held together by pins and luck.

Cedric sat eye level with her hem, which he was attempting to sew. Mary knew that this was certainly not the case, but she felt as if every pull of his needle somehow went through her skin. She feared that at the end of this fitting, she would look down and find that she and the skirt were one. Sara apparently found it all hilarious, for she stood to the side in her own Cedric Errol creation, unsuccessfully hiding laughter behind her hands. Their grand premiere was merely days away, and the costume situation was still uncertain. Indeed, trying to pack ten characters into a cast of two was a herculean undertaking, which Cedric was quick to point out with each of what Mary considered to be helpful critiques.

"Scene ten needs some work," Mary said in order to distract herself from the feel of his needle brushing the skin of her ankle. "And the soliloquy. Do you think we'll have time for the scene change?"

"We are still keeping the scene change?" Cedric asked, looking up at her. As predicted, his needle landed squarely on her Achilles tendon.

"Ouch! By heaven, Cedric, stick me again, and I'll kick you."

"We ought to unionize, Sara. The way this company is treating us is downright medieval." At least, that's what Mary thought Cedric had said. She couldn't really tell with the pins sticking out from between his lips while he pinched a bit of fabric before sewing in a crease.

"And of course we're still doing the scene change," Mary said. "How else are we supposed to show the transition between the mine and the governor's palace? The audience will be utterly at a loss without a clear distinction between settings."

Mumbling, Cedric said, "They will be at a loss for a few other reasons, no doubt."

"What was that?"

"Nothing, General." Cedric beamed up at her with a smile like a mummer's mask. His hands moved with a bit more care and deftness, but she considered kicking him anyway.

Mary looked up and saw Sara attempting to hide a deep yawn behind her hand. She took in her friend standing before them in a moment of usually hidden vulnerability and understood how exhausted she must have been. Up before dawn, asleep well after dark, and naught but work and labor for all of the hours in-between. Mary was instantly ashamed, ashamed of her own inconsideration.

"We can continue this tomorrow," she said. She extended her hand down to Cedric, who helped her from the pew. A train of loose threads trailed behind her. "Cedric and I shall remain and work on sets and costuming."

Sara must have realized her lapse in maintaining that shield of contentment, because she instantly squared her shoulders and smiled, even though that alertness did not reach her eyes.

"No," Sara said. "I am quite well, let's continue."

"My star actress carries the play. Cedric and I can keep going, while you take some much-needed rest."

Sara's protestations were brief and quickly struck down. Eventually, she bid them good night. Mary turned back to Cedric after watching to be sure Sara made her way through the woodlands surrounding the chapel safely.

"So," she said to him, striking her Robin Hood pose. "Shall we get started on the governor's mansion?"

Mary's sewing scissors once again snagged on the thick paper that served as the main canvas for the production's set design. It was normally used to wrap meat, fish, and other raw materials in the seminary kitchens, but over the weeks, Mary had managed to collect enough to give Cedric something to work with. He'd taken the role of artistic designer with more seriousness than she expected, having stayed up all hours sketching, painting, and cutting away without any of the resources that a true designer could hope for. Mary considered Cedric as he sat across from her, painting what would ultimately be the sitting room where the great climax of the play would occur. His face was drawn in deep concentration, his hands moving deftly and assuredly. His legs were stretched before him, his back propped against the seat of a pew. So rarely did Mary see Cedric out of his chair, it was disconcerting to watch him now, appearing as limber as any other student.

"What color for the drapery, do you think?" he asked. The paintbrush—borrowed from the art room where young women practiced their watercolors—was held poised for a decisive stroke.

Mary leaned over her own forest of columns and chandeliers to assess his work.

"Something delicate," she said. "Like a lilac or robin's-egg blue. There were rarely any dark colors in the bungalows, in an attempt to stave off the heat. Could you create the illusion of transparency?"

Cedric frowned and tilted his head like a bird. The light created a glare across the lenses of his spectacles.

"I could," he said, and that was all. It made Mary smile. Cedric was the most likely to oppose her, challenge her, question her every decision. And yet, whatever understandably mad request she made was answered with quiet acceptance. She had asked him to manifest her imagination out of thin air, and he had yet to disappoint.

"Do you think this will work?" she asked. It was a question she'd kept herself from asking, especially in Sara's presence, yet it always hung heavy in the air between them all.

When Cedric did nothing but sigh, not even look up to acknowledge her, Mary rushed ahead to add, "So much rests on the success of this performance. If it is a triumph, then Sara will be free and independent and the darling of the world. If it is a failure, then Minchin's wrath will be all the more absolute. We sit here and paint sets while Sara lives in utter despair. I mean, my dearest friend rarely has a moment to herself, and yet she sacrifices her time to humor my delusions as if she hasn't a care in the world. You and I could even be expelled."

"Is that a threat or a promise?"

"Cedric!"

Cedric's eyes shot up to Mary's face. Something felt close to erupting in her. A fear, a sadness, a desperation.

"Is this—all of this—incredibly foolish?"

Cedric maintained his hold on her gaze, then slowly set the paintbrush down. He reached across the distance between them, having to stretch his body to do so, and took hold of Mary's hand. She actually started at the contact. This was something that he would normally offer Sara, this physical companionship. It didn't seem improper or out of place with them, but natural. This, with her, felt terribly serious and strange. There were calluses on his fingers. From hours with his charcoal and sketchbook, Mary assumed. Or embroidery.

"To answer your question," he said. "Yes. This is all incredibly foolish." Mary let out a short, barking laugh. "However. You are doing it—*we* are doing it—to help someone we care about very deeply. It all might, possibly, crumble to pieces, cause us lasting embarrassment, and ruin all of our lives." Mary actually felt a sob rise up in her chest. "*But* it may also liberate Sara from her circumstances and renew all that has been lost. That is the madness of your brilliance, I suppose."

Cedric gave her hand a reassuring squeeze before withdrawing to his side of the aisle. A few seconds of comforting silence only interrupted by the sound of scissors and paintbrushes stretched between them until Mary was suddenly hit by a realization.

"Did you just say that I was brilliant?" she asked, feeling herself blush with the flattery.

Cedric smirked, which looked interesting on a face that was usually so stoic and appraising.

"I also said you were mad, Miss Lennox."

Mary could have exhaled with relief. This was the Cedric she knew; this was a rapport she could understand.

"Ah. Well. All of those who are truly brilliant are a bit mad, anyway."

Cedric smiled and shook his head, but kept his biting remarks to himself.

"My father thought my mother was mad," Mary said. She didn't quite know where the statement came from. It had been months since she'd thought of her mother. Years since she'd spoken of her. "Apparently, she used to walk the halls of our home at night, talking to herself. Full conversations, as if speaking with a completely separate person. Her voice would change, from a Welsh man's to an American woman's. Even a little girl, once. It would give the servants a terrible fright. Perhaps this play is just my own way of speaking with the people in my head?"

"Or perhaps your mother was denied her time as a playwright," Cedric said. "Perhaps her head was full of heroines."

Mary sighed. "I've been so angry for so long I don't know how else to think about her. I mean, heroines who ignore their children and heroes who disappear for days at a time?"

"Sometimes it is better to be ignored," Cedric said in a low voice.

"At least you had sisters, right?" Mary asked. "I had only my ayah. Then only my father after that, which was similar to having no one at all."

Cedric shrugged and did not raise his head to meet her

questioning gaze. "They were already of age and married by the time I was six," he said. "So, yes, I did have sisters, but only in theory."

"What is it like? Having siblings?" Mary asked with all sincerity. Cedric seemed to pause and take time to answer the question genuinely.

"It is . . . active," he said. "Until it is not. My sisters were not in the house long, but when they were, there was a sense of constant movement. What is it like being an only child?"

"Exactly the opposite. There! I believe I am finished."

Ten paper columns lay before Mary, ready to be painted and mounted onto the wood salvaged from the walls and pews of the chapel.

"What do you think?" she asked.

Cedric looked over her work and grinned.

"Not bad at all. See, you did not even need my help creating the sets."

"Please, this could not be accomplished without you, dearest Cedric." She tried not to notice the charming color that dusted his cheeks. Still, even as they smiled and worked cheerfully, the question was heavy on Mary's mind.

"This *will* work," she said. "Won't it?"

"It must," Cedric said. "For Sara's sake. For all of our sakes."

9

The morning of Parents Day came and went almost unnoticed by Sara. In fact, so much was required of her in the
kitchens the previous night that she saw dawn without a wink of
sleep. She and Becky passed the evening helping prep what might
as well have been a wedding breakfast. Much chopping, stirring,
cooking, and baking was required. In order to allow Becky a
moment of uninterrupted rest, Sara volunteered to keep constant
vigil over the fruitcake that demanded upward of eight hours to
bake overnight. To keep herself awake, she reviewed the (what
she hoped to be) final script for *Bejeweled Paramour*. Mary had
labored over it intensely, and even though entire scenes were
changed, characters removed and added, and monologues that
Sara had painstakingly committed to memory now completely
rewritten, Sara had to admit that it was a stunning piece of work.
Dramatic, tender, romantic, and somehow more empowering
than anything she had read before.

With nothing but Becky's soft snores to keep her company that night in the sweltering kitchen, Sara spoke to the darkness: "You would adore this play, Mama. You too, Papa, even though I fear it may be rather too melodramatic for you. Oh yes, you're right, Mama. How could a man whose favorite play is *Othello* decry anything else as melodramatic?"

THE PARENTS WOULD be arriving almost immediately, and the school was caught up in a terrible flutter. Sara only had moments to hurry upstairs to the attic and change into the proper housemaid attire Minchin had rented for the occasion. This morning, more than any other, the stairs seemed to stretch before her, and she had to constantly remind herself that sleep was not the reward for mastering the climb. If she even reflected on the thought of her bed, she would be resolved to fall into it as soon as it was within sight. When she opened the door of her attic, she even had her eyes closed to avoid glancing in her cot's direction.

"Why on earth are your eyes closed? Were you expecting me?"

Sara's eyes popped open. Mary sat primly on the edge of her cot, looking quite comfortable and in control. It was barely seven in the morning, and she was already fully dressed in pink, of all things, with a big pastel bow in her short-cut hair. *Pink*. Sara didn't even think Mary was aware of the color.

"Mary," Sara said, as if reminding herself of her friend's name. "What are you doing up here?"

"I knew things would be frightfully busy once the parents

arrived, but I had to tell you the good news as soon as possible."

Mary rose from the cot, an unfolded piece of paper clutched to her chest. The overwhelming shades of pink seemed to wash out her normal color, as if rouge replaced the blush of her pale skin. In fact, upon closer inspection, Sara saw that Mary *was*, in fact, blushing. Her entire body was flushed with excitement.

"What has happened?" Sara asked. She crossed to the stool with the broken leg and sat down, having mastered a means of sitting on it without toppling over. Her eyes burned from lack of sleep, and she had to pinch herself to keep her lids from drooping.

"Goodness, Sara, you look half dead," Mary said. "Will you be ready for the performance?"

Sara nodded. "I'll be ready. Now, tell me what has roused you into such a state so early in the morning."

Mary beamed again, then thrust the paper into Sara's hands. Sara looked down and saw that it was a letter, written in that same impatient hand she'd seen so often in her friend's manuscripts, only more masculine and practiced. Addressed to Mary, signed by Mr. Joseph Lennox. Sara struggled to scan the contents, but the ink seemed to bleed one word into another.

"Your father is coming to Manchester?" Sara asked, grasping at straws.

"Not just that," Mary said. "He is coming to *Parents Day*. Today! Damnable English post, the letter was written almost a month ago and just arrived this morning. Now our scheme shall surely succeed." Mary tried to sit on the upholstered chair across from Sara and almost fell directly through the hole in the bottom.

"My word, this place is horrid," Mary mumbled.

"Unimaginably so," Sara agreed.

"I would say Mistress Minchin should be ashamed, but one must be capable of shame to begin with. Anyway, what was I saying? Yes, my father, he is coming today. I have written him countless times about you and your situation, and he has shown nothing but the purest sympathy. He will meet you, and Cedric, and be instantly charmed into committing a portion of his fortune toward our company's West End debut. We may not even need to perform during the breakfast, but of course we shall after all of this hard work—Forgive me. I am letting my excitement run away with my words."

Mary suddenly stopped herself and reached across the expanse to grasp Sara's hand.

"What I mean, dearest Sara, is that we have a champion now. My father may be absent and neglectful, but I have never known him to be hard of heart. He invests his money in everything from abandoned diamond mines to textile dyes, so why not this? Why not *us*? He will make our past month's work worthwhile. I know this to be true."

Sara looked into her friend's wide, expressive eyes and saw a faith that almost brought her to tears. This Mr. Lennox would pass months—whole seasons—without confirming whether or not his only child was dead or alive. He manifested nothing, no proof that he existed to do anything other than pay her way until a husband could be found. From what Sara understood, Mary was packed up and shipped off to her first boarding school in Calcutta mere days after her mother's funeral. Then another boarding school after that, and another after that, farther and farther away from her only remaining parent until the man finally managed to locate the only school in perhaps the entire world that refused to allow students to leave until graduation. Sara saw nothing worth adoring in such a father. And despite it all, Mary loved him, and her heart swelled to bursting at the prospect of seeing him. It was an infectious kind of hope, and Sara could not help but bask in it.

"I am sure you are right," Sara said. "I cannot wait to meet him."

"He will adore you," Mary said. "He won't be able to resist helping you, I am sure of it. Now, he is a bit of a sad, serious man, so don't be offended when he refrains from smiling. It's just his way." Then, as quickly as Mary had sat down, she was up.

"I must go. Today is the only day out of the entire year when they conduct head checks. You remember where to meet Cedric once the breakfast is underway?"

Sara nodded.

"Wonderful. He promised to have everything assembled and prepared, and I'm slow to doubt him. Indeed, he seems to be taking all of this more seriously than I am."

"He is enraptured with the play," Sara said. "He discusses it as if he were discussing Marlowe. For all his teasing, I believe young Cedric is quite impressed with you, Miss Mary."

Mary responded to that with a raspberry blown between her lips.

"He could stand to say as much instead of questioning my every action, as if each step I take is some kind of moral offense.

One of my closest friends and most ardent enemies, that is Cedric Errol. But I am sure he cannot carry everything himself from his dormitory. Perhaps I should—"

"Mary, dear, you're rambling," Sara said calmly. "Everything will be fine. Better than fine! A glowing success. Now please, I must change before the parents start arriving at the school. Mistress Minchin wishes for me to be right at the door and ready to greet them." And essentially do the job of a servant, she did not add.

"This will be the last day you will ever have to do anything that awful woman tells you to do," Mary said. "I swear it."

And Sara knew that Mary believed that with her entire heart. It was something Sara loved about her friend, that confidence and assuredness. It was also something Sara feared. Sara was prepared to take the future as it came. Mary, however, would never allow herself to be constrained by something as frivolous as uncertainty.

10

Three Hours Later

W e really must stop meeting like this, Mistress Minchin. It is bordering on the improper."

Mary once again found herself standing in the headmistress's salon, staring down the barrel of her ire. And goodness, was she furious! Since all but dragging Mary from the dining hall—not even allowing time for her to change out of her costume—Minchin had spoken barely a word or even chanced a glance in Mary's direction. Even now, the older woman stood with her back to Mary, staring out of her narrow window into the gray afternoon air. This quietude actually made Mary rather uncomfortable. She would prefer being verbally admonished, beaten even, to this tense silence. She could take a direct challenge, a direct attack. Now, in this moment, she felt like the frog sitting in the tepid pot, waiting for it to boil.

"I am sure you have come to this conclusion for yourself, but this was all my idea," Mary said, again struggling to defuse the tension with words. "Cedric and Sara had nothing to do with this. I mean, of course, obviously they *did*, but the origin of the scheme was mine."

"Oh, that I do not doubt," Minchin said at last. Her voice fell heavy, like a stone into a still pond. There was an evenness to it that put Mary on edge. She did not even sound particularly angry. Mary knew how to respond to anger in the headmistress, quite enjoyed it really. In this light, Mary was being addressed almost as an equal.

"What I cannot comprehend," Minchin said, conversational, back still turned, "is what you could possibly hope to accomplish with this spectacle. I have analyzed it over and over again in my mind, and I find it truly impossible to understand. If this was a simple act of singular disruption, I would not be quite so surprised. Yet, involving Miss Crewe and Mr. Errol implies something a bit grander. Am I right?"

Minchin turned for the first time in many minutes to look at Mary. Again, she had the sense of being addressed as a point of fascination, not as a worrisome student. The headmistress's expression was one of true curiosity.

"If I am to be punished, please do make it quick," Mary said. The turn of this inquisition was becoming unnerving.

"Have a pressing appointment, do you, Miss Lennox?"

"Yes, of course," Mary said, struggling to not sound doubtful of her own words. "My father will wish to see me."

For a moment, this strange, elevated, unwavering mask that Minchin had been content to wear showed a crack of changeability.

"You saw your father in the dining hall?" the headmistress asked.

"I was rather preoccupied." Mary could not help the smirk of satisfaction that graced her face in answer to, finally, a moment of frustration in Minchin. "I am sure I simply missed him. He is prone to lateness, anyway. He is probably waiting in the dining hall for me now."

"So, you *did not* see your father enter the dining hall?"

"Is that not what I said?"

"Then how could you possibly know whether or not he is here today?"

"He said as much. In a letter I received this morning." Mary's hand twitched toward the pocket in her skirt where she felt the minimal weight of the folded letter against her thigh.

Minchin looked suddenly very confused, as if Mary were speaking in an unknown language and the woman was struggling to pick out clues in her speech to devise a meaning. Perhaps Mary was speaking in Farsi, for all the sense Minchin herself was making.

"When was this letter of yours dated?" Minchin asked, the words rushing out of her now. "When was it sent?"

"I do not see how that is any of your—"

"Now, Miss Lennox, please!"

Mary's mouth closed like a steel trap. She suddenly felt as other students must feel: that she was in the presence of an authority that had the right and privilege to command her at any point.

Much against her own principles and will, Mary answered,

"Almost two months ago. It just arrived this morning, delayed by the post."

Minchin closed her eyes. Her constantly leveled shoulders seemed to sag, and a soft bow appeared in her back. She reached up to cradle her forehead in the palm of her hand, and Mary for an instant realized Minchin's age. The wear to her skin, her muscles, her bones. She was never able to estimate the headmistress's year of birth. She only knew for certain that she was a woman grown, older than her mother ever was, and yet younger than Cook, a woman with wrinkles as deep as desert canyons. Now, seeing something heavy and terrible settle over Minerva Minchin, she could tell the woman was older and more exhausted than Mary had ever guessed. It made Mary tired just thinking of the hassle, the hustle. The sleepless nights. It must all be terribly burdensome.

Mary would not admit this to herself for months or years to come, but in that moment, she was deeply grateful for her father and his money. She would never know the suspended terror of an earned income. She would never be asked to compromise herself to survive. She would never have to stand across from a young hell brand such as herself and plead for compliance just to ensure the smooth passing of a day. Whatever responsibility Minchin now felt, Mary would never be required to feel. She suddenly, desperately, wished to be close to her father, safe in the shadow of his privilege.

"I did not wish for this to happen this way," Minchin said. Again, there were no notes of superiority in her tone. Maybe, rather, a begrudged respect. "No matter our . . . disagreements, you must believe me when I say that to you. I did warn you that such a day would come, Mary Lennox. I told you, and still you persisted in challenging every basic expectation that a young lady of your station might have. Sit still and look pretty, that is all that has ever been required of you, and yet it might be the singular thing you are incapable of achieving. And now our Lord is testing you in the cruelest possible way."

Minchin was speaking quickly, barely directing her speech to Mary at all. Mary had to physically step into the woman's space in order to be heard and addressed.

"Mistress Minchin! Mistress Minchin, what are you going on about? You are behaving in the most peculiar way."

"Oh, Miss Lennox. Do you not feel the ax hanging above your head?" Minchin pleaded. She then took a deep, steadying breath, and spoke: "Your father, Mr. Joseph Lennox, is dead. He passed away in India from a fever some weeks ago."

Mary did not mean to react the way she did. She knew how it looked, how it felt, but she truly could not help herself. How else was she meant to respond to such foolishness? What else could Minchin possibly expect her to do but laugh? A full, deep, round-bellied laugh like an old man's. It made her throw back her head and clutch her stomach. It tilted her balance and caused her to reach out to steady herself on the back of a chair. She couldn't recall a time when she had laughed so hard. Not even when Sara snorted during breakfast and sprayed milk from her nose, or when

Cedric did an uncanny impression of Lavinia right down to the manufactured London accent. Those were jokes, teasing among friends. This was pure farce.

All the while, Minchin looked at her as if preparing at any moment to douse her in holy water and perform an exorcism.

When she finally had the breath to speak, Mary said, "Goodness! Minerva Minchin. I admit, I would never expect this of you. How could I know that you were a fellow thespian? I must say, this is a masterful production, especially considering the time constraints."

"Miss Lennox, did you not hear me?" Minchin asked. "I just told you that your father is dead."

"Yes, I know! It is absolutely brilliant, the gall of it all. With a, perhaps, more gullible student, this would have the desired effect. I admire your commitment. All of this, just to make me learn my lesson? If I were not already standing, I would give you an ovation. And my father, is he in on it, as well? I know he must be. He thinks himself a very serious man, but I have always been able to make him laugh." Mary quickly tiptoed to the heavy curtains draped around the window and swept them aside. "Father? Father, come out now, your scheme has been discovered!"

"Enough of this." Minchin began to fumble about her skirts, searching, it seemed, for a pocket. Meanwhile, Mary could catch a few mumbled phrases, such as *delusional, ridiculous, prideful,* and *no one to blame but herself.* After much rustling, Minchin's long, black-draped arm jutted out toward Mary, a piece of paper protruding forward, like an extension of herself. Minchin's face was drawn down in a complicated mix of solemn, good Christian pity and notably un-Christian satisfaction.

Mary took the letter in her own hand and found it crisp, even hard between her fingers. It was weighted paper, thick with importance. Of course, Minchin would be the type to fold her letters into perfectly cornered little squares that required Mary to meticulously pull back one edge, then another, then another. It wasn't a long letter by any means. It took up less than half of the paper. And Mary recognized the stationery. She recognized the handwriting. She had received many such letters over the years in lieu of direct correspondence from her father.

"Are you well acquainted with my father's lawyer, Mistress Minchin?" Mary asked. "Well enough, I'd imagine, to gain access to his stationery like this."

Mary grinned conspiratorially at Minchin, but the woman did not grin back.

"Shall I recite?" Mary flicked her hand and the letter spread out like a fan. She cleared her throat, held it at eye level, and began to read aloud.

*"Attention: Mrs. Minerva Minchin, Headmistress of the Select Seminary for Young Ladies and Gentlemen in Manchester, England—*Ah, look, that is you!—*My name is Basil Shepherd, Esq. I am writing on behalf of a mutual employer, Mr. Joseph Lennox, whose daughter, Mary, is currently attending your school. It is with great regret that I must inform you of Mr. Lennox's very*

recent demise. On the sixth of November, Mr. Lennox succumbed to a fever—"

At this point, Mary stopped reading aloud. She rushed forward through the rest of the letter in silence, grasping at words and stitching them together into some kind of understanding. Mr. Shepherd was not a verbose man. For a lawyer, he had a surprisingly lax command of the English language and preferred to arrive at the point quickly, efficiently, and without any room for misinterpretation. That preference was used to sobering effect in this letter. Here were the key points that Mary managed to draw from the customs of correspondence: Her father was, indeed, dead. His fortune—such as it was—was utterly depleted. Mary's prospects were now buried with her father's ashes in Calcutta.

Mary allowed herself to go limp and landed with a *thump* on the closest chair. Even though she knew all this must be true, somewhere in the basement of her heart, Mary strived to find an angle that made her former conclusions the proper ones.

"But his letter," Mary said, more to herself than to Minchin, who watched her warily as if Mary were an injured animal that might strike out at any moment. "He said he would be here. He said he was making preparations to be on his way. How could he be dead and alive at the same time?"

"It appears that he succumbed to his illness very soon after writing," Minchin said. "It is only a cruel fate that allowed one letter to be delayed and one to be expedited so as to arrive on the same day."

Quickly, as if on reflex, Mary said, "I don't recognize fate."

Minchin's grunt was deep and crude. The noise reminded Mary of a fishmonger she'd seen bartering on a market trip with her ayah once.

"Well, fate certainly recognizes you, Mary Lennox."

Even in the midst of her confused grief, something in Mary was flattered by that. How many could say that they were the apple of fate's fickle eye?

"Now that you have at last come to terms with your situation," Minchin said. "We may address the question of what is to be done with you."

Oh yes, well. Mary supposed she should be concerned with that.

"I expect you must be feeling very pleased with your turn of luck, Mistress Minchin," Mary said with a lift to her chin. "You will be getting two former students to torment for the price of one."

Minchin looked confused for only a moment before realization and a bloom of relief crossed her face.

"Oh dear Lord, child," she said. "You *will not* be remaining here. You did not imagine that I would have you and Miss Crewe running about, causing mayhem for all eternity, did you? You may be disappointed to know that you are not nearly as clever as you think yourself to be, Miss Lennox."

Mary was immediately hit with a violent pain in her chest. Later she was slightly ashamed when she realized that pain had not come with news of her father's death. The pain of separation from Sara and Cedric was altogether unacceptable and devastating. The death of a parent—*her* parent—felt more like an eventuality than a tragedy. She was sad for the loss, of course. She loved her father in the way all children were told to love their parents. But in her friends, she had found family, home, a true sense of meaning. The pain of being away from them felt more absolute than death.

"If I am not to stay here," Mary said, "where am I to go?" She was struck by a terrifying notion. "Am *I* being sent to debtor's prison?"

"A part of me only wishes that I could have the honor of packing you off to a place that might break you of your belligerence in a way that I obviously failed to do," the headmistress said. "But, alas, your father managed to maintain good standing with my ledgers before falling into destitution, and just barely. Apparently there is this uncle—"

"Uncle?"

"Yes, and do not sound so shocked! Mr. Shepherd said as much in the letter. Ah, how very like you to only read what you wished to read and entirely ignore everything else." Minchin snatched the letter from Mary's hand fast enough to leave behind paper cuts. Reading it aloud with a clarity as crisp and white as fresh laundry, she said, "*Miss Lennox is to be deposited into the care of her distant uncle with all haste. A Mr. Jeremiah Lennox who now resides in the American state of Tennessee and a township called Knoxville. The man in question has been notified of his brother's death and the forthcoming arrival of his niece. I shall rendezvous with Miss Lennox in London and ensure she safely boards a fast steamer to America. Please forward all inquiries, requests, or remaining balances to me.* There! Let that be the end of it."

If Mary had been the type to scream, she would have screamed. She knew from her brief stint singing in the seminary's choir that she had powerful lungs and could carry a note for a long while, even if it wasn't a pretty one. She even felt herself filling her lungs with air and unlocking the hinges of her jaw.

"I can see that this is a lot for you to absorb—"

"A lot to absorb?!" The beginning of Mary's wail carried into this question, raising her voice and for an instant perhaps making her a tad bit intimidating. Minchin, to her credit, did not look intimidated.

"Do contain yourself from falling into hysterics, Miss Lennox."

"Why should I?" Mary shot back, with a hard step forward. She liked raising her voice and speaking with a loud, demanding tone. It was rather cathartic. "This appears to me to be the perfect time for hysterics! I am to be packed up like an ugly hand-me-down vase and shipped off 'with all haste' to the middle of nowhere thousands of miles away. In a war zone, mind you!"

"Now you truly are in hysterics," Minchin said. "The War for Southern Independence ended months ago; you will be perfectly safe."

Mary could not be more pained if she'd been shot with an arrow.

"You mean the Civil War in America? Certainly you cannot have sympathy for the so-called Confederate states?"

Minchin's demeanor became steely, showing Mary that she'd been asked to defend this mindset before.

"I admire any people that strive to better themselves."

"They were slavers!"

"As we in Great Britain were not very long ago, Miss Mary. Judge not, lest you be judged."

"I *cannot* have this conversation with you right now." Mary began to pace the room. The hem on Cedric's hastily made costume that she still wore had begun to unravel and loose threads dragged behind her. Mary knew that she absolutely could not leave Sara behind, not under any circumstances. Minchin was merely an older, poorer version of Lavinia; the only things she accepted were battle lines and chosen sides. If Sara had no allies in this fight for her dignity, Minchin would only grow more brazen in her torment.

"There is nothing to be done for it, Mary," the headmistress said. "It is just the way things are. Be grateful that you have an uncle to claim you. Knowing your father's unique penchant for squeezing gold from a stone, I am sure this other Mr. Lennox is just as enterprising. Why, you may even expect to continue being kept in the manner to which you are accustomed."

"That doesn't matter," Mary said, knowing that in many ways, it did. "If I cannot be with my friends, then none of it matters. I won't go, I tell you. You cannot make me!"

"Make you? Dear girl, it is already done. You are to pack your things and leave this place tomorrow, and never return, if I have any say. You may go under your own steam with all the dignity and decorum I would expect of a seminary girl, or I shall have our gardener truss you up in a sack, throw you over his shoulder, and toss you on a train like a piece of luggage. That choice, I'm afraid, is the only one you have."

Even as Mary fumed at the idea and was insulted that Minchin would even threaten her with it, she knew that it was the utter truth. She was no longer a student at this school and Minchin had no one to answer to. If she indeed wished to throw Mary in a sack and physically haul her onto a train, there was very little Mary could do to stop her. She started when she felt something wet and stinging slide down one cheek and then the other. She wiped the tears roughly away with the back of her hand. They continued to well up in her eyes and a true cry of distress bubbled in her chest, and then her throat.

Even Minchin looked surprised at this sudden show of emotion.

"You know, I truly cannot tell if you are crying for your father," she said, "or crying because you cannot have your way. I hope you can tell the difference."

Mary gasped, again both insulted and aware that Minchin may well be speaking the truth.

"Do you truly think so little of me? You, a supposed caretaker of children who should never carry such bias?"

"That is not fair!" Minchin asserted. Her voice actually

lifted up from its bottom-dwelling tone to something nasally and even girlish. "I did everything I could for you, Mary Lennox. I strived to give you a purpose, guidance, the structure that clearly no one up to this point had bothered to give you. I even attempted to cure you of this strange affliction that makes you out to be such a sallow, unattractive child. Your father entrusted your well-being to me, and I did my best by him. May God rest his soul. But I shall not have you speaking to me as if you were some Cinderella, pure of spirit and maliciously, unfairly tormented. For the past four years, you have fought me at every turn. I attempted to teach you how to dress as a young lady should, and you come down on your very first day in a boy's clothes. I expose you to some of the most learned teachers in the area and you read—and sleep!—during class. You challenged my every rule, pushed back against every request. For heaven's sake, you just attempted to put on an entire performance in the middle of this school's most essential event! How many parents will see your display as representative of the caliber here at the seminary and immediately remove their children? This place does not run on bread alone, child!"

At this point, Minchin was near gasping. Her planklike chest rose and fell so rapidly that Mary felt she might excite herself and topple over. Indeed, the woman had to reach out and support herself on the edge of her desk.

As the last echoes of Minchin's diatribe began to fade, Mary said, "Perhaps. Yet you manage to treat Sara Crewe—the one person in this entire school who endeavored to please you—like dirt under your shoe. Yes, perhaps I am unreasonable, unstable, and belligerent, then pray tell, Minerva Minchin, what is she?"

What happened next happened very quickly.

In one moment, Minchin was yards away from Mary, at her desk. In the next, she had crossed the length of the room, stood directly before her, and drawn her hand back. Mary did not feel the strike itself, but she felt the sting it left on her cheek. It started small, then the pain spread across her face like an angry red tide. Minchin stood tall above her with her hand still raised, a not-so-veiled threat that she could do that—and would do that—again. But her eyes were uncertain, even fearful. She knew that striking a student, even a former student, was madness, and if word got out, no theatrical performance would match the level of her ruin. Mary knew this. She knew that Mary knew this.

Mary felt herself grin with the glow of victory. As all great generals know, after all: you can lose every battle except the last.

11

*S*ara could not help but feel a sense of unnerving familiarity as she sat in Mary's room and watched her stamp about, throwing clothes into trunks and cases.

It felt like a memory, or a dream of a memory, as if she were watching a version of herself, a version that took a different path. Or rather, had a different one offered to her. They were both orphans. Both without homes or means. Both left to the mercies of a delusional and vindictive matron. Yet, there was one notable difference. Mary was being allowed to leave, forced to leave even. Sara, on the other hand, had nowhere to go as soon as she stepped outside the confines of the seminary. Again, this smelled of a memory, but one from someone else's life.

"I thought you said you had no family," Sara said in a hollow attempt to maintain conversation, to keep Mary's mind somewhere useful.

"As did I!" she screamed. A lace petticoat landed hard in the bottom of her trunk. "No one ever spoke of an uncle in America, or anyone, for that matter. No one left alive, that is. For a time, my first nurse actually managed to convince me that I was not born but rather my parents had me grown in a pot like a flower. And I believed her! For *years*! And why shouldn't I?" Another petticoat. "My father rarely spoke to me about himself. Of course he would fail to inform me about his secret relations scattered to the four winds."

Her father. They had yet to truly talk about that. As soon as Sara came to Mary, she went in on the whole problem of the uncle in America who was to be her new guardian. She spent barely any time at all explaining that her father was absent from the celebration because he was dead. Sara knew that Mary's relationship with her father was complicated at best, and that pretending that he had never existed was the easiest route for her to take. But still, inside she must be breaking, just as any child would be.

"What of your father's remains?" Sara asked, immediately wishing she had begun with a more delicate question. "Are they to be left in India?"

"Oh." Mary stopped her angry packing and stood still a moment. Her brow creased when she said, "I am not sure." Her voice slowed and her eyes took on that distant screen that came when she was lost in a memory. "I vaguely recall some discussion between my father and the vicar who served English families about returning my mother's body to England to be buried in her family plot. In the end, it was decided that the disease that killed her was too dangerous. They pretended that her body was in that grave, but I knew she was burned. I suppose that is what they've done to my father, to stave off contamination. They take such things quite seriously there, you know."

Sara sat stock-still as she listened to Mary, her mouth slightly agape. She'd never heard her friend speak so much of her mother, and certainly not of her death. And all in this far-off tone, as if she were describing the cremation of historical figures and not her own parents. It seized her with a sudden urge to rise and embrace her friend, to confront the grief with her. Yet she knew such a blatant showing would only drive Mary further into herself. Instead, she kept her seat and gave Mary her undivided attention.

They both jumped when the close air in the room was shattered by a knock at the door. Sara and Mary exchanged glances.

"Students come to pay their respects?" Sara asked. Mary's laugh had jagged edges.

"More likely that Mistress Minchin has employed the local constable to have me forcibly removed," Mary said. Then, with a raised voice, "I do have my rights!"

There was a pause as if someone were dissecting what they just heard, then came another more wary knock.

Sara did the polite thing and answered.

"Cedric!" she exclaimed. "How on earth did you get up here?"

Cedric sat before them in his chair, slightly out of breath and darting his eyes around to make sure the coast was clear.

"Quick wit and imagination, of course," he said. Then, in a lowered voice, "Is it true?"

Sara glanced back over her shoulder to see that Mary had

accelerated her frustrated packing and was making some low noise in her throat not too dissimilar from a growl.

"Let us assume that it is."

Behind Sara, Mary yelled, "Does the entire school know already?"

"Only those who are easily entertained," Cedric said. "So yes, the entire school."

Mary let out a cross between a sigh, a sob, and a scream.

"Mind letting me in before I am caught out here?" Cedric asked. Sara had the wherewithal to hesitate. Young men in the girls' dormitory were strictly forbidden and the rule was militantly enforced. Still, it was only Cedric. She opened the door wider, giving him room to pass through.

Mary must have heard the door close behind her, for she turned around and the expression on her face was fully scandalized.

"You *cannot* be in here!" she said sternly, and for a terrifying moment, she sounded very like Minchin.

"You are worried about decorum? You of all people?" Cedric asked. Then he reached out for her hand. Reflexively, Mary placed it in his. He gave her arm a firm tug that brought her down into a crouch. At once, Mary was wrapped in a hug. Sara could see Mary stiffen like a rabbit caught in a fox's maw. She even flinched, but Cedric did not loosen his grasp. Then the most extraordinary thing happened. Mary's face contorted in a mask of vulnerable, pained sadness. She closed her eyes and tears leaked down her cheeks.

"I failed both of you," she whispered, almost too softly to hear.

"You did no such thing," Sara heard Cedric insist. "This world failed *you*, Mary Lennox. And that is the truth of it."

Mary closed her eyes tighter and, like a child, secured her own arms around Cedric's neck, returning his hug. Sara was taken aback. This moment between her two friends seemed to be something not made for her eyes, or any other eyes, for that matter. Quite a few things suddenly made great sense to Sara. Quietly, she averted her gaze and allowed Mary to release the staggering frustrations of the day against Cedric's shoulder.

THE SUREST SIGN of the looming winter was the speed with which the night fell upon them. There were barely even proper sunsets anymore, just a harsh transition from light to darkness as quick and absolute as the extinguishing of a flame. Mary's room was draped in long, thick shadows and filled with the sounds of her restless sleep. Sara and Cedric insisted that Mary lay herself down—she had been standing for Lord knows how long—and they took up the somber task of packing her things. It hadn't taken her long to curl in on herself like a dried leaf and fall into fitful slumber. The two carried on their work without even lighting a candle for fear of disturbing her. Sara was in the process of slowly folding one of Mary's gowns when Cedric caught her eye. He gestured toward the door. Sara followed him into the hall, softly closing the door behind her.

"I cannot believe this is happening," he said as soon it was closed. The hallway was dark, and his voice seemed loud in the hushed space. It seemed the entire school had shut itself away and retreated to some shadowy corner.

"We three just found each other and now we are to be separated," he said, fierceness in his voice. Cedric was as cool and still as a shallow pond under normal circumstances, but this new development sent ripples racing across his visage.

"I worry for Mary," Sara said. "I fear she doesn't quite understand what has happened. It won't come to her until she's sitting in a train car headed to London. Or perhaps even later than that."

"We can't let this go that far."

Sara's brow rose skeptically, warily.

"What are you saying, Cedric?"

"I am saying that nothing has changed. We can still go through with the plan."

Usually, Mary was the one plowing ahead without any heed for the reality of the situation, while Cedric held her back with words of caution. Now, here was Cedric, jumping to conclusions miles ahead of where they were.

"Perhaps you failed to notice," Sara said, "but none of the parents leapt to their feet in exultation when the curtain closed. Producers and benefactors aren't rushing to support the Player Princes and bring us out of this place. The one benefactor we were told to rely on is—pardon my language—on a pyre somewhere in the Orient."

Cedric waved his hand, dismissing everything Sara had just said with an almost offensive casualness.

"We don't need them. We shall leap over them entirely and go straight to Paris."

Sara's jaw unhinged and fell directly to the floor.

"Paris?"

"Yes, of course. Why do you look so surprised?"

"Cedric, you just suggested that we run away to France. What response should I have, other than surprise?"

"Sara." Cedric reached up and took her hand in his, a common gesture between them now. In the early months when their friendship first began to bloom, Cedric carried the shield of social propriety before him as if facing down a dragon. Now, that shield was naught but dust and he proved himself to be touchingly affectionate.

"Sara, how much hope have we had since first beginning work on Mary's ridiculous play? How close have we been? There seemed to be a future for each of us, something complete and worthwhile. We cannot let all that work and hope shatter without a fight. Besides, we're all brilliant artists now, and artists abscond to Paris all the time. How hard can it be?"

Impossibly hard. Sara knew this unequivocally, the same way she knew that Mary's play would not be the great salvation that they once dreamed it would be. Yet, looking at Cedric—glowing from the inside like a lantern—Sara found herself thinking perhaps, no, it wouldn't be so impossible after all.

He must have seen the consideration of his proposal playing behind her eyes, for he grinned in a way that was almost in homage to Mary.

SARA RETURNED TO her attic rooms for the first time since that morning. Outside of these cramped, dark spaces, so much had changed. Yet within, everything remained frozen in a miserable sameness. The haphazard, broken furniture, the barely there bed, the fast-burning candles. Sara could even hear the rush of mice as they scurried back to their respective holes. The familiar—no matter how terrible—is always comforting, and as Sara began to limp under the load of the day, she felt a sudden desire to curl up on the hard mattress and sleep until Becky came to wake her. *Becky!* The memory of her partner in this terrible journey hit her with stunning force. All these great plans had been made without consideration for her, or how she might ever hope to escape this life. Sara was ashamed at her own selfishness and resolved to use these last minutes under this roof to correct the lapse.

She found Becky in the adjoining rooms, separated by not a wall but a thick, hand-stitched curtain that allowed for the illusion of privacy. She was awake and reading from a thin primer. Becky had been illiterate, and Sara thought it especially cruel that Minchin would have her live, work, and sleep in a school without even attempting to offer her an education. Sara could easily borrow primers from the children she minded, now all quite comfortable with reading in English and moving on to other languages, and she spent what empty time she had working with Becky. Becky was exceptionally bright and moved through primer after primer with that same efficient quickness that she employed in her work. It was a sincere joy teaching her, and it was something that Sara would miss in the months to come.

"Oh, Miss Sara!" Becky said when she noticed Sara standing in the shadows on the edge of the room where the spindly candle flame couldn't reach. At night, when Becky was free to move about without her veil, Sara could see just how lively her brown eyes were. They complemented her head full of auburn hair, and in the candlelight, they danced like a campfire.

"I did not expect you to make our lesson," Becky said. "With all the excitement 'round Miss Mary, and all."

"I would have come for our lesson regardless," Sara said, crossing to Becky. "How are you enjoying the tale of Joan of Arc?"

Becky looked down at the primer and shrugged her small, too-thin shoulders.

"It's interesting enough," she said. "But it's awful sad that a lady must die in order to make a difference."

Sara smiled and said, "Quite right. But, Becky, that is not why I've come tonight. You see, Mary, Cedric, and I are running away to Paris."

Becky's eyes were wide. Her arms went lax and the primer fell to her lap, forgotten.

"Lord in heaven, Miss Sara! Have you lot lost your wits?"

"Yes, most likely," Sara said without a pinch of jest or sarcasm.

"Running away is not what these pampered sorts think it is,"

Becky said. "I knew children who ran away from home and ended up in prison, dead, or disappeared altogether. It ain't like these primers, all pirates and sword fights."

Sara could see that part of Becky was deeply offended. And Sara thought that perhaps what they were planning was, all in all, quite offensive. They had everything they needed to live and grow, and yet they proposed to flee as if held prisoner. Again, Sara felt ashamed, but no less resolved.

"I know that," she said. "Or at least I think I do. What I *do* know without a doubt is that I cannot remain here. It's very likely that we may take five steps from this place and fall to misfortune and regret every decision we've ever made. Or we may find the purest kind of happiness. We won't know if we don't try. You can leave, too, Becky."

"Oh no. No, miss, I cannot. I have little trade, no family, no prospects, and a pox upon my face. Too many young'uns out there hungrier than me who need to work. After all, Mistress Minchin ain't bad as all that. Least I know I'll never have cause for idleness here."

Becky meant that as some kind of joke, but the joviality didn't reach her dancing eyes.

"Mistress Minchin is a horror," Sara said firmly. "Before she was tormenting me, I know for a fact that she was tormenting you. As soon as I am gone, her reign of terror will become more absolute, and I would be no true friend to leave you to such a fate. Here." She handed Becky a calling card, still ivory white with gold lettering shimmering in the light. "This is the calling card of a gentleman named Mr. Ram Dass. I met him some weeks ago in town. He showed me the greatest kindness and told me that if anything could be done to help me, I was to find him at the Duckworth Hotel. I've made inquiries since then, and I know he still resides there. Go to him and tell him Miss Sara Crewe sent you with this message: any and all kindness he might have bestowed on me, bestow on you. I do not doubt he will rise to the occasion."

Becky looked down at the calling card, back up to Sara, then down again to the calling card.

"Miss, I cannot accept this."

"You must! I cannot in good conscience leave tonight without knowing there is some hope for your happiness. You must go to him at first light. Pack what you can—take my overcoat and the books and the biscuits that are left—and make quick work of putting this place and Mistress Minchin at your back. This Mr. Dass is a good man, and sincere. I cannot imagine he would, but if he does refuse to offer you a home and some worthwhile employment, ask only for means to travel away from here."

"Away from Manchester?" Becky asked, her voice wary but hope glittering in her eyes. "Where on earth would I go, Miss Sara? What would I do?"

Sara smiled and attempted to make it as vibrant and hopeful as possible.

"Whatever you want. That's what I intend to do."

"This is madness," Becky said, even as she clutched the calling card to her chest. "You are mad, Miss Sara Crewe, as mad as Mary Lennox!"

That made Sara throw her head back with laughter.

"Ha! Lord preserve me, never that mad, I pray. Still, I take that as a compliment."

Becky suddenly reached out and held Sara's hand in her own. Sara could see the tears appearing in her eyes.

"Is this to be goodbye, then?" Becky asked.

Sara grasped Becky's hand just as firmly and said, "I certainly hope not. You have been a blessing to me these many months, Becky, and whatever peace I find, I pray that you find it in scores."

Dabbing at her eyes with the sleeve of her nightshirt—looking somehow, even in the darkness, brighter than Sara had ever seen her—Becky said, "Paris, huh? My, what a grand adventure you will have. Like a lost princess in a story."

12

*M*ary was jolted awake quite literally.

Someone had grasped her by the shoulder and commenced to shaking her back and forth. She was dislodged from sleep so suddenly that she was momentarily afraid because she didn't know where she was or even who she was. Then she saw Sara's face floating above hers. The light in the room had changed, now shifting to a soft and blushing blue.

"Oh, good, you're awake," Sara said. Mary had half a mind to scream at her dear friend.

"Of course I am awake," she said. "That is usually what happens when one is woken by an earthquake."

"You *can* be dramatic. We don't have time to dawdle; you must get up immediately. It will be first light within an hour."

"Why? What's going on?"

Mary quickly rubbed the sleep from her face, then sat up straight to take in her surroundings with awakened eyes. Sara was not wrong; dawn would be upon them soon. And in this light, Mary took in her friend fully. Now, Sara was known for quite the menagerie of outfits in the old days. She was one of the very few students who actually had the option of putting on full formal dress for dinner. *Every* dinner. But this costume had to be the most peculiar Mary had ever seen on her friend, and that included the whole galoshing getup. Sara was dressed exactly like a young boy, in tweed pants, cotton shirt, and buttoned vest. A wide cap sat snugly on her head, so when Sara stood with her hands on her hips, she could at once be mistaken for one of the lads outside of hotels and places of business who shouted the news to sell papers.

"I repeat myself," Mary said. "What's going on?"

Beaming like an absolute fool, Sara said, "You won't believe it. Cedric has had a wonderfully absurd idea."

Once it all was explained to Mary, she had to agree that the plan was outrageous. But it was also glorious. She honestly hadn't expected such a thing from Cedric. Apparently, Minchin's fear that Mary would rub off on him was not a baseless one.

"Becky actually came up with the scheme of dressing as boys," Sara said as she helped Mary look through the loose and formless boys' clothes she had found in a pile of newly laundered garments, waiting to be sorted and returned to their owners in the dormitory. "She is reading the tale of Joan of Arc and was inspired. Of course, we can find proper dress once we're in Paris, but we shall doubtlessly be questioned if we travel as ourselves. A troupe of young rascals traipsing across the countryside shouldn't raise a hint of suspicion."

"I may not wish to return to 'proper dress,'" Mary said. She was testing a pair of trousers by going through what she remembered of her ballet positions, clumsily and with a distinct air of ridicule. "There is so much room to move in these things, and not nearly as much to weigh you down. I feel I could run for ten miles without catching my breath. How on earth do women allow themselves to be cinched into something that resembles a tool of medieval torture more than an article of clothing when they could have this! Although, the shoes do present a problem."

"Yes, I thought the same. I believe we'll have to wear our boots for now," Sara said. "The boys' shoes that needed to be polished were in a terrible state."

Mary wrinkled her nose in question, and Sara nodded in answer.

"Lord bless Cedric," Mary said. "He is the best of his breed."

As if summoned by magic, there was a knock at Mary's door. Sara rushed to open it, but then stood in the doorway, staring.

"What's the matter?" Mary asked, immediately assuming that Minchin had come to personally escort her to the train station and now their plans were unraveled.

"Could you look a little less like someone bedside at a miracle, please, Sara?" Mary heard Cedric ask.

"This *is* a miracle! Cedric, you are walking!"

"*What?*"

Mary all but pushed Sara out of the way to see for herself, and sure enough, there stood Cedric Errol. Mary had to make an immediate adjustment; she was so accustomed to looking down to address him that she was visibly confused when she came eye to eye with his chest instead. Then her head rose as if operated by some crane, and kept rising.

"Goodness, but you are tall" was all she could think to say.

Cedric smiled a daunting smile and actually—for the first time in the many months Mary had known him—looked bashful.

"I know," he said. "It's a funny kind of irony, is it not?"

"But how is this possible?" Sara asked.

Cedric lifted his shoulders and Mary noticed that underneath his arms were solid wooden crutches. She saw the considerable strain in his forearms and hands, veins pronounced and muscles shaking with effort to keep him standing straight. So it was not a complete miracle after all. Still, she was not disappointed. Far from it. The very fact that this could be possible was beyond expectation.

"I cannot use them for long," Cedric said with a turn in his voice that sounded almost like an apology. "But they should get me to the train and then onto a boat, at least. I shall not be of much use outside of a bed after that. Once in Paris, I shall find something more suitable, somehow. Mary, you do realize that you are staring, don't you?"

Mary closed her eyes immediately, childishly, and spoke to him in darkness.

"I am terribly sorry. It is just, you are so very tall, it is a bit disconcerting."

She did not speak in flattery. When standing erect, Cedric towered above them both, even Sara, who outmatched most of the young men of the seminary.

"Speaking of trains and boats and suitability," Sara said once Cedric was in the room and seated on the edge of Mary's absent roommate's bed. "Has anyone considered exactly how we are going to *get* to Paris? I imagine it is not as simple as approaching a train conductor and asking for a ticket."

"We could stow away," Mary said while scratching at the rough material of her new trousers.

"Aren't stowaways usually arrested?" Sara asked in that teacherly, maternal tone that implied Mary already knew the answer to that question. Mary sighed loudly, causing her still choppily cut bangs to fly up over her eyes. Of course, stowing away was practically illegal in most counties and those who dared found themselves in prison or worse. But still, there was something awfully grand and romantic about hiding in the storage car and watching the world rush by in great gulps through the open train doors.

"I have some money," Cedric said. Sara and Mary looked at him as if he had only recently joined the scheme and was not the architect of it himself. Seeing their expressions, he rushed ahead. "A small allowance, but I have been saving. It should get us all farther than far enough."

Sara glanced over the room at Mary and a conversation passed between them without words. Sara was asking if she should be the one to bring this up. Mary was saying that it was up to Sara. Sara then made the decision for them both.

"Cedric," she said, slowly, as if speaking to a startled child. "You have not mentioned your parents throughout all of this. Mary and I, we now only have each other. But you may yet have those who love you and will miss you if you run away."

"My family may live and breathe," Cedric said, "but they didn't send me to this place because they would miss me. It is a school designed for families who have a specific desire to forget they ever had children."

"But still, perhaps we should leave them a letter," Mary said. "Some way to find you if—"

"Perhaps I do not want them to find me."

Cedric's eyes were hard, even pleading. Mary and Sara were resolved never to push him on the subject of his parents, but this was something entirely different from avoiding the question of why he didn't receive regular care packages like so many of the other students. Even though Mary's father was chronically absent, he had a presence, like a ghost in a room. For Cedric, there wasn't even the hint of a presence. It broke Mary's heart, truly, for her friend to be an orphan by choice, not by fate.

"Very well, then. Heaven knows we'll need that money," Mary said. She let her voice rise and lilt as if on the wind to keep up Cedric's spirits and her own. "We shall board the first train heading east, then the first ship across the Channel."

Cedric and Sara exchanged brief glances.

"Are you sure it's east?" Sara asked.

"Of course. France and Europe are east, toward the rising

sun, America is west, toward the setting sun. Don't look at me like that. I may fall asleep in most of my courses, but I know at least that much."

Not an hour later, they were all standing in the shadow of the train station, awash in the gentle blue of the early morning. They had no bags, no luggage, nothing to distinguish them as the whirlwind travelers Mary felt they were. Cedric gave the ticket agent all the money he had and told him they'd like three tickets east, as far as the rail line went. The agent looked upon them curiously and seemed to momentarily doubt whether or not he should be giving three odd children the means of boarding a train and disappearing into the fog of the morning. Then he must have figured that it was none of his business anyway and granted them the tickets they needed.

Mary was glowing with excitement and pride, and even fear, as they settled into a secluded box toward the back of the mostly empty train car. Cedric was panting from the effort of traveling by crutches from the station to the train, but a grin still danced in his eyes. The train jolted forward, giving them a start, before easily shifting into a loll. It didn't take long for Cedric to be rocked to sleep by the swaying train carriage. Mary considered following Cedric into sleep, but Sara's solemn glance out of the uncovered window kept Mary anxiously aware.

Finally, she built up the courage to say, "You're regretting this, aren't you? Running away?" Mary watched the young woman who had grown to become her very best and dearest friend as she looked out as dawn touched the countryside rolling by.

Sara took her time to answer.

"I am thinking of my parents," she said at last. "My mother especially. She was loath to ever turn from a chance to prove herself. Her Spanish grandfather never accepted her because her mother had married a Filipino. Thinking of her determination to prove she was worthy makes me wonder if she'd be disappointed in me for running away."

Ever since this grand scheme was imagined only hours before, Mary had tried to not think of her parents. She didn't know whether or not they might have been offended by her lack of commitment or proud of her refusal to settle for a situation that was less than ideal. Her parents were two people who saw their own happiness as the sun around which the universe turned. Perhaps they would be proud after all; they would applaud her selfishness. They would call it sacrifice.

"You are not running away, Sara," Mary said. She reached out and grasped Sara's arm in a firm, almost-mad grip, strong enough to force Sara to look her fully in the face. "You are running toward something. Not away. I mean, look at the sunrise."

Sure enough, as Mary spoke those words, the sun broke free of its slow crawl above the horizon and the world was awash in a brilliant yellow light. The rays touched their faces and reflected in Sara's eyes, a color so startling it caused Mary to stop and stare, even after all this time. Mary knew—buried under all of her cynicism, doubt, and blatant refusal to care about the conventional—that she should be using this time to mourn. Her father was dead. Her mother was dead. Her prospects were dismal, her future was uncertain, her only remaining family more a stranger to her than Minchin. And yet, she found herself smiling, truly smiling.

"We go with the sun on our faces," she said, almost giddy with hope, with excitement. "And by God and all the saints, I am glad to put the damnable seminary at our backs!"

Sara was shocked enough to snort, then to laugh and to keep on laughing.

13

*S*ara was woken with a rough shake of her shoulder.

Her head jostled on her neck, landing with a resounding *thwack* on the wooden armrest that served as her pillow. A noise like a bell rang out in her ears, making her clutch her head and clench her eyes. She could not remember a more uncomfortable nap, and her body throbbed from the strain of being twisted and turned into a position that awkwardly created a bed out of a stiff-backed train chair. Someone shook her shoulder again, harder this time, if at all possible.

"What? What do you want?"

Her voice sounded grave, terse, and heavily accented, even to her own ears. She was reminded of her grandmother—a woman whose shadow covered miles while her physical stance barely topped five feet—and how angry she sounded when startled awake after a fretful sleep. It stopped Sara cold, for a moment. That was perhaps the last memory she would ever have of her grandmother. She took a brief moment to take note of it, log it away with the sound of her father's laugh and the smell of her mother's hair.

"I said, up with ya, you vagrant!" said a gruff and overly loud voice. Sara looked up through eyes squinty by poor sleep to see a uniformed man staring down at her. Only then did she notice that she was alone in the box.

"Where are my friends?"

"Already thrown off for leaving the train to buy food at the station, and I'll do worse to you if you don't remove yourself at once. Don't know what you all thought might happen, stowing away."

"Stowing away?" Sara said, only now beginning to fully come to terms with where she was and what was happening. "No, sir, we paid for passage."

"And where did you think a few pence would take you? Singapore? Now, I don't want to mishandle no young girl, but I'll toss you over my shoulder and haul you off this train if you don't get moving."

Sara was not *completely* surprised to discover that her "clever" disguise was transparent as glass, but there was still some disappointment.

When Sara stepped off the train, the sky was overcast and the air wet, heavy, and gray. She could not tell what time of day it was, and the train station was as nondescript as any in the English countryside. Passengers milled about—stepping from one train to another—and colors blurred dully together like dripping paint drying on an old canvas. Sara was momentarily so disoriented that she thought she might still be sleeping. Then she saw Mary and Cedric huddled together on a bench, neck deep in a furious argument, and knew that she was fully awake and something had gone terribly wrong.

As she drew closer to them, the conversation became clearer.

"I cannot *possibly* be blamed for this!"

"No, in fact, you can *irrefutably* be blamed for this. You're the one who put us on the wrong train!"

"Please, Cedric, you speak as if I loaded you onto the car at the end of a pistol. And if this is anyone's fault, it is yours. What exactly did you tell them when you bought the tickets?"

"I asked for three tickets on the first train heading east."

"And you didn't clarify exactly how far those tickets would take us? Honestly, it's as if you have never boarded a train before! Just because you buy a ticket does not mean you can get off and on at any point in the trip, you pay by distance."

"Do not speak to me as if you are the chief inspector of Her Majesty's Railway Inspectorate!"

"I swear, Cedric Errol, I have half a mind to demand satisfaction."

"A duel? Well, that's just my luck! I can tell you to meet at dawn and you will doubtlessly show up at sunset!"

"What has happened?" Sara took this moment to step into the conversation before things truly came to blows. Knowing Mary's temper and Cedric's unhealthy predilection for stoking that temper, a duel was not completely implausible.

Both began speaking at the same time, but Cedric was the louder.

"We are the witless beneficiaries of Mary's disdain for formal education," Cedric said. "That is what has happened."

Mary's face was cycling through shades of red when she all but yelled, "Oh, *really!*"

"That is very clever," Sara said. "But truly, where are we? Is this the coast?" She looked about the train station as if a flock of seabirds would suddenly appear in the sky or the smell of ocean water would waft over them. Instead, she looked up and saw only spindly black birds, and only smelled the industrial scent of burning coal.

"We are in Sheffield," Mary said. "Which is, admittedly, not anywhere close to the coast."

"*Sheffield?*" Sara asked. She rushed to recall detailed images of maps outlining the varying regions and counties of England. She was the only girl allowed to take geography courses at the seminary, but for some reason, her teacher neglected to spend much time on England and was more concerned about the possible location of ancient Troy.

"I think we're going the right direction, but this train isn't going to take us all the way unless we cross at Dover."

"Funny thing, geography," Cedric said, and this time, his usually dry and dismissive wit managed to break Sara's composure.

"Bloody hell, Cedric, you *live* here!" Sara asserted, allowing the rare curse to slip through. "Mary can at least plead ignorance, having passed her formative years in India, but you grew up in this land."

Cedric looked between Sara and Mary, mouth open in an offended and affronted shock.

"I cannot believe you," he said. "Either of you. Just because I was born and raised in England does not mean I traversed the country on foot to the point of memorizing every hill and dale before enrolling at the seminary. I beg you to not force me to explain the obvious reasons why that could never be possible. Just because you grew up in the Philippines, Sara, does not mean you know the topography by heart."

"Actually, yes!" Sara said. "It does! That is what happens when you truly live in a place, you learn it. When you proposed we run away to Paris, did you not have any clue of how we would get there?"

"I am sorry, did you expect me to have a fully detailed itinerary? A list of historic sites to visit, restaurants to patronize? Mary comes up with mad plans every day, and no one accuses her of being irresponsible!"

Even in the midst of what was their friendship's first real, possibly devastating argument, Mary flashed her catlike grin and the tone of the exchange was instantly lifted.

"That, dear Cedric," she said, "is due to professional experience."

Sara did not feel like laughing—in fact, she felt like crying, screaming, raging at the ridiculousness of their collective situation—and yet, she found herself giggling. Mary did have a point. Still, the obvious could not be avoided.

"So." Sara let out a long exhale and forced the frustration to flow out with it, or at least the most present frustration. She settled in a tight spot on the bench between her friends and felt slightly comforted by their close, familiar presence. "We're here. In Sheffield. Should we go back?"

"No!" Cedric and Mary said very ardently, in unison.

"No," Mary said again, calmer. Sara could see her mind working behind her eyes. "Going back to the seminary is not an option. We couldn't afford train tickets at this point, even if we wanted them. Paris is still our goal."

"As much as I agree with that statement," Cedric said, "we cannot very well walk to Paris. Not to mention the swimming that would be required."

"Is it exhausting, being so insufferable?"

"That look on your face, Miss Lennox, makes it all worthwhile."

"Silence!" Sara said in a raised voice, calling on the skills she'd gained as the caretaker of the seminary's youngest students. "We must think seriously here. We are essentially stranded in a place none of us fully understand. We have no money and no hope of acquiring any more. No clothes, excepting the clothes on our backs. No possessions. No food."

"Neither of you brought food?" Cedric asked. Sara was almost disappointed by the surprise in his voice.

"I'm sorry, did you expect me to have a fully detailed itinerary?" she shot back in turn.

Cedric visibly deflated as he said, "Touché."

"We are three capable, well-educated young people," Mary said. "It cannot be so difficult to find work. At least something that will earn enough for a new train ticket. Sheffield must have a city theater or a traveling troupe we can join. After all, let's not fail to acknowledge what we've done here!"

Mary stood and began to spin about the train station, barely avoiding confused passengers and making a fine spectacle. Dressed in some boy's old and odd-fitting clothes, Mary looked like a street performer seconds from doing flips and dancing a jig for coins. In fact, that wasn't a half-bad idea.

"What exactly did we do that is so exceptional?" Cedric asked, even as he laughed at Mary's display. "From my perspective, boarding the wrong train is not deserving of top marks."

Mary finally stopped spinning and teetered a bit, almost knocking over a very serious-looking gentleman.

"Please excuse her, sir!" Sara said. "She has only just recently lost her mind."

"I have not even begun to lose my mind."

"Appearances would say otherwise."

"What we have managed to do," Mary reaffirmed, "is escape a terrible situation. Yes, perhaps we are in a respectively worse situation, but still. We are free of the seminary. Of Mistress Minchin. We could go anywhere from here."

Mary bent down to steady herself and noticed something on the ground below her. She practically yelped when she righted and extended her hand to display her findings to Sara and Cedric. The bright metal of a farthing glinted in the low light.

"If this does not validate our journey, I don't know what will," she said. "Jostled from the pockets of that gentleman, I'm assuming. Not enough to buy us a ticket to the coast, but enough to get us a warm meal, surely."

Sara held out her hand for the farthing and Mary dropped it into her open palm. It was heavy and bright, newly minted perhaps. It would probably *not* be enough to get them a warm meal, but Mary didn't need to know that. Not right now. Let her ride this strange high of being lost and yet found, free and yet trapped. She was right, they could go anywhere from here. The future was uncertain, but they were together, and they were loose of the binds that tied them to a school, or a place, or a people.

It might have been foolish to think in such a way, but Sara couldn't very well help herself. After all Mary had experienced in her lonely time on this earth, if she could see something worth hoping for, so could Sara.

14

*I*t did not take them long to discover that the city of Sheffield had no formal theater. At least, not one that was looking for additional actors or members of their company.

Mary began asking passersby and shopkeepers as soon as they exited the train station where the nearest theater was, or if there was an active troupe about looking for help. The first time someone laughed off her questions, she thought it an anomaly. The second time, it was a coincidence. The third time, it was a pattern. And it had begun to rain in waves of these big, round, cold raindrops that seemed so particular to England. Rain in India was reserved for certain seasons, and even then, it was warm and refreshing. Rain meant life in India, and hope. Rain in England meant the absence of hope. The boys' clothes became heavy when wet, but they were well-made and warm enough to stave off the chill. However, Mary's society boots were not made for town streets, and Sheffield's muddy puddles leaked through her laces and somehow made their way between her toes.

Her deepest instinct was to complain, but when that impulse rose up in her, she'd look at Sara—who walked into the rain with squared shoulders while everyone else looked stooped and hunched—and thought of the discomfort she had endured under Minchin. If her dearest friend could bear being reduced to a servant after a lifetime of wealth and respect, then Mary could suffer through wet socks. Cedric, however, was another matter. Mary could see the strain the crutches caused him. He attempted to stay quiet, but even over the sound of rain on rooftops, Mary could hear his low groans of pain. They had to find *something*.

"I cannot believe England claims to be the center of Christian morality," Sara said quite suddenly.

Attempting to hide another grimace, Mary assumed, Cedric smirked and said, "I thought that moniker had passed on to the United States. Merry Old England hasn't committed much to holding on to the title."

"The United States just recently outlawed slavery, and only after years of bloody and senseless war," Mary said. "I highly doubt they're ready to be the moral center of anything."

"And neither are the British," Sara said. "There can be no more than four blocks between here and the train station, and I have already lost count of the homeless children. A city this big, a country this wealthy—an alleged empire—cannot manage to take care of their own?"

Mary's eyes had been directed upward, watching for street signs that might lead them toward food and work, but she now allowed her gaze to drift down to the street level. She didn't have to strain her eyes to see what Sara saw. Urchins were everywhere, as gray and washed out as the stone of the buildings under which they huddled. Some held out hands or upturned caps, asking every person who stepped within three feet for alms and a few shillings for food. Some focused their energy on staying warm, or staying as warm as they could in nothing more than worn, homespun frocks and trousers with holes in the knees. And others still didn't even shiver, did not blink. Their skin was made black by the factory coal dust that mixed with the rain, the fog, the snow, the air. They stared back at you with hollow glares, like the eyes of a taxidermic deer. Mary had seen such eyes in the poor of India, on those very few occasions she was permitted access to the outside world. But never before in England, or, at least, she had never allowed herself to see such eyes in England.

"They are like ghosts," she said.

"Living ghosts," Sara added. "More dead than alive, but too alive to be dead. It breaks my heart."

"One gets used to such things."

Sara and Mary swiveled their heads, full of judgment, to Cedric. Mary could not believe some of the things that came out of that boy's mouth. It was difficult enough putting some kind of label on his thoughts, categorizing his actions, predicting his behavior. Even his character sometimes shifted like a reflection in a disturbed lake.

"How could you say that, Cedric?" Sara asked. Mary didn't hear any anger in her friend's voice, which was surprising after the subdued fury she unloaded on Cedric at the train station. Instead, she sounded sincerely curious.

Cedric was in such pain that what would usually be a teasing grin on him looked twisted into a sneer. "And you say I am the sheltered one?"

Mary spoke up: "Being sheltered has nothing to do with it. Just because you have seen something before does not make it any less wrong, or real."

"I'm not saying that it is not wrong," Cedric said. "Only that it is the way things are, especially in big cities like this. A plague of cholera swept through Yorkshire not long ago, killing thousands. Mostly factory workers and their families. Not a year later, the city's population was replenished twice over, all by new workers coming in from the countryside. The churches honored the lives of the lost annually for a time, but eventually, the community moved on. More factories were being built. More people were flocking in for work. More cholera epidemics that may not have killed as many but still killed. When things change so quickly, even when they are terrible things, it is easy to focus on the most immediate, the most personal. I imagine it is like swimming in calm waters in one moment, then fighting the tide the next. In both cases, your only goal is survival."

Cedric spoke with a calm assuredness that unnerved Mary. He never claimed to be an actor, but he recited the speech with a bard's practiced confidence. As if they were lines that he learned long ago and had since committed to heart.

"'Tides change' is no excuse," Sara said. "I learned how to swim in an ocean, so I know something about tides. You do not fight them, you ride them."

Mary suddenly cried out in excitement, capturing everyone's attention.

"Well, this tide has certainly lifted our boat," she said. "That is the first street vendor I have seen all day."

She pointed forward and directed them toward a sweet-bun cart in the center of a private, sheltered square. The smell of baking bread cocooned the area and created an oven of sweet delights for the senses. All stomachs seemed to growl as one.

"We only have one farthing," Sara said. "We surely can't afford enough for everyone."

"We can share it," Mary said. "They're large buns, enough to get us through the day until we can find something else."

Sara had the farthing and thus volunteered to purchase the sweet bun. Mary kept her focus on Cedric, who was leaning against an alley wall. Every inhale and exhale seemed to echo through his entire body. Sweat coated his brow, and Mary saw him in more pain than she'd ever seen him in before. He was always the collected and unperturbed one, even compared with Sara. But now Mary could feel his frustration.

"You are showing a considerable lack of decorum, Cedric," Mary said, attempting to ease her own anxiety with the banter on which their friendship was built.

His eyes were closed and clenched in a type of focus, but he managed a grin.

"This is not exactly the drawing room of the Prince of Wales. I think I can spare a moment of vulnerability."

"Is this the longest you've gone on the crutches?"

Cedric shook his head and said, "My father was rather resistant to the concept of having his only son using a chair. He had aspirations toward a soldier, I think. He used to dress me up in his old uniform and make me march the estate. Or, at least, march as well as I can. He had me on the crutches for eight hours once. Rode me out in a carriage to the middle of our land, counting the distance in leagues like the Roman soldiers did. He left me there, told me if I wanted to come home, I needed to march back like one of Caesar's men. I made it home, but I could not walk again for almost a year after."

Mary listened to this all in rapt silence. When Cedric released information about his family, about his life, it was as rare an experience as spotting a unicorn in the garden. She was always afraid of asking too many questions or passing some unintended judgment. She did have questions—scores of them—and an inherent desire to dive down into the depths of something until she found an answer that satisfied her. Controlling that impulse with Cedric was difficult, but also entirely necessary.

"I am sorry" was all she could say, and perhaps all that was needed to be said. Cedric smiled. It was a handsome smile, when it was sincere.

"Don't be," he said. "I am not. This is an adventure of a lifetime. One of the most exciting things that has ever happened to me."

That made Mary laugh from a very genuine place. She said, "If running away from finishing school, boarding the wrong train, and ending up lost and penniless in Sheffield is the most exciting thing that has ever happened to you, you have lived an un-extraordinary life."

"Ah well," Cedric said in that old man voice of his, sighing with the weight of a person three times his age. "I suppose that is the benefit of having friends like Sara. Like you. What with your being extraordinary and all."

The honesty and offhandedness of the compliment took Mary by surprise. Her first instinct was to bite back with something witty and devastating, as was their way. But something stopped her, allowed her to bask in his kindness and its implications.

Sara returned, beaming as the steam from the freshly baked pastry rose up around her face and chased away the wetness of the rain. The smell was intoxicating and reminded Mary of just how long it had been since she ate a full meal. Her stomach concaved with the anticipation.

They divided the bun between the three of them, and it crumbled apart easily. Mary wanted to be considerate and responsible, eating slowly and saving the rest for later since there was no promise of future meals, but her hunger got the better of her. She consumed her section in one clean bite. Looking very much like a chipmunk, she glanced over to see Cedric staring at her as one might stare at a newly discovered Egyptian beetle featured in a museum exhibition.

"Did your jaw just unhinge?" he asked.

Rather than shoot back a biting retort, Mary actually stopped and considered just how she did manage to take a third of a massive pastry and eat it at once.

Cedric was eating his portion with the meticulousness of an engineer, Mary was licking her fingers, but Sara had not touched her portion. Instead, she stood, staring intently into the square. Mary followed her gaze and saw a girl sitting as flush as possible against the wall of a building in an attempt to shelter herself from the cold and rain. She couldn't be a day older than they were, but her face portrayed a tragic age. She looked hungrily at the bread cart and the people who passed with their own buns, no more than a midday snack for some. However, her eyes didn't read envy. They read acceptance of the shadow that loomed over her short life.

"That girl is hungrier than I am," Sara said.

Mary looked from the girl to Sara, then back again.

"Do not do it, Sara." Sara cut her eyes at Mary, but the resolve still hung about her face. Mary's shoulders drooped. "Please. We don't know when we'll have enough for another meal."

"I am certain that it will be sooner for us than it will be for her. I can take another missed meal. I doubt the same could be said for that girl."

Mary reached out her hand to stop Sara, but it was too late. She was already on the move, walking with determination across the square, in the drizzling rain. When the girl realized that Sara was approaching her, she scurried away, as if expecting to be kicked or struck. Sara slowed her pace. Mary could not hear what transpired, but she saw Sara bend down to the girl and speak to her softly. She held out her portion of the sweet bun, and although it took the girl some time, eventually, she snatched it away with wild hands.

Mary heard Cedric chuckle wryly, then say, "She really is a princess, isn't she?"

When Sara came back to them, Mary was shaking her head and somehow managing to look very disappointed.

"I don't see what you're so upset about," Sara said. "If you hadn't already eaten your pastry, you would do the same."

Mary made a crude, scathing noise and said, "No, I wouldn't. After all we have been through, you should know that by now."

"Hey, you there!"

A rough, aggressively authoritative voice crashed into the square as if dropped from a great height. All heads turned. Those who Mary assumed knew what that voice meant—mostly bedraggled children and threadbare grifters—made themselves scarce.

"What is happening?" Sara asked.

"I'm not sure," Cedric said. "But I feel that it may have something to do with us."

Two constables burst onto the scene like two large bears bursting into a meadow. They were red-faced and thoroughly put out, moving with all haste toward the three of them. One of the constables pointed at Sara with a stocky leather cudgel.

"You little thief," the first constable said with such ire that spittle flew from his mouth.

Sara actually held her hand to her chest in shock.

"Sir, you are mistaken," Cedric said, the picture of polite company.

Mary was a bit less compromising: "What the bloody hell are you talking about?"

"Shut it, both of ya!" The second constable lifted his cudgel and twitched, as if he might strike Cedric. Sara moved in front of him immediately, blocking him with her body.

"Leave him alone! And I am no thief."

"Lying ain't gonna help you none. We saw you give that little hoodlum a sweet bun, and we know that only way the likes of you could get one is by stealing."

Laughing, Mary said, "That certainly is a leap in logic."

"I said quiet!" This time, the cudgel was turned on her. It was a strange and curious sensation, for she had never been threatened with violence before. She didn't even have enough experience to be intimidated.

"I said I am no thief," Sara said, putting herself between the man and her friends. "I did not steal that sweet bun, I purchased it."

"Don't lie to us, you thief," the officer said. "We know damn well that your kind don't buy nothing that can be stolen." The slight seemed to sail right over Sara, but it hit Mary directly in the chest.

"How dare you!" Mary said in all of her righteous fury. "You ham-headed fools, you cannot say that to someone."

"You *will* shut your mouth, or I will shut it for you," the other said to Mary, and there was no room for doubt in his tone.

Things began to transpire very quickly. There were hands on Sara, then on Mary, pushing her away, and hands on Cedric, pushing him down. They all spoke together in cacophonous and panicked voices. Mary could see and feel Sara being dragged away, and Mary felt an old impulse rise up in her like the heat of boiling water in a kettle. She couldn't watch horror stare down those she loved and do nothing. It was the impulse to do something, even if it was foolish and ultimately useless. She heard the genie's voice again in her head, daring her to be brave.

"I stole the sweet buns!" Mary suddenly shouted out. Everything stilled and people stared. "I did," she affirmed again. "I stole them and gave them to my friends. They had nothing to do with it."

"Mary, what on earth—"

"Hush, Cedric. If you must take someone away, take me. I go willingly."

The two constables watched this play out with obvious confusion. The young street urchins and pickpockets they were used to didn't converse among themselves about which of them was the criminal. They usually scattered, ran, then denied everything as soon as they were discovered. Still, a confession made their work less strenuous. Without much to-do, they released Sara and took Mary into their custody. Mary saw that Sara looked near tears as she struggled to help Cedric to his feet.

"Go! Both of you!" she whispered harshly as the two men dragged her between them, each holding firmly to an arm. One gave Mary a stiff tug, forcing her to face front, and that was the last she saw of Sara and Cedric.

Well, she thought as she was led away to she knew not where. *At least the rain is letting up.*

15

*S*ara wanted to run, but with Cedric's weight hanging heavy on her back, she could only limp away quickly.

She found herself continuously looking over her shoulder, expecting to see a constable pursuing them. She also, more than a few times, expected to see Mary rushing to catch up, flush with excitement after having escaped captivity. She would be so proud of herself and thrilled that she could now use the introduction "Mary Lennox, the Fugitive." But no one was either running to catch them or running to join them. Sara wanted to cry, but every time she heard Cedric groan in pain or saw him droop in exhaustion, she swallowed that sadness and kept her back strong.

However, the point came when she couldn't bear Cedric's weight any longer. They collapsed against the side of a building, both panting and on the edge of tears. People passed them without sparing a glance. Some even went as far as to step over one of Cedric's crutches, which had fallen haphazardly into the middle of the narrow street. Perhaps they'd become so familiar with the sight of children leaning against buildings and huddled on curbs that another two didn't raise any alarm. It gave Sara a deeply unsettling feeling of being unseen. They were lost in a strange place, Mary was dragged away to God-knows-where, and now people were looking directly past her fear and frustration as one might look past a piece of rubbish in the street. In a few minutes she would vanish entirely.

"We have to help her," Sara said as soon as she had breath to speak. "We have to get her back, Cedric."

"Get her back?" The strain in Cedric's voice brought to mind distant memories of those early days in the seminary infirmary. Back when Cedric was just another patient, frail and bound to that bed in a cold corner of the room. It jarred Sara briefly out of the place, out of the moment they were in. In only a few months, Cedric had grown to be the pillar of their friendship. Now, seeing such a withered, worn, and pained child before her made her want to cry for a whole new myriad of reasons.

Cedric took a long, steadying breath. Sara could hear the air rattling around in his chest, but in time, he seemed to have steadied himself enough to speak with the clarity and decorum to which she had become so accustomed.

"Mary has been arrested, Sara," he said slowly. Even though he struggled to stay even, his voice cracked when it tumbled across *arrested*. "She's been taken to prison. Or some kind of workhouse, more like. It's hardly as if we could break in like some hero in an American cowboy novel and spring her. Stupid,

stupid! I should have taken the fall for her. I could have worked my way out of this, but she—"

"There's nothing you could have done," Sara said. "Either of us. But that doesn't mean we should let this just happen now. Mary would create a way to find and free one of us. A thousand times over. We just need to think grandly, like her."

"You mean insensibly?"

Sara slapped her hands against the hard cobblestones in an effort not to scream.

"If you have a better solution, Cedric, share it! Now, we could do something to get ourselves arrested, as well. Then they will take us to wherever she is, and we'll devise a way to escape together. Or we could beg some kind of statement from the proprietor of that bun cart. They will no doubt remember me and clarify for the authorities that the bun was not stolen, and this is all a terrible mistake. Maybe we are overestimating this entire process. She could be released in hours, minutes even, once the constables realize their error. Are you listening?"

Sara stopped in her very Mary-esque rattling of far-fetched ideas when she noticed Cedric looking off into the distance. His eyes were unfocused, lost somewhere in the time and space between the world that exists around you and the world that exists in your own head. His smudged spectacles sat low on the bridge of his nose, and he did not once attempt to correct their position. Sara was initially offended by Cedric's level of distraction. Now she was suspicious of it.

"Cedric?"

When he spoke next, he did not look at her. In fact, he closed his eyes.

"There is something I need to tell you," he said. "Many things I need to tell you. It would be better if it was done in stages, and not all at once. I shall start with the most believable, the most digestible. And then build up to the truly disturbing."

Sara had the good sense and instinct to be afraid. Then she remembered whom she was speaking to and collected herself. What could be disturbing about Cedric Errol?

"Stages may be best," she said. She folded her arms and nodded for him to begin whatever tale was resting so intently on his heart. Cedric nodded and raised himself with only the strength of his arms until he sat rod straight against the wall of the building.

Still refusing to look at her, he said, "I have been here before. To Sheffield. I have been here several times, in fact."

This did cause a small, brittle feeling like flaking paint to scurry up Sara's spine. She had to roll her shoulders and stretch her neck to dissipate that touch of confusion mixed with betrayal.

"When?" she asked, instead of hurling accusations, which would be Mary's immediate response.

Cedric exhaled, causing the long, uncut hair that hung about his face to sway like gossamer shades in a light breeze. Sara's lip turned up with a twitch. So often had she seen a similar gesture in Mary. She wondered briefly if he'd adopted it from Mary or if Mary had adopted it from him.

"Many times, over the years. My family has had . . . business here for generations. I know what you are thinking: How is it possible for us to become so lost if I've been here before?"

"I am glad you brought it up before I had to."

"Please believe me when I say that I am not familiar with this area." Cedric held up his hands pleadingly. "My previous travel has always been via coach. My father has a zealot's hatred for trains. I have never had an inclination to look out of the window when visiting Sheffield, never mind walk the streets for miles on end. You may see me as awfully silly and more than a little bit spoiled for admitting as much, but it is the truth, Sara. Do you believe me?"

"Well, of course. Of course I believe you," Sara said.

An eagerness to defend himself and validate his actions radiated off Cedric in hot waves. There was fear in his eyes, fear of rejection. If they were different people, under different circumstances, this would have been an unforgivable lapse in trust. But they were too far out at sea for such things to matter. She grinned and fumbled clumsily at lightening the mood.

"This is not by far the most startling confession I have ever heard. Once, Mary told me *exactly* why Lavinia despised her so much. That confession would make a vicar's toes curl. If that is the most shocking thing you have to tell me, then consider me underwhelmed."

Sara offered a laugh, but Cedric's face betrayed nothing but sobering earnestness.

"Then I recommend bracing yourself for what is to come next."

With a sudden burst of strength and energy that Sara knew he didn't have, Cedric righted himself and slid his back up the wall until he was in a standing position. He gestured to his crutches, and Sara darted quickly in and out of the street to fetch them. Cedric did his best to appear calm, comfortable, aristocratically unbothered. Yet the pain came through his eyes clearly. To look into them was to look into a boiling pot. He inhaled, then allowed his weight to settle on the crutches.

"Where we are going next is not far," he said. "However, be advised that I have never traveled there by foot. Five minutes' worth of travel in a coach will likely take much longer on crutches. I may need to lean on you."

Sara stood to her full height, brushed the mud from her trousers, and held out her arm to him.

"You may lean on me now," she said. "You may always lean on me."

THEIR JOURNEY CERTAINLY took more than five minutes. They were walking for almost an hour before Sara and Cedric stumbled gasping upon the threshold of a clean, orderly townhome in the midst of an industrial district. Such a respectable building of red brick and green shutters seemed starkly out of place among the factories and warehouses. Outside of the building—squeaking as it waved in the passing storm's dwindling wind—was an embossed plaque displaying the names **HODGSON & BURNETT**.

"Is this the place?" Sara asked.

Cedric was indeed leaning against Sara by this point. His arm was hooked securely over her shoulders and his body slumped heavily toward the ground. His breathing came in long and labored, and Sara could feel his strength ebbing. It had been many months since Cedric had succumbed to the tremors—not since the night on the frozen lake—but Sara suspected that so much strain over such a short amount of time would set him back to bed-bound if this continued. She didn't care what revelation lay within this mystery location; she was just grateful for a place to rest and ask for help.

Cedric lifted his head only marginally, enough to glance up at the plaque through pale lashes.

Sounding far more anxious than optimistic, Cedric said, "This is it."

Sara looked to the sky and saw that the sun had begun its descent along the western horizon. Was it the end of the day already? Had so much changed in such a short time? Sara felt a new and staggering compulsion to sit down and rest on the cool cobbles of the Sheffield streets until the day wound back and this whole misadventure could begin anew, the proper way, the right way. They should be settling into the cabin of a ferry bound for the French coast right now, if they'd just boarded a different train. Cedric would be complaining about the standard of the accommodations instead of fighting to stay conscious through numbing pain. She would be preparing to pass a night in a real bed, on a real mattress, and would kneel to pray on a soft rug instead of splintered wood. Mary would be telling the story of their great escape to a dining hall of eager listeners from all over the world instead of . . . well, instead of wherever she was now. Doing whatever it was they were no doubt forcing her to do. Sara shook her head. She couldn't think about it. Not until Mary was safe and their odd little family was whole again.

Sara leaned against the front door of the establishment, and it swung inward. Instantly, the change of temperature overwhelmed her. While outside there was a slight chill, sharp wind, and wet air, this interior was as dry and cloistered as an oven. The air was smoldering and close, causing her to inhale and exhale rapidly, struggling to catch her breath. It was a place of claustrophobic and constricting discomfort. The sole resident—sitting alone at a large desk in the very center of the cramped room—only heightened the bizarre feel of the place. The man was sallow, thin-skinned, and pale, like many of the citizens of Sheffield who were bound to desks, offices, and assembly lines. He continued scratching away at a ledger, even as Sara stood halfway through the door with an entirely immobile Cedric in her arms.

"Excuse me." The man did not move. His ears didn't even twitch. Sara cleared her throat and said again, "Excuse me!"

The sallow man jumped at the interruption and seemed even to be on the verge of a scream. He bounced up from his seat and looked upon them with saucer eyes, as shocked as if they'd appeared out of smoke.

"What the devil?" he exclaimed. "What on earth do you two think you're doing? We have nothing for you here. Get out! Get out, I say, or I shall summon the constables."

The man began to round the desk, and Sara was instantly on edge. Here she was, dressed as a boy, roughed up after a day wandering the open streets, barging uninvited into an obvious place of business with a near-unconscious young man in her arms. This fellow had every right to summon the constables.

"I need to speak with Mr. Hodgson," Cedric said. His voice was hollow and almost indecipherable. If not for the relative silence of the room, he wouldn't have been heard at all.

"'Mr. Hodgson'?" the man shot back, incredulous. "You cheeky scamp, how dare you!"

"What is the problem here?" asked a new man, whom Sara assumed to be Mr. Hodgson, as he entered the room. He was more substantial than his colleague, barrel-chested and round, but his skin was just as transparent.

"These ridiculous children are asking for you, Mr. Hodgson! A mad day when hooligans off the street can ask unprompted after one of the best lawyers in Sheffield."

Lawyer? Sara risked an inquiring glance at Cedric, who was beginning to come back to full consciousness.

"I say, who are you?" Mr. Hodgson demanded. He walked directly up to them, charged toward them, really. Sara had to take a step back to avoid being run over. "Explain yourselves at once, damn it!"

"My father may take much offense at your speaking to me in such a way, Samuel."

Cedric's voice had suddenly transformed. Sara could still hear the strain and the pain in it, but the tone had dropped to a new register. It was authoritative, refined, and completely in control. Even as he continued to distribute most of his weight onto Sara, his presence displayed a millennia's worth of entitlement.

Even Mr. Hodgson appeared momentarily put out and put in his place.

"Does your father know me, boy?" he asked, pulling his waistcoat down over his significant stomach.

"Indeed, he does," Cedric said. "The Earls of Dorincourt have employed the solicitors of Hodgson & Burnett for over two hundred years."

The tension in the room seemed to freeze. Sara found herself exchanging questioning glances with the lawyers, as if they were all victims of the same joke.

"The Earl of Dorincourt?" Mr. Hodgson's question wilted toward the end, as if he feared the answer.

"Yes," Cedric said. In a sudden and remarkable display of strength and will, Cedric drew himself to his full height, only managing to balance himself with a hand on Sara's shoulder. "You see, I am Cedric Errol, or Lord Fauntleroy."

"What?" Sara couldn't help herself. Her cry came from a place of shock and disbelief. This was surely one of Mary's farfetched and overwrought dramas. It had to be. Cedric Errol was no lord. The son of some country knight or village vicar, *maybe*, but a peer?

Cedric cut his eyes quickly at Sara, wordlessly imploring her to keep her composure, then continued. "The earldom is my inheritance, and since the firm Hodgson & Burnett is employed by the earldom, I believe, by association, you are employed by me."

Mr. Hodgson's mouth opened and closed like a gasping fish. He immediately looked penitent, a mortal standing before a spiteful god. Sara fully expected him to fall on his knees and plead for mercy.

"Young Master Cedric," he said, stuttering. He looked back at the other man, who was even paler than before. "Marley, you witless creature, did you not recognize the son of our dearest benefactor?"

Marley gasped at the slight, then gestured fiercely at Sara. "How was I to know? He came in with this queerly dressed half-breed—"

"You will address Miss Sara Crewe properly in my presence, sir!" Cedric said, practically yelled. "She hails from one of the finest families in the Philippines and could own this entire block in an instant if it fit her fancy. She will be treated with the utmost respect, or my family will find a new firm to employ."

Sara had never heard him raise his voice above a polite, conversational timbre. This was something new altogether. He held a power, even an anger, that made her jump where she stood.

Mr. Hodgson was apparently the only one taking these threats seriously. He approached Sara and Cedric slowly, back now curved in submission and hands clasped in placation.

"Do forgive my new associate, Lord Fauntleroy. He has only recently joined the firm, and since your father has been away, we have not had the opportunity to familiarize him with our more established clientele—"

"I have no interest in your excuses. Please ensure such a lapse does not occur again."

"Of course!" Mr. Hodgson glared pointedly back at his associate.

After a moment's hesitancy, Marley inclined his head and said, "Of course. My deepest apologies, Lord Fauntleroy. Miss Crewe."

Sara did not gift the man with a response. Only lifted her chin and felt her pride in self, and her pride in Cedric, rise like a strong tide.

Mr. Hodgson rushed to salvage what might have been—and might yet still be—a fatal encounter. He snapped at his colleague, motioning for him to bring chairs for her and *young Master Cedric*. Even when repeating the moniker in her head, Sara could not make sense of it. Such deference and respect and fear from these people. Back at the seminary, students and teachers alike had barely spared him a second glance.

Once Cedric was comfortably seated in what must have been the building's most heavily upholstered chair, and Sara perched on a much less accommodating stool beside him, Mr. Hodgson leaned close to Cedric and spoke in a much less self-important whisper. "However may we be of assistance, Lord Fauntleroy? We are humble servants of the Errol family."

"Your supposed humility aside," Cedric said. "We are in need of your services. We require a new wardrobe of clothes. My father's tailor on High Street should suffice, and I believe my mother often visited the modiste Madame Accambray for her frocks. Are you not writing this down?" Mr. Hodgson tripped over himself to get paper and a charcoal pencil. Cedric continued undaunted. "My family's four-horse coach will need to be summoned from the estate. A hansom cab will be acceptable for now. I have exhausted my traveling cash; please reach out to our banker concerning a withdrawal of five hundred pounds so I may properly entertain my guests. Within the hour, if you please."

"Yes, of course, Lord Fauntleroy," Mr. Hodgson said as he scribbled fiercely onto a loose leaf of paper. "All within the hour. Within the *half* hour."

"Mr. Hodgson, the banks are closed for the day."

When all eyes turned with fire on the young associate, Sara felt sure that he instantly regretted speaking at all.

"Forgive the young man's impudence, sir," Mr. Hodgson said. "However, I am afraid he speaks the truth. Your family's bank will not be open for business again until nigh on eight tomorrow morning."

Sara saw that Cedric didn't risk breaking the aristocrat's laws of decorum by displaying disappointment on his face, but she could sense it in the way his hand squeezed so tightly into a fist that it began to shake.

"Very well," he said with a sigh. "First thing in the morning, then."

The hapless lawyers clearly did not have the bravery to say no.

"Accommodations will be necessary for the night," Cedric said while inspecting his shirtsleeve. "Please have the Sheffield house opened and made ready for our arrival. I have strained myself on our journey here, and need Dr. Presley's aid. He will know what to bring."

Sara listened to this all transpire around her, but she found herself numb to much of it. She felt as if she were falling down and down into some sort of topsy-turvy dreamland where up is down, in is out, and her friend Cedric is the lord of the land. If she hadn't been so dumbfounded, she would have insisted that she was still asleep in a train car.

"Very good, Lord Fauntleroy," Mr. Hodgson said. Then— slowly, warily—he asked, "Might you and the young lady require anything else?"

Cedric snapped as if alighting upon a sudden realization.

"Ah yes! I almost forgot. How experienced is your firm in criminal law?"

16

*I*t was dark by the time they arrived. The city looked even more uncooperative in the twilight hours. The buildings seemed unimaginably tall, and the shadows stretched their hands out to snatch at hems and shirtsleeves. Wet cobblestones reflected the hazy glow of streetlamps, making the ground one walked on shift and pulse. It was hard to be certain of where one stepped, if the next footfall would be solid or an unexpected plunge into oblivion.

Soot from the factory chimney stacks had mixed with the rain, shrouding everything with a disturbing black coating. When Mary touched a wall or a doorknob or a chair, her hand came away stained, as if by an oily ink. Then her mind would drift to Cedric and the look on his face as she was being dragged away. It was an expression of unrestrained panic, of a child's in the midst of separation from everything it has ever known. She would not allow herself to believe that such a face would be her last memory of him. Not even as they roughly escorted her through the iron gates of a great, windowless black box—stooped low to the ground like a hunched prehistoric beast. Not even as those gates closed behind her with the finality of a funeral bell.

The lack of windows made things difficult to discern. Mary had to squint her eyes, not only to adjust to the minimal light, but also in an attempt to shield them from the dust in the air. Tiny fragments of something hung about her like a fog. It scratched the back of her throat, made her eyes water, and soon she was coughing to the point of breathlessness.

"Quiet, you."

The constable to her right was the mean one, Mary had come to discover. The one to the left seemed more ornery than malicious, but *this* man took a twisted satisfaction in the process of seizing children, tossing them around, then depositing them into a cruel new reality.

Once Mary was able to see clearly, she realized that this place was nothing more than one long room. Closest to the door was some kind of office. A setup for desks, chairs, and paperwork. Farther back were long rows of tables, one of which was covered by a massive quilt. Farther back still were distant bodies moving about in a mass. The sounds of talking and even laughing reached her ears as if from a great distance.

Sitting at the desk to their immediate right was a woman who could very well be Minchin's relative but for her all-black robes and bleached-white wimple. She carried that same unearned air of authority and that same hidden propensity for pettiness.

"Good evening, Jerry," she said to the constable on the left.

"Evening, Mother Superior. I have a new one for you. Picked her up in a square in Highfield with stolen goods."

"A thief? Wonderful. It's been some time since we've had one of those."

Mary did not appreciate how they all spoke around and over her like some cat they found sniffing at the rubbish.

"That is a matter of some contention," Mary said. "You see, when these so-called lawmen abducted me—"

"I said, quiet!"

Before Mary could think to react, a hand came down hard on the back of her head. Her teeth snapped together and made her ears ring. In the last few days, she had been struck more than ever before in her life and she was determined to never let another person lay hands on her again.

"She's a mouthy one, Mother," the constable on the right said with a note of amusement.

"Yes, I see. No matter. We have had mouthier than her, and they broke easily enough. This child will be no challenge. Welcome to St. Christopher's Home for Indigent Girls," the superior said, addressing Mary directly for the first time. "You have been brought here in lieu of being turned over to the authorities. Here, we shall use the honest work of making quilts and the love of Our Lord to cure you of the faults of character that led you to such a life. Only a select few young ladies are given the blessed chance that this home offers. I trust that you are in full knowledge of just how lucky you are, and you will take this experience seriously."

Mary certainly did take the experience seriously. For one—staring into the eyes of this woman who believed wholeheartedly in every delusional word she said—she knew that she was in some serious trouble.

"I take your silence as acceptance," the nun said. "If you maintain this attitude, we shall get on swimmingly. Jessie!"

A girl—shorter than Mary, but certainly older—rose up from what looked to be her work of collecting scraps of fabric from the long worktables. Her face was one of hard lines and solid, unbroken composure. But her eyes were kind. Tired, but kind.

"This is Jessie," the superior said. "She will give you your new clothes and acquaint you with your new situation."

Jessie gave Mary a quick and critical once-over, then shook her head.

"This'll be hard for you," she said very matter-of-factly. And Mary did not disagree.

JESSIE ESCORTED MARY past the worktables, through a labyrinth of metal-framed cots, some of them occupied by one or more girls. A few appeared to be older than Mary, well into what Minchin might call "society age," while others looked barely old enough to speak. They all wore the same rough gray gown that Mary had been forced to change into after her other clothes and possessions were confiscated. She did not think anyone deserved such a fate.

The other girls stared at Mary as she passed. Curious glances, filled with questions and pity, and more than a little bit of annoyance. *Here comes another one to take up more of the food, more of the warmth, more of the attention.* Not so different from the seminary, really. Not so different at all.

Jessie came to a short stop at an empty cot at the far end of the building. There was nothing on the cot but a dingy straw mattress. Not even a thin square foot of blanket to keep her warm, or a pinch of pillow on which to rest her head.

"Is this it?" Mary asked. What started as an honest question came out sounding much more imperious than she'd intended. She could see the offense plain on Jessie's face.

"What more were you expecting?" the girl asked. "A chambermaid and a butler?"

Mary used the good sense she had left and kept her mouth shut.

Jessie left her in peace, and Mary made herself comfortable on her pallet. Or as comfortable as she could be. Every other second, she felt something tickling her hand or her knee or her leg; however, when she snatched her hand away, she would see nothing there. Whether or not invisible, minuscule bugs actually danced across her skin, she carefully folded herself into her baggy dress in order to avoid touching the mattress.

She suddenly heard a noise somewhere next to her that might have been a laugh if not for the labored, gasping tone. She looked over to see a girl stretched out on the neighboring cot. Mary had spent enough time in the seminary infirmary to know a very sick person when she saw one.

"Itches like the devil, doesn't it?" the girl asked. Her voice was so soft it was difficult to hear, and heavily flavored with an accent.

"I cannot tell if there are bedbugs," Mary said, "or fleas or just my own imagination."

"Whatever your imagination can create is probably better than the truth." The girl began to laugh again but soon fell into a fit of body-shaking coughs. Even with the distance between their cots, Mary could hear the phlegm rattling in her chest. It took the girl a long time to catch her breath, and once she did, some of her strength was visibly gone.

"Consumption?" Mary asked. She didn't want to do the girl the discourtesy of beating around the bush.

"Maybe," the girl said. "Maybe scarlet fever. After a while, doctors stop telling, and you stop asking. Is this your first time in a place like this?"

Mary winced and said, "Is it that obvious?"

"You're clean. Usually, girls get a bit more scuffed before ending up in a workhouse. What'd you do, run away from home?"

"Close," Mary said. "Ran away from school. It's rather silly, really. We thought we were going to Paris, but we ended up getting kicked off the train here in Sheffield."

The girl grinned through thin, chapped lips and said, "You are right, that is silly. I'm Anne, by the way."

Mary dipped her head. "Mary Lennox. Pleased, charmed, and all of that."

"Mary?" she said. "I knew a Mary once, I think. But that was months ago."

"How long have you been here?" Mary asked as she studied the dirty floor and the low ceilings, encrusted with even more soot.

"You know," Anne said, "I can't remember. Perhaps a year, or even two. No windows in this place, you see. The days blend together."

"A year is not possible! What on earth did you do to be committed to a year in such a prison?"

Mary could see Anne's eyes begin to droop. Her arms—light and delicate things, spindly as bird's wings—seemed to sink into the mattress as if made of steel.

"I don't . . ." Space stretched between her words. "I don't remember . . ." Anne's last word was barely out before she slipped into sleep. It was a quick descent. She must have been very tired, or very sick, indeed.

Mary started at the jarring of a bell. The sound bounced off the metal walls, causing her teeth to chatter. She cupped her hands over her ears, but still felt the ceaseless ringing in her bones. Anne somehow managed to sleep through it all.

"What is that?" Mary yelled, or at least, she thought she had yelled. She couldn't even hear her own voice.

"Food," a close-by girl said. She was older, fuller of body, and taller even than Sara. "Get moving. If you ain't at the table when the bell stops, you don't eat."

Mary was on her feet, but felt a need to linger by Anne's cot. The bell continued to ring, but Anne had not moved.

"What about her?" Mary asked.

The older girl looked down at Anne, shrugged, then kept moving. Mary's principles forced her to stop and think. If the choice was to move or go without, and Anne was too sick to move, then Mary would go without. But she *was* hungry. A third of a sweet bun wasn't going to get her through the night, the morning, or however much time she had to create a plan. And she didn't really know Anne, didn't know anyone here. She could do more on a full stomach, she decided. Whatever she could bring back for Anne, she would.

Supper at St. Christopher's Home for Indigent Girls was not supper at the seminary.

The five courses Mary was accustomed to were narrowed down to one. In no more than a day, she had gone from roast duck with vegetables and pudding for dessert to a single serving of some kind of wheat-based gruel with flecks of . . . what? What was that? Pork? Chicken? It floated at the top of this savory porridge, which Mary found suspicious.

She sat at a long trestle table that stretched the length of a room. Every girl across from her and to either side ate their food savagely, as if this were their first and last meal. They swallowed so quickly that Mary wondered whether they could even taste what they were eating. Perhaps that was the way of things here. To fill one's stomach and not worry about what one ate or how it tasted. Mary felt her own stomach grumble. Even though her better character knew that this was not food that anyone should feel compelled to eat, her basic instincts recognized the nourishment. She brought her nose close to the cooling bowl and sniffed. It didn't even have a smell.

"Eat." The girl next to her was sharp-faced with a nose like a hawk and striking dark eyes. She spoke to Mary without glancing in her direction, but Mary knew that she was being addressed.

"What is it?" Mary asked.

"Does it matter? They don't feed us again till tomorrow night, so unless you can go a day without food, you should eat. Don't be a hero; no one cares."

Mary looked back down at the food. The hawk-nosed girl was right. No use trying to make a statement or hold a position; no one was watching, no one was listening. Not eating would help no one, especially not herself. Using the large metal spoon that came with her bowl of gruel, she guided the smallest portion into her mouth. She was relieved that it tasted just as bland as it smelled. If it truly had been unbearable, she would have spit it out across the table, heroics notwithstanding.

Even though Mary had never been more exhausted, sleep would not come to her. It was at once too quiet and far too loud in the barracks. The sounds of girls coughing, snoring, groaning, talking, and even crying in their sleep made for a disturbing and disheartening symphony. And then, after what felt like hours of continuous noise and twitches of activity, there would be silence like that of the grave. Not even the rats would move. Mary was halfway immersed in a dream when one of these bouts of silence seized the barracks, and she started awake, gasping for breath after dreaming that she was buried in a deep hole in the middle of the desert. It was enough to drive her mad, and all of this only after a few hours. She could barely comprehend a few months of this, never mind a few *years*.

"Mary . . ."

Her name was whispered in a far-off, pleading tone. Mary looked over from her cot, and there Anne was, still asleep. Her mouth moved as if speaking, but Mary could only pick up bits and pieces.

"Mary . . . Mary, wait for me," Anne whispered again.

"I'm right here, Anne. Anne!"

Mary reached out to touch Anne, but she snatched her hand away when she felt the texture of her skin. It was somehow both hot and cold. Burning up from within but still clammy and wet as the walls of a cave. This girl wasn't just sick, she was in true distress. Moving quickly and relatively quietly to avoid detection by the matrons who patrolled the rows of cots like prison guards, Mary slipped out of bed and crawled to Anne's side. She touched Anne again, with more insistence. Anne jostled a bit, but her eyes only opened a sliver. They were glassy, like the eyes of a taxidermic animal.

"She didn't wait for me," Anne said. "I begged her to wait, but she left whilst I was sleeping."

It did not take much for Mary to realize that Anne was talking about someone else entirely. And she wasn't really speaking to Mary at all. Someone else was the receiver of this tale, someone far away, beyond the veil. But Mary listened as raptly as a child hanging on a parable. Without hesitating or pausing even to think

over her actions, Mary searched for something to write with. She—
perhaps cruelly—assumed that many of the girls in the workhouse
were illiterate, and that the staff of St. Christopher's did not hold
the same torch for education as they did for hard labor. All to say
that pen and paper were hard to come by.

Over Mary's shoulder, Anne mumbled, "Mary, you said you
wouldn't leave without me, you *said* . . ."

Mary struggled to pay attention to Anne's words as she
searched. She would need to remember whatever was left to write
down. Finally, she found a piece of flint stuck in a crease between
her mattress and the iron frame. It was no bigger than her finger-
nail, but it left a residue like chalk. She had no paper or anything
remotely similar, but the floor of the workhouse was littered with
scraps of fabric from the textile work the girls were forced to
endure. Mary found one light enough to let the flint show through,
then skittered back to Anne's side.

"Who is Mary, Anne?" Mary asked. Her finger was already
moving over the fabric, recording Anne exactly as she saw her.
Weak, worn, and unmistakably a child.

Anne inhaled, and it was the sound of wind through bare
trees.

"My sister," she said. "My oldest sister. There were five of us,
when we came from Galway. No work, Papa said. No work, no
food. No family left alive. We hoped for chances here in England.
Mama hoped for passage to America. Ran out of money long
before that."

Mary continued to write, tripping over spelling and

punctuation and grammar. There was no need for drama and imagination here. So much of what Anne said was too much to believe and too much to create from one's head alone.

"When did you come from Galway?" Mary asked.

Anne's eyes drifted up and away, as if looking back into time.

"There was no food, you see," she said, seeming to have not heard Mary's question. "Papa said we had no choice. We landed in Liverpool and walked. Walked for days. We told stories about home and the family. There were so many of us, once. They all melted away. Even Granny Cane. Her house always smelled of salt and sea. I can't smell the sea here. Naught but ash in this air. Ash and soot and dead things . . ."

She drifted off again, wilting on the end of her sentence. Mary leaned closer, close enough for her breath to jostle Anne's limp brown hair. She rested a hand against Anne's arm and tried not to be repulsed by the texture, thin like wet paper.

"What happened to them?"

Mary suspected that this was a delicate question. Why bring up something so certainly painful? But there was a ticking clock on this girl's story. If someone did not take the time to record it, save it, cherish it, it would be gone forever. Just like the stories of so many others who came in and out of this place.

When Anne spoke again, her voice sounded choked, as if an invisible hand were clutching at her throat and stoppering her mouth.

"Papa went first," she said. "A sickness in the drinking water. Mama made it to Bradford before typhoid set in. Mary said to head for factory towns, like here in Sheffield, so we could get work. We made matchboxes in a one-room tenement with ten other children. Baby Liam was so small, and weak. He didn't last a night with the pox. Marcus robbed the wrong merchant. Hung from the gallows like ivy from a tree."

Mary's hand halted.

Anne took a deep breath, then continued. "Laura walked out in the night and didn't come back," she said. "Not long till it was just me and Mary. But we couldn't pay the rent on the room, and we were put out. Then winter came. *Mary, it's so cold.* So much snow, no place dry to be found for love nor money. No place dry, no place soft. Sleeping on stoops. Eating old carrots rotting in the gutter."

Anne's speech reminded Mary of a preacher in a pulpit. Voice growing in power, in fear, with each word. Mary could only write as Anne spoke, struggling to stay on top of every word. It was a trial to keep tears from gathering in her eyes.

Anne looked directly at Mary when she spoke again. "You said that there was only space for one of us under the blanket. A storm was coming, and the snow would be ten feet high by morning. You said you wouldn't leave me. That I could sleep in peace 'cause you would be there, keeping watch. You made me a promise, Mary!"

Then Anne was crying. It was a broken cry. Not enough energy for sobs, too malnourished for tears. Just an openmouthed, silent wail. Mary couldn't keep her distance any longer. Without much minding where they were or how sick Anne was or how tragic this whole sorry tale had become, Mary climbed onto the cot next to Anne and wrapped herself around her. She held the girl as close as possible with strong, secure arms.

"I'm not going anywhere," she whispered as Anne cried tearlessly onto her shoulder. "I shall be right by your side when you wake up."

In time, Anne's cries ceased, and her breathing became even and touched with a contentment that Mary was sure she hadn't felt in some time. In her hand, Mary clutched the triangle of cloth that held only a portion of Anne's life story. She closed her fingers around it until the fibers of the fabric rubbed against her palm. She resolved herself to make proper use of it when she got out of this place. No play or drama, but a proper narrative. An article, perhaps, submitted to a society paper where those vapid souls who thought of nothing beyond their own wealth and recreation would be forced to acknowledge it. That would make a real, true impact. As she allowed her own frenzied mind to succumb to sleep, she thought of how supportive Sara would be of the notion. Cedric would cut some snide remark about Mary's stubborn righteousness. He would be right, of course. Cedric was always right.

THE SUPPER BELL was sounding again, but Mary was certain it wasn't supper time. She couldn't have been asleep more than a few hours. She opened her eyes wide, disappointed to find that the light in the room had not changed. The same gas-lamp glow was suspended high above in the rafters of the workhouse. It could still be night for all she knew. Mary marveled at the cruelty of such a policy. You could tell the girls that it was seven in the morning, when in truth, it was only a couple of hours after midnight. They could be worked for twenty hours straight through and have no idea. Anne was right, there was no way to measure the passage of time in such a place.

Anne!

Mary sat ramrod straight in a cot that was not hers. The speed of the movement made her head throb, and she had to pinch her nose to dull the ache and bring the memory of last night back with full force. She remembered hearing Anne wake in the night. The horrid tale of her time in England and the grief that had followed her steps like a wedding train. It was decided in Mary's mind: Anne would not spend another day bed-bound and starving. They would get up together and greet the day. Anne would get better and survive this, as she had so much else. Mary had a namesake to honor, after all. She turned toward Anne with a grin on her face, prepared to tell her the very same thing, but something stopped her short.

It was the stillness with which Anne lay. No twitch of the hand, no flutter of an eyelid. The gaps between her inhales and exhales were so long that it would be easier to say that she wasn't breathing at all. In fact . . . Mary leaned in closer, listening with pricked ears for the telltale sounds of a beating heart or expanding lungs. And there was nothing. Mary inhaled herself, deeply, as if in homage to the air that Anne would never breathe again.

Mary always thought that if caught in such a situation—sitting next to the corpse of someone she'd spoken to mere hours ago—she would begin screaming and pulling at her hair. Like an actress in an operetta, Mary was prepared to fall into a dramatic and elegant faint at the sight. But Mary did not scream. She wasn't even sure the beat of her heart had altered. Outwardly, she was the picture of calm. Inside, however, a sadness fueled by terrible anger rolled and crashed against her mind and soul as waves crashed against a cliffside.

Once Mary had enough strength of limb to stand and fall in to the queues of other girls, she discovered that St. Christopher's was expecting a very important visitor. The Countess of Lumley, the girls whispered in excited, hushed tones as they dressed and made ready for the day. The wife of the Earl of Lumley, some benefactor of the workhouse. The matrons buzzed around like flies in an effort to make presentable the pretty and healthy girls, and to hide the sick and disfigured ones. Because she was clean and new, Mary was hustled into the group of pretty and healthy girls. They were given faded blue aprons to put over their frocks, and lilac bonnets with fraying lace for their heads. It was a weak pretense. Anyone with eyes would be able to see that under the doll clothes and hastily brushed hair, the girls assembled in a neat row toward the front of the workhouse were not picturesque examples of the good that hard work could do. And Mary had yet to tell anyone that Anne was dead. She wasn't sure if she could stomach the apathy that would be reflected in their eyes.

"Quiet now!" the matron ordered once all rows had been

made straight and tidy, and all of those who might risk causing discomfort were swept away. "Lady Lumley is a great supporter of this house. You show her your best, likely you'll get a new dress or new shoes or better food. Disappoint her—make a bad impression in any way—and every pound we lose will be a day without supper for you. Am I understood?"

"Yes, matron," the girls intoned as one. The similarities with the seminary were becoming more obvious with every passing second, in Mary's eyes.

The matron nodded and said, "Right. That's my girls."

She motioned at one of the older girls by the main doors. With a groan of effort, she opened them and allowed a beam of morning light to erupt into the workhouse. All the girls winced; some even covered their eyes to protect them. Mary adjusted quickly, but with that adjustment came clarity. In the stark light of day, the girls looked even thinner, weaker, younger. The light seemed to go directly through their skin, illuminating rivers of red and blue pumping beneath the surface. Eyes were bloodshot; teeth were yellow. Mary was briefly frightened at such a sudden change. These weren't girls of all ages and faces with whom she stood, but wraiths. The walking dead, hanging on to existence by a tenuous thread. Mary likened the experience to the kinds of visions that the old prophets and mystics claimed. An instant of truth in a world of illusion. Then the door closed, and darkness closed in again. The ghosts faded away but the bodies remained.

For a long while, the countess was only a voice and a silhouette approaching Mary at a leisurely pace. She spoke with the Mother

Superior—the director of this place, Mary assumed, the one who had oriented her. Mary could hear them speaking of trivial things such as the weather and the prospects for the London season. They weren't even discussing the workhouse—the very thing Lady Lumley had come to appraise. Mary had the immediate sense that this was just another stop on the road from country to London Town for such a grand woman. A ticking-off on a list. The money would come to St. Christopher's, Mary had no doubt. Perhaps it was the House of Lumley's annual act of philanthropy. Nothing any of the girls did or didn't do would change that.

Now that she'd come closer, Mary could take in exactly how glamorous Lady Lumley was. She wore a gown of deep evergreen, as vibrant and lush as the eyes of a wood sprite, and the matching bonnet framed her diamond-shaped face like a halo. There was a sharpness to her polite smile, an intelligence in the simmer of her eye. As much as Mary wanted to despise this woman for her role in the demeaning of St. Christopher's girls, she found herself drawn to her. For some reason or another, she saw an ally buried under all the velvet and lace. As suddenly as if she had been struck by Zeus's thunderbolt, Mary remembered the piece of fabric that was still clutched in her hand. Cedric's main criticism of *Bejeweled Paramour*—one of many he had shared over their weeks of planning and rehearsal—was that it didn't reach past the pretense. Once Mary finished admonishing him for daring to criticize her masterpiece, he would go on to explain that the drama was not a truthful rendering of its subject matter. It was a caricature of it. As entertaining as it was, that was all it would ever be:

an entertainment. If Mary wanted to really reach into someone's heart and compel it to change, she would have to try harder.

"Good morning, girls," Lady Lumley said to the collection of young women. "Thank you for having me at your lovely home this morning."

That is when Mary took a step forward.

"Lady Lumley," she said, raising her voice to ensure that she wouldn't need to repeat herself. "Did the matrons tell you that a girl died here last night?"

A gasp rose up around Mary. To keep her focus and her nerve, she did not allow her eyes to stray from Lady Lumley's. They were midnight blue, like her mother's. To the countess's credit, she did not laugh at Mary or dismiss her. Instead, she held up her hand when the superior seemed prepared to whack Mary with her cane.

"Really?" she said. "No, I was not told. Who was the girl?"

That was exactly the invitation Mary needed. She approached Lady Lumley with her hand outstretched, the crumpled corner of cloth protruding before her.

"Her name was Anne," she said. Lady Lumley reached out with long, gloved fingers and took the cloth from Mary. "She came from Ireland with her family some time ago. She was sick with a bad cough for months and nothing had been done about it. Instead of taking the time to have her diagnosed properly, they ignored her and let her suffer. Because she was too weak to rise out of bed, she did not eat."

"That is entirely untrue!" the superior, red-faced and sinister, said in a huff. "I know of the poor soul this impudent thief speaks of, ma'am. She was beyond healing, and each doctor we summoned said that nothing could be done for her. We gave her every comfort in her final hours."

"Is it true that she was not permitted to eat?" Lady Lumley asked the superior. The woman stumbled some over her words but recovered her professional composure quickly.

"Well, my lady, we have a policy here at St. Christopher's. When we sound the supper bell, if a girl is not at the table by the time the bell stops, she goes without. It gives them an incentive to be on time. If we had known Anne was so ill, we would have—"

"You did not know?"

This, Mary and Lady Lumley said in unified disbelief.

"You are lying," Mary said, "and you are unspeakably cruel."

This time, the nun appeared ready to launch at Mary, propriety be damned.

"How dare you!" she glowered. "You ungrateful little—"

"I am inclined to agree with this child," the countess said in a tone that was both casual enough for a drawing room but as authoritative as a judge. "And I cannot work out what would offend me more: your cruelty or your untruthfulness." The lady then turned to face the rest of the girls, who watched all this unfold with the wariness of a deer trapped in a hunter's gaze.

"Do any of you know of this?" she asked.

It did not take long for someone to speak up.

"Anne been sick since she came here," one girl said—the hawk-nosed one who told Mary not to be a hero. "I heard tell that the doctor they brought for her—that they bring for all of us—is no doctor at all. He shoes horses for a mill down in Stockbridge."

"And it's true 'bout the supper bell," another girl said. "I tore up my hand once, cutting fabric. I was down with infection for a fortnight. The only food I ate was the food others snatched for me."

In the way of all aristocrats, Lady Lumley did not let the look of shock reach her face. She simply arched an expertly plucked eyebrow and inclined her head.

"Thank you for your honesty, girls. Mother Superior, the funds my husband and I bequeath to this home have been specifically earmarked for the provision of health and medical care. Is a farrier from . . . what was it?"

"Stockbridge, Your Lady . . . ship," Mary supplied helpfully.

"Yes, thank you. Is a farrier from Stockbridge the best that ten thousand pounds a year can buy? And what of this foolishness with a dinner bell? I understand the need to instill promptness and respect for one's time in these girls, but if one is physically unable to take a seat at the table, I fear the lesson may become a moot point."

"My lady," the superior began, "these are isolated circumstances."

"Indeed. Well, I cannot wait to hear about them. I believe I shall extend my review of St. Christopher's from an afternoon to a week, if you do not mind. After hearing of these *isolated circumstances*, I am eager to ensure what these children speak of is not a pattern that needs correcting."

The superior did not argue or object. Instead, the life seemed to drain from her face until she seemed as sun-starved as the girls in her care.

Lady Lumley then returned to face Mary. She glanced down at the cloth on which Anne's story was penned and appeared to give it a serious if speedy once-over.

"You wrote this, child?"

Mary said, "I only wrote down what Anne told me."

"Even so. This is quite a good accounting of her life. Very . . . truthful. You do the poor girl a great honor. What is your name?"

"I am Mary Lennox, my lady," Mary answered, before giving her best imitation of a proper curtsy. Much against her own will, she felt her chest inflate with pride.

"A pleasure to make your acquaintance, Miss Lennox. Pray tell, how did you come to be here? You do not strike me as an urchin or wayward child."

"Please believe me when I say, Lady Lumley, that I am no different from any other girl here. Yesterday, I was a student at the Select Seminary for Young Ladies and Gentlemen in Manchester. Today, I am a prisoner here at St. Christopher's Home for Indigent Girls. Yesterday, my father was very alive and very wealthy. Today, he is dead, and all his wealth depleted. I am just as much a wayward child as Anne is . . . was. Mere moments separated our fates."

"My word," Lady Lumley said. Then she smiled. "Quite well said, Miss Lennox. Perhaps a better question might be, how did you come to be arrested and deposited into the custody of this girls' home?"

"Oh. Well, that was a complete misunderstanding."

"It was thievery." The superior seemed to have recovered some of her courage, or at least some of her pride. "The local constables spotted her selling a stolen sweet bun."

"Is *that* what they saw?" Mary asked. "That certainly explains a lot. For you see, in truth, my lady, that sweet bun was purchased in all fairness and legality. And the sweet bun was not being sold. It was being shared with someone far hungrier than I. I would have been happy to explain as much if anyone bothered to ask."

Lady Lumley's marble exterior suddenly shattered, and she burst into peals of laughter like silver rain.

"Miss Lennox, you do charm me. Is this Select Seminary where you picked up such wit? I must be certain to send my girls there."

"I wouldn't, my lady. There is not much difference between the seminary and St. Christopher's except the price you pay to be there."

"Duly noted. Mother Superior!" When Lady Lumley turned her full attention back to the nun, her heels clicked together like a soldier's. "How much is Miss Lennox's debt to society?"

"Debt? To society?"

"Heaven's gates, woman. I mean, how much for the sweet bun she allegedly stole? There is no way for us to prove what she is saying right here in this room, but I am inclined to believe her. My father was a leading member of Parliament, after all. He taught me to separate truth from fiction."

"I could not say," the superior said dismissively. "That is for the city barrister to decide."

"You mean Judge Kidd's eldest son, of course. We grew up together, dear Brigsby and I," the countess said with a casualness that hid inherited confidence. "Whatever Miss Lennox's debt is, consider it paid. I am sure he'll understand."

It took Mary a few seconds to comprehend what was happening, but once she did, she genuflected until her head began to spin.

"Thank you, Lady Lumley!" she said over and over again.

"Oh, do stop that, Miss Lennox. You curtsy like a pigeon, and I mean that in the kindest way. And do not fret over Anne's story. I shall make sure it is heard."

"Thank you," Mary said again, even as she was backing away toward the door. "I promise to remember you in my prayers, my lady."

"And I shall remember *you*, Mary Lennox. Look me up in London, if you are ever in town. A talent such as yours should not be lost to history."

Mary could not agree more. After one last curtsy of thanks, she turned and practically sprinted for the door.

Behind her, she could hear Lady Lumley say, "Jessie is your name, correct? You seem to be a bit of an authority here. It appears I'm in need of a more thorough tour of this place."

MARY HAD NEVER been more relieved to see a blue sky. Even though she'd only spent a night in St. Christopher's, her arms reached out for the sun like a person entombed for years. For a while, she simply allowed herself to stand there, basking in the warmth and the glow. She knew truly now what it was to be imprisoned, and she knew what it was to be free. She vowed never to confuse the two again.

"Mary?"

Mary opened her eyes wide at the sound of her name, then found herself squinting in confusion at the sight before her.

Cedric Errol was in the process of being helped out of the most ornate private coach Mary had ever seen. It was drawn by four striking white horses with silver manes, dripping in livery and regalia. The carriage itself was painted entirely in gold leaf; it shimmered in the sun like Apollo's chariot. The man helping Cedric was someone she'd never seen before. A large man with a round belly and an obvious desire to enthusiastically fulfill Cedric's requirements. Cedric himself was dressed better than most kings. Expertly tailored, the richest fabrics, gold cuff links winking at his wrists. He looked every bit the prince instead of the pauper he was only a day—*less* than a day—before.

"Cedric?" she said. There were so many questions. Her thirsty mind was foaming with them. Yet, when the time came to ask, she could only say, "What are you doing here?"

Cedric looked at Mary as if she were the one appearing out of the morning fog in an enchanted carriage, dressed more stylishly than Queen Victoria herself.

"I'm rescuing you, of course," he said, as if that explained everything.

"I appreciate the gesture," Mary said. "But it is not necessary."

Then Sara popped out of the carriage. It was as if she'd traveled back in time, for she wore almost exactly the same blue dress she had been wearing on her first day at the seminary.

"Mary Lennox," she exclaimed with breathless happiness. "You will not *believe* what Cedric has been hiding!"

17

*Y*ou cannot still be upset with me, Mary."

"I am not upset. I am disappointed."

"That is just a more evasive way of saying you're upset."

"You would know a great deal about that, wouldn't you? Being evasive?"

"Please, both of you, we have been in this coach for three hours. How much longer can this go on?"

Mary and Cedric stopped glaring at each other long enough to look at Sara. She sat against the window of the coach, her head in her hand. She massaged her temples slowly, like a mother might when surrounded by unruly children. Her head throbbed and the rocking of the carriage did not help dissipate the pressure building in her skull. Ever since they fetched Mary from the workhouse, an argument that wasn't an argument was transpiring between Mary and Cedric. Normally, Sara would be able to bear these sparring sessions that they seemed so eager to engage in. If anything, she'd simply move to a different room or space, and when their feud died down, she would rejoin them. But they were in a coach designed to comfortably seat no more than four. They were traversing a great distance from Sheffield to Cedric's family seat farther north in the wilds of York. There was no escape, and Sara was coming to realize something rather specific about her dearest friends: just as Newton proclaimed that unless acted on by an outside force, an object in motion would stay in motion; unless acted upon by an outside force, a tiff between Cedric and Mary would stay a tiff.

"I'm not asking for some overwrought apology, Sara," Mary said. "I am grateful that he would go through the trouble of breaking his charade to liberate me."

"There seems to be a criticism in there somewhere," Cedric said while waving his finger like a conductor.

"But what I do want," Mary continued, "is some kind of explanation. How long has this been going on?"

"You mean my being a lord?" Cedric asked, dripping with irony. "I would have to estimate about sixteen years."

"I mean pretending to be a normal person, you bane of my existence!" Mary said rather loudly.

"I *am* a normal person! Nothing about me has changed!"

"Cedric, *everything* about you has changed! All this time we have known each other, never once have you told us where you came from. And now, not only are you the heir to a peerage, you're heir to the wealthiest peerage in the realm! You could have paid Sara's debts, spared her these past months of heartache and torment. And even if you somehow were not able to pay Sara's debts, you could have paid our passage to Paris five times over, at least. You are not the same as Sara and I. We have nothing and no one, whilst you have half the world at your disposal. Did it truly take my being dragged away and imprisoned for you to realize that?"

"All of this secrecy was for a reason," Cedric said. Sara could not help but note how he bypassed Mary's question. "I certainly have not always agreed with those reasons, but they are reasons, all the same."

"Such mystery, Master Cedric. It is not as if you are the man in the bloody iron mask; you are a future earl. That is nothing to hide from or keep concealed, not to me. I mean, am I wrong? Sara?"

"Oh no!" Sara held up her hands and rapidly shook her head. "No, no, no! You two will not involve me in your bickering *again*."

"This isn't bickering," Mary and Cedric said at once. It was enough to make Sara laugh. It was also enough to make her head hurt.

"Cedric assured me that his father initiated the farce," Sara said, at last allowing herself to be dragged into what would doubtlessly turn into months of snide remarks and biting comments. "He clearly would have told us the truth if it was within his power to tell. Right?"

"Of course. Of course, Mary." Cedric's hand shot out and grasped firmly on to Mary's. He held it fast, as one might hold a lifeline. Sara did not doubt that this was more than just another point of contention for Cedric. If he lost Mary's trust over this, a part of him would chip away and never recover.

"I believe you, Cedric," Mary said. She did not tighten her own hold on Cedric's hand, but she didn't push him away, either. "You say my being disappointed is evasive, but it is no exaggeration. I *am* disappointed. Sara and I are your closest friends, and yet, you couldn't even tell us your deepest truth?"

"You two are so . . ." His eyes shifted between Mary and Sara. His mouth twitched, as if the words were fighting to make their way out. "You are so exceptional. India and the Philippines. Parents who were merchants and revolutionaries. I am just the unwanted heir of the son of a second son. My past is as unremarkable as my future will undoubtedly be. You both so easily and eagerly accepted me into your wild hopes and imaginations. Things that I would never see in myself, you saw in me. My father did not tell anyone at the seminary other than Mistress Minchin who I was to preserve *his* pride. I suppose I maintained the illusion for the same reasons. I am not proud to be Lord Fauntleroy, heir to the Earl of Dorincourt. I would much rather be just Cedric Errol."

Sara could see how Cedric was beginning to suffer. His shoulders were curved, bent with a sadness that she assumed he carried with him every day. He did not want to lie, clearly. But he was deeply fearful of the truth. She could not in any good conscience allow him to bear all of that alone.

Sara crossed to the parallel bench in the carriage, directly next to Cedric. She wound her arm through his and rested her head on his shoulder. She could feel his spirit open up to her and, with a sigh of thanks and contentment, let her in.

"You will always be just Cedric Errol to us," she said. "Wise, creative, talented, and cynical Cedric Errol. And Mary feels the same."

Sara gave Mary a pointed look, proclaiming the end of this round, and Mary rolled her eyes in acquiescence.

"Yes, of course I feel the same way," she said. She kicked her leg out and hit Cedric lightly in the shin. "You are a terribly serious fellow who aggravates me to no end. But I suppose I can forgive you and accept the apology you have yet to deliver. In truth, I am rather grateful for this change of fortune. After what I saw in the workhouse, I do not think I could spend another day on the streets. Where exactly are we going, by the way? It feels as if we have been traveling for an eternity."

Cedric laughed. "Not quite an eternity, no. But close enough. We are going to my home, my family's home, Maythem Hall. It has been the country estate of all Earls of Dorincourt since the Wars of the Roses."

"Oh, fascinating!" Mary said, sitting up. "Which side were you on? Was it Lancaster? You seem like a Lancaster type."

"Do not insult me," Cedric said. "We were for York. Obviously."

"Will your family be home?" Sara asked.

"Oh no. My sisters are all married and mistresses of their own estates many miles away. My father is never home. I expect my cousin will be there, though. He does linger about, like an unpleasant odor." Cedric's nose actually wrinkled at the mention of him.

"Sounds like someone worth meeting," Mary said, winking at Sara.

"More likely someone worth avoiding," Cedric said. "His name is Dr. Craven, some distant relation from London. When he heard that I—being weak of limb, as I am—was my father's only son and he had no plans to have any more, he descended upon the estate. He attempted to endear himself to my father and has been rather successful. The seminary was his idea, after all."

"My Lord," Sara said. "Not worth meeting at all."

"But you will get to meet the dogs," Cedric said, enthused. "And to see the main house, which is a beautifully grand old property, even though it is drafty and leaky and always cold. Still, every window looks out onto the North York Moors. There is nothing keeping you from constantly enjoying the beautiful sunrises."

"I'm sure they are lovely," Sara said. "I am excited to finally see one of these great English country homes I have heard so much about. Ballrooms and drawing rooms and gardens that extend for miles. All so romantic and heroic."

"Maythem is a great English country home," Cedric said. "But it is . . . well, I would not want you to be disappointed. My father was never one for domestic endeavors, and since my mother died, the place has fallen into some disrepair. Not even my sisters were married at Maythem; they preferred to host receptions at the homes of their stylish new husbands."

Mary said, "That is entirely their loss. Why, who wouldn't want to conduct the happiest ceremony of their life in a run-down, most likely haunted country mansion?"

"Oh, there is no 'most likely' about it. Maythem is certainly haunted. But they are amenable ghosts. They are very content keeping to themselves."

"Should we not devise some reason for our presence at Maythem?" Sara asked. "You are, of course, the master of your home, Cedric, but someone will inquire as to why we aren't at the seminary. We are technically runaways, after all."

Mary took on her traditional pose of deep thought. Her arms were crossed, and her eyes were directed toward the sky, as if waiting for inspiration to strike.

"There must be some excuse for Mistress Minchin to release students from that place," she said. "I cannot believe her senseless rule about no one leaving campus before graduation. It cannot be legal, let alone probable. The parents must insist at some point."

"It would have to be something completely beyond Mistress Minchin's sphere of control," Sara added. "Whilst in that woman's service, I realized that many of the rules she created were for her benefit, and her benefit alone. She most likely believed that keeping the students away from their families would prevent them from realizing what they were missing at home, so she never lost students and their tuition."

"A force of nature," Cedric said. "The only thing Mistress Minchin could not possibly argue with is a force of nature. Or an act of God."

"Ha!" Mary exclaimed suddenly. She held up a finger in realization and triumph, like a detective in a novel reaching eureka. "That is it exactly, Cedric! An act of God. If there was a cholera outbreak at the seminary, Mistress Minchin would have no choice but to send everyone home, and with all haste. She would barely have time to alert the parents. Students would need to leave immediately, and those with families in far-off places—such as Sara and myself—would need to rely on the hospitality of our local friends. Enter you, Cedric Errol, our savior."

"As endearing as that role seems," Cedric said, "there are certain laws of propriety that we are expected to uphold. It is downright devilish to allow a young man to escort two young ladies, alone, across the country to his private home. If Mistress Minchin were truly evacuating the school, she would insist you stay with a girl's family."

"Perhaps for two young ladies, she would insist," Sara said. "But not for two orphans, one an indentured servant and the other a penniless troublemaker."

"*Recently* penniless, longtime troublemaker," Mary corrected. "But in any case, Sara is right. Mistress Minchin would be just as quick to throw us out with the slop as to let us go home with you. She would be absolutely charmed by your Christian charity, then pray that she would never have occasion to see any of us again."

Sara felt herself humming with a childish excitement at the familiarity of it all. The three of them, gathered close together and making far-fetched and adventurous plans. Only months ago, they were lounging in the summer sun and devising ways to secrete biscuits and cool cider from the kitchens. They were not much younger then, but somehow, that felt so long ago. The world had become at once much smaller and much larger; things that were once absolute were now tentative, and realities that went unquestioned were now constantly doubted. The world Sara inhabited today was not the world of yesterday. The sun had gone cold and the night sky was drained of stars. And yet, even amidst so much uncertainty, some things were mercifully the same.

"All right, then," Cedric said, giving the whole plan the finality it needed to be set in motion. "The seminary has been evacuated due to a cholera epidemic, and I invited you to seek shelter with me until other arrangements could be made. That should buy us more than enough time to come up with a real plan."

"Are you implying that my plan is not realistic?" Mary asked.

"Not unrealistic," Cedric replied quickly. "Just not based in a present reality."

Before they could launch into another sparring match, Sara extended her arms between them and shouted, "Oh, no you don't! No more arguing for at least another hour, please!"

"Your timing is exceptional, Sara," Cedric said, his attention now directed outside. "We have just arrived."

Both Sara and Mary rushed to opposite windows, expecting to see a stone castle materializing in the distance. Instead, they saw the same thing they had seen since leaving Sheffield: miles and miles of treeless hills. There was something frightfully beautiful about this country, for Sara. In many ways, it reminded her of the Philippines. In many ways, it did not. Parts of the Philippines could be just as wild and untamed, sometimes more so. Yet those wildernesses teemed with life. Even when you were miles away from the nearest town or settlement, you did not feel alone. The birdcalls kept you company; the hum of bee wings trailed your steps. High trees shaded you from the sun, and fruit on shrubs gave you food when you were hungry. But this place provided no such comforts. The land was silent and brutally exposed. Sara felt that to be alone in such a landscape was to be truly alone.

"Either Maythem Hall is a rabbit warren made up of tunnels and halls built entirely underground," Mary said, "or there is nothing out there."

"Your wit is infectious," Cedric said dryly. "But alas, my family seat is not a rabbit warren. Perhaps I should have been clearer. We still have a few miles to go before reaching the hall, but *this* is Errol land."

"This?" Sara asked. "How much of this?"

Cedric gestured broadly with a hand, taking in everything stretching into the horizon.

"All of it," he said. "For all intents and purposes, I am home."

Sara stared with newfound, wide-eyed wonder at the vista before her. It could not be less than ten thousand acres of untouched land. It would be easier to say that Cedric was the heir to a quarter of the world.

"Hell's bells," Mary whispered. "I admit, I secretly imagined that 'wealthiest peer in the land' was an exaggeration."

SARA THOUGHT THEY had reached Maythem Hall when they passed through a small village of thatch-roofed homes and a one-room chapel, but that was not the case. She was *certain* they had reached their destination when they approached a large lodge with lights twinkling in the windows. She was wrong again. It wasn't until they passed through massive iron gates and traveled another two miles up a tree-lined drive that Maythem finally appeared before them.

It immediately struck Sara as something out of one of Miss Austen's novels: Pemberley in all its finery, largesse, and grandeur. The hall was long, stretching endlessly from the east to the west. The entire building was wrapped in pale stone that glowed in the minimal light. The hall was built in the Palladian style, as far as Sara could discern based on her brief period of infatuation with architecture. Massive columns held up the second floor and figures stolen from Greek myth stood guard at the roofline. As magnificent as it was, Maythem Hall in actuality was not what Sara had expected. Knowing Cedric—and knowing of his father—she could very easily envision a stony old castle with crumbling towers and the whisper of long-ago battles sounding on the wind. This was altogether more stylish and intentional. Maythem Hall had been created to make a statement, that was clear enough. What that statement was precisely, Sara had yet to work out.

"Cedric, this *cannot* be your home!" Mary said. Almost half her body was extended out of the window, and she had to yell to be heard over the sound of the wind rushing by.

"The style is a bit indulgent, I know," he said. "About one hundred years ago, my ancestor—the twelfth Earl of Dorincourt, I believe—wanted to bring the old homestead into the new era. The fortress that our family had once used to fight the Lancasters, the French, and the Scots was demolished, and this country manor was built in its place. The twelfth earl was quite a vain man, apparently. He didn't feel that Dorincourt Castle represented his likeness accurately."

"Let no one doubt the man's vanity," Sara said. "This house is a manifestation of Narcissus's reflection."

The coach stopped at the entrance of Maythem Hall. Before Sara could even collect herself, a footman was there, opening the door and bowing to Cedric.

"It is wonderful to have you home, my lord," the footman said.

Mary looked to Sara and mouthed, *My lord?* Sara could only shrug. There were some things one never became used to.

"It is wonderful to be home, Eric," Cedric said, sounding every bit the kind and considerate landowner. Cedric was smoothly lifted from inside the carriage and placed into a new wheeled chair, this one far lusher and more advanced than the chair he'd used at the seminary. Sara could see clearly how this one allowed him more independence; he could turn, stop, and roll the wheels with the use of a crank attached to one of the arms. The wheels were especially thick, like the wheels of a draft cart, so as to allow him freer movement over the stone drive. Even still, something in the way Cedric carried his head made him seem more uncomfortable than he had been on their journey from Manchester, when he had nothing but wooden crutches to hold him up.

"Eric, these are peers of mine from the seminary," Cedric said. "Miss Mary Lennox of India and Miss Sara Crewe of the Philippines. They are to be given every courtesy and comfort during their stay."

"Of course," Eric said. He bowed to each of them in turn. However, Sara did not miss the way his eyes lingered on her. "Miss Lennox. Miss Crewe. Welcome to Maythem Hall."

Sara extended her hand and allowed the footman to help her out of the carriage.

"Thank you," she said. "Eric, yes?"

"Yes, miss."

"Wonderful. I'm Miss Crewe and this"—she gestured back at Mary, who seemed content to climb out of the carriage on her own—"is Miss Lennox."

"Charmed," Mary said, but her attention was entirely focused on the expanse of Maythem. "This is your *home*, Cedric?"

"Has been since the day of my birth," he said. "And probably will be until the day of my death. Is that really so unbelievable to you, that I could live here?"

"I just never imagined that you, of all people, could live somewhere like this. It is not nearly as serious and stuffy as you project to be."

"Oh, well." Cedric rotated the crank, and the wheels on his chair began to roll forward. "Just wait until you spend a night here. You two go on through the front, Eric will escort you. There is a ramp assembled for me toward the back."

After Cedric took his leave, Sara and Mary made their slow ascent up the wide sandstone steps that led to the main entrance of the estate. Upon closer inspection, Sara could see some of the disrepair Cedric had spoken of. Years and years of rainwater flowing without direction had created patches of mold in the creases of the building. Cracks were beginning to show in the marble, and the windows looked dingy and unwashed. Sara could only guess how majestic Mayhem was in its prime. Queues of carriages stretching up the drive designed for the purpose, and candles burning in each window. It must have shimmered like a jewel in the queen's crown.

When they finally made it to the top of the stairs, an entourage was there and ready to meet them. The most prominent figure was a woman. She was stout and looked to be strong of limb, standing as rooted as a tree. Her cheeks were apple red and her eyes flashed like black onyx. She wore perhaps the deepest shade of purple Sara had ever seen in a dress outside of a ball or gala. Her bonnet was the same black as her eyes, and wilting purple flowers stuck out from it in haphazard sunbursts. She wore a monocle over the left eye, and the tempered glass of the lens made that eye appear larger and even more appraising.

With this woman stood two men, each drastically different from the other. One was extremely tall, taller than Sara by half, and thin as a bamboo stick. He had Cedric's eyes but none of his charm or ability to hide his emotions. A tense anxiety pulsed around him, hot enough for Sara to feel from a distance. He did not look at all happy to see them. The additional man, on the other hand, looked enthused to the point of skipping. He was an older gentleman in a gardener's cap, back hunched from years of kneeling in flower beds and vegetable patches. He smiled at them fully, with gapped teeth, and remembered himself enough to remove his hat when Sara and Mary were within speaking distance.

"Presenting the Misses Mary Lennox and Sara Crewe," Eric said from somewhere behind them. "They are guests of Lord Fauntleroy's."

The woman took a step forward, presenting herself as the head of this house, if not in name, then in presence.

"On behalf of the Earl of Dorincourt and his family, I welcome you both to Maythem Hall," she said. She did not smile as she spoke to them. In fact, her mouth seemed very intentionally turned down in a frown. While she was doing an admirable job of trying to hide her accent, Sara could detect something heavy and layered lurking beneath. "I am Mrs. Medlock, head housekeeper. I must say, when young Master Cedric summoned the coach to Sheffield, he made no mention of guests."

"Lord Fauntleroy is doing us a great service," Sara said. "You see, there has been a devastating cholera outbreak at the seminary. Mary and I have families abroad, with no means of contacting them in time. Lord Fauntleroy was kind enough to offer us sanctuary on his beautiful estate until arrangements can be made to ferry us to a more final destination."

The corners of Mrs. Medlock's lips wrinkled in a type of sneer.

"*You* are a student at the young master's boarding school?"

Sara knew what the true question was—she was quite prepared for it—but before she could answer, Mary spoke up.

"She is the *premier* student," she said. "The very top of our class in all subjects. She was, in fact, tutoring Cedric in Greek before the school was evacuated."

Sara knew this to be a bold-faced lie. She never had occasion to tutor Cedric in anything, and certainly not in Greek. She was barely a novice with the language herself. However, Sara knew what Mary was attempting to do, and she appreciated it more than she could say.

"Of course," Mrs. Medlock said. "I do beg your pardon. Any friend of Master Cedric's is a friend of this house."

"I certainly hope that is the case, Mrs. Medlock." They all turned to see Cedric rolling toward them from within the depths of the manor. "These young ladies have been through quite an ordeal, fleeing the school in such a rush. No time even to collect their personal items. I want them to be treated not just as friends, but as family whilst they're here."

Mrs. Medlock curtsied stiffly. Cedric nodded in turn, then directed his attention toward the tall man with the pained expression.

"It is good to see you again, cousin," Cedric said. His tone was leaden and lacking all the warmth of family.

The man's response was no brighter: "And you as well, cousin. I see you could not manage a full year in school before rolling home, eh?"

Ah, Sara thought. *So this is the infamous Dr. Craven.* Cedric's earlier words regarding him seemed all the clearer now, and she could see no reason not to heed them.

"Probably disappointed Cedric did not perish in the outbreak," Mary whispered directly to Sara's left. As slow as Sara was to think the worst of people, she had to agree with Mary.

"I for one am cheered to have you safely home, my lord!"

Or at least, that's what Sara thought the old man had said. Unlike with Mrs. Medlock, there was no hiding that accent.

Cedric reached out and clasped the man's hand in a companionable, respectful embrace.

"It is excellent to see you up and well, Ben," Cedric said. "You were suffering from the grippe last I heard, is that right?"

The old man looked to be almost blushing when he said, "It is kind of you to remember, my lord. I recovered just last month and have been getting on better than before. Dickon manages quite well without me, the good lad. He has the makings of a fine head gardener for this estate. It is a sad business that you missed the tulips this past spring. A beautiful sight and didn't lose a one to the April frost."

"I am sorry I missed them, as well," Cedric said. "It is strange to think that I have been away so long. Has my father been home?"

At the mention of the earl, all echoes of excitement or even happiness died down. Eyes lowered, postures became stooped and fearfully respectful. The earl was miles away, and yet his presence loomed as large as Maythem Hall itself.

"The earl has not been in residence since you left for school, Master Cedric," Mrs. Medlock said. "Your sister Lady Beatrice had correspondence from him in the fall. Apparently, he is on an expedition in the Nordic fjords."

Cedric appeared to be chewing on that news, literally clenching and unclenching his jaw before speaking: "I see. And has Lady Beatrice any knowledge of when he might be returning?"

Mrs. Medlock only shook her head. With a sigh that betrayed the disappointment that he was sure to be feeling, Cedric said, "Very well. Then I suppose my return home is fortuitous. I am sure many items require my attention, in my father's stead. Cousin." Cedric smirked up at the young doctor. "Would you perhaps walk me through the year's ledgers? As you are the relative who shows the most interest in our accounts, I expect there is much to update me on."

"Whatever discrepancies there may be," Dr. Craven said with oozing sarcasm, "I am sure your keen young mind will ferret them out."

Dr. Craven stepped to the side and, with a great flourish, extended his hand out in a motion for Cedric to proceed.

Before disappearing back into the dark void of the house, Cedric finally gave Sara and Mary his full attention for the first time since their arrival to the threshold of the estate.

"I am sorry, I may be occupied for some time," he said. His speech was so formal, so odd considering how casually they spoke to one another normally. It made Sara feel that she must stand up straighter or hold her head higher. She was not addressing her dearest friend; this was a man of great wealth and prestige, and he not only deserved but demanded her greatest respect.

"We entirely understand, Lord Fauntleroy," Sara said. She could hear the way Mary's neck snapped when she swiveled to look at her. Sara knew what Mary was thinking: yes, it was bizarre for her to be calling Cedric "Lord Fauntleroy," but Sara's mother had been thorough in her training before sending her to England. Peers must be properly addressed at all times, especially among those deemed socially inferior. It was an archaic tradition, but it was tradition nonetheless.

"Thank you, Miss Crewe," Cedric said. "Mrs. Medlock will see that you both are situated. If you have any needs whatsoever, they will be accommodated."

Then he was gone, swallowed abruptly into the gloom of the great house. And without Cedric present, Mrs. Medlock's chilly manner immediately returned.

"We are not prepared for guests," she said. "You will have to share a chamber until further arrangements can be made."

"We can share!" Mary said, nearly tripping over her words. "We would never wish to inconvenience the staff."

In truth, Sara assumed that the coldness of Maythem unsettled Mary. It unsettled Sara, as well. She did not wish to test whether or not she could sleep in peace on her own in such a house.

Mrs. Medlock did not wait to say whether or not this met with her approval. She turned and walked briskly ahead of them, and Sara assumed they were expected to follow. The gardener—Ben, Cedric had called him—was the only one left with them on the threshold.

"Don't you lasses mind Mrs. Medlock," he said. "We never get no visitors to Maythem that ain't part of the family. If the young master thought enough of ya to offer sanctuary in your time of need, then she'll warm up to you quick as a bee. Enjoy your stay." He tipped his hat to them, then left them truly on their own amidst the overwhelming loneliness of Maythem Hall.

SARA WOULD HAVE loved to stop and reflect on the details of Maythem's architecture or the furniture as they were led through its halls toward what she presumed was to be their new room. However, even if Mrs. Medlock had stopped long enough for them to marvel at where they were and what they were seeing, the hall was shrouded in so much darkness that much of it was impossible to see. The afternoon had turned overcast, and as the day turned steadily to night, the long shadows of the great house stretched and filled like spilled ink. Sara knew they had passed through a great entrance hall when the stone busts of philosophers and emperors stared back at them with eyes like the empty sockets in a skull. The manor was two floors, but the first floor, excepting the kitchen and the servants' quarters, felt as if it stretched on forever. No matter how far Sara felt she had walked, there was always more to go. There was a library, possibly two—both of them with unlit fires even though a chill was coming down from the hills—then a very long gallery. Every few yards or so, there was a single candle lit in a sconce. In those small pools of light, Sara caught occasional glimpses of massive portraits. In each of the faces she passed, she tried to see Cedric. She would recognize his eyes or his chin or his nose or his hair. But none of these people held any of Cedric's kindness in their frozen visages. Their eyes betrayed nothing but judgment and disgust. *Who are you? How dare you presume to walk where we walked, stand where we stood?* Sara could not imagine passing a weekend in such a place, never mind a lifetime. And as a child, no less. How Cedric grew to be the caring soul he was, Sara could not entirely say.

Finally, Mrs. Medlock came to a hard stop in front of a large, solid door. Sara could hear the clang of keys on the chatelaine at her waist, the turning of a bolt lock. The door opened on creaking hinges. Mrs. Medlock went in first, then Sara and Mary followed. Just like with the rest of the hall, this room was dark. The only light was muted, and it came through the large window on the far side of the room. Sara could see the outline of a bed and drapes and furniture. Then a single candle was lit, and light danced out across the floor.

"Welcome to the East Room," Mrs. Medlock said.

Mary and Sara looked about in a kind of horrified awe.

"I certainly see why they call it the East Room," Mary said.

Every inch of the heavily upholstered bedroom from the bedding to the wallpaper to the rug on which they stood was thematically inspired by an English stereotypical view of China. A fortune's worth of pagodas and cherry blossoms and women in robes with flutes. Mary actually began to laugh and had to cover her mouth with her hand.

Mrs. Medlock clearly noticed this and didn't seem to appreciate the slight.

"Is this not satisfactory, Miss Lennox?" she asked.

"It is more than satisfactory, Mrs. Medlock," Sara said. "Thank you for preparing it on such short notice."

While Mrs. Medlock's back was turned, lighting a candelabra, Sara elbowed Mary in the side and implored her to behave. The last thing Cedric needed, from either of them, was complaints from the staff. By the time Mrs. Medlock was facing them again, they were both standing at polite attention.

"The maid will bring your dinner trays up," Mrs. Medlock said. "I shall also set her to finding some appropriate clothes."

Sara immediately looked down at her own attire, which she considered to be rather fashionable. For all their general incompetence, Cedric's lawyers were surprisingly adept at shopping for women's clothes. Then Sara remembered Mary. Although Cedric had the forethought to purchase clothes for Mary once she was liberated from the workhouse, the two of them were so intent on bickering throughout the entire trip that she was never given an opportunity to change. She was still wearing that hideous, handmade gray gown. So much of Mrs. Medlock's behavior seemed slightly more validated.

"Oh," Mary said. She looked down to herself, then to Sara. "Please excuse my attire. I was volunteering in the infirmary at the seminary as we were forced to leave. This is the uniform that all caretakers were assigned. We fled in such a hurry, there was no time to change."

Sara exhaled, and felt sure she could see Mary doing the same. This seemed explanation enough for Mrs. Medlock. At least for now.

"I believe the young master has purchased some ensembles for your wardrobe," she said. "The maid will bring them up with your dinner."

Finally, Mrs. Medlock left them in the dark, old-fashioned, cold room. Sara felt suddenly very exhausted and likely would have fallen to the floor if not for the vanity stool shaped like the head of a Chinese dragon that caught her. Mary went a far more direct route and launched face-first onto the sole bed, which creaked loudly and sent up a cloud of dust when Mary landed.

"This room is indecipherable," Sara said. She initially assumed that the wallpaper was attempting to tell some type of narrative, but the repetition of the same pagoda in the same location made her anxious to find the seam.

"This entire situation is indecipherable," Mary added, her voice muffled by a pillow. "I still cannot understand why Cedric kept all this from us."

"We accepted Cedric as one of us; think of how difficult that would have been if we knew him first as the heir to a wealthy title."

"I don't care about his title!" Mary said with a loud stamp of her foot.

"Oh, yes you do."

There was silence on the massive bed for a moment, and then a heavy, resigned sigh.

"You're right. I do."

Sara smiled. In a way, she was proud of Cedric. He was ignored at the seminary. Everyone assumed he was either weak or unintelligent or even unimportant because of his reliance on a chair. It warmed her heart to think of their faces when they found out that the young man they'd called cripple was more powerful in his own right than any of their self-aggrandizing *nouveau* parents could ever hope to be. And that afternoon, when Sara watched him speak with his oily cousin and his staff, Sara saw the earl he would be one day. The vision was very bright, and she was quietly honored to say that she had been there at the beginning.

A loud groan from Mary split the room, and Sara could not help but roll her eyes at a girl who had to inject drama into every situation.

"You are just upset he has more to do now than lick at your heels like a puppy."

"I resent that remark, and I reject it! I'm happy to see Cedric busy, occupied. He is brilliant, and I am grateful to no longer have to carry the burden of harnessing that brilliance."

Sara had been observing the intricacies of the room, but the drop in Mary's voice made her turn her head. She sat on the edge of the massive bed—feet hanging over the side like a small child— and her short hair stuck out in all directions. Her head was bent, and Sara could feel a sudden sadness radiating off her. In seconds, she was next to her friend. Closer to her now, able to look directly into her eyes, Sara could see that the sadness Mary felt wasn't just about Cedric's confession. It was then that she realized that they hadn't once discussed Mary's time in the workhouse. When they picked her up outside of the old warehouse that seemed more suited to storing bricks than unclaimed girls, she became immediately fixated on the hows and the whys of Cedric's new status, and her entire evening in custody appeared to be irrelevant. Yet, looking at her friend now, Sara realized that Mary's past twenty-four hours weren't irrelevant at all.

"Mary, what precisely happened when—"

Then the door opened. Sara was startled enough by the interruption to jump. Even though the house was quiet and one could hear spider legs rushing across the floor of the opposite wing if they listened closely enough, Sara hadn't heard any footsteps before their bedroom door was opened. There wasn't even a preceding knock.

"Yes?" Sara called out. "Who is it?"

A youthful female voice responded, "Don't mind me, miss! Mrs. Medlock sent me up with supper and frocks for ya."

Neither Sara nor Mary gave this person whom Sara assumed was the maid any clearance to enter the room, but in she came. First through the door was a rolling trolley filled to brimming with plates and cups and teapots, followed by a young woman. She was lean and long, and the freckles that dotted her face collected in crowded clumps under her eyes, which somehow reminded Sara of war paint. The uniform she wore appeared hastily put on: the ribbons of her bonnet weren't tied, her apron was inside out, and her dress may have been missing a petticoat. There was a clear impression that none of this—the uniform, the tray, the food—was normal for her.

"Do forgive me for the delay," the maid said with the same heavy accent as Ben. "The poor kitchen weren't quite prepared for—"

The maid's sky-blue eyes landed for the first time on Sara, and she stopped short. The trolley rolled on ahead of her, slowly, into the middle of the room. She stared at Sara with an absolute shock that might only be reserved for seeing a bear in your bedroom. Her mouth was slightly open, and her eyes were wide and hardened in a way Sara recognized.

"They didn't tell me," the maid finally said. She took a step back as if she might bolt for the door at any second. "They didn't tell me you were one of 'em."

Sara felt tension rising in her chest. It was a familiar sensation, developed after months living among people who had never seen someone who didn't look like them before. And if they had, it was only during a traveling show, from the other side of iron bars.

"One of whom?" Sara asked, standing to her full height. She was eager to hear this answer and already had a series of responses prepared and ready for whatever bigotry this maid was foolishly about to reveal.

"You know!" The maid looked at Mary, as if looking for an ally. "One of those . . . those . . ."

"Actresses?" Mary inserted herself into the exchange with a bright energy that superficially promoted informality, but underneath simmered with a threat. "I assure you, Sara is a marvelous actress. I understand that they may be rare this far north, but don't allow your eyes to deceive you. You are indeed in the presence of one of the finest thespians this side of the Thames. The name Sara Crewe will be worth remembering, mark my words."

Mercifully, the maid remembered herself. She lowered her

eyes in a show of respect, then dropped into a brief, brusque curtsy.

"I'm honored," the maid said. "You're right, Miss Lennox; we don't get much of Miss Crewe's kind on the moors."

Sara smiled her brightest, warmest, most accommodating smile. She forced herself to recall a mantra that her mother used often when faced with those who despised her or—more commonly—underestimated her: "We must be like Jesus and ask God to forgive them, for they know not what they do."

"Is that our dinner?" Sara asked, pointing to the trolley that now sat alone between them. Even the inanimate piece of furniture seemed aware of the slowly dissipating tension.

"Yes, ma'am," said the maid. She moved quickly and repositioned it until it lined up with a small lacquered dining table framed by the room's window. Sara did her best to put on an elevated air and not look at the maid as she sat down. If this girl wanted to play caste and color, then Sara would play caste and color. She was no lady, but she was bloody close.

"Is this . . . what is this?" Mary asked of the lukewarm plate before her. The dish was such a vibrant shade of red that it seemed notably out of place in the faded room. It smelled of the earth, and it was served in a shallow bowl with a large soup spoon.

"Rhubarb, miss," the maid said. "A specialty here at Maythem."

"This massive estate with centuries of legacy, host to kings and queens and dignitaries, is known for a vegetable?"

Sara knew that Mary's question was sincere, but her tone came across with such derision that it made Sara grin.

"Cook didn't have much notice of guests, Miss Lennox," the maid said. "We had fresh rhubarb—quick and easy to make, a delicacy 'round here—so Cook made rhubarb. Tomorrow's menu will be much more to a city-dweller's liking, be assured."

Sara heard her stomach growl in disappointment, but she kept her peace. Yesterday, they were rejoicing at the chance to share a sweet bun. Rhubarb might not have been part of a twelve-course Parisian dining experience fit for Versailles, but it was filling and free. Without waiting for Mary, Sara lifted her spoon and took a bite. She was surprised to find it sweet and tart and slightly chewy, like a candy.

For the first time since she entered the room, Sara gave the maid a true smile and said, "It's very good."

Mary tilted her head like a bird.

"Is it really?"

Once Mary began eating, she ate with such vigor that Sara assumed her doubts were gone. The maid still stood quite awkwardly at the edge of the table, either very curious or very astute.

"What's your name?" Sara asked, just to break the awkward sounds of people chewing.

"Martha, ma'am," she said. "Martha Sowerby."

"Have you been here at Maythem long?"

Martha shook her head, causing the ribbons of her bonnet to swing like rabbit ears, and said, "Only a few years, since the young ladies of the house left. My family lives on the estate, though.

When my pa died, the earl took on my little brother as an apprentice gardener to cover the rent my ma couldn't pay. We've been happy here. Happy enough."

Martha's words were polite and grateful, and perhaps for those who knew no better, they would have been enough to convince someone that she truly was happy. But that fondness was shallow and rehearsed. Her tone was stiff in the way an untrained actor's tone might be stiff when performing their first monologue. It made Sara feel like a mouse scurrying through a room with evidence of a cat, but no cat was to be found. Not until you felt its teeth closing around your neck.

"If that is all," Martha said, "I'll take my leave. In the morning, I'll assist you with your frocks. I understand if the hour's too late to fool 'round with all that now. Good night to you both."

Martha gave another curtsy, then left the room. As soon as the door closed behind her, Mary burst out in laughter.

"Well, well," she said. "And they say I'm contrary."

18

$\mathcal{M}$ary could not sleep.

It wasn't that she didn't want to sleep, didn't need to sleep. However, every time she closed her eyes and stilled her body, her mind kept running like a rabbit pursued by hounds. For so many years, her life had moved with leisure. Every day blended into the next with few expectations or surprises. Then Sara Crewe came to the seminary and things changed with lightning speed. Suddenly, Mary had friends—the closest of friends—and a new passion in theater. She was now an orphan in truth, not just in sentiment, and the seminary felt far behind her. And to top off the whole strange affair, she was sleeping in one of two dozen bedrooms on an ancient estate owned by a boy that she still couldn't visualize owning a pony, let alone a title! And yet, her shock could only go so far before it became gratitude. If not for Cedric's position, they would still be starving on the streets of Sheffield. There was no space to breathe amidst such change. Mary felt like a bal-lerina forever lost in a pirouette.

Of course, there was also the workhouse. And Anne.

No! Mary shut her eyes tight until she saw white spots behind her eyelids. She could not think about that. It all had transpired so quickly, like a dream, but it was a dream that clung to her after waking. At times throughout the night, listening to the wind bash against the windows until the beams of Maythem Hall groaned, Mary would turn on her side and for an instant see Anne's thin, gray face on the pillow next to her. Mary would start, blink, then once again see Sara sleeping peacefully. Unlike Mary, Sara appeared to be utterly content in sleep. The lines of her face had gone smooth, and her breathing was deep. Mary assumed it was the most peaceful sleep she'd had in months. She was happy for her friend, but also extraordinarily jealous.

At last, she could take the stillness no longer and resigned her-self to being awake. She wrapped herself in one of the many quilts piled on top of the mattress and stood up in the cold, dark room. The light coming through the window was a shadowy blue; Mary had seen these early hours before and knew that sunrise was still maybe four hours away. Only a few months before, at the semi-nary, Mary would use this time to write. If she was awake, she was awake for a reason, and that time was worth taking advantage of. But she didn't want to risk waking Sara, who desperately needed the rest.

"I believe I could find my way to the library," Mary said to the twilight. "Perhaps a little reading would help me fall back to sleep." She usually didn't need an excuse to explore; however, in this case, it felt necessary. After quietly slipping on her shoes, lighting a candle, and wrapping the quilt more securely around her, Mary slipped silently out into the hall. She was instantly struck by how dark the house was beyond her candle's weak sphere of light. There were no other lights, for the house was asleep, but there were also no windows. The darkness around her had mass and form, smoothly filling in the crevices as water did when poured into a glass. A part of her was afraid. Sleep or no, all proper sense would demand she go back inside their room, get in the bed, and close her eyes until morning light. Mary, however, had never been known for proper sense. She brandished the sole taper before her like a shining sword and walked forward.

To Mary, portraits never looked more surreal than at night. The East Room was obviously surrounded by some kind of gallery, for every inch of wall Mary passed displayed a portrait of one sort of Errol or another. Some were portraits that you could hold in the palm of your hand; some, informal sketches from battlefields and drawing rooms. Others were sprawling panoramas that took up entire walls, and one depicted every living member of the family from the earl down to his spaniel. There was Cedric as a little boy. They were created to be seen in the full light of day, where the artists and the subjects could ensure their perspective was the only perspective. Yet the light of the night revealed so much more. Cast in such a muted glow, the most beautiful looked haggard, the strongest looked weak, the richest looked poor, and the loving looked entirely hateful. Mary walked this endless, lightless hall for what felt like miles, studying the portraits. Without the horizon, she couldn't determine whether morning was drawing closer or further away. Everything seemed to stand still, like the subjects of the paintings themselves.

Then there was a break in the monotony. She came upon a tall portrait—nearly stretching from the floor to the ceiling—that at one time had been fully covered with a black velvet sheet. Due to time or neglect, one corner of the sheet had fallen, revealing a face hidden underneath. Even with her limited view, Mary could instantly tell that this portrait was different from the others. The strokes were less meticulous, the colors less vigorous. Mary assumed that whoever the subject was, they had wished to be painted delicately, without the gravitas of their station hanging about them like royal robes. The face that Mary could see was that of a woman. It was striking, the similarities she saw with Cedric. Not so much in his physical makeup—the shape of his face or the shade of his skin—but more in the aura she exuded. It was an atmosphere of happiness and wonder, something that Mary saw more and more in her friend; here was the only portrait subject she'd seen so far who smiled. And not that thin-lipped aristocratic smile but the kind of smile that someone would flash mid-laugh. Teeth and all.

"Who are you, lady?" Mary asked. To her full shock, surprise, and even apprehension, a laugh answered her. She started so violently that she almost dropped the candle.

"Hello?" she called out. She looked up the hallway and back

down again. A stone sank in her stomach when she realized that not only was she alone in the hall, but there were no doors. Had she not just passed a door? Not to mention the room where she was staying with Sara, which was a long way behind her. She held the candle aloft, hoping the light would extend down the hall and show a way out. However, the darkness continued on and on. It was like standing in a cave or a tunnel with no beginning or end. And there again, laughter, which seemed to come from within the walls and without at the same time.

"Mrs. Medlock? Martha?" Mary called out again, praying for an answer. There was none. She took a long, deep breath to steady her fraying nerves.

"All right, Lennox," she said, mainly to fill the silence closing in around her. "You are dreaming. Yes. That's it, you are still dreaming. All you have to do is wake up. Wake up!"

She shouted and her voice echoed, almost shouting back at her. She blinked her eyes, stomped her foot, and shouted again. Every time, she found herself still standing in the gallery hall, not sleeping soundly in her bed.

"Stop this, you're being foolish. Just turn around, you will stumble upon a door, eventually."

And so, she began to walk. However, was she moving farther out or farther in? Had she passed this painting before? Were those footsteps behind her? Soon, she was running. The echo of her own hurried steps resounded around her, making her feel as if an army were pursuing her. She trailed her hand along the walls, searching for a door or even a curtain that would let her out. Her hand grasped at paintings, furniture, empty space, but at last landed on a doorknob. Mary heard her heartbeat pulsing in her skull as she shimmied the knob open.

All she had to warn her was a gush of chilly air before she was falling face-first into a rosebush.

19

Somewhere in the world beyond her dreams, Sara heard a rooster crowing. She squinted her eyes and begged the morning to go away. She had been sleeping so deeply, and there were such wonderful dreams. Dreams she hadn't had since childhood, of mermaids and silver lions. But she knew, even in her sleep, that if she didn't rise soon, her mother would be in to wake her. She'd throw open all the curtains and start singing hymns very loudly until Sara had to get out of bed in order to escape the light and sound. Perhaps it was warm enough to go swimming. Perhaps she would at last see the mermaids from her dreams.

When Sara finally opened her eyes, she was confused, but only for a brief moment. Of course, she wasn't at home in the Philippines. There would be no swimming in the sea this morning, or any morning for a long time.

Not only was Sara not in her light-filled room in Manila, but she was alone. She could have sworn Mary had been next to her when she fell asleep.

"Mary?" she called out into the room. Outside, she could hear the chatter of birds, but nothing else. Beyond the seam of the curtain shielding the room's one window, a golden light filtered in. When Sara crossed to the window and opened the curtains, she saw the sun breaking spectacularly over the horizon. The colors were vibrant, stunning, and altogether different from what she expected of York. All her musings and readings had prepared her for rainy bogs and moors capped in thick fog. The colors that painted the sky now were colors she'd only seen breaking over the ocean. When Sara realized what she'd assumed was a window was in fact a door leading into the garden, she easily and willingly stepped out into the chilled morning.

Dewy grass crunched under Sara's feet as she walked. She felt small, flying bugs tickle her ankles and land on her hands. Even though the winter was in the midst of a slow roll over the land, Sara's thick cotton sleeping gown cut through the cold. The solicitors of Hodgson & Burnett really were quite capable in a modiste; they might even consider expanding their firm's offerings.

As Sara walked through the lonely and finely manicured gardens of Maythem Hall, and the sun continued to rise, she could not help thinking of home. The smell of tilled earth brought back memories of planting perennials with her mother and harvesting vegetables with her grandmother. The cold air felt bracing and clean, and the view of endless, unmanned land begged her to run. Begged her to race the wind and dare herself to win.

She wondered briefly if this was why Mary wandered off. She would not put it past her dear friend to find the nearest gale and pursue it into the sunrise.

By God and his angels, Sara wished she could share this sight with her parents. She wanted desperately to run back inside, sit at a writing desk, and pen a long letter describing everything that she had seen, heard, and experienced since leaving the seminary. Papa would applaud their escape from the school; her mother would request more details about Cedric's title and subsequent availability. They would both pine over every description of the extraordinary Maythem Hall and be on a steamer to York within hours of reading the letter to see it for themselves.

Much to her own surprise, Sara began to cry. She felt the tears gather under her lids and roll slowly down her face. She didn't once attempt to wipe them away. To erase her tears would be to erase their memory, and Sara didn't want that.

"Castle! Castle, here!"

She heard the voice only seconds before she saw two massive collies with manes like lions burst through the shrubbery and run directly at her. Sara was not one to shy away from animals, but in this situation, she had to fight her natural instinct to flee. Not that she would have made it very far. In no time at all, the dogs were upon her, barking enthusiastically. She did not know whether to talk to them or try to pet them. Even though she'd spent her entire life growing up with farm dogs and even scared off a wild dog who'd come for their chickens, the shrill barks of the collies did their duty and kept her frozen where she stood.

"Stop that now, the both of ya!"

Sara tore her frightened gaze away from the dogs long enough to see a boy climbing over a tall hedge. He was long-legged, so it didn't appear to be difficult for him. Sara was immediately struck by how clean he looked. Not a freshly laundered clean, but a washed-in-rainwater clean. His hair was as red as the sunrise and tied back with a thin ribbon. It was a very old-fashioned style that Sara had only seen depicted in portraits and pictures. His cheeks were tinged in red, probably from the cold, and his eyes were a shade of summer-sky blue that Sara had never seen before.

"Aye, leave off!" he yelled at the collies. Instantly, they ceased barking and sat in unison, demure as puppies.

"Well, that's better," Sara said. "That display before was entirely unnecessary."

"I apologize for them," said the boy. His accent had rhythm and tone like a poem. "Maythem doesn't get many visitors, and they don't know how to act. Did they frighten you?"

"Oh no," Sara said. "I mean, a little, but it's quite all right. I was raised on an estate, so I'm accustomed to barking dogs."

Sara did not know why she was speaking so fast, or sharing so much. There was something about this boy's presence that begged her to share. It was as welcoming as an old, bent tree.

"Even still, they should know better, but the second Master Cedric is home, they're puppies again."

Sara held out her hand, and one of the collies touched its wet nose to her fingers. Now that she had permission, she began to scratch it behind its ears and marveled at how soft its fur was.

The other dog, not one to be left out, pushed its head under her other hand. Without once considering the rules of propriety when in the presence of a young man, Sara dropped to her knees and allowed the dogs to lick at her face and neck. Soon, their earlier suspicion was transformed into all-out adoration.

"What are their names?" Sara asked as she basked in the unbridled joy that dogs could bring to any scenario.

"The big one is Castle. Lodge has the white star on his head. They're brothers. You can also bet that Castle will find trouble, and Lodge will follow him into it."

The boy smiled. He had a wide, red, curving mouth, and his smile stretched over his entire face. Unlike so many of the young men she'd met since coming of a certain age, his smile held no hint of pretense or expectation. It was given as freely as it was received.

"Forgive me," he said suddenly. He looked down and Sara thought that he might even be blushing.

"Whatever for?" Sara asked.

"The dogs and I have been following you for some time."

"Following me? Since I came into the garden?"

"I saw a shape moving through the roses, ya see. I know it's right foolish, but with ya being dressed in white, and your hair dark as a storm cloud . . . I thought you were a fairy."

Sara did not mean to, but she began to laugh. That was certainly a first.

"No apology necessary. I'm rather flattered. I always wanted to be a mermaid, so a fairy must be the next best thing. I suppose it's my own fault either way for coming out dressed like this."

He was blushing again, and Sara had to bite the inside of her cheek to keep from laughing.

Instead, she asked, "I think I may know of you. Are you Dickon?"

"Have we met, miss?" he asked slowly.

"Not before this moment, no. Only, I have heard your name mentioned by others. Mr. Ben, the gardener?"

After letting out a relieved sigh, the boy—Dickon—said, "Ah! Yes, Old Ben. I've been apprenticing for him since he fell ill in the spring. Dickon Sowerby is my name, miss."

Sara held out her right hand in the American fashion. Dickon hesitated for a moment, but in time, he welcomed the handshake and clasped her hand in his. It was large and textured by years of blisters. It was a warm hand, Sara realized. She was hesitant to let it go.

"Sara Crewe," she said, still holding his hand. "I am a guest of Cedri—that is, Lord Fauntleroy."

"A pleasure to meet you, Miss Crewe." The boy flashed his full-faced smile again. A wordless exchange passed between them before they finally drew their hands apart. There was a warm throbbing to her right hand where he had touched it. "There has been talk amongst us about Master Cedric's visitors. We don't have many, you see. It is all rather exciting."

"Everyone has been very . . . welcoming," Sara said, searching for the proper word. Dickon seemed to pick up on her obvious wariness; a trickster's smirk hid in the corner of his mouth.

"Mrs. Medlock was a bit cold, was she?"

"Yes! Immediately! She has been perfectly respectable, a credit to this house, but I feel she'd be happier with Maythem Hall quiet and to herself."

"Eh, she means no ill by it. Lady Fauntleroy's death brought a dark shadow over this place. I reckon that cloud still lingers over Mrs. Medlock, even after all this time."

Cedric had never divulged details about his family, especially his mother, but Sara knew that her death was a knife that was forever lodged in Cedric's chest. Hearing how it impacted the lives of others made her even more curious to learn more.

"I feel I must apologize again, Miss Crewe."

Sara was sitting fully on the ground now, with the large, pointed head of a collie in her lap. The other was doing tricks for attention, so when Sara said, "What do you mean?" she wasn't really listening.

"I have never seen someone who looks like you before."

Sara turned her head sharply to look up at Dickon, to see if she understood him, and he was staring directly at her. His face wasn't masked in the cruel shock that she had seen on Martha, Lavinia, and so many others in this country. She didn't see that perverse fascination that others had flashed her way, either. He was legitimately curious. Somehow, Sara felt embarrassed.

"It is strange," she said. "I have seen thousands upon thousands of people who look like you."

Dickon scratched at his head, nervous, and Sara knew immediately that she had said the wrong thing.

"I am sorry, that did not . . . I didn't mean to sound—"

"Please, I understand," Dickon said. "You're not some new flower I found growing on the moors. You are a person, same as anyone else, and should be treated as such."

Something inside of Sara exhaled at that. Not even Mary or Cedric had gone as far as to express that they were all the same. With them, she still managed to feel like something held aloft, to be marveled at and observed and analyzed. A layer fell away with this boy, Dickon, who had appeared out of the fog. It was easy, speaking with him, being in his presence. It hadn't been easy for a long time.

"You are clearly an accomplished gardener," Sara said, looking about her. The sky was full of light and the small winter flowers were beginning to bloom. "This land is beautiful. It reminds me of my home, in a way."

Dickon sat down next to her, completely bypassing the wall that kept young women from young men in this society. Outside of Cedric, Sara had never been so comfortable with a boy who was not in her immediate family. She found herself wondering if the way her hair was continuing to grow in was attractive, or if her toes looked as mismatched as she thought they were. She even felt self-conscious about her skin, something that her mother all but begged her never to do. Then Dickon smiled, and that self-consciousness melted away like spring frost.

"Where are you from?" he asked. "America?"

"The Philippines, actually," she said. "It is a colony of Spain in the Pacific Ocean, a country made up of seven thousand islands. I came to England for my schooling."

Dickon's eyes sparkled with excitement. It was as if God had taken a cup of the clear summer sky—birds and all—and poured that color into them. Sara found herself staring and had to consciously focus on something else. Like his hair. Or his hands.

"The Philippines? I can't properly envision that. I have never been fifty miles from the place I was born. And seven thousand islands? That ocean must be a wonder to behold."

"It is," Sara said. "There is nothing that compares. Except maybe that."

Sara nodded out toward the moors. They flashed in shades of brown and green and orange and purple and red. More colors than Sara would ever expect to see in a place such as this. Dickon followed her gaze, and as if by one of Mary's directorial demands, a beam of soft light landed on his face and made him appear to glow from the inside out. His smile was one a proud parent would give a child.

"If anything is as majestic as the sea, it must be the moors of Yorkshire. I have passed each of my days walking these wilds, and still there is so much to learn."

A silence passed between them. It was as comfortable and delicate as the morning itself. The dogs had even gone quiet and still, drowsing by Sara's knees. The sun was warm and reminded her of the lazy summer days she'd spent with Cedric and Mary. She closed her eyes and could hear their collective laughter, smell the blooming flowers. It felt like falling asleep, slipping back into those better, happier days. And it was like waking up, realizing that so much had changed. Sara opened her eyes, and Dickon was looking at her again. His eyes were suddenly darker, deeper. His smile was soft and contented. Appreciative. Sara allowed herself to stare back. The air—which was once buzzing, vibrating with the hidden life of a garden—became heavy. Sara felt her heart beating rapidly, but her breathing was steady, almost lethargic. Sara was extraordinarily efficient at monitoring, categorizing, and managing her emotions. But this feeling was something new. There was no managing this.

"I would love to show you the moors that I see," Dickon said. His voice was almost a whisper. Sara even had to lean in closer to hear him. "From here, in the garden, it all is still so distant. Once you are out amongst the bell heather, and the tall grass, and the sparrows . . ."

"Yes," Sara said instantly. She did not even allow him to finish. "I want to see it, all of it."

Dickon's smile was radiant. Sara saw his hand itch, as if containing a desire to reach out and touch her. Sara knew that she shouldn't, had no reason to, but she wished that he would.

"Dickon?"

The voice was loud, practiced in extending itself to be heard. Dickon jumped like a dog who had been kicked. In seconds, he was up and standing, leaving Sara on the ground with the dogs. Just as Dickon was wiping the wet grass from his knees, Martha turned a corner on a stone path. She looked dressed for a long walk in a hand-spun wool dress and thick overcoat. Her hair was loose, and it was the same fiery red as Dickon's, and with the same blue eyes.

"Christ, there you are!" Martha said. "I told you to meet me by the kitchen. No time to pick through these gardens looking for you, not when there is work to do."

Martha stopped short when she saw Sara. A curtain fell instantly over her and she was once again an attentive maid in a grand house.

"Miss Crewe," she said. Even her tone of speech had changed. "What are you . . . did you require something?"

Looking between Dickon and Martha, Sara said, "Not at all. Just out on a morning walk."

"In your nightshift, miss? With no shoes?"

Sara did not have much of a response for that. By anyone's standards, her sitting in the middle of a garden in a cotton sleeping gown, dirt between her toes, was peculiar. Mistress Minchin would have had a lot to say about such a blatant lack of decorum.

"I suppose I forgot myself, with the magic of Maythem," Sara said. "I shall go back to my room and dress for breakfast."

She began to stand, and Dickon offered his hand. He was strong; with only a slight tug, she was up on her feet. They were standing close, close enough for Sara to smell the dew in his hair.

"Meet me back here, midday," Dickon whispered. His hand still held hers. "Dress for a walk, not for sleep."

Then Dickon winked one of his blue eyes and Sara felt that she could have swooned. And she never, *ever* had any inclination to swoon. She didn't have the breath to answer him; all she could do was nod. Dickon squeezed her hand, almost hard enough to hurt, then let it go.

"I see you have met my brother Dickon, miss," Martha said. Out of her mouth, it sounded like a warning.

"Yes, he stumbled upon me wandering through the rosebushes," Sara said. "I would have become quite lost without him. And Castle and Lodge, of course." The two heroes in question perked up at the mentioning of their names.

"Well, Dickon certainly is helpful." Martha narrowed her eyes at her brother. "Do you need an escort back to your rooms, miss?"

"I managed to get myself lost, I am sure I can manage to get myself found again. It was wonderful to meet you, Dickon. Martha."

Sara nodded her head at the Sowerby siblings in farewell—her gaze lingering on Dickon—petted the puppies one last time, then made her way back through the gardens toward her room. Behind her, she could hear rushed, aggressive whispers. The farther away she drew, the less she could pick out, but she thought she heard the words *half-breed* and *inferior* and *uppity*. Then she heard quite clearly, "Don't talk to her again." Sara had to laugh to herself. Little did Martha know . . .

THE MORNING WAS fully broken by now. The day had begun, and Sara was eager for breakfast. Her mind had drifted back to Dickon. She tried to avoid thinking of him, but while a full breakfast was appetizing, Dickon was intriguing. They'd only spoken for a few minutes, yet their conversation felt imprinted on her memory as if they'd conversed for hours, for days. He almost did not seem real. None of this seemed real. Strapping young men, manicured stately gardens, ancient estates. These were scenes out of a fairy tale, and girls from the Philippines were not featured in fairy tales. The desire to speak with her parents struck her again, hard enough to steal her breath. She needed their grounding presence now more than ever. In moments such as these, surrounded by the sensual smell of winter roses, the ability to become untethered and float away felt as easy as singing a song.

But the illusion was broken when Sara turned a corner and saw Mary—covered in scrapes, brambles sticking out of her hair—pinned up against a wall while Mrs. Medlock pointed the barrel of a musket directly at her chest.

"What is going on here?" Sara asked and was rather suspicious of the answer.

"Sara, thank the Lord!" Mary exclaimed. She was also wearing only her nightdress, and the circles under her eyes made Sara think that she'd been out all night. "Please tell this woman who I am. She is under the impression that I am some kind of vandal."

"How else am I to explain you wandering about in the early morning in naught but your nightdress, looking as you do?" Mrs. Medlock asked without lowering the musket. It looked to be an absolute relic, something the housekeeper fetched from the wall of a library. "Are you one of them sleepwalkers? Is it an illness?"

Sara moved to stand in front of Mary, shielding her with her body.

"Mary does not sleepwalk," she said. "I am sure she has a perfectly reasonable explanation."

"I am a guest of this house! Why do I need to explain myself?"

"Mary, please, try not to make this worse."

"She is being utterly unreasonable!"

"And what are *you* wearing, Miss Crewe?" Mrs. Medlock asked. She finally lowered her musket, giving Sara room to breathe. She had never been on the receiving end of a weapon before, but she had heard enough stories of terrible accidents. Once she and Mary were out of danger, she remembered to address Mrs. Medlock's question.

Somehow, the most sensible answer turned out to be, "I am a guest in this house, and I do not need to explain myself."

Mrs. Medlock looked at Mary and Sara with profound disbelief. She herself was clothed in only her robe and a sleeping bonnet, probably having rushed outside when she saw the "vagrant" nosing around in the gardens. Sara felt for the woman, truly. The last twenty-four hours for her had probably been more exciting and aggravating than the last ten years.

She finally asked the question that had most likely passed through the minds of every authority who spent an hour in Sara and Mary's company: "What manner of young ladies are you two?"

20

*M*aythem looked different in the light of day. Gone were the grasping shadows and endless halls and disembodied voices and doors that led to nowhere. Every room was filled with light and color, and Mary found it infuriating. The house was mocking her, and she never appreciated being mocked. Also, the more she tried to explain exactly what had happened to her in the witching hours of the morning, the more she sounded like the mad sleepwalker Mrs. Medlock thought her to be.

"You keep asking me how I found myself in the garden, and I keep saying that I am not sure!" Mary said for what felt like the hundredth time. Both Sara and Cedric gave her queer looks across the dining room table.

"It sounds like you were sleepwalking," Cedric said.

For the first time in a long time, the sound of Cedric's voice felt like claws scratching against Mary's ears. That condescending tone grated on her to no end, and as he sat at the head of the long table looking every bit the proper little lord, she wondered if she had the strength to throw something at him. He was dressed in finer clothes than she had ever seen on him. His hair, usually hanging loose and even shaggy, was combed back, slicked to his skull. His spectacles looked to be rimmed in gold and the buttons of his waistcoat shone like sterling silver. When Mary and Sara first made it to the dining hall for breakfast after dressing, Cedric was already there, and had been for hours. Ledgers and loose papers were scattered about him. An older man who turned out to be the estate's steward sat close by him and they spoke in serious tones. Cedric smiled when he saw them standing in the twelve-foot doorway. It was a sudden and surprised smile. As if he'd forgotten they were in his house at all.

"So, you fell into the rosebush," Sara said. "What happened next?"

Sara looked the most at home in the state dining room. She knew how to sit, how to eat, how to speak. Sitting between her and Cedric, Mary felt like a stray dragged in from the street. Neither Cedric nor Sara would ever intentionally make her feel that way, but still, the dining room's soaring ceilings closed in around her like a coffin.

"What happened next," Mary said in answer to Sara's question, "is confusing, even to me. I remember the candle going out. The night was dark—I could barely see my hands extended in front of me. The door I had stumbled through jammed behind me, and I feared having to walk the acreage of Cedric's lands for hours until the sun rose. Then I saw a lantern light, strong, in the distance. I thought it was perhaps Ben or a footman patrolling the garden. I followed the light, even called out for it, but I could never reach it. It floated like a fairy light, bobbing in the ether, as if by its own will. That's when I ran into the well."

Cedric visibly perked up at that. He shifted in his chair, and even dragged his attention away from the report he had been reading. Finally, Mary didn't feel like the annoying child at the adults' table anymore.

"I literally ran into it; it was rather tall, almost to my shoulders. There was a severe chill in the air, but the stone of the well was warm. I pressed my body to it and felt as if I were being hugged. When I looked down into its depths, I saw starlight. The water was so black, and so still, that the night sky was reflected in it like a mirror. The stars shifted and I saw shapes. Faces. At least, I thought they were faces. My mother. My father. My ayah. Ghosts, reaching up with taloned hands."

As Mary spoke, she could see those faces floating before her. They were not peaceful, contented ghosts. Their eyes were as black as the water itself, and their mouths were turned down in snarling frowns. They were angry with her, it seemed. Furious. They were all stuck back in India, dust burned on a desert pyre. And where was she? What was she doing to mourn them? What vigil had she stood? She felt the talons scratch at her face and her throat. It felt as if they were dragging her down, back to India, back to a life of loneliness and insignificance.

"Mary?"

Mary blinked and the faces dissolved. Sara was looking at her from across the table. Her hand was flat and stretched out toward her, reaching for her. Cedric was giving her his full attention now, as well. Forgotten were the reports and papers, and even his breakfast. It was not until Mary looked down to observe herself that she realized her hand was at her throat.

"I'm fine," she said. She moved her hand away and curled it into a fist. Her fingers felt stiff and resistant. The strain made the muscles in her forearm shake. "Where was I?"

"The ghosts in the well," Cedric said. For once, he didn't sound demeaning.

"Right. So, yes, I became so frightened that I reared back and fell. I leaned against the warm walls of the well until I had my bearings again. I suppose I dozed off. When I woke, the sun was shining, and Mrs. Medlock was pointing George Washington's musket at my face. And that's the whole of it."

Mary didn't mention the key. She'd found it half-buried at the base of the well's wall, as if someone had failed at throwing it away. Like the walls of the well, it was warm. Like the floating fairy light, it called to her. Never before had she withheld anything from Cedric and Sara, and she didn't intend to keep it a secret for much longer. But something told her that this key was for her alone to find. She would tell them when it was time.

"I am so sorry, Mary," Sara said. "That sounds like a harrowing night. I understand why Cedric assumed it was a dream."

"I wish it had been a dream," Mary said. "Perhaps then it would make more sense."

"It was no dream. I know that part of the garden, Mary,"

Cedric said. He'd removed his spectacles and sat with his head in his hand. "Although I have no idea how you managed to find it. My father went to great lengths to make sure only he and perhaps Ben Weatherstaff could enter. It was my mother's garden. Or part of it, in any case. She adored gardening and my father must have bequeathed her three miles to make her own. It was actually where they found her, when she died."

Mary felt her heart beat hard in her chest. She looked at Sara, who had a hand pressed over her own heart.

"I have never been in the garden myself. It takes some athleticism to reach it now, clearly, and I . . . well. I have never been called athletic. My sisters have been there, however, and they have seen this well."

Cedric returned his spectacles to their rightful place and took a deep breath.

"I think it is time I told you about my mother, Lady Lilas Fauntleroy."

Lady Lilas Fauntleroy was no one's first choice for mother of the future Earl of Dorincourt. According to Dickon's tale, the family had a mile-long list of points against her. Not only was she a widow with two daughters of her own, but she was significantly older than the earl at the time of their marriage—she was thirty-five and he was but twenty. The union was saved by the fact that her father was an American captain of industry. The money she could potentially bring to the earldom was astronomical. However, she had that senseless American habit of independence. She was not the demure daughter of a minor lord who had been raised with the expectation that her life and everything in it existed for the betterment of the family. Lilas's aspiration extended beyond that. When Cedric's father, then Lord Fauntleroy, met Lilas, she had already visited Africa, Asia, Europe, and South America *twice*; she was famed throughout New York City and beyond for her award-winning roses; and she was a successful amateur polo player. Those were only a handful of her accomplishments.

Then, of course, there was her background as a member of a prestigious Jewish family. The Earls of Dorincourt and their households had been Protestants since Henry VIII made it fashionable, and Catholics before then. Although Lilas was ready and willing to convert in order to marry Cedric's father, the association was too close to appease the grandparents and uncles and aunts. Only after Lilas's father increased her dowry—all but sold her to the House of Errol—did they decide to forget her ancestry entirely. Cedric himself didn't know he had living family still in America until recently.

"They sacrificed a lot for their marriage," Cedric said. The breakfast plates had been cleared away, and the three of them sat close together with mugs of hot cocoa, listening attentively as Cedric told his story. It was the closest the three of them had been since arriving at Maythem Hall. No staff, no stewards, no housekeepers with guns. The fireplace was lit, giving the already-bright room a living glow.

"Was it a happy marriage?" Sara asked.

Cedric shrugged.

"As happy as a marriage between two opposites can be," he said. "My father adored my mother. Hung on her every word and gesture. But he didn't love her for herself; he loved the *idea* of her. He had one chance to rebel against his family, and marrying her was the greatest defiance he could muster. That alone seemed to be enough for him. My mother, for all her strength and independence, had a harder time. She grew up in New York City, the most populous and active city in the world. North York was like a desert island for her. She had her garden and her children, but that wasn't enough. For someone with such grand goals, how could it be? *Oh.* But what a garden it was. She made things grow that had no business growing in York. Roses, ferns, lilies, fruit trees. I was not alive at the time, of course, but the queen actually visited when she was young and proclaimed hers to be the finest garden in England. Before long, my mother began to spend all her time in that garden. She would rise before the sun and not return to the house until the moon was high. My sisters had to help plant and prune if they wanted to spend time with her at all. My father was the Earl of Dorincourt by then, and had new responsibilities." He chuckled darkly, shaking his head. "Apparently, there was no time for his lonely and suffocating wife. Especially when they had no children of their own to show for all the money and sacrifice.

"When she came to be with child, the doctors told her she was too old. That there was a considerable risk. Nothing to be done for it, though. Things proceeded, and I was born. People, especially my father, say that she died giving birth to me, and technically, they wouldn't be wrong. It was not instant, however. She managed to walk, bleeding, from the birthing bed to her garden, carrying me the entire time. It wasn't until some hours had passed that they realized what had happened."

Mary didn't think she took one breath throughout Cedric's entire speech. After months and months of pieces of a life doled out like rations, for him to unload it all to them at once was nearly overwhelming. And he told it all so casually, without any of the gravity and sadness that such drama demanded. Perhaps this was not the first time he'd told this story, whether that be to others or just to himself.

"After that, everything changed," he said. "Maythem Hall became more of a monastery than a country home. No more dinners, or balls, or guests. The staff was reduced drastically since there were so few of us. Really just Mrs. Medlock, Ben, a few governesses and tutors. And my father decided that he'd rather be anywhere else in the world than here, with us. Literally anywhere, especially when he realized I would never be his decorated soldier. The frozen north is his most recent obsession. I know when he looks at me, he sees his greatest failure. Failure as a father and as a husband. I sometimes feel that he would have preferred us both to die on that day instead of leaving me here as a living memory."

"Cedric, you cannot think that way," Sara said. "Your father is still your father, and for all his rigidness, I am sure he loves you."

"Of course he loves him. Though love means almost nothing at all when it is not demonstrated," Mary said, a little more harshly than she had intended. Mary knew from personal experience that a parent's love might be unconditional, but it was also complicated. Perhaps her own father hadn't resented her the way Cedric's father resented him. But he was also just as willing to leave Mary's rearing to others, even up to the moment of his death.

"Thanks, to both of you," Cedric said. He reached and grasped their hands, one in each of his. "So much of this is in the past now, buried in that well. Somehow, Mary, you managed to dredge it all back up."

Mary laughed.

"You know me, dearest Cedric," she said. "Intent on bringing a level of drama and adventure to every situation."

That brought a laugh out of them all. The weight of what Cedric had shared still hung in the air, but their laughter chased that darkness away.

"So!" Mary said brightly, bringing the palms of her hands flat on the table and jarring them all into a lighter, more adventurous mood. "What shall we do with our day? I have obviously already made the greatest discovery in Maythem history; what else does your estate have to offer us, Cedric?"

"I could give you a tour of the west wing," Cedric said. "There is some storm damage on that end of the hall that I need to review, anyway. I would be honored to have you both join me."

Unexpectedly, Sara pushed back from the dining table and moved to stand.

"Forgive me," she said while smoothing the wrinkles from her dress. "But I already have plans."

"What?"

"Already?"

Mary and Cedric looked at each other, feeling more than a little bit abandoned.

"Sara, we've been here for less than a day," Mary said. "When on earth did you have time to make plans?"

"You are not the only one who has gone exploring. I walked the garden earlier today and saw a chapel not far away; I would like to take some time to pray for my parents. Mistress Minchin never gave me the opportunity."

Again, Mary looked to Cedric, grasping for a response but not finding one. There was no arguing with that, and Lord knew Sara deserved the time and space to honor her parents. So much had changed for Sara, and so fast. This time at Maythem Hall was a time of peace, and perhaps even tranquility in solitude.

"Cedric, do you know if the chapel is open for visitors?" Sara asked.

"Oh! Of course, Sara, it is always open and available to anyone. The vicar is in town currently, I believe, but I can summon him—"

"You are a prince of a host, dear Cedric, but that won't be necessary. I am sure there is more need for him in town, anyway. I shall see you both back here, for dinner?"

"That is *hours* from now!"

"Mary." There Cedric was again, with his disapproving tone. "I think we'll be quite fine on our own until dinner, won't we?"

Mary knew that to be true, but still. Mary and Sara had not spent a day apart since meeting. It was a strange and admittedly juvenile feeling, knowing that they might be on separate adventures.

"Yes," Mary said regretfully. "We'll be fine. See you at dinner."

"Thank you, Mary," Sara said. "Besides, you two will enjoy this. A chance to get to know each other a little better."

Sara grinned at them, then made a hurried exit from the dining room. If she had been moving any faster, dust would have been left in her wake. She was certainly eager to get to that chapel.

21

*W*hen Sara said the only thing that might rival the splendor of the ocean was the moors, she was not exaggerating. Standing on a high hill overlooking the valleys and plains, she felt as if she were standing at the edge of the world. The wind was high and beat against her in a way that reminded her of the tropical winds off the Philippine coast. It was an exhilarating sensation that made her laugh with joy and adrenaline.

"Oh, Dickon, this is more than I could ever imagine," she said. "More than worth the hike."

And it had been quite a hike. Sara had followed Dickon's directions to the letter and dressed in the most durable, comfortable dress she could find in her new wardrobe. She tied a thick scarf around her shoulders and wore a wide-brimmed hat to block out the sun. Dickon had said very little when she appeared in the garden so attired; he only grinned and nodded his approval. He himself wore nothing more than a shift, trousers, and boots. Not even an overcoat to block out the cold.

"Is that all you're wearing?" Sara had asked.

"I was prepared to ask you the inverse," he'd said. "Are you wearing all of that?"

Sara looked down at her ensemble, which she felt was ideal for walking about the moors like Catherine in *Wuthering Heights*.

"It is almost December, after all. I have to be warm, else I shall surely freeze out there."

"Now I can believe that you are from an island. I did bring this for you. The footing on the hills can be treacherous for those who aren't half goat like myself."

Then he presented her with a solid oak walking stick. It stood taller than her, and the treatment on the wood made it feel almost as soft and pliable as cotton in her hands.

"My father had a walking stick," she said, thinking back to the walks through the brush or on the beach, trailing her father like one of Dickon's collies. "He always said that he would find the time to make one for me."

"Where is your father now? In the Philippines still?"

Sara did not know quite how to answer that, so she chose to say the truth. "Yes. Yes, he is."

That all occurred many hours ago. They had walked for miles through deep valleys where crystal creeks ran to the river, and then on to the ocean. They walked over rocky hills, through herds of sheep that looked upon them as if they were the animals who had strayed too far from their pasture. Dickon insisted on taking her to the perfect peak from which to observe the

Errol estate for miles around. And he was right; it was perfect.

"We can rest a moment before returning to the hall," Dickon said, taking her scarf to lay out a picnic space. "I brought bread and cheese, if you're hungry."

Sara was in fact starving. They'd been walking since breakfast, and while she considered herself to be a relatively physical person who never shied away from a climb or a walk or a swim, Dickon's pace tested her resolve.

"This is a place ripe with potential and adventure," Sara said as she nibbled at the cuts of brown bread and cheese Dickon offered her. "And it is all so unknown to me. I want to see every fox hole and rabbit burrow. It must have been a dream, passing your childhood here."

"It is strange to spend time with you, a stranger to this place," Dickon said. "You see adventure and dreams, I see where my father shepherded goats. Where my mother tried to make turnips grow. Do not mistake me; I love the moors. It's where my family has lived for two hundred years. But life here can be as hard as it is beautiful."

"I am sorry," Sara said. "I forgot myself. The things I said are how people often look at *my* country. Especially people from here, from England. They only see the beaches and the sunshine from the porches of their grand hotels. They never see the poverty, or the pain. But why would they? They only stay for a month, through the winter at the longest. Just enough time to enjoy oneself before it becomes . . . uncomfortable."

Dickon shook his head and said, "You sound like my sister."

"Not Martha?"

"Martha, precisely. She has nothing but terrible notions about ancient old estates like these. Saying things like 'they don't belong here' or 'this is our land, not theirs.' All kinds of radical ideas that give my mother the vapors. Martha only went to work at Maythem because our family needed the money."

Hearing that, Sara was again surprised by Martha's behavior. By all accounts, they should be on the same side.

"How about you?" Sara asked. "Do you feel the same about places such as Maythem Hall? Families like Lord Fauntleroy's?"

"Not the same, no. I do wish that there was more to experience and discover, as you said. My father was born and raised on these hills. On the same farm as his grandfathers and great-grandfathers, tilling the same land. Destiny states that my fate will be the same."

Sara instantly thought of Mary, and her personal philosophy regarding fate.

"Do not be so quick to assume what destiny has in store for you, Dickon Sowerby. I have seen more things that disprove fate's plan over the past few months—the past few days—than I have that prove it."

Dickon's eyes flashed, and the rosebud blush returned to his cheeks.

"You may be right, Miss Crewe," he said. "I certainly didn't anticipate meeting you today. I'm glad I did."

Sara's heart skipped a foolish, girlish beat at that. She felt like one of Mary's melodramatic heroines, batting her eyes at every compliment and falling in love with every gentleman who brought her a flower.

"I am glad to have met you as well, Dickon. I must confess, since coming to this country, I have done nothing but pine for home. But being here today, with you, you have shown me a part of this land I never expected to see. I understand now why my parents sent me here, and I wish they could see it with me."

Sara could all but feel the question brimming in Dickon. She appreciated his consideration, but the curiosity was there, and she didn't wish to keep him in suspense.

"My parents were killed not long ago," she said, struggling to keep her voice even and contained. The more she was forced to have this conversation with strangers, the more real it all became. This was not just a fancy known only between her and her friends; it was a reality that was dictating the course of her life.

Dickon inhaled slowly before he said, "I am so sorry, Miss Crewe."

"Thank you. I suppose I have not yet come to terms with it. I haven't even seen their graves. The headmistress who bound me in servitude made me feel as if they'd been disposed of like something rotten."

"Will you return home now, to the Philippines?"

Sara had not thought this was a question she would be allowed to ask herself, not after Minchin bound her to the seminary with the threat of debt. Now she was free from that debt, and with Cedric's help she might have the means to go wherever she wanted, whenever she wanted.

"I do not know," she said in all honesty. "A part of me is afraid, I think. Afraid to see what is left of my family and my home. Here, all I have is my own grief and imagination, and a distance from the truth. If I went home, there would be no hiding from it."

"There is no hiding up here," Dickon said, looking about him at the steadily darkening sky.

"You are right," Sara said with a soft smile. "I believe that is why I enjoy it so much."

"I'm afraid we must make our way back, Miss Crewe. A storm is gathering to the north."

Sara could see it for herself. From such a distance and such a height, the black clouds looked like a creature crawling over the hills. She could even see the rain beginning to fall, as sheer as a veil. And it was moving as fast as any tropical storm. It would be upon them within the hour, if even that long.

"We won't have time to return to Maythem Hall before the storm hits, will we?" she asked Dickon.

"No," he said. "No, we won't. I would not dare lead you through such a gale."

"Do you not think I can stand to walk in the rain?" Sara asked with a smirk.

"I think you may be more capable than I," he answered, throwing back a smirk of his own. "But that looks to be more than a trifle of rain. It would not be safe to attempt walking the miles back to Maythem."

The wind began to pick up; Sara had to hold her hat to keep it from flying away, and if her feet had not been planted, she could have gone sailing into the horizon herself.

Raising her voice to speak above the rising storm, Sara asked, "What shall we do?"

She could see Dickon's eyes move quickly, intelligently over the terrain. Even with the winds from Odysseus's fateful bag bearing down on him, he appeared solid and entirely unfazed. It was something out of myth, his confidence and comfort in such a wild place.

"I have a suggestion." He did not raise his voice, but Sara could hear him clearly. "It is not what you might call proper, but it would offer us shelter. My family's home is less than a mile away from where we stand now."

Sara knew what he was asking and appreciated his concern for propriety by not stating it clearly himself.

"Are you asking me to stay in your home?"

He jumped in quickly with "My family's home! My mother, sisters, all my siblings are there. It would be chaperoned, of course. Your honor would not be . . . there would be no question of . . ."

His flustering was almost humorous, in a touching way. Sara struggled to remain as serious as he was endeavoring to be.

"I understand," she said. She looked out again at the storm, already miles closer than it had been just moments before. If she didn't make a decision soon, they would be stranded.

"One thing you must promise me," Sara said.

"Of course," Dickon said with unfiltered earnestness. "Anything."

"You must not ever, *ever* tell Mary. She will use it as fodder for some scene in a drama, and thus never let me live it down."

22

*C*edric, you *must* be joking."

Mary of course knew this was no joke, but if it was, it would make Cedric the greatest trickster since Loki.

"How long has this been here?" she asked, her eyes still on the marvel before her.

"For the last hundred years or so," Cedric said. He had the most self-satisfied smile on his face, and if Mary hadn't been so enchanted, she would be furious. "There was a devastating plague in London, and those who could were encouraged to quarantine in their country homes until it passed. My same ancestor who demolished the old fortress also loved the opera and did not want to sacrifice his exposure to the London season. As a result, he converted the second ballroom into a theater."

Mary did not think a modern-day opera house could compare with such luster and elegance. Even though the seating for the audience could only accommodate ten, maybe twenty, the stage was a proper size and trimmed in gold. Angels watched from the banisters, and golden laurels hung over the stage. Bloodred curtains too heavy to lift were tied back with rope as thick as Mary's arm, and there was even room for a small orchestra pit that might accommodate a stringed quartet and a harpsichord. Up above was the largest chandelier Mary had ever seen. What must have been hundreds of crystals hung like raindrops suspended in the sky. Mary knew it must have been as brilliant as the sun when fully lit. Although she had no idea as to how someone would find their way up there to light them and dim them again. In any case, that must have been a logistical detail that those who could install a royal opera house in their personal residence need not concern themselves with.

"It is absolutely caked in dust," Mary said as she ran her hand over the stage. A long line in the grime was left behind. "When was the last time someone used this place?"

Cedric took a moment to consider the question.

"Years and years," he said at last. "Not even my mother could restore it to its former glory. Too much of an expense, according to my father."

"For such a wealthy family, nobody seems particularly capable of managing the household."

Mary meant that only partially in jest. Cedric's tour of the west wing had revealed much, including the true state of Maythem Hall. Years of neglect were difficult to hide in such a large home.

The paint had faded, the dust had gathered. The storm damage that Cedric had spoken of earlier turned out to be a massive crater that took out half of a ceiling. Mary could feel the frustration in the walls of a home that was once the jewel of the county, possibly even all Yorkshire. It wanted desperately to be beautiful, and the beauty shone through in the way light fell across the marble floor. This luxurious theater stood as proof of that potential.

"It is the burden of all families like mine, I think," Cedric said. "We have land, art, all manner of inheritances. But renovations such as these require something that the British aristocracy has never been able to achieve: cash savings. I have spent months of my life thinking of all the ways we could return Maythem Hall to its glory, especially this wing. It gets the best light by far, but it has been uninhabitable since the days of my grandfather."

"Does your father have any plans for improving the grounds, seeing as he is the earl?"

"Oh, my father. He probably wishes this whole place would fall into the sea or be swallowed up by the earth. When he's off on his adventures, I doubt he gives Maythem a passing thought. My cousin, on the other hand, has all kinds of recommendations. Selling this painting or renting that acre. He even proposed demolishing this wing to cut down on maintenance costs: can you believe it?"

"You should tell your father *your* ideas about what to do, Cedric. This is his home, after all, just as much as it is yours. He will want to save it."

Cedric gave Mary an almost pitiful look.

"Home reminds him of my mother, and he would be happy to never think of my mother again."

Mary found this to be ridiculous, this refusal of Cedric's father to accept things as they were, not as he wished they could be. Mary knew what wealth was. Until very recently, she had no inkling of what it meant to go to bed hungry or wake up cold. Her every need was provided for ten times over. However, if she could have the legacy that Cedric and his entire family had laid out before them as an option, she would take it over her father's now-depleted wealth in an instant. If she did have that legacy, perhaps she wouldn't feel quite so lost now.

"We can raise the money," she said suddenly. She saw the doubtful look on his face and rushed to bypass it. "No, listen, Cedric! We can use this wonderful opportunity. A fully outfitted theater just waiting for a willing and eager audience. Yes, it may be in need of some modern fixtures, but a stage is a stage. Just wait there, you will see."

Mary ignored Cedric's protestations and hiked up her skirts so she could maneuver herself onto the stage. She bounced lightly on the balls of her feet, testing its strength. There was a bit of a sag, but nothing that she didn't see as ordinary wear. No rot, no holes. A hundred ballerinas performing *Giselle* wouldn't make that floor cave in.

"Can't you just visualize a real set, fully illustrated backdrops? Your work would shine on this stage, Cedric, truly. Come up here, see for yourself."

"Mary, do not mock me, please."

"I am not! Cedric, I would never. There is a ramp here, most likely for moving large set pieces. If it can hold my dancing, it can certainly hold you."

Cedric hesitated for a moment, but in time, he moved his chair around the edge of the stage. There was some difficulty getting enough momentum to maneuver up the ramp, but he refused Mary's help. He was exhausted and more than a little bit frustrated, but he was on the stage next to her and not entirely pleased to be there.

"There, the stage has not caved in," he said. "I think your theory has been proven. Can we move on to the next room?"

"Don't be silly. There is nothing for it, we must dance."

Cedric immediately began to laugh. Full-bodied, throw-your-head-back-and-clutch-your-middle laughter. When he noticed that Mary hadn't cracked even the smallest of smiles, he stopped laughing.

"Now, *you* must be joking."

"Not at all. Do you know how to waltz?"

"In *theory*."

"Then that is enough."

Without even stopping to ask for permission, Mary folded her wide skirts around her legs and sat down in Cedric's lap. She looped one arm over his shoulder and used the other to hold his hand. It was not the waltz that Minchin taught, but it was close enough. Mary smiled at Cedric, but he was staring at her with something close to fear.

"Don't look at me like that, I'm not going to eat you."

"Are you quite sure? I assure you, that would be considerably less frightening than this."

Mary rolled her eyes, then took Cedric's left hand and placed it on her waist. He gasped as if she'd just thrust his hand into a roaring fire.

"I'll hum," she said. "You spin."

Mary had only ever waltzed to "Minute Waltz" by Chopin, so that is what she began to hum, or at least as much as she could remember of it. For a long time, Cedric just stared at her. Then, at last, he used the crank on his chair to begin to move. Mary was instantly reminded of that first night on the frozen lake. The sensation of gliding, even flying, was replicated here. And yet, there was something different about this moment. She was close to Cedric, closer to him than she had ever been. She could see the small beads of gold reflected in his eyes and the freckles across his nose, usually hidden by the bridge of his spectacles. They were on an equal level in this position. She could look directly into his face; he could look directly into hers. If the stage was going to cave in, it would already have caved in. After a while, Mary stopped humming and focused instead on the heat radiating from the hand on her waist. She had danced with young men before, when the students of the seminary were brought together to rehearse the correct drawing-room techniques. Then it was like dancing with a wooden board or an article of clothing; she could have been dancing with anyone, with anything. But in this moment, dancing with Cedric was not like dancing with a wooden board. Not even close.

This was a real, living person whom she knew better perhaps than she knew herself.

"This is nice," he said, and it was the first thing he'd said since they'd begun to dance. He spoke in a true whisper. If Mary hadn't been only inches from his face, she wouldn't have heard him.

"You are a very good dancer," she said.

"That is good to know considering that no one has ever asked me to dance before."

They both laughed, but it was a private laugh. Intimate enough that their breaths briefly merged.

"Well, that is a shame, because you are performing admirably."

"That means more than I can say. Especially coming from you."

"Why? Is it because I am the only one brave enough to say it if you danced like a cornered badger?"

"Yes," Cedric said. "That is true. But it is more than that, I think. If ever I was to dance with someone . . ."

Cedric's voice suddenly caught, as if in a sob or a choke. Mary could feel the hand that she held begin to shake.

"Cedric?" she asked, concerned. Was this one of his tremors? Of course, she would be the one to push him too far. "Let's stop. We should stop."

"No." He flexed his hand, and Mary found it to be stronger than she imagined. She was suddenly pulled even farther into him. It was close. Possibly too close.

"Cedric, what is wrong?"

"Nothing! Nothing is wrong. Everything is wrong." Then

they stopped moving. Cedric's breath came in deep, long passes. Mary was close enough to feel his heart beating rapidly in his chest. It was fast enough to worry her, and she actually pressed her hand against it as if she could calm its pace.

He placed his free hand over hers on his chest. "There is something else I must tell you," he said. He did truly sound like he might cry. Mary had never seen Cedric cry before, didn't even consider it as a possibility. She wasn't sure how she'd react.

"Do not tell me that you are actually a duke."

Mary meant that to be a joke, to lift Cedric out of this doldrum he'd fallen into, but he did not even pretend to laugh with her.

"Oh no," she said. "You are a duke, aren't you?"

"No, worse than that. I am engaged."

Oh.

Well.

That was considerably worse.

"You are *what*?"

"I said that I am engaged."

"Yes, I heard you! I am sitting right *on* you. What I mean is, how did this happen? Is that where you were all last night, off proposing to someone?"

"Of course not, don't be foolish."

Mary was up out of his lap faster than if he'd been on fire. Her skin tingled and itched as if she wore an old sweater. Everything on her felt exposed. She wanted to take all of the feelings and moments that they had just shared and grab them out of the air, then stuff them back into her own heart where they belonged. She shivered, but the room was not cold. She wrapped her arms about herself to contain the way her muscles flexed and cramped from *something*. Was it shock? Was it anger? Embarrassment? Or something else altogether.

"I am not being remotely foolish," she said. "I am responding quite naturally! How many secrets do you have exactly, Lord Fauntleroy? Yesterday, it was an earldom. Today, it's a betrothal. What will it be tomorrow? Are you Napoleon's long-lost heir?"

Cedric, to his credit, was remaining as cool and calm as stone while Mary felt like she was holding her skin together with just her hands.

"I did not want this, Mary. I had no choice in any of it. It all occurred long before I was born."

"Your lack of agency does not make it easier, Cedric! Who is this person, anyway?"

"I have never even met her! The daughter of some minor lord in the next county over, heir to five hundred acres. My father saw a chance to consolidate our families. At this rate, I probably never will meet her, I hear she may be eloping with an Italian prince or some such—"

"Why are you telling me this?" Mary screamed. It was a glass-shattering scream. The diamonds on the chandelier far above actually shook, clanging together like an opulent bell tower.

"Because I love you!"

Cedric's voice launched at her, and she felt that it might knock her over. She even wavered on her own feet, wishing desperately for a stool or a chair. Or a fainting couch. A fainting couch would be better. One of Mary's leading ladies would have poured herself into Cedric's arms and proclaimed her love to the stars after such a confession. But Mary had no desire to do that. She had a desire to run.

And so she did.

THE STORM WAS loud and clouded Mary's thoughts and steps. She was grateful for that. The crashing thunder and blinding lightning filled her head with something other than what she had just experienced. He body jittered and shook from the chill of the torrential rain, not from the shock of hearing that one of her best friends was not only engaged, but in love. *With her.* What did that even mean? She knew what it meant in novels and in plays. It meant swooning sighs, illicit rendezvous, and elopements in Gretna Green. None of those things seemed appropriate for her, and certainly not for Cedric. They were two people who found heated debates that would easily devolve into arguments exhilarating. They existed to make note of each other's flaws. Everything one did would, without a doubt, aggravate the other. That was not love, it couldn't be. And even if it were, he was *engaged.* Even though the rain fell in sheets thick and strong enough to wash away the side of a mountain, they could not wash that knowledge from her consciousness. Out, out, damned spot. Reverse time and make it as if it had never happened.

Mary did not know where she was going or even where she was coming from, so when she finally raised her head to take in her surroundings, she was not at all surprised to find that she was completely lost.

"These damnable gardens!" she shouted into the storm. The thunder clapped back at her in answer.

Just like with the night before, Mary began to feel the stone walls around her, looking for a door. She could not see anything, but her hands felt stone, wood, wet ivy and other vines growing up and up. But no doors. Now she was beginning to feel truly cold. Every breath made her chest ache, and a wetness clung to her throat when she coughed. Sleeping outside at the base of some well wasn't an option, not tonight. She could forgo dinner in order to avoid looking at Cedric, but she could not pass the night in this weather without risking real illness.

Finally, her hand grasped at a heavy metal ring. She pulled, hard, but the door did not budge. Blinking away the water in her eyes, Mary leaned forward until she could see the details of the door. There was a handle and rusted hinges. But there was also a keyhole. Mary could feel its imprint and even stick her finger through to the other side. She dropped down onto her knees, sinking into the mud and ruining the otherwise very nice dress. She placed her eye against the keyhole, and what she saw, she could not rightly believe. It was sunlight. Not a lamp or a candle or even a chandelier: true midday sunlight in the middle of a late-day storm. She also saw colors, colors so explosive that they could only exist in nature. All of this was of course impossible. Mary knew this in her bones. And yet, here she was.

She reached into her pocket and pulled out the iron key. It

was solid, once a shining silver, now turned brown and dull by time. It was a substantial key, as long as Mary's hand from the tip of her middle finger to the base of her palm. It was such an important-looking key. When Mary first found it, she assumed it opened a trunk filled with treasure, or a door to the old fortress. A garden door to a hidden land where the sun shone at night and flowers bloomed on the eve of winter, what could be more important than that?

Mary eased the key into the keyhole without resistance. She turned it once and heard a loud, metallic *click*. With only a slight push, the door began to swing open. The sun touched Mary's face and the world in all its magic and beauty opened up to her.

23

*D*ickon and Sara did not outrun the rain. It moved with a force only nature could summon, catching them as they made their way down into a shallow valley that housed a sole building with grass growing on the roof and smoke filtering through a narrow chimney. By that point, Sara wouldn't have minded the Tower of London's dankest dungeon. More than anything, she wanted to be warm and she wanted to be dry. Rain had a marvelous ability to make one feel as if they would never be dry again.

"It's not much," Dickon yelled over the gale. "But it will give us shelter until the storm passes!"

"It looks glorious," Sara answered, and she did not speak out of flattery. Unlike Maythem with its marble and sophistication, this place spoke of true home, not just a building made to house the sleeping.

Sara heard the dogs bark as they approached, and when

Dickon opened a door, light and warm air came rushing out, along with the bounding forms of Castle and Lodge.

"Down, boys!" Dickon demanded. "Down, leave us be!"

"Is that you, son?" a woman called out.

Under the sound of barking dogs came the joyous clamor of children at play. Wafting over it all was a smell that set Sara's mouth to salivating. When her stomach growled, she felt sure that the entire estate could hear it, along with the thunder.

"Yeah, Ma, it's me," he said. "Got caught in the storm."

Dickon closed the door behind her, and it was like stepping into an oven. Sara felt instantly heated from the inside out. The house seemed to be made up of one or two rooms, with a massive hearth fire burning at its center. Herbs hung from the low-hanging rafters, and the trappings of a busy life were strewn about everywhere. Homemade toys, chopped vegetables, tools, and laundry to be washed. A crew of small children ran past her in pursuit of one of the collies, nearly knocking her over. It all brought a smile to Sara's face. So much of this reminded her of the Philippines and the life she left behind.

Dickon must have observed her standing as still as a caught deer, observing everything with wide eyes.

"As I said, it's not much—"

"It's perfect, Dickon," Sara said imploringly, even as her dripping clothes made a puddle on the plank floor. "It is better than another night in Maythem by far."

"And who is this?"

Sara straightened her back and reapplied her expression of respectability when faced with a tall, windswept woman with Dickon's fiery hair, shot through with streaks of gray.

"Ma, this is Miss Sara Crewe," Dickon said. "She is a guest of Master Cedric's."

"Oh, Master Cedric is back?" the woman Sara took to be Mrs. Sowerby asked.

"There was an outbreak at our boarding school," Sara said. "Lord Fauntleroy was kind enough to offer sanctuary. Your son Dickon is offering a similar kindness. He was showing me the moors, and the storm caught us off guard."

Mrs. Sowerby listened to this with a quizzical brow. She took in all of Sara, from her hiking ensemble, to her soaked shoes, to her brown skin. Sara did not feel judged, as she often had when standing before strangers in this strange land. Just taken in.

"Well," Mrs. Sowerby finally said, "any guest of Master Cedric's is certainly a guest of ours. You did well, Dickon, bringing her here. Are you hungry, lass?"

Sara exhaled and allowed herself to be comfortable in this woman's presence.

"Very much so, ma'am," she said. "It smells delicious, whatever it is. I'd be more than grateful."

"Such manners, Miss Crewe!" Mrs. Sowerby exclaimed. "'Bout time we had some class 'round here. Prepare a plate for her, Dicky. I'll see if we can find something to get you out of those wet clothes."

SARA SPENT MORE time laughing than she had in months. Her belly was full twice over, and the homespun frock she wore was warmer than her galoshing getup by far. The antics that came with a house full of children were foreign to her, so she watched closely as they played nonsensical games, chased one another endlessly, and used Dickon as a human pincushion. They asked her all sorts of questions ranging from where she was from to why her skin was darker than theirs.

"Mind yourself, Lily," Dickon said to his sister, who appeared to be the youngest of the group. "You don't ask people questions like that."

"No, it's all right," Sara said. "I'm quite used to it."

And she was. It was one of the many things she'd become accustomed to after months looking after young English children who had never seen a dark-skinned person before.

"You shouldn't have to be," Dickon said.

"I rather someone ask than assume," she said. "Or speak from cruelty."

"I understand, I suppose. I cannot count the number of times some fine lord or lady staying at Maythem called me a cur or vagrant just because they saw me trimming hedges. I could be the next Earl of Dorincourt for all they knew."

That made Sara laugh, and not out of a feeling that such a thing would be impossible. Dickon, she felt, would make for a very caring and engaged landowner.

"Thank you, again," she said. "For welcoming me into your home."

"I should be thanking you," Dickon said. "My sisters and brothers will talk of nothing else for months. The day a princess from another land came to visit."

Sara tried not to betray on her face how much that sentiment stung. Where before, being called a princess appealed to her subdued desire for flattery, now, it only reminded her of what was lost.

With her head bent down, eyes focused solely on her empty dinner bowl, she said, "I'm no princess. My parents did the hard work. Hard work that afforded me access to certain privileges. From there, I just do what I'm told. Smile this way, speak that way. I don't even have money to claim anymore, not that it mattered."

Dickon leaned in close, close enough for the heat of his breath to flare across Sara's cheeks.

"That is not why people call you a princess, Miss Crewe," he said. "It is something in your spirit. The way you address people, the way you look at people."

On the edge of a whisper that felt all too private in such a crowded home, Sara said, "And how do I look at people?"

The corner of Dickon's expressive mouth turned up in a grin.

"The way you're looking at me now," he said. "Without judgment. Without expectation. As if I am the most important person in the world."

Sara wanted to say that in this quiet moment, he was. She even opened her mouth to affirm as much, but a massive yawn that stretched her jaw and made her ears ring came out instead. Sara rushed to cover her mouth, embarrassed by how close Dickon had been in the midst of such a faux pas.

"Goodness!" Mrs. Sowerby said from her deep rocking chair directly next to the fire. "Someone has had a long day."

Working to tamp down another wave of exhaustion, Sara said, "I suppose so. I feel I could sleep for a fortnight. I hate to be such a trouble, taking up space in your home."

"Think nothing of it!" Mrs. Sowerby rose limberly, with the dexterity of a cat. "Martha is staying at Maythem tonight, so there's a space. And even if there weren't, we'd make one."

Sara was squeezed between two of Dickon's younger sisters on a wide, low cot spread across a portion of the floor. She thought she'd feel claustrophobic, surrounded on all sides by shifting, breathing bodies. But that wasn't the case at all. She felt secure and strangely comforted. The closeness implied a togetherness that the largest bed in the roomiest house could never match.

From her place on the floor, Sara watched Dickon stoke the fire, Castle and Lodge snoring loudly at his feet. The flames matched the shades of his hair, and the flaring embers danced in his eyes, still alert after what Sara knew to have been a grueling workday. Sara did not pry, but from what she could tell, there was no other man in the house of proper age. No support for his mother, for his household. She wondered how long he sat up minding the fire while the others slept.

She felt her own eyes begin to become unfocused. She could not be certain, but she thought she saw Dickon turn to her and smile.

"Sleep, Sara," she heard a voice that sounded an awful lot like Dickon's say. "Nothing will harm you. Not whilst I'm here."

And Sara did sleep. It was the soundest sleep she'd had since Manila, and maybe before even then.

24

*I*n the morning the garden was still there.

Mary slept bathed in sunlight, a trickle of sweat at her temple, so filled with warmth and so comfortable and safe that for the briefest of moments, Mary thought she was back home in her bed in India. Softness beneath her, not the hardness of a seminary bed nor the filthy straw pallet of the workhouse; not the cold and damp of the north of England but the warmth and heat of her native tropics, a comfort she thought she'd forever lost.

The illusion was so complete that she even smelled the musky, slightly bitter fragrance of the marigolds her ayah used to plant outside the windows to keep the insects at bay, along with several scents she thought she'd never encounter again: the cloying richness of jasmine, the watery sweetness of sacred lotus. She could almost hear her ayah calling her: "Mary, Mary."

No, not her ayah. Her mother. A scream like a woman's, a low and throaty *aww*, followed by *ayyy-yah, ayyy-yah, ayyy-yah*.

Conscious thought began to return. A peacock? She hadn't heard a peacock's call in years. Her mother was dead, and her father was dead, and the house with the marigolds was empty by now, most likely full of dust and rodents and the snakes that hunted them. Her ayah had said goodbye to her a lifetime ago, when she'd put Mary on a train to Calcutta.

When she opened her eyes, she wasn't entirely certain she wasn't still dreaming. She was not in India at all, but in a place infinitely more strange, like in a Jules Verne novel. The center of the earth.

The garden she had seen through the keyhole the night before was real—light in the literal darkness, lush and strange—only now she was inside. The heavy iron key was still in her hand. Behind her, the gate was shut.

She didn't remember removing the key from her pocket nor coming inside, and yet she must have done so. She didn't remember crossing the threshold and coming within the garden's high walls. Outside there had been the same northern gray stone, the same dull color of the great house, a monument to wealth and title, invulnerability and the empire. Yet inside, the walls glowed in the sunlight, thick with ivy and creeping flowers of every color, blue and white and violet, dripping not just with purple wisteria like clusters of grapes but brilliant pink-and-orange blossoms shaped like trumpets, and bushes with clusters of small white flowers so sweet she wanted to push her face into them and drown in their scent.

A brilliantly colored hummingbird not much bigger than a butterfly flitted past, its feathers bright green along its back, splashed with brilliant red across its throat. A ruby-throated hummingbird—she was sure she'd heard the name somewhere, sometime. Surely such a creature had never been seen before in dreary old England.

"What is this place?" she whispered.

Then the cry of the peacock came again, that same haunting note she'd heard in her dream: *aww*, then, *ayyy-yah, ayyy-yah, ayyy-yah*. A flash of brilliant blue and green in one of the trees. She hadn't imagined it. Hidden in a secret garden in the far north of England, so far from its native land it was practically unimaginable, a peacock—a bird whose calls she'd heard every day of her faraway childhood—cried for its mate.

Above her a beam of sunlight shot through heavy gray clouds and bathed the garden in the same warmth she'd felt in her dream. Beyond were curtains of rain, gray and damp with the first breath of winter, but here in the magic garden all was sunlight and spring.

Joy filled her like the first deep breath after reaching the surface of water. She followed a stone pathway through the garden, past pools where golden fish flashed their bellies, past clusters of prickly, barrel-shaped plants she'd seen in a book once—cacti, she thought they were called—to a patch of green where a carved wooden bench sat as if it had been put there especially for her. The seat was smooth and polished as if many people had sat there once, but Mary was entirely alone. She sat and looked back down the garden path: the stones, the pond, the peacock, the riotous colors of the flowers in pink and purple, orange and white.

The joy in her chest expanded and rose within her like a

bubble. It was as if a costume had fallen away, the mocking and cantankerous version of herself she'd been playing since the moment she boarded a steamer for England, since her ayah had clutched Mary to her one last time and put her on the train that took her away from home, away from her father and the house with the marigolds, all the disappointments she'd felt like small blows to her spirit. Her spirit was fighting back. Here she was herself again, the Mary she remembered from long ago, the one who had waited for her mother to come home, whose patience had been rewarded with disappointment and then grief.

Her strongest urge was to pick up a pen and put her thoughts to paper. To write of her adventures at the seminary, standing up to Minchin and her cruelty, the police on the streets of Sheffield. Or perhaps life in the poorhouse with Anne, whose own tale of woe was even more cruel and cramped than Mary's. Or the woman in the painting. Cedric's mother, the Jew brought here from her home in America, a fate that to Mary was utterly sad and familiar.

She tapped her fingers impatiently against her leg. Her kingdom—such as it was—for a pen and paper.

It was the place, this place. Here she heard shades of things long gone, her fingers itching with the urge to write and write until her inkwell ran dry. The feel of the words flowing out of her onto the page. It was the place that made it seem possible: this place, alive with magic, with hope and possibility.

Then, even more strongly than the urge to write, she had a sudden and irrepressible thought: she must find her friends and bring them to the garden.

— ❦ —

"Sara, there you are! Come with me at once."

Mary had spotted Sara coming over the rise of a distant hill, the sun at her back, and she ran half the way to meet her. She didn't walk alone, however. A strapping boy, close to Sara's own height, with fire caught in his hair, accompanied her. Mary noticed the way he looked at Sara, as if the rising sun rose for her. Indeed, it was hard to miss.

"Who is this?" she asked once she was close enough to speak to them properly.

"Mary," Sara said. "You ask who *I* am with when you yourself look as if you've done battle all night?"

Mary took the moment to take in her appearance, and yes, Sara was quite right. She was so covered with dirt from her venture the night before that the original blue of her dress was barely visible. She felt the blotches of dirt on her cheeks and in her hair, and she knew what they were seeing: she looked like a creature of myth, a bog monster.

"Oh, never mind this," she said. "And don't pretend like you haven't seen worse. And I ask again, who are you?"

The young interloper in question removed his cap and dipped his head in a sign of feudal deference.

"Dickon Sowerby, miss," he said. "Apprentice gardener."

"Good for you," Mary said. "That doesn't explain what you're doing with Sara."

The boy began to stammer; something about a hike and rain and staying somewhere through the night . . .

"Why were you coming to find me, Mary?" Sara asked, interrupting Dickon's very poor attempt at explaining himself. Mary must have looked quite intimidating indeed.

"I have something to show you," Mary said. "You and Cedric, and I guess you as well, Dickon. As an apprentice gardener, you may be able to explain all of this."

THEY FOUND CEDRIC in the dining room, surrounded again by all manner of papers and ledgers, still in his dressing gown. When he saw Mary—tailed by Sara and Dickon, who apparently had never been inside Maythem before and found it all to be dazzling—approaching him with the speed and authority of agents of the Crown, he just about dropped his toast.

"Should I even ask?" he said to Mary, instead of probably the hundred things he wanted to say instead.

"Probably not," she said. "Just come with me. And quickly!"

They followed Mary outside, Sara pushing Cedric in his chair, a slow crunch over the gravel walkway, a rattle of wheels.

"What is going on?" Mary heard Cedric ask. "And aren't you Dickon Sowerby?"

"We don't have the slightest idea what is going on," Sara answered. "Something has upset her, apparently. And yes, this is Dickon Sowerby."

"Wonderful to see you again, Master Cedric."

"Upset?" Mary demanded from the front line, a place where they obviously thought she could not hear. "Quite the opposite!"

She was back down the path before she could wait for Sara and Cedric to catch up. Goodness, but her friends were slow when there was a world-changing discovery at hand. She took the iron key from her pocket and turned the lock on the great gate, making the gears grind.

She was almost afraid to look, to see that the sunlight that'd bathed the garden when she awoke that morning was an illusion caused by an errant sunbeam, the riot of flowers and birds nothing but her overactive imagination getting the best of her. Then how Sara and Cedric and Dickon would laugh at her for getting herself worked up again over nothing.

When she pushed open the door, though, it was all still there. The sunlight. The flowers. The birds. The pond with its glimmer of golden fish. She had not imagined it.

She breathed it in deeply, took the scents and the warmth into her lungs, and only then stopped to look down at her clothes. In the brightness of the garden, she looked like a troll. The mud had dried to dust in the warmth, so she slapped it off, great clouds of it gathering around her until she could see the glimpses of blue beneath.

When she straightened up, she could feel them behind her: Cedric and Sara and Dickon. Could feel their awe.

"What is this place?" breathed Sara.

Dickon cried out in delight, rubbing the petals of a huge pink-blossoming bush between his fingers. "This is bougainvillea, this is. I ain't never seen it in person before, only in the pages of a book. I thought it only grew in the tropics."

"It does," said Sara, smiling. "I thought I'd never see it again in this lifetime."

"Nor I," said Mary.

Then the voice of the peacock, deep in a tree: *aww*, followed by *ayy-yah, ayy-yah, ayy-ah.*

"What in heaven's name was that?" said Cedric.

"A peacock," said Mary. "Native to India. I grew up with them."

"I didn't know my father had imported peacocks. I daresay he told me nothing of this place."

"There it is, that bit of blue: look!"

They stood and watched the brilliant blue bird flap from the tree branch down to the ground, where the duller, gray peahen pecked at some unseen insect. Then the peacock unfurled his astonishing fan of feathers, iridescent greens and blues, and shuddered with pleasure in the female's direction.

Beside Mary, Sara breathed in with pleasure. "Oh! How beautiful!"

The peahen ignored her mate and walked off in search of breakfast, but the four friends in the garden were not so unaffected. Every sight was an astonishment, every turn of the corner bringing some new, rare delight. Mary took them to the pond where the fish flashed like gold coins in the depths, the bench where she had sat and wished for pen and paper. Her friends followed behind her, touching the flowers, stopping to marvel at the hummingbirds drinking from the trumpet vine, listening to Dickon name the plants and flowers, the birds and strange beetles that crawled under leaves and over vines.

He particularly stopped to look at the cactus, a pink blossom bursting from its side. "Th-this shouldn't be here," he said. "England's far too wet for these. I ain't never seen them except in a book about the West, in America."

"Surely it's not too wet for them, since here they are," said Cedric.

"None of these should be here."

"You're telling me you've never been in here before, Dickon?"

"Never, sir." He took off his cap and slapped it against his leg. In the sunlight his hair gleamed red. "I didn't know it was here."

Sara shaded her eyes in the sunlight and looked up. "Isn't it strange that the clouds don't cover the garden," she said, pointing at the sheets of rain that were just visible beyond the walls. "It's as warm here as the middle of summer, and yet it's nearly winter."

"So strange," Dickon said, running his hands over the sweet-smelling white bush opposite the cacti. "Honeysuckle, I think, though I've never seen this variety. And it shouldn't be blooming this time of year." He shook his head in wonder and laughed. "Nothing should."

Mary beamed in triumph. The only thing better than discovering such a place was sharing it with those she loved most in this world. Even Cedric was flabbergasted, saying over and over that he hadn't known. His father had never told him this garden was here.

Mary felt her fingers itch again, longing after pen and paper to write down everything she had seen and thought and felt.

A sharp cry behind her, and Dickon said, "Master Cedric, what on earth are you doing?"

Mary turned to see Cedric standing. On his own, without crutches. Without his chair. Tall and strong he looked, his face beatific.

"I can do it," he whispered. "I always wondered if I could, someday. If I wanted it badly enough."

He took a step forward, then another. His feet shuffled across the grass—he was still afraid to lift them too high—but then he picked one up and brought it down. Picked up the other, and brought it down again. And then in three remarkable strides, he crossed the distance between himself and Mary and grasped her by the elbows.

"I knew I could," he said. His hands were cold, clammy, and shaking with a long-repressed hope. His entire body seemed seized from muscle to marrow, but the joy in his eyes took Mary's breath away. "I knew it could be possible here! I just knew—"

He took one step back, and it was a step too far. In the next moment, he collapsed in a heap on the ground.

25

*H*ow short the moment of delight; how long the season of suffering. As Mary sat through the night watching Cedric groan and shiver, cooling his fever with a wet cloth and his terrors with a friendly hand, she could not forget the days she had waited to learn if her mama was coming home. If her hoping and waiting would be for naught.

After the delights of the garden, the sickroom was an oppression she would not have been able to bear, except that it was Cedric who was ill, and she to blame for it. For those few minutes in the garden, hope had penetrated them all. It was hope that had caused Cedric to stand and walk. He'd been pulling her toward him at the moment he'd fallen. His eyes were bright with it; he was more alive than she'd ever seen him before.

In those long and terrifying moments after he'd fallen and lain unconscious on the path, she saw a stillness in him that frightened her in a way nothing else had in years. It was the stillness she'd seen once in a rat bitten by a cobra; it had twitched several times and then collapsed. It was the same with Cedric—just a moment before, he'd been there, offering her his hand. Then he was not.

It was several long minutes before Dickon and Sara managed, with some difficulty, to get him back into his chair. They'd been shouting for her to help them, but for the first time in some while, Mary Lennox hadn't the slightest idea what to do.

Not Cedric. Everyone she'd lost in her young life she'd been able to bear, so far. But not this. Not him. Seeing Cedric pale and limp, imagining him dead, chilled her absolutely even in the lush warmth of the secret garden.

But he was not dead, thank God. And would not be, if she could do anything about it. Mrs. Medlock supervised, but it was Mary who sat by his side. She was the one who tended him hour after hour, talking to his fluttering eyelids, the weak and impulsive rise and fall of his heartbeat. She could see it, barely, in the flesh at his throat and the insides of his wrists, the veins blue beneath his ash-white skin. He was sick, far sicker than he'd ever been before.

Curse that infernal garden—it made one believe in things that were impossible.

Martha brought him a broth, and Sara urged Mary to go to her room and get some sleep. "Let's take turns tending him through the night," she said, and put a gentle hand on her arm. "Please, Mary. You mustn't blame yourself."

Mary looked up into Sara's kind, pleading green eyes.

"I can't leave him," she said.

"You're not leaving him. I'll be here. You're taking care of yourself so you can help him again tomorrow."

"But if he dies in the night, and I wasn't here—"

"Hush, now," said Sara. "He won't die in the night. Don't talk nonsense, this isn't one of your plays."

Another Mary, in another time and another place, would be offended by that insinuation. This Mary could not care less about plays or actions without consequences.

"You don't know it's nonsense," she said.

"He exerted himself too much. The garden overwhelmed us all."

"You're not a doctor. You're only trying to make me feel better. But I won't feel better. I can't."

"Mary, please come away," Sara said. Her arm around Mary's shoulder was warm and healthy, unlike Mary's own sallow complexion and half-frozen limbs. "This room is like an icebox; you haven't been seeing to the fire at all. Please let me help you."

But Mary would not. Her fault, that they had all gone into the garden. Her fault, that he had dared to stand and walk too far. More of her fanciful, foolish ambitions dragging people down like a riptide. And now she might lose him forever. This was her fault.

At some point, she blinked and looked around, and noticed that the light had dimmed outside. Sara was gone, but the fire was stoked and burning brightly. A single candle stood in its holder by the window, the glass reflecting the double light into the room, in which Mary could see, palely, her own distraught reflection.

— ❧ —

Mary heard someone say her name. She'd fallen asleep with her head on the bed, her arms tucked beneath. The fire had burned low.

"Mary," said the voice again, a thick rasp that reminded her of a dying hearth and a creature made of fire who once stoked her imagination and calmed her fears. She squinted at the hearth, sure the genie was there looking at her with his burning-coal eyes, speaking her name with his tongue of fire. But there were only the last embers of a log, crumbling.

"Mary," rasped the voice again, but this time, it was behind her.

Mary spun her head around to see Cedric staring up at her. She was reminded of another sickroom and another bed on another cold evening when she mistook his charcoal-smudged fingers for evidence of a tropical disease. Even though less than a year had passed since then, she felt so much older now, in this moment.

Cedric's brow creased with pain. He reached out his hand, which she took and held. It was cold and pale, like the rest of him, but more dear than anything in the world. "Poor Cedric," she said, and rubbed his knuckles with her thumb.

He tried to smile. "I truly am at death's door, then, if Mary Lennox offers me comfort and pity."

If he hadn't been splayed out and suffering from unimaginable pain, Mary would have thumped him.

"I'm trying to make you feel better, you dimwit," she said.

"Ah, here we are. I'm a dimwit again, apparently on the path to recovery."

That made Mary laugh quite against her better judgment.

"Are you in much pain?" she asked.

"A bit," he said. "Did Sara come in a while back with some tea? I thought I heard her."

Mary had been so absorbed in her own misery that she hadn't heard Sara, though clearly someone had lit the candle.

There—hanging on the hook over the remnants of the fire— was the iron kettle. Mary lifted the lid with the cloth and smelled the heady aroma of willow bark, which would ease his pain. The green smell of the tea brought back memories of the garden, and her shame. But Mary swallowed that feeling.

"She did bring it, the dear. Always ten steps ahead. Let me pour you a cup."

While the tea cooled, she helped Cedric sit up so he could drink it. His hands curled around the steaming cup for warmth. Another failure—she hadn't been tending the fire, and now the room was so cold, Mary could see her breath. She knelt and poked up some embers, putting on a fresh log and blowing on the coals until they glowed red, then redder.

"Ah," said Cedric from behind her. "That's nice. It's warmer in here already."

"Let me get some more wood," Mary said. "I'll send Sara up to you. She's a better nursemaid than I am. At least she won't call you names."

"Don't go," Cedric said. He reached out to her, grasping at air. "Please. I need you."

Need her? That was a first for Mary; more often than not, people implored her to leave.

"You wouldn't rather have Sara?" she asked. "She's so much more patient and gentle than I am—"

"Whatever your bedside manner," he implored. "It's what I need right now."

Mary chose to ignore the yearning turn to his voice. She chose to ignore how it made her feel. She couldn't help thinking back to the hall's theater and their silent waltz on the stage. His eyes were heavy-lidded and deep then too. Just like they were now. But this was not the place, and it was certainly not the time.

"Is the tea helping at all?" she asked, a clumsy attempt at changing the subject. The English always loved to talk about tea, she'd found. They would abandon talks of God, war, and famine to comment on the mellowness of the chamomile.

"A bit," he said. "It—ahh!"

He cried out in pain, dropping the cup and soaking his shirt with tea. His face contorted for several long seconds during which all Mary could do was dab at his shirt and watch him shiver.

She helped him change into something dry and poured him another cup, but his face was pinched and he didn't drink. She put the last log on the fire and was about to go down for more wood, but he said again, "Don't go. Please."

"I'm being reasonable," she said. "It'll be like the North Pole in here when the fire goes out. What kind of a nurse would I be if I let you freeze?"

She sat on the edge of the bed, close enough to smell the sweat on him and feel the tremors that ran through him when the fever or the pain were too much. The pulse at his throat throbbed. He must be in unbearable pain.

"In a minute, then," he said. "Stay and talk to me."

"I don't know what to say."

"Will miracles never cease? Tell me a story."

Mary kept one eye on the fire, watching the last log burn up. She should leave before things became too dire. Send up Sara instead, who had the reason and the caring hand that Cedric needed right now more than anything. But who would she be, truly, if she turned down an opportunity to tell a story?

"Did I ever tell you I once met a genie?"

Cedric's eyes didn't open, but he gave her a small, tight smile. "So I am to be the Shahryar to your Scheherazade. Is, then, this one of the three wishes he granted you? To freeze to death in your friend's sickroom on the moors of northern England? I know you're impulsive, but even I would have thought you'd have chosen more wisely than that."

"Not at all, you ridiculous boy," she said. "He didn't grant me any wishes whatsoever. He told my future. He predicted everything that has happened to us so far. That I would travel far and witness the wonders of the world through a keyhole. He said I would win the friendship of a princess and the love of a prince."

Even though his eyes remained closed, Cedric's brow—dotted with sweat—creased at that.

"Did he?" he asked. His voice was soft, fading like music heard at some great distance. "Sara is the princess, no doubt. And whatever we experienced in that garden is certainly a wonder. And am I . . . ?"

Cedric's eyes opened. The unspoken question hung between them, bound them together with all the destiny of a genie's promise. *Yes*, Mary said without speaking a word. *Yes, I believe you are.*

Cedric sighed and sank down into his blankets. The log was burning low; she would have to go soon, very soon, and get as much wood as she could carry if she were going to keep him alive through the night.

"What was the price he asked?" Cedric looked at her. "Your genie, for this great gift of prophecy?"

"Bravery. He said I must be brave and face my future."

"I suppose the story is true, then," Cedric said. "Because you are the bravest person I know."

"I was already brave," she said. "Or at least, brave enough. But I don't think I'd ask for the same now."

"Oh no?" Cedric's eyes closed again. His words came out slow, labored, every breath a trial. "Pray, what would you ask for now, if this genie were to appear to you again?"

Even though they were alone in the room—possibly alone in the entire mansion, in the entire county—Mary leaned down until she spoke in a whisper made to be heard amidst the clamor of an unforgiving world.

"I'd ask him to take your pain away," she said. "To let you stand and walk, and run, as far as you'd like." She squeezed his hand, tight as she could, tight enough to make him cry out. But he made no sound. "Cedric. Did you hear me? You could present me with every genie in creation, offer me as many prophecies as there are stars in the sky. That would still be my dearest wish in all the world."

"I do not need you to save me," Cedric murmured. "Only to love me."

Mary brushed a hand across his brow and said, "Your father might want you to marry a countess, but no one will ever love you more than I."

26

*D*awn was still half an hour away when Mary stole out of the house and back to the garden, once again taking the heavy iron key from her pocket and opening the gate. The creak of the hinges was loud and felt artificial in such a restful, fantastical place.

The possibility that she loved Cedric the way he loved her had settled over her throughout the night, quietly at first, then like a riot. She'd never considered love or marriage to any man, ever. But Cedric wasn't any man; besides Sara, he was her oldest and dearest friend. Their futures had always seemed full of possibilities: they would go to Paris; have careers on the stage; make their fortunes; and raise scandals. She always imagined—hoped, really—that her life would be as infamous as Ellen Terry's, who at sixteen made her living on the stage until she ran off and married a man thirty years her senior. The kind of life that made the gossip pages of the newspaper. The idea of living with a man like Cedric—quiet and respectable and familiar—had never once occurred to her.

Perhaps it was better it had never occurred to her. What with his betrothal and all, to Lady Five Hundred Acres. It had surprised her, how much that cut. Foolish boy that he was, he never realized that Mary had feelings too.

Yes, it was better this way.

Inside the garden it was already dawn. She went down the path to the bench once more, tipping her face back and letting the sun wash over her.

The woman who'd made this place, Cedric's mother, Lilas, had come from America, the very place Mary had nearly been shipped in exile. Her face in the painting was as joyful as the garden was joyful, but tinged beneath with something else: all this color, but hidden away, secret. Something that had to be looked for, dug after. Not daily joy, but a hidden heart of pure bliss that the outside world couldn't touch. What kind of a woman had made this? What kind of a woman would have found it necessary, to hide her joy in a secret place, so secret that the servants and her own son never knew it was there?

Mary, Mary, quite contrary. How does your garden grow?

The words came to her like a song. Around her, a thick fog began to form, blowing in off the moors, covering the sun, hiding the birds and the bright flowers. Shapes moved in the fog, shapes with arms and legs and heads that congealed into something with sad-eyed, almost-human expressions.

It was as if the shapes in the fog were performing a play just for her. The woman in the painting—Mary recognized her eyes—enduring shame at the hands of her husband's family, especially his disapproving mother, who did everything she could to get Lilas to leave Maythem. The dowager even struck Lady Lilas once. Confined her to her room for an entire week and fed her nothing but bread and water while her husband was away. She swore that she would disinherit her son and their children if Lilas didn't return to her family in America and divorce her husband.

Mary saw the lady weeping on her bed, clutching her belly—the future Lord Fauntleroy, Cedric—while her cruel mother-in-law told her the child in her womb was a half-breed, an abomination. Saw Cedric's father throw his mother from the house, comfort his wife. The earl had loved her, despite his family's cruelty—maybe more, because of it.

As her belly grew, Lilas would talk to the child, whisper secrets to him, sing to him. She'd been happiest in the garden, taking Cedric's father to see this or that plant, and he indulged her. He sent for plants and flowers from every corner of the globe, brought in birds from India and the Americas to make her smile. And smile she did—but only here in the garden, away from her husband's unforgiving family.

On the day of Cedric's birth, when her pains began, she'd been planting a wild white rose right where Mary stood. She couldn't have known that day was her last, that Cedric's birth would end her life—or that her husband, in grief, would shut up the garden, refusing to set foot inside the walls his wife had loved. The plants and animals there left to their own devices. And the much-wanted son, sung to every day in the womb by his mother, doted over by his father, would become a neglected and unloved boy, the one whose very existence had snuffed out his mother's life.

The shades before Mary dissolved, but not before she startled to see Lady Lilas turn and speak to her directly, with just as much life and clarity as that genie almost ten years ago. She spoke two words Mary felt rather than heard: *Don't forget.*

27

*T*he fire in Sara's room had burned down to nothing when she finally woke. Martha hadn't come up yet with more wood, so it must be very early, maybe an hour before dawn. She'd only meant to close her eyes for an hour or two when she'd come back to her room and crawled into bed.

She poked her head inside Cedric's door: he was still asleep, but his fire was burning still, at least. Mary must have stepped out for just a moment. Sara took the kettle from its hook and brought it with her to get more tea from the kitchen. When Cedric woke, he would likely be in pain and needing more willow bark.

The house was silent in the still hours of morning. Outside, a fox cried. Rain pattered the windows, so fat and heavy and cold that Sara was grateful for Cedric's drafty house, that her dear friend had a place where they'd been welcome when they left the seminary. If Sara had still had a home to go to, she wouldn't have hesitated.

It was with some surprise that she came out of the kitchen and bumped into two men in top hats and dripping mustaches, both of whom were leaving a huge puddle on the marble floor of the entry.

"Don't stand there gawping, girl," growled the older of the two men, the one who (to Sara's very trained and careful eye) was the more finely dressed. "Take my coat and bring us towels at once."

"I'm sorry, sir," said Sara. "I am not one of the servants; I am a guest of the young Lord Fauntleroy. I need to fetch this tea to Master Cedric. He's been ill. I'll have Martha or one of the others come to you right away."

This caused both men to look upon her with a harsh and appraising eye. She did not doubt the concept of a brown-skinned lass who was anything but a servant eluded them completely.

"Not a servant?" one of them said. "Who are you then, girl?"

Sara straightened her back and said with all the pride her parents had instilled in her, "I am Sara Crewe. Master Cedric is a school friend who has graciously offered sanctuary in his home whilst we wait out a sickness at school. Who, may I ask, are you?"

The two men exchanged a look. The first man said, "I am Fitzwilliam Errol, the Earl of Dorincourt. You're standing in my hall, girl. You might show me a little respect."

You might show your guests a little respect, Sara thought. Instead, she curtsied.

"Welcome home, sir."

The earl shook off his greatcoat and dropped it in a pile on the floor. The other man took his off and handed it to Sara, who promptly draped it over the seat of a nearby chair.

"Not there!" the earl shouted. "You'll ruin the upholstery."

Sara remembered her education and the proper decorum she should use when addressing the peerage. But just barely. "As I said. I am your son's friend, not a servant, but I'll see who is up to tend you. Excuse me."

She turned to head up the stairs, but the earl's voice stopped her.

"Where is my no-good son? He has a bit to answer for."

"He's been unwell, as I am sure you understand," she said. "You might be able to see him later today, if he feels up to it."

"'If he feels up to it.' No, I daresay he'll see me now." The earl squinted at Sara. "You said you're Sara Crewe? Where is the other one, Mary Lennox?"

That the earl knew her name—hers *and* Mary's—did not bode well.

"I do not know, my lord," she said. "She might be asleep. What do you want with her?"

"This"—nodding toward the other dripping man—"is a Mr. Shepherd, a solicitor in the employ of a Mr. Joseph Lennox of India, recently deceased. Apparently, Mr. Shepherd was supposed to put Mr. Lennox's daughter, Mary, on a steamer to America, but the girl slipped off with Cedric and some servant girl named Sara Crewe."

"I am not a servant." Sara came down hard on each word. "My parents died, and Mistress Minchin insisted that I work at the school for my keep."

"My dear, that is the very definition of a servant," Mr. Shepherd said, speaking for the first time. "Legally speaking."

The earl fixed Sara with a determined eye.

"So, it appears you've been living on my good graces for many days, Miss Crewe," he said. "Would you kindly lead me to my son? I have several things I need to discuss with him."

"LET US OUT! You ridiculous tyrant, let us out, at once!"

"Mary, please. You are wasting time."

Sara watched as her friend beat with both hands against the door of their room, screaming at full volume. The solid oak did not budge, and not a sound could be heard from outside. The windows had been sealed, and they were left without even food to eat or water to drink. When the earl ordered them confined to their rooms, he was clearly not speaking lightly. Martha was only too happy to turn the locks herself, giving Sara a cruel smile as she turned and went out.

The earl announced that Mary was to travel to London with her father's lawyer in all haste, to begin her American exile at last. Sara was to return to the seminary. If Minchin refused to have her, the earl announced, she'd be sent to a workhouse very like the one Mary experienced in Sheffield.

"They can't send you back to that house of horrors," Mary cried as she continued to bang on the door. "I won't stand for it."

"It looks like we don't have much choice," Sara said, "barring Cedric standing up and walking to our rescue."

Mary's voice went silent for a moment. Both of them were remembering the sight of Cedric walking in the garden. How glorious that had been, how short-lived! As had happened many times before, that moment of freedom cost him dearly, and it might be many days—weeks or months, even—before he would get out of bed again at all, much less manage such a feat.

"He'll be all right," Sara said.

"I know *he* will. Little Lord Fauntleroy," Mary said. "I'm more worried about what will happen to you and me."

Sara smiled. She knew perfectly well that Mary was worried about Cedric. Waving off her worry was simply her method for managing it.

"What do you suggest?" Sara asked. "Scurrying up the chimney?"

Mary had the pure, distilled gall to consider that notion. "Not a bad idea," she said. "It should take us all the way to the roof, or at least the second floor."

"Mary, I was not being remotely serious."

"You are typically more helpful than this."

Sara knew that to be true, but she didn't bother debating. In the blink of a fly's eye, their situation had gone from blissful to dreadful. Cedric was still ill, for all they knew, probably locked away in his own heavily upholstered dungeon. Lawyers had been summoned, ultimatums made, plans for their immediate future drawn out and signed. Sara was foolish to think that there was any true escape. Even as her mind turned to Dickon, the warmth of his home and his smile, she knew even that was no better than another of Mary's fantasies.

Mary herself was now up and pacing, something Sara hadn't seen in what felt like a long time. She looked a holy terror, still a tad muddy and dressed in the same gown she'd worn in the garden almost two days ago. Her hair stuck out in all directions, and the whites of her eyes had a pinkish tinge. She reminded Sara of a tiger she saw with her father in a London menagerie, only hours after their arrival in England. A beautiful, powerful creature as old as the earth itself, unsettlingly aware of its own captivity. Terrified at the loss of control.

Suddenly, Mary stopped in her pacing. She looked about the room, just south of frantic. Then she darted like an alarmed cat and began to pull things from the walls. The pagoda tapestries, the paintings, she even tore at the wallpaper.

"Mary, dear heart," Sara said. "What are you doing?"

Hurling books from a built-in shelf, Mary said, "As old as this place is, there has to be a secret passage somewhere. Doors in walls, rooms behind paintings, that sort of thing."

Of course, Sara thought. *She would be the one to suggest a secret passage.*

"Maythem Hall isn't even that old," she said. "Cedric himself told us it was built only a hundred years ago."

"Secret passages are always fashionable, Sara," Mary said. She had now taken hold of the massive rug covering a quarter of the room. "Help me move this; there may be some kind of trapdoor."

Sara did not move. Not that she didn't wish to rise and assist Mary, but she was tired. Tired of waking up in the middle of beautiful dreams.

"Help me!" Mary screamed. Then, taking in Sara's face and posture of dejection, "Please. I can't do this without you."

Mary was never one to give up. It was something Sara at times detested about her closest friend. It was also something she had come to love beyond all measure.

"Of course you can," Sara said as she stood. "But what kind of friend would I be to let you try?"

THE TWO OF them tore the bedroom asunder. They moved with the speed and force of a typhoon, releasing what Sara considered to be a cathartic amount of destruction. It wasn't until they used their unnatural, furious will to move the bed that their destruction reaped results. Built directly into the wall behind the headboard was a door. It was a door made for fairies, only coming to Sara's knee. It was clearly underused and poorly hung.

"Well, that explains the chill in here," Sara said.

Beaming, Mary said, "And if that draft is any indication, I know where this door leads." Mary pulled the great iron ring set into the door, and it came away with a groan and great billowing of dust.

The passageway extended before them like an abyss. Black as

night and cold as frost, littered with the remains of unfortunate mice and the spiders who lived off their folly. But it was a way out. And that was more than enough.

Seemingly to herself, Mary said, "When *will* they learn?"

"Learn what?" Sara asked.

"Why, that we're unstoppable, of course."

She winked, and that lit a hope in Sara like the striking of a match.

28

*M*ary was pleased to discover that her suspicions were once again correct.

After crawling on hands and knees through all manner of unpleasantness—having to ditch both of their petticoats halfway through in order to fit—Sara and Mary emerged in the garden. Within its walls, nothing had changed. They could very well pass the rest of their lives there, undisturbed and unnoticed, while the rest of the world spun on. But that wasn't an option. Not with so much at stake.

"We should split up from this point," Mary said. "I assume Cedric is where we left him. I'll start there. If you can find some horses or a buggy, we could leave before anyone notices."

"I doubt no one will notice me trying to drive a two-horse buggy," Sara said. "I'll find Dickon. He may be able to help."

Even in the midst of their grand escape, Mary managed a proud, even suggestive grin. She hadn't seen much of the two of them together—Sara and this tall Dickon Sowerby—but what she had seen made her bubble over with a wicked happiness. Leave it to Sara to find a suitor in less than a day, and a capable one at that.

"We have yet to discuss that development," Mary said.

"And we won't begin now." Sara picked up her skirts and began to run. Over her shoulder, she cried, "Meet us back here in an hour."

Mary watched Sara's receding back and steeled herself with purpose. This might yet be her greatest performance.

Mary made her way around to the back door and up the servants' staircase, where she knew Cedric's father would be unlikely to encounter her. To the second floor she went, careful to check every corner, listen for every footfall. She most certainly did not want to be confined to her quarters again, though the thought of the key still in her pocket made her feel more brave. That, and the knowledge that Cedric needed her.

On the second-floor landing she heard raised voices: the low boom of Cedric's father berating the boy, Cedric's own dear voice answering, less strong in volume but certainly not in conviction.

"I won't have it, Cedric!" said the earl. His voice was muffled, but Mary could make out bits and pieces: ". . . dare to run away! . . . shame on the family name . . . clear I made a mistake. Those two girls—"

At that Cedric interrupted.

"Those two girls are my dearest friends," he said. "I won't let you say a word against them."

"You certainly cannot stop me from saying what I choose," the earl thundered. "Running away to Paris . . . a life on the stage?"

Cedric said something in a low voice that Mary could barely make out, but what it sounded like was this: "I was thinking of making my own choices for once. Not letting others determine my lot in life."

More words she couldn't make out—*gratitude, duty*—but still Mary nearly burst with pride. Cedric was every bit a match for his father . . . and then some.

The sound of the door opening and the earl's heavy footfall. Mary ducked into an empty bedchamber nearby in time to avoid him, listening to his booted feet stomp off down the hall toward the front stairwell, then down to his study. He'd probably be down there for hours, brooding. Just as Mary had hoped.

The Earl of Dorincourt had his say. Now Mary Lennox would have hers.

She turned the handle on Cedric's door so quietly that he didn't hear her come in. She had time to see him sitting on the edge of the bed in his dressing gown, staring into the last embers of the dying fire. His face was wet with tears and red with anger.

"In the mood for company?" she asked.

His face bloomed with happiness when he saw her. It was enough to make her run to him, as silly as the sentiment felt.

"How did you . . . ? No, never mind. I am sure I don't want to know. Now quickly close the door before my father sees you. Where's Sara?"

"Gone to find help," Mary said as she closed the door behind her. "I am not going to America, you are not staying locked up in this room, and Sara is certainly not going back to the seminary. Not after all that has happened."

She came and sat next to him, not too close but not too far away, either. Instinctively, he reached for the blanket to cover his legs.

"Don't," she said. "I was just thinking, if you'd been completely healthy, your father would have never sent you to the seminary, and our paths might not have crossed."

A bitter smile touched the corners of his mouth but not his eyes. "And if you weren't such a cantankerous midge, your father might never have sent you to the seminary, either. And if Sara hadn't been so—well, herself—her parents might have never considered her for British boarding school. We were all only one choice away from never knowing the others existed."

"To tell you the truth," Mary said, "I would not wish that for the world, Cedric. After everything, I'm glad I met you."

"So, our natures became our fates."

"I don't believe in fate."

"Miss Lennox, you *are* fate. The sooner you come to terms with that, the infinitely easier your life will be, I am sure."

She picked up his hand and held it. It was smooth and soft and a little cool. "And where is your fate taking you next, according to your father?"

"Eton," Cedric said. "He's declared the seminary far too liberal, if you can ever believe that, and insists that I receive a proper Christian education, as befitting a lad of my station."

Mary scoffed.

"It could have been worse," Cedric said. "He could have said he was sending me to Rugby."

She scoffed again, but clutched his hand a bit tighter. He was making a joke out of his bitterness. Either school—with their emphasis on sport, with the older boys torturing the younger ones for fun—was likely to be a torment to Cedric. She shuddered, thinking what he would have to endure. But then she considered Maythem. Its vastness and history. Its dilapidation. Of the Errols Mary had met so far, Cedric seemed to be the only one to care about the ancestral home and who strived to maintain it. What would become of Maythem without Cedric? What would become of Mrs. Medlock and Ben and Dickon? Ten thousand acres, dotted with homes and families who depended on the land. Mary never had the burden of legacy. She was not made for it. Cedric, on the other hand, seemed created solely for that purpose.

"I think you must stay, Cedric." Her own voice sounded far away and solemn, as if speaking from the bottom of a deep well.

Cedric considered her a moment, then began to laugh.

"I know they called you contrary at the seminary, Mary, but this is altogether difficult."

"I am not being contrary, Cedric. I have thought more clearly in the last two days than I have in my entire life. You are the heir of this title, of this place. In two years, you will be done with schools and these ridiculous expectations. A man by all accounts, with all the world before you. The next Earl of Dorincourt. I imagine even Eton might be worth that."

Cedric gave her a startled look. "I'm not going to Eton! I'm going to Paris with you."

Mary sighed. "You most certainly are going to Eton. It's time you did take your place, Lord Fauntleroy. As the Earl of Dorincourt."

Cedric was nearly on his feet. "Absolutely not, I—"

"Don't argue with me! I offer none of this lightly. You know how Dr. Craven has mismanaged everything here. Your father, he . . . he will run from the pain he feels forever. And the people in this place—Dickon, Martha—they depend on you. You can't abandon them."

"But, Mary . . ." His hand curled around her wrist, his thumb rubbing circles into the skin of her arm. "You know what will happen if I stay. I thought that we—"

She stopped him before he could say things that would break her heart.

"I thought that too. But it was wrong of me to try to take you away. We got ourselves into trouble just getting on a train. We forgot to bring food; we got on the wrong train! There's no way we'd scrape together enough money to get passage across the Channel and all the way to Paris."

He said nothing. She knew he was registering the truth of what she'd said, or perhaps it was just the serious manner in which she'd said it. No more wild and reckless plans, only sober judgment. For once.

"Besides, you're no actor." She poked him in the ribs with her elbow. "You remember your lines well enough, but you recite them like an alderman who's late for tea."

A smile, finally. Sweetness and resignation in his face.

"You could have chosen a better man for your troupe, that's true," he said. "Although I shall defend my set design, especially on your terrible budget. But no one could be more devoted than I. You know that, don't you? I know I gave you nothing but criticism, but the Player Princes offered me a chance to be so much more than I had been, and for the first time."

"I know," she said, and it was all she could say.

The things she'd realized about the two of them the night before—that she would gladly give her life for him, and that she couldn't ask him to follow where she now had to go—weighed on her heavily. She loved him dearly. She would always love him. But she could not ask him to give up his inheritance to follow her. He would embrace his role in this life, someday. As she would have to embrace hers.

"You're better off without me in charge anyway," she said. She felt tears building up inside of her, but an immovable pride tamped them down. She had cried once in front of Cedric, and she was resolved to make that time the only time. "Though I'll write you from wherever I land and tell you all about my adventures there."

"Just be sure you point yourself in the right direction this time. West," he said, "toward the setting sun. Which is always where I'll look, when I think of you."

She let herself lay her head on his shoulder just for a moment, just while they were alone. "And I'll always think of you when I face east," she said. "You'll be the dawn to me. Now and always."

29

*L*eaving the garden, and Mary, was a tricky business. When Sara emerged beyond the walls, the early hour meant the fog was still heavy on the moor. She wasn't entirely certain she could find her way, but braced with determination and fearful for Dickon, she squared her shoulders, pointed herself downhill, and went slowly through the haze.

Down a gully she went, past a thin, bare larch. She remembered it from before, this sapling, and kept going. The bottom of the ravine was thick with pebbles but dry after the autumn season, and though the way was not at all smooth, she was sure she was going in the right direction. The ravine widened and grew more rocky until the gully came to a fork, where the path went steeply uphill while the gully continued downhill. She tried to remember the way she'd come before but had no memory of this place. Up, or down?

She turned and looked back the way she'd come, but the fog

was so thick she couldn't see more than a few feet behind her. No larch. There could be wolves on the moor, and she wouldn't know it until they were upon her. Were there wolves in Yorkshire? Probably not, but there were thieves, and worse. She could easily become lost, unable to find her way back to Maythem, to Mary and Cedric. She might stumble and break her ankle, and no one would ever find her.

As if the place had read her thoughts, she heard footfalls in the gloom, a shuffling of rock and vegetation, a swift intake of breath—and there was Dickon, with a bundle of twigs tied to his back and a startled look on his face.

"Sara!" he exclaimed. "Are you mad? What're you doing all the way out here on your own?"

She nearly wanted to fling herself on him in relief.

"Looking for you," she said. "I was starting to think I was lost."

"Another step in that direction and you might've been," he said. "That there leads down to the River Esk, which runs through some awful lonely country. But where on earth have you been? Martha said something about you leaving. Are you . . . are you going home, to the Philippines?"

That was almost enough to break Sara's resolve.

"No," she said. "No. I don't know if I shall ever see my country again. But the earl plans to return me to Manchester."

Dickon's eyes went wide, almost fearful, and the muscles in his arms seemed to clench and unclench rhythmically. It was an expression of physical shock.

"You cannot," he said. It was a firm statement, laden with purpose and conviction beyond his years.

"Yes, I know," Sara said. "Mary and I need your help, to leave. Do you have access to Maythem's stables? Its horses?"

"Even if I did," Dickon said. "Stealing from the earl would be—"

"A death sentence," Sara finished. Of course. Even as she traipsed through the moors, she never once stopped to consider what the ramifications of their actions would be, especially for Dickon. They wouldn't make it past the hunting lodge before a battalion of constables were upon them. Nothing would change for Mary and Sara. Dickon would carry the brunt of the consequences. And then there was his family.

Suddenly, there was no containing it, any of it. A year's worth of frustration and dashed dreams struck Sara in the chest with all of the stinging power of the moor's gales. She turned her back to Dickon and, for the first time ever, surrendered her control. How far had it gotten her, anyway? Did control and decorum save her parents? Did it stave off Minchin's bigotry? Did it paint her as anything other than rubbish to be tossed aside in the eyes of the earl? No, of course it didn't. She suspected that nothing would.

Sara opened her mouth and screamed. The wind took her voice, lifted it, and carried it far away. She hoped it resonated over the whole of the British Isles, the whole of Europe. She prayed that they heard her even in the Philippines, and that they knew she remembered them.

The need to breathe was the only thing that stopped her

screams. She inhaled long, deep gulps of wild air. It really was beautiful, this place. Sara imagined that the world looked quite similar in the early days, before man discovered fire and greed.

"What am I going to do?" she spoke to the endless skies.

"Marry me."

It took Sara a moment to realize that those words came not from the spirits of air and water, but from Dickon.

She turned to look at him, and his essence portrayed nothing but resolution. He made a frivolous offer, but nothing about him in that moment seemed remotely superficial.

"What?"

"I said, marry me, Miss Crewe."

If Mary was present, she would have laughed. Sara felt like laughing herself, but something told her that this was not the time.

"You don't mean that," she said.

"I'm being quite sincere, Miss Sara. Never mind that I care for you, because I do. Most ardently. If we were allowed another month, another week, I would offer myself to you still. It would be more proper. Appropriate, what a lady of your standing would deserve. I would even have a ring by then, hopefully."

Sara could barely even comprehend what he was saying. Offer himself to her? A ring? She took Mary for the insane one earlier, but perhaps she'd been mistaken.

"We cannot be married, Dickon," she said. "We are too young. We barely know each other."

"My cousin married at sixteen," Dickon said with great confidence. "So the matter of our age is no matter at all, not out here. And in regards to our familiarity . . . I'll not say that we are friends. Even passing acquaintances. And yet, I feel I have known you forever. I look at you, and I see my past, present, and future. How could I otherwise?"

If Sara hadn't been so confused, she would have swooned. He spoke with such earnestness, such truth. One may go their entire life pining for a person to pour out their soul at one's feet. But when that moment actually comes, it is always a surprise.

"Why?" Sara asked. Possibly not the most romantic response to what he'd said, but it was the appropriate one in her eyes. "You say you care for me. I would be speaking falsely if I said I did not also, by some stroke of destiny, care for you too. But why offer to divert your entire life and ask for my hand?"

Dickon smiled, and it was a radiant, brilliant smile.

"Marry me, and you are no longer Sara Crewe. You are Sara Sowerby. My claim to you as your husband would outweigh any headmistress's claim. So are the ways of things in this land."

"Well, that's frightfully old-fashioned," Sara said. "Could it possibly work?"

Dickon's long legs brought him to her in three quick strides. He smelled of the ancient earth, and dew water clung to his red hair. Sara's hand itched to reach up and run her fingers through it, but she withheld.

"I'll defend you, no matter what," Dickon said. "As a friend. As a husband. You will never return to that awful place again. Not whilst I live and breathe."

"But you have a whole life before you!" Sara implored. "A

family, a trade. There will be other girls whom you will fancy, surely. There always are."

"None like you."

In an act of unquestionable scandal that would set old matrons throughout the empire to fainting, Dickon took both of Sara's hands in his own and kissed them. Sara gasped, whether from the act itself or what it represented, she could not say.

"Marry me today or marry me thirty years from now, Sara Crewe," he said, looking directly into her eyes, leaving no room for misinterpretation. "I am yours if you'll have me, either way."

Sara felt the walls of her throat closing with unspent emotion. Her eyes burned with unshed tears. This was absurd! It was foolish and desperate and impulsive, all things she was not prone to. And yet, standing in the shelter of Dickon's embrace now—listening to him offer up his life to preserve her own—she knew that there was no other option. Nothing that felt this right or this absolute. Mary would tell her to be brave, and so she would be.

"Yes," she said. "Yes, I'll marry you."

30

*W*hen she left Cedric, Mary decided that before she departed from England for good, she would set right at least *one* injustice. She marched down to the earl's study and rapped firmly on the door.

"Sir," she said. "It's Mary Lennox. May I have a moment of your time?"

The earl came to the door with a scowl. "I see I shall have to find a more secure location for you, Miss Lennox," he said. "How did you break out of your room?"

"Never mind that. I have no intention of running away or fighting my passage to America any longer."

At this the earl seemed truly surprised. "Oh? Whatever changed your mind?"

"Maythem did."

"Pardon? I don't think I understand."

"Come with me and I shall explain." When he didn't move, she said, "If you *please*, sir. It will take just a moment."

Grumbling about the impertinence of English girls raised in the far-flung territories of Her Majesty's empire, the Earl of Dorincourt followed Mary Lennox out the front door and down the path to the secret garden. Taking the large iron key from her pocket, she turned the lock and opened the gate, standing back to let the earl go inside first.

Inside was soft light and warmth, a blissful midsummer evening of long sunlight. Here and there bees flitted, covering themselves with the flowers' yellow dust and buzzing drunkenly back to their hives. In the middle of the garden the great white rose that Mary had seen in her vision—the one Lady Lilas had planted the day of Cedric's birth—bloomed extravagantly, so heavy with blossoms that the climbing vines sagged with the weight.

"What is this?" asked the earl. "Some kind of trickery? A hypnotist's fancy?"

"This is your wife's garden," Mary said. "I see you don't recognize it."

"No, Lilas had gardens. Many of them, all over this estate. But this . . . I do not think I've ever seen this place. And this has been here all along?"

"Since the beginning," Mary said. "It was her sanctuary."

The earl wheeled on her. "And how would you know that?"

Mary could very easily have told him the truth. That the spirit of his wife walked these grounds without peace, crying out for someone to hear her, to acknowledge all she was and all she could have been. But perhaps that would be too impertinent, even for Mary.

So instead, she said, "Is it not obvious to you? I did not even know Lady Lilas, and yet I can see her in every bud and stem."

The earl looked stricken, his face changing from anger to skepticism and finally to grief. He was a young man by all accounts. Barely forty. And yet, age clung to him like rust. When he moved forward to take a rose from its branch, his steps seemed pained and weighed down.

He held the bloom to his nose and inhaled. His eyelids fluttered closed, and his sigh was one of absolute contentment.

"They're real," he said. "*Rosa laevigata.*"

Mary could not help herself when she scoffed and rolled her eyes.

"Of course they're real," she said. "Just as Lady Lilas was."

"These were her favorites," he said. "She had grown them easily in America, but here she would spend hours digging in the soil, trying to help them survive this frigid place. I had them shipped in every week, expedited so as to preserve the bloom. But no matter how much I paid or whom I invoked, they always arrived dead. Even on the day of her funeral. I put them in water, tended them as she taught me, but they would never. I just couldn't—"

A sob rose up and out of the earl. At once, he was no longer the arrogant, imperious Earl of Dorincourt, but a man who'd lost a much-beloved wife. Who looked very lost in the world without her.

Mary put a hand on his arm, a gesture that she was sure not a soul had made toward him in years.

"It must have been terrible to lose her. And I'm sure Cedric reminds you of her death. But it isn't his fault. He lost a mother that day. He has never known the world with her in it."

A darkness overtook the earl's face once more. She had over-stepped—or so he must have thought. But she would not back down from this fight. Not when she was giving up Cedric forever.

"He's never known a day of your love and kindness," she said. "Please. It would mean so much to him to just know that it isn't all in vain."

The earl removed the offending hand from his arm. Even the magic of the garden could not turn his heart in an instant.

"Don't presume you know anything about me," he said. "You've been under my roof less than a week, girl. What you know of my family, of our history, amounts to less than that."

"I know your son," she said, not backing down. "I know how unhappy he is, enough that he was willing to follow my foolish scheme to go to Paris rather than staying at the seminary or even coming home. Rather than taking up the duty he was clearly born to embrace. It was desperation that drove him here."

The earl raised his chin. "I have given my son everything he needs to take his place in the world. Money, prospects, a world-class education—"

"Not everything," Mary interrupted. "Not yourself. Lilas gave up everything to be with you and make her home here. To have a family with you. You dishonor her sacrifice by blaming your son for her death when all she wanted was for you to appreciate something for once in your life."

"Why, you high-handed little—"

"Father."

They turned to see Cedric standing on the path in nothing but his nightgown. His chair was back at the entrance, by Sara and Dickon, who stood close together by the gate. Mary had not known they had an audience. Indeed, it seemed as if, during their exchange, she and the earl stood alone in the world.

Even though their argument was enough to bring down thunder, it was Cedric, standing strong in the middle of the garden, who commanded everyone's attention. How tall he was, how noble-looking as he took another step, then another, getting stronger with each one.

"Cedric," the earl said as he watched what he surely took to be impossible becoming real before his eyes. "Son, look at you."

"Yes," Cedric said. "Look at me. Really look at me, Father. Is this—all this—what it takes for you to see me?"

And so, the earl did look. He looked his son in the eyes, unflinching. He blinked, as if clearing a fog from his vision. He observed his son as if he was something once lost but found again.

"You look so much like her," he said. "More so than even her own daughters. Your hair. Your eyes. Both so intelligent. So much wiser than me."

"I would like to know her," Cedric said. "I would like to hear what you remember about her."

"She was so patient, so good. She made me a good man." He

smiled, and it brought to Mary's mind the image of sunlight breaking through stone. "She—she would have loved to see this place. To see you stand and walk. I always knew you could do it if you wanted to, that if you tried you could make it happen. I knew it was all in your hea—"

"It's not in my head, Father," Cedric said. "You do not know the strain I am under, the pain. I do not have the strength of my legs, but that doesn't make me any less of a man, or any less worthy a son. Whatever hopes you and my mother had for me, they can still be real. We can make them real. Together."

Cedric extended his hand to his father, shaking with the effort, and for a moment, it floated suspended there. Mary watched Cedric closely, waiting for a sign that he would fall. But that sign never came. The earl exhaled, and a lifetime of loss seemed to flow out of him. He took Cedric's hand in his own and gave it a firm, respectful shake.

"I've wronged you, my son," he said. "You may never believe me, but I am ashamed of myself. For the pain I've caused you in your mother's name. I have always seen your brilliance, Cedric. Your empathy. Your compassion. You are more the Earl of Dorincourt than I shall ever be. Whatever I can do to help you walk into your destiny, I shall do. Perhaps I shall earn your respect, along the way. I could never hope to earn your love—"

"You have it," Cedric said. "You always have."

Mary watched them, watched them all, with her cat eyes. She saw the way Dickon reached for Sara's hand, slowly so as not to be noticed. She saw the way the earl dipped his shoulder to take up his son's weight and ease his burden. She saw the way sunlight bursting through a gray sky turned the white roses to orange, then to pink. She saw the wonders of the world, not in the beauty of the garden, or the magic that dwelt there. But in her friends. And their iridescent happiness.

31

The earl, in a gesture meant perhaps to make up for having imprisoned them both in their rooms, ordered a set of new clothes made for Sara, as a wedding gift, and a new traveling dress for Mary's trip to America.

"New clothes make every new adventure feel like a fresh start," he said.

He wasn't wrong, but as Sara Crewe stood and let the dressmaker pin her hem, she felt the weight of the decision she'd made to marry Dickon and stay in England settle around her like wet cloth. The sacrifice he was making. That she was making. To marry Dickon may mean avoiding a life of hardship under Minchin. But it also meant that she may never see her home again.

She'd always assumed she'd go back one day. When she'd boarded the ship in Manila with her father and waved goodbye to her mother on the shore, watching the blue-green hills fade into the horizon, it all felt so temporary. A journey with a clear beginning and a clear end. She expected to be with them again within the year, perhaps for Christmas or her grandmother's ninetieth birthday. After an adventure in a foreign land, she'd come home to the warmth and light, the smells of the sea, the taste of coconut and mango, to fields of delicate sampaguita flowers that had covered their lawn when she was a child. She wondered when those images would start to fade, replaced with fields of heather and Mrs. Sowerby's wood smoke.

Sara flinched when she felt a pin land hard on her ankle.

"Do stay still, miss," the dressmaker said dryly, without a hint of remorse for causing her pain. Apparently, no one had told her that Sara wasn't some county girl with flowers in her hair. For the first ten minutes of the fitting, the dressmaker made a considerable effort not to touch her skin directly, lest something rub off.

It was a pretty dress, though. Sara observed her reflection and found that the sunflower yellow was flattering against her skin tone. The design of the corset accentuated her height. Her mother would like the dress. She would like Dickon too. Her father would adore him, adore his self-reliance.

She could make a life with Dickon, if she tried. He was honorable and true, and he loved her. That was not nothing, as Sara had seen every day of her life. Her parents had loved each other, and her grandparents before them, even though that marriage was forced upon them by those who thought themselves masters. To enter into a love marriage, rather than something arranged for money or position—that was something she hoped for, but didn't expect. Her father had plans for more. Plans that would keep her safe, if not happy.

Her father. Her father had made a terrible mistake sending her to the seminary, but his decision meant that she had not died in the volcano eruption, with the rest of her family. She might be the last, the very last, of her line. She owed it to them, all of them, to live and to live well. To be their story, the one they could no longer tell themselves.

"I am Sara Crewe," she whispered to her reflection, seeing her mother's eyes reflected in her own. Her grandmother's eyes, her great-grandmother's eyes. "I am the daughter of Richard Crewe of Munster, Ireland, and Munich, Bavaria, and Matea Reyes, of Manila and Pampango, the Philippines. This I do not for myself, but for those who came and those yet to come."

"What's that, miss?" asked the dressmaker.

Sara suddenly remembered herself. Remembered where was.

"Nothing," she said. "Just saying a prayer."

IN THE MIDDLE of the afternoon on the girls' last day, just as the sun was lowering itself into the horizon for its nightly rest, a knock came at the door of Maythem Hall.

The residents and guests—the earl, Mr. Shepherd, Cedric, Mary, Sara, Mrs. Medlock, Martha, and Dickon—gave one another questioning looks, for surely no one was expected today. And the arrival of strangers usually had the effect of turning everything upside down.

Mrs. Medlock answered the door to find a lady on the

doorstep, a fine lady in a very fine carriage, dressed all in silks and shivering in the raw English weather. "Excuse me," said the lady to Mrs. Medlock, "is this Maythem Hall? The seat of the Earl of Dorincourt?"

"It is, madam," said Mrs. Medlock, making the deepest of curtsies. "May I tell the earl who has come?"

"My name is Mrs. Matea Crewe. I was sent here by Mistress Minchin of the Select Seminary for Young Ladies and Gentlemen to find my daughter, Sara. She seemed quite put out, but said if I insisted on finding Sara, this would be the only place she could think to look."

Upstairs, Sara, who had been watching Mary pack her trunks to leave for America in the morning, heard a voice in the hall that she thought she'd never hear again. She was up and on her feet, running down the stairs before she could remember herself.

She stopped on the landing and looked. There stood her mother in cream silk, paler than Sara remembered and definitely more wet, but unmistakably Matea Crewe, smiling. She was wearing an elegant Maria Clara dress, the very same one that Sara had last seen her wearing on the dock in the Philippines. "It's you!" Sara breathed, and threw herself at her mother.

THE STORY WENT like this: The volcano erupted, but Matea had been traveling out of the province when it did. She returned to bury her husband, her mother, and her cousins. But she survived, as had the family estate in Batangas and their many holdings in Nueva Ecija. The onion farms were intact, even though they had lost the sugar plantation.

On hearing the news—sitting in the drawing room at Maythem with the earl, Cedric, and Mary—Sara did not faint or cry out or even weep with joy. She sat ramrod-straight with her hands folded in her lap, looking at her mother but not entirely seeing her, consumed with anger.

The elation she felt at seeing her mother was replaced by a hideous regret. Not only was Sara no longer an orphan, but she was also wealthier than before. The status and wealth that had been stripped from her at her parents' supposed death was restored, but at what cost? Why, for them, for their family, was there always a cost?

"Sara," said Matea Crewe. Her voice, after so long, felt like salve on Sara's wounded heart. "*Ija*, I've come to take you home."

32

*I*t was early, not yet light, when Mary went through the hidden door behind the bed, down the hidden staircase, and outside. The morning was cold but clear; the blue light of false dawn was starting to rise when she returned to the deep old well she'd found that first night in the manor.

She leaned over and looked down into the depths. This time the dark water did not show her the sad faces of the past. The visions were strange but exhilarating: a long vista of blue mountains covered with trees, majestic rivers crashing over rocks or spinning down from great heights. Adventures far beyond anything she'd experienced thus far.

Then she saw herself, or what she supposed might be herself one day: a lady with messy curls and an impatient expression with a pen and paper in her hand, writing. Then a ship tossed in a wild and stormy sea, a theater with a gilded ceiling and a beautiful lady onstage, her face obscured in the brightness of the stage lights.

Then, strangely, Cedric, much older and wearing a fine dinner suit, laughing. He looked happy. He would be happy, and that was all she could ask for.

She was leaving Maythem, leaving Cedric and England, but at least she knew he would be all right without her. He would take his place on the estate and learn to be an earl, now with his father's love and blessing.

Never again would Lady Lilas's memory be locked away. The genie had asked Mary to be brave, and so she would be. She took the iron key and dropped it into the well.

SARA PACKED FOR her return to the Philippines with her mother. Hearing Mary slip out through the hidden passage, Sara decided to follow her outside and into the garden one last time.

When Mary turned and went past the garden, Sara turned into it and opened the iron gate. The grass was no longer luscious and green, but the expected brown for that time of year, the vines and flowers dried up, the birds quiet. There was no sign of peacocks in the trees, no bees lazily buzzing from blossom to blossom. They'd vanished as if they'd never been. Even the great white rosebush in the middle of the garden lay dormant, only the carpet of brown petals surrounding it giving evidence that it had been, until this morning, so luxuriously in bloom.

Sara was reminded of a quote: "I and my fellows / Are ministers of fate." And so they were. Each had made their choice.

Now the future was laid out before them, not like a magic carpet to sweep them away to lands unknown, but to their own sober futures. Mary to her uncle in America, still soaked in the horror of a bloody and hideous war. Sara to her family and home in the Philippines, many thousands of miles away. Only Cedric would stay in place—not to Eton, not even to the seminary. But home with his father and his duty, which he must now learn to take up.

Sara crumbled the brown rose petals in her fist. Now that Cedric's place in the family was restored, Lady Lilas's garden had gone to its rest at last.

She was turning to go when she found Dickon still kneeling on the ground, tending to everything as if it were still the fairyland Mary had first discovered.

He looked up at the sound of her footfalls.

"Sara!" He hurried toward her only to stop short at the sight of her clothes, the dress her mother brought her of fine gray silk and wool, a vibrant pañuelo about her shoulders.

"You look lovelier than I've ever seen you," he said. He started to reach for her, then looked at his dirt-covered hands and thought better of it.

The clothes were like a shield, a wall separating her from Dickon the way the walls of the garden kept out the outside world. They'd had a future only so long as they were equal, Sara as poor and needful as Dickon. Now that she was a lady again, he was formal, even shy. How much had changed in the few short hours since she'd seen him last.

"It's true, then," he said, eyes lowered. "Your mother has come for you."

"She has," Sara said. "With news of my family, and my . . . my father's death."

Dickon reached out for her again, and she did not stop him. The dirt stained the silk, leaving a clear imprint. "I'm so sorry," he said. "I mean, I was already sorry, of course, but to get such good news followed by such bad—"

"It's all right. This news for all of its disappointment is better than anything I could have imagined. Dickon. This doesn't mean . . . This doesn't change anything."

"Don't, Miss Crewe."

That took Sara aback. She thought they were beyond this, beyond the pretending.

"It's *miss* now?" she asked. Chuckling, she said, "I thought that *dearest* would be more appropriate. Or *beloved* or *darling*—"

"You do not need me anymore, Miss Sara. You don't need the marriage. You are saved, truly saved, and I could not be more happy for you."

He certainly did not sound thrilled. He sounded like a creek running dry.

"Don't need you? Dickon, I would not have made it to this point without you. Without what you were willing to give up for me."

"You speak as if proposing to you was a sacrifice. I would do it again, in an instant, and for no reason other than the fact that you're—" Dickon stopped himself, and it seemed to require all his effort to continue. "But this is as it should have been all along. I knew you were too fine a lady for the likes of me. Now with you leaving—"

"Dickon! I wasn't planning to leave you behind."

This seemed to surprise him most of all. He took several steps back and bumped against the base of a tree with enough force to make it shudder.

"Come with you to the Philippines?" He breathed the words as if she'd suggested a trip to the moon. "Oh no. I couldn't possibly."

She came toward him again, closing the distance between them. There was no reason why they couldn't still be together. As a lady, Sara could choose her own fate. Now Dickon could choose his as well, if he came with her.

"You showed me the moors, and I said it reminded me of the sea," she said. "Let me show you my world now. It can still be the two of us, Dickon. My mother will buy passage for us both. You would never want for anything again. And perhaps we could maintain our engagement. Until the day we know each other as well as we know ourselves."

For a moment, she thought for certain he would say yes. How glorious it would be, how much he might be able to do and discover there.

Then some determination crossed his face and settled there like a stone.

"Afraid I can't do that, Sara," he said.

Sara did not want to admit that her heart was broken. But that didn't make the pain of it shattering any less.

"Why not?" she asked, terrified of the answer. "Do you not care for me anymore?"

Dickon seized her with such pressure that it took Sara's breath away. It was not violent, not in the least. It was intense and honest and overwhelming.

"I'll care for you until the day I die," he said. "I know that now, as sure as I know every creek and valley of these hills. But just as your place has always been in the Philippines, my place is here. You have a family and an estate of your own. I would— I would feel like I was taking advantage."

"You were willing to rescue me," Sara said. "Now let me rescue you."

Dickon smiled and said, "You cannot be rescued from where you belong, Sara. I have my own battles to fight, and they aren't across the sea. My family needs me. They need an opportunity to do better than those that came before."

She clutched his hands tightly. "But then we shall never see each other again," she said. "How can I live with that?"

"The same way I can," he said. "Whenever I look upon the moors, I'll think of the sea and remember you." He picked up her hand and kissed it once, lightly. "What will you look at to remember me? A pile of dirt, maybe."

"Not at all," she said. For so long she'd wanted to go home.

Now that the moment had come, she found it impossible to leave. Though leave she would.

She pressed her palm to his cheek and felt him lean into her touch. "The voice of the birds," she said. "When they wake me in the morning and bid good evening to me at night, I shall think of you, Dickon. Now and always."

33

*N*ow I know what they mean by London fog," said Sara, standing next to Mary on the deck of the steamer set for the Philippines by way of New York. The ship—anchored just east of London Bridge and its five heavy stone arches—juddered as the engines started up, steam pouring out the smokestacks and into the leaden-gray sky curling around the dome of St. Paul's, the Tower of London. The hour struck noon, which they could tell by the tolling of Big Ben, but the clock tower itself was hidden in the gloom. It was hard for Mary to comprehend that this land of choking smog and perpetually gray skies existed in the same land as the clean vastness of the Errol estate.

Mary held a handkerchief to her face in order to breathe.

"London fog isn't true fog at all, but coal smoke," she said, and coughed to prove her point. That—combined with the smell of river water, the steam from the ship, and a passing fishing vessel laden with eels—made for a pungent and dreary fare-thee-well to England.

There was no one at the dock to see them off. Cedric and Dickon had stayed behind in Yorkshire, coming only as far as the train station to wish them well. It had been a hard goodbye, knowing that they were unlikely ever to meet again. There would be another goodbye in New York, when Mary disembarked with Mr. Shepherd for the train to someplace called Knoxville, Tennessee, and Sara and her mother continued south to circle Cape Horn, then the long crossing of the Pacific via Hawaii to the Philippines. One more goodbye among many.

The steamer passed banksides deep in mud, mussels crusted onto wooden pilings, factories belching coal smoke into the air. But gradually the countryside began to change, the air growing fresher, the banksides greener. Finally, a breath of sea air blew over them—salt and tang, freshness, cold. They had reached the mouth of the Thames. Soon they'd pass through the English Channel and head out to sea.

"I had an idea for a story," Mary said as they passed the white cliffs at Margate. "I could use your help on it."

"You know I'm no writer, Mary," Sara said.

"Perhaps not. But you're a character in the story, so I should like your help nevertheless."

"A character?" Sara asked. "A dull one, I imagine. Please, I beg of you, not a princess."

"Not at all, you goose," Mary said. "Even though, as much

you disdain it, the comparison is apt. It's a true story, actually. I want to begin with my journey from India to Manchester, to Maythem Hall, to now, and all I have learned along the way."

Sara hugged her thick cape around her, the tails of her headdress waving in the sharp wind.

"A thrilling tale, then," she said. "The kind no reader will believe is true at all."

"I'd rather they not believe it," Mary said. "Only learn from it. As I have. What do you think of this line: *'I stand in the clothes my father gave me, orphaned, but not alone. An adventure as wide as the sea stretches before me, but my heart feels as warm and safe as a garden. I feel as if the whole world might indeed be as warm and safe as a garden.'*"

Sara could have taken wing and floated away with pride. For as long as she had known Mary, she seemed intent to be anywhere but where she was, anyone other than who she was. Now listening to her embrace everything she had become and may yet be, Sara understood that Mary's bravery wasn't directed outward toward Hamlet's slings and arrows. It was directed inward at the doubt and loneliness that seized her own heart. A loneliness that she rejected and rose against every day.

"The world *is* as warm and safe as a garden, dear Mary," Sara said. "Not for all. But for some. And for me. Due in part to the love and bravery of friends like you."

Epilogue

1879: Revere House, Boston

$\mathcal{S}$ara dressed quickly for afternoon tea, so eager to see her friend after many long years that she almost forgot her shoes. Only her maid, Alice, was able to stop her long enough to remind her to put on her slippers, tut-tutting "that a lady such as yourself would think to go barefoot!"

Normally Sara was not so impatient with Alice, but today was a special case: she had traveled to Boston from New York specifically for this meeting, unable to pass up an opportunity to see the former Mary Lennox in the flesh after so many long years of nothing but letters. Huffing somewhat at her maid, Sara stuffed both feet into her shoes and flew out the door. She didn't want to miss a minute of Mary's time.

In the drawing room, Mary and her friend were already deep in chatter, their voices low in the high-ceilinged space. Still, Sara could make out the unladylike cackle that had always accompanied

Mary's tales, the rising tide of her whisper doing little to hide that she was asking a question just this side of indecent. "And it was all she could do to hide the evidence!" Mary said in her not-whisper just as Sara came up to the two women.

"Still weaving tales, I see?" Sara said. Mary's head whipped around to stare up at her old friend, and although the years had turned her from a sallow young girl into a thriving, mature young woman, that childish excitement still showed in her eyes.

Mary was up and throwing herself into Sara's arms before either of them could stop themselves.

"Sara Crewe!" she exclaimed. "I was starting to think you were *never* coming down."

Sara laughed and blushed, standing back a little to look at her friend. Fourteen years had done little to tame her wild locks, her energy and expressions, but her clothes were the finest Sara had seen all season, even among the New York set that treated fashion as a religion. However, just one cuff was a little torn, no doubt from one of Mary's wild exertions.

"My goodness, it is good to see you, Mary," Sara said, embracing her friend. Then she remembered herself, stepped back, and dropped into a curtsy. "I do beg your pardon. I should say, Lady Fauntleroy, Countess of Dorincourt."

Mary all but dragged Sara to her feet.

"Oh, pish, don't go on like that, Sara," she said. "I'm still the same troublemaker I always was. Just ask the unfortunate fellow I married."

Sara looked around but didn't spy the other member of their

once-eternal trio. "Where is dear Cedric?" she asked. "Has he grown too proud to pass an afternoon in the company of women?"

"Not in the least," Mary said. "He's out on business. Insisted on getting as much done as possible before we embark on our trip to India. He'll be back to join us for dinner. He can't wait to see you either."

The two sat beaming at each other until they remembered they weren't alone. A woman of nearly exactly their age—and much like Mary in wildness of appearance, her hair also coming half undone from its knot—looked from one to the other and said, "Lady Fauntleroy, aren't you going to introduce me to your beautiful friend?"

"Goodness, what a nincompoop I am. Of course. Sara Crewe, this is Jo March, the authoress. Jo, my friend Sara is an actress on the London stage."

"Of course she is," said Jo, offering Sara her hand to shake. "The whole world knows about your Juliet, Miss Crewe. A revolutionary performance, if I do say so myself. What brings you to Boston?"

"Please, call me Sara. Only the chance to see Mary and Cedric, of course. I know your books well, Miss March. Or should I say Mrs. Lawrence?"

"My dear Teddy still calls me Jo March, especially when he's cross with me. Which is often." She gave Sara's hand a gentle squeeze and turned to Mary. "Now, Mary won't let me even peek at her highly anticipated memoirs—"

"Only a fool would unleash your biting wit on an early draft,

Jo. I swear, she's worse than my editor, and she has a penchant for making cuts with shears," Mary said.

"But," Jo continued, "from what I heard, you two and Cedric had quite the collective upbringing. Did you all run away and join the circus when you were young?"

"Not quite," Mary said. "We were heading to Paris, as I remember, only we never made it farther than Sheffield."

"And then North York Moors," said Sara.

"How could I forget!" said Mary, beaming.

"You started those memoirs years ago," Sara said. "You must have written a thousand articles since then, and still the tome is unfinished?"

"Oh, it's been through several drafts. I'm still not happy with it, though. Never will be, I imagine. Jo insists on helping me, and I fully intended to devote my summer to it, but I have the *Saturday Evening Post* asking for something new."

Sara had to smile. That Mary Lennox had her choice of publications would have been a scandal in England, where she was known only as Lady Fauntleroy, wife of the Earl of Dorincourt. But their business and their travels rarely brought them to England these days. A passionate writer and successful entrepreneur, Mary was known throughout the States for her plays and dramas. She'd launched into international fame when she submitted an article to the *New York Herald* about the mistreatment of Native American children at an assimilation boarding school in Tennessee. Her old friend Lady Lumley had read the article and instantly recognized

Mary's name. The article was shared throughout the social circles of the West, even finding the hands of the queen, and making Mary Lennox a household name.

"What's this about a trip to India?" Sara asked. "Going to visit old friends?"

"Goodness, no," Mary said, screwing up her face. "You know me better than that, Sara. No, your old friend Ram Dass has asked me to write about the abuses by the British in that corner of the empire. He saw my article about St. Anthony's and found many similarities with some of the schools in India. You of all people know I couldn't refuse him. You were right, about his intensity. It's an inspiration and also a terror."

"What about you, Miss Crewe?" asked Miss March. "Mary tells me that you are preparing for a new rendition of *Antony and Cleopatra.*"

"Amongst other things," Sara said. "My heart is now in a school for young girls in Manila. I know all too intimately what it means to be a gifted brown girl in an abrasive world, and I wish to offer those like me a safe place to grow and learn. It is the least I can do."

"Sara won't tell you this, Jo, but she's one of the richest women in the Philippines," Mary said, whispering loudly. "This is already, what, the fourth such school?"

"The fifth," Sara said. "And as I said, it's the least I can do. If you know of any teachers looking for work, Miss March, I would be very much obliged."

"I'm swimming in teachers!" said Jo. "I can have you half a dozen by the end of today."

"Would they be willing to move to Manila?"

"Why not?" said Jo with a twinkle in her voice. "But first, I want to hear about this Paris adventure. Start at the beginning and leave nothing out!"

It was really no wonder Mary and Jo were friends. They had the same ceaseless exuberance.

"It all began when this very elegant young lady arrived at the school where my father had dumped me," Mary began. "A dreadful place called the Select Seminary for Young Ladies and Gentlemen in Manchester. One day, we hear word that a princess has arrived with half a dozen trunks and a French maid . . ."

Sara smiled, hearing Mary call her *princess* once more. But it also made her want to weep. For all of their happy endings, one still hung loose, battered by the air like a thread on a gown. Dickon and Sara had stayed in communication for years—he even made it all the way to London to see her perform—until letters from him ceased. She later discovered that he'd joined the army to help support his family and been deployed to a remote part of Africa. When he refused an order to shoot into a crowd of villagers, he was court-martialed and executed. Sara made the journey to Yorkshire for his funeral and stayed until his mother had the strength to stand again.

Despite many offers, Sara Crewe never married. To the world, she was a young savant bound to her craft. But in her heart, she was still bound to Dickon's promise. If she couldn't have him, she would have no one at all.

For an hour Mary regaled Jo March with tales of their adventures, including the poorhouse, the garden, Sara's reunion with her mother. Jo March exclaimed over all of it, begging Mary to finally conclude her memoirs so audiences around the world could experience it.

"Posh, and what would they all say?" Mary asked. "That the respectable and unsinkable Mary Lennox has gone from writing of injustices and foul play to fantasies? People will think I've gone mad."

"They think that anyway," said Sara, sipping her tea and giving Mary a wicked look. "But you haven't even told Miss March the best part."

"What's that?" asked Jo.

"How Mary and Cedric were reunited."

"Do tell!"

This time it was Sara's turn to tell the tale: how only five years ago, Cedric had appeared in Knoxville, strong enough to walk upright with the help of a cane, and living well off the fruits of the revived Maythem estates. He'd grown even taller and more handsome, and arrived in Knoxville with the intention of liberating Mary from a terrible situation. Possibly even slaying a dragon or two. When he came to the dry-goods store of a certain Jonathan Lennox, however, he discovered that Mary was in fact the owner of the establishment, which had grown from a small storefront to a major operation with locations throughout the state. When he asked to see her after so many years and so much unspoken anticipation, he was told to wait until "the boss" was ready for him.

When she finally appeared, dressed in the region's best finery and brimming with knowledge and capability, she said to Cedric, "If you have come to save me, you are truly wasting your time. I have managed perfectly well with saving myself."

"Indeed," he said. "And I have come for your heart anyway."

"You have it already," Mary told him.

Even she could not have penned a better ending.

The three women laughed and made toasts to one another as well as to love and enduring friendship, and their happy chatter filled the room with joy for many hours until at last it was finally time to part.

— ⚘ —

Co-Author's Note

MARGIE AND I are huge fans of Frances Hodgson Burnett. Our copies of *The Secret Garden* and *A Little Princess* were dog-eared and reread over and over. We loved the stories of Colin, Dickon, and Mary, and of Sara's many adventures. How fun to read about Cedric in *Little Lord Fauntleroy*! However, I always felt a twinge of sadness, of missing something, as I was so sorely unrepresented in them.

Growing up as a young girl in the Philippines who loved to read—especially classical stories filled with sweeping vistas and overtures of friendship—I often found myself rewriting scenes to reflect my culture, or inserting characters that looked like me. This was not an act of disrespect for the original work, but rather an act of love. I adored these stories enough to strive to find a place for myself within them.

I was hesitant at first, wondering whether there was a place for a Filipino girl in these classic stories. But as Margie and I wrote *The Secret Princess*, I felt more and more confident that recasting Sara Crewe as a wealthy, beautiful, intelligent, and unapologetically Filipino girl in 1860s England was the right choice. She was the face I never saw in Frances Hodgson Burnett's original work.

Writing her fights the stereotype that writers and readers have to this day about immigrants and people of color knowing nothing but poverty and noble suffering until the modern era. Yes, people of color in historical fiction can have wealth and prestige and position. They can be more than set pieces to be propped up in a corner or living metaphors sacrificed to give the main character some kind of moral dignity. They can drive a story set in any era, while also staying true to the realities of the time.

Sara Crewe in *The Secret Princess* is not meant to discredit what the original Sara Crewe represents. Burnett's character provides young readers with incredible lessons around humility and kindness and grace under pressure. However, the time has come for a fresh interpretation that takes into consideration the millions of readers who could benefit from the hope Sara Crewe's story inspires, to show that we can be princesses too.

I could not have done this without my co-author and best friend, Margaret Stohl, who urged me to write Sara as Filipino from the very beginning.

—Melissa de la Cruz

— ⚘ —

Acknowledgments

A SECRET GARDEN full of thanks to our amazing team: Ari Lewin, Jen Klonsky, Jen Loja, Elise LeMassena, Anne Heausler, Elyse Marshall, Emily Romero, and everyone else at Penguin! Thank you to Richard Abate and Sarah Burnes. Thank you to our friends and family.